OUT OF ANYWHERE

ANDREA NOURSE

Paperback ISBN: 978-1-7353325-2-9

eBook ISBN: 978-1-7353325-3-6

Proofreading and editing by Jacqueline Hritz

Cover Design by Maria Ann Green & Jeff Jacobs

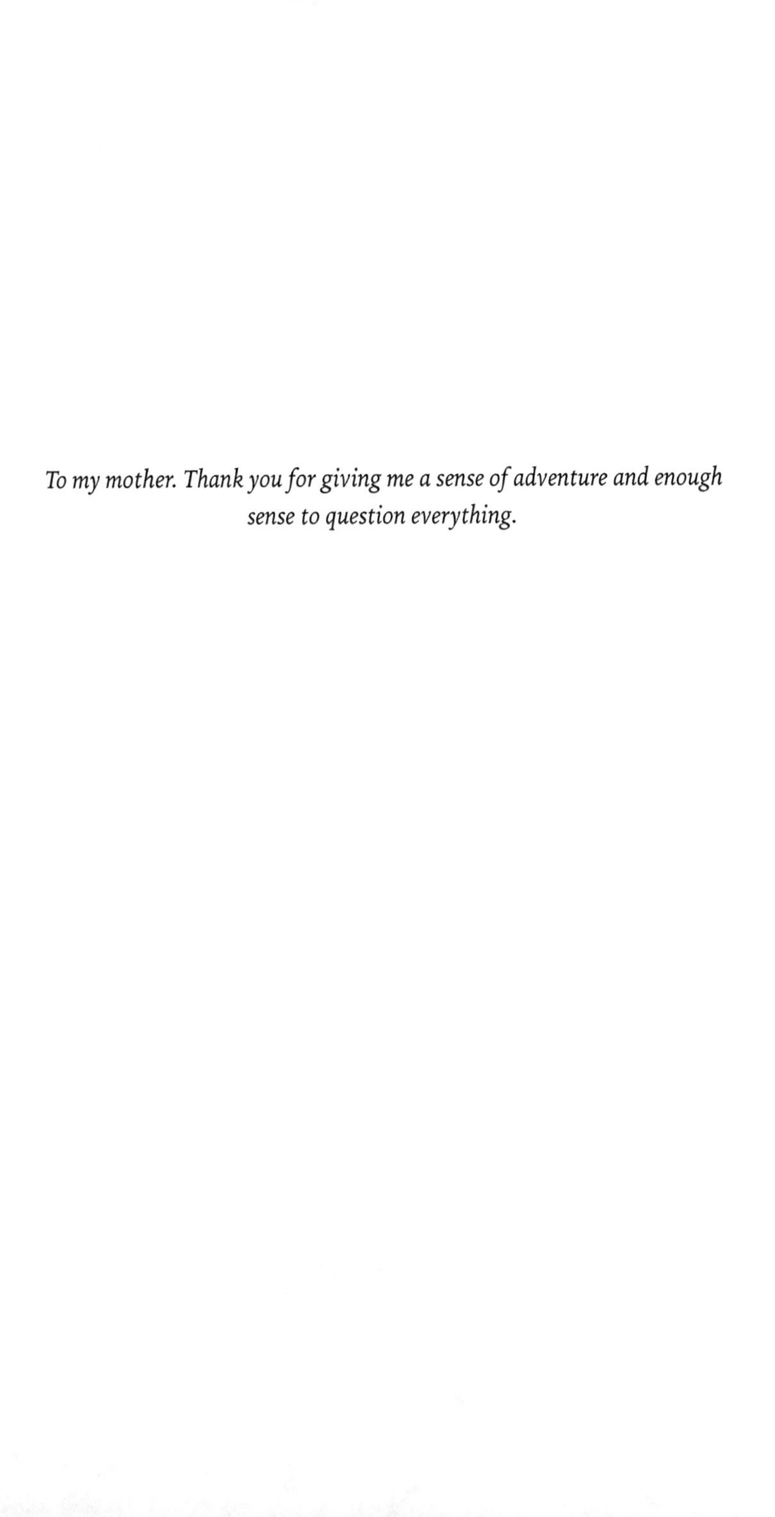
To my mother. Thank you for giving me a sense of adventure and enough sense to question everything.

ONE

Trusty Rusty was dead and determined to abandon me. Just like everyone else. Dark gray smoke billowed from underneath the rusted hood. I pulled towards the shoulder and took extra care to ensure the car was off the road entirely—exactly how my mother had taught me. My ancient but always dependable car shuddered as she jolted to a stop. She gave up on life at the exact moment I needed her most. The dashboard lights flickered once before dimming completely. I dropped my head forward and winced when my forehead slammed against the steering wheel. *Of course.*

"Shit!" I screamed into the darkness.

Well after midnight, the only illumination came from stars millions of miles away; the two-lane road ahead of me empty and pitch black. A shiver ran up my spine as I stared into the abyss in front of me. I'd spent my entire life on the road but never became accustomed to the emptiness of a black sky. I couldn't remember how much time passed since I'd last seen another vehicle. Minutes? Hours? Did it matter? I was alone and stranded somewhere in nowhere Missouri. That is, if I was still in Missouri.

Tears had blinded my sight when I'd left Kansas City hours ago; the water blurred the signs and lines ahead of me. The orange glow of the city lights faded long before I reached this unfortunate road. With no map beside me and no destination in mind, I wasn't even sure what highway I was on. 71? 60? Or was it one of those lettered county highways that went nowhere and everywhere all at the same time?

It didn't matter. None of it mattered. I couldn't let it matter because I couldn't break any more than I'd already broken. Trusty Rusty had been with me longer than anyone or anything. She was the first thing that was truly mine. I didn't have much, but I had her. She'd taken me thousands upon thousands of miles, and she'd done so without complaint. Now she was dead, and I had less than $200 to my name. Two hundred dollars wouldn't cover a tow truck and a motel, and it certainly wouldn't cover the engine I was certain had blown. I might be able to swing for one or the other, but not both. Food or shelter? Gas or a shower? My life was nothing but a constant rotation of either-or options, but never enough for both. It's the only life I'd ever known. I always had enough to survive or enough to tease a dream, but not enough to actually live a life worth living.

Arching my back, I stretched forward to work the kinks out of my neck. The kind of knots that persisted after weeks of sleeping in a car. The kind that waiting tables and cleaning toilets aggravated. The kind that permanently haunted my twenty-five-year-old body. My fingers attempted to knead the knots, but as usual, the tension held firm, balling up under my grip. I rested back into the seat; I had no other choice but to spend one final night curled up in Trusty Rusty. Closing my eyes, I sighed and silently cursed the road and everything it had ever done to me.

To be perfectly fair to the road, it hadn't actually done anything wrong. It was all the small towns, cities, judgmental eyes, and lack of progress along its edges. The road itself was my sanctuary. It's where I was raised, and it's likely where I would die. The thought sent a chill down my spine. I shook it off.

What I wouldn't give for a hot shower and sheets that didn't itch. A bed that was big, soft, and stain free. A bed that was mine for more than a night or two. If I really let myself get crazy, perhaps one inside an actual hotel—with an *h* not an *m*—with a complimentary hot breakfast. Even if said breakfast was bland oatmeal. Maybe one with a coffee bar and fancy creamers. Now *that* would be the stuff of nomad dreams.

Tomorrow I would decide what to do next. I was in no state to make decisions or dream at the moment. For now, I was grateful it was summer and not winter. The air inside the car was warm, but not as suffocatingly hot and humid as it usually was this time of year. There wasn't a cloud in the sky, only the moon and stars. Morning was still a few hours away. As badly as I wanted a shower and a bed, I needed my car to carry me a little further. If I could drive just a few more miles and find a town with an odd job or two to fill my pockets, I might make enough to limp forward for another month.

Before I was allowed to drift off into the nothing I craved, a knock on the window startled me. My eyes flew open, and I sat up straight, ignoring the pounding in my chest. I wiped my mouth, clearing an imaginary trail of drool, and turned to the window. The bright light of the officer's standard-issue flashlight nearly blinded me. Blinking, I reached for the handle to push the door open. The windows, cracked and caked in dirt, had stopped rolling down sometime in the mid-1990s, long before she was mine.

"Miss?" the gruff voice said. "Please step out of the vehicle." I recognized the authority immediately.

"Yes, sir," I said as politely as possible given my current situation. Being raised on the road taught me many things. The most important of which was how to talk to police officers. Unfortunately, I'd had ample opportunity to practice.

I swung my legs through the open door and stood slowly with my hands visible. My back protested. I'd been sitting in the car for far too long. "How are you this evening?" I asked, fighting back a yawn. Goosebumps rushed up and down my exposed arms. For late summer, the midnight air held a slight chill when not confined within a closed car. I rubbed my hands over my skin in an effort to warm myself.

"I'm good, thank you," he drawled. His voice was tired, but pleasant. "License and registration please."

I reached into the console behind me and pulled out the tattered papers.

"What are you doing out here so late?" He scanned the license and did a double-take and he mouthed my name.

"I left Kansas City last night, and I've been driving ever since. My car just up and died," I said. The forced lady-in-distress whine made me want to roll my own eyes but appearing pathetic usually worked. Sympathy was a powerful emotion that my mother taught me to use to my advantage. I wasn't sure whether I wanted him to leave me alone or help me get to the nearest motel. I'd play it by ear. Men could be useful at times.

Standing to my full height—all five-foot-two of it—my eyes hit just at his chest. I tilted my head back to get a good look at him. His eyes, though soft, held the same exhaustion as his voice. His stereotypical small-town cop beer gut protruded over his standard-issue slacks and was held up by his belt. The gun on his hip was at the ready, but his hands were relaxed.

"Shay Lane?" he asked, his voice filled with something I couldn't quite identify. I nodded in response. "Where ya headed?"

That was the million-dollar question that I never had an answer for. Home wasn't an option, no matter how much I wished it was. "I'm not entirely sure," I answered honestly. His presence calmed me. He had a gentleness and a trustworthy nature about him. It almost felt familiar.

When our eyes met, he flinched slightly. I ran my fingers

through my sandy-blonde hair, knowing it was a tangled mess. I kept it short to avoid just that, but it wasn't quite short enough. Did I look that bad? Perhaps it was my breath?

"Could you tell me where we are?" I asked.

"Wishing, Missouri. Well, a few miles north of town. You're in Paris County, to be exact."

"Wishing, Missouri?" I repeated, trying to hide the cynicism in my voice. What kind of name was Wishing? It sounded fake. Maybe I was still dreaming. Or maybe I was in Missouri's version of Mayberry.

"Small town. Only about three hundred of us. Lived here most my life. We've got a motel that's cheap, and it's decent. We're famous around these parts for our Wishing Well Festival. It's every March," he rambled. He rocked from leg to leg. His eyes darted across my face. For a second a flash passed over them, but it was gone as quickly as it appeared.

When your entire life depended on trusting your gut, you learned to read people. Their eyes. Their body language. The deeper implications in their words. It could mean the difference between a safe night's sleep and a night of running. Quite often, it held the delicate difference between life and death. My mother taught me to never trust a smile but to always trust the eyes. Truth lived in the eyes, and this man's eyes held a world of truth. Honesty. Sadness. Kindness. The blackness of them a stark contrast to the softness they held. I imagined he was well-liked and respected in his town.

"Officer," I said with a quick glance at the name stitched on his shirt, "Officer Trigg, how far of a walk is this motel?"

"About five miles or so," he answered without pause. "Your car—it's a 1980 Toyota?"

I nodded, following his eyes back to Trusty Rusty. "A Corolla. She started smoking a few miles back, then sputtered and died. I knew it was coming. Has been for the last decade."

"Let me radio in for a tow," he said. I started to protest,

knowing I couldn't pay for a tow and a repair, but I couldn't bear the thought of her being left on the side of the road. She'd been there for me longer than anything else. For nearly six years, she'd been mine. Aside from the small collection of books she held in her trunk, this car was my one constant companion. The idea of relegating her to an abandoned burial on the side of the road nearly broke me.

"Sure," I said with the slightest hint of reservation. "I just have a few things I want to get out."

"Let me help you, Shay."

"Thank you." I lifted the suitcase of books from the trunk, but he took it from me before I could get it out.

"Geez, how many bodies you got in here?" he asked. His lips twitched into an ornery smile.

"About fifteen," I joked. "Books."

"Ah."

I swung my backpack over my shoulders, cringing at the sharp pull of my muscles. "Aside from the books, I travel light."

"I can see that. Well, why don't I give you a ride into town? I'm sure Mr. Harper has a room open. The motel is never full. Clean beds and a hot shower, though. If you ask nicely, he'll even brew you a hot cup of coffee."

My mouth watered. "That sounds amazing. Thank you, Officer Trigg." I followed him to his cruiser, his head turning back every few seconds to make sure I was still behind him. Each time, I offered a small smile. He winked and turned back. We loaded my suitcase and all my worldly possessions into the back of his car. When he held the front door open for me, his eyes studied my face for a moment. Though they still held the welcoming kindness, something about the way he watched me made me want to pull back. He didn't look at me like other men. My body was fully clothed in his mind, but he was reading between the lines as if he'd seen the pages before.

"You're lucky I was caught up at the station tonight," he said as he settled into his seat. I pulled my seatbelt over my lap but didn't respond. "I'm sure you'd have been safe in your car, but you never know out here."

"Bears?" I asked. My mother once told me she'd encountered a brown bear on some random back road in Missouri.

"Bears. Troublemakers. Drunk drivers." He said it so pragmatically; I just nodded along in agreement, though I was certain I'd have been just fine. It wouldn't have been the first time, or the last, that I spent a night on the side of the road. I could handle myself.

We rode in silence the rest of the way. He opened his mouth to speak a few times, but the words never came. I rested my head on the window and closed my eyes. It was nearly two in the morning, and I'd been awake twenty-four hours.

Officer Trigg pulled into the dimly lit parking lot of the Wishing Well Motel. The plain white building stood starkly against the predawn sky. Bright blue doors lined the single-story motel, each with a gold letter hanging haphazardly in the center. There were no more than five doors. Curtains blocked whatever life was inside the rooms, but all were dark.

"Well, here we are," he announced and put the car in park. He clicked his seatbelt free, and I did the same. Outside, he retrieved my suitcase and backpack from the car.

"I can get it," I said.

"It's no bother," he replied and pulled my pack over his shoulders and lifted the suitcase. "Eddie Harper and I are old friends. He owes me a favor or fifty."

The meaning of his words sunk in. As much as I wanted to argue that I could cover my own room, I was grateful for the offer. I never turned down a free meal or bed. Unless, of course, it came with strings attached. Officer Trigg didn't seem to be the sort to attach strings. I followed him into the dark office. He rang the bell, and we waited in silence.

A short, pudgy man with a handful of white hairs protruding

from his large head popped out from a back room. He wore faded red flannel pajamas. I fought back a snicker as I imagined him turning around to reveal a classic pajama butt flap. "Trigger, whatcha doin' out this late?"

"Miss Lane here broke down over off Highway 5 and needs a room for the night."

"Miss Lane?" he asked with a raised eyebrow. "Certainly. I've got Room C open. Cleaned it myself."

Officer Trigg nodded an approval, and Eddie handed me an old key attached to a giant, plastic, diamond-shaped keychain. Other girls might be accustomed to fancy key cards. Not me. The familiarity of the chunky key was comforting as I held it tightly in my palm.

"Thank you," I said once we reached the room. "Who should I call about my car?"

"I'll get word to you sometime tomorrow, if that works."

"Is there a bus station nearby?" I asked. Officer Trigg handed over my backpack.

"About sixty miles away, up in Springfield." That ruled out walking.

"Alright, well, thank you again." I yawned. My eyes blinked like bricks, heavy with exhaustion. I shut the door behind me, confident I'd be able to track down a solution tomorrow. Tonight, I was done. Wishing, Missouri, was as far as I'd make it.

I slipped the prepaid phone from my pocket and dialed the familiar number, knowing full well she wouldn't answer. She hadn't picked up in more than six years, but I dialed anyway. It rang once before clicking to voicemail.

"Hey, Mom," I said once it beeped. "I left Kansas City today. Ran out of money and my welcome. Remember Greg? We broke up. Well, 'broke up' isn't the right word since we were never together. Anyway, his wife found out about me, and he kicked me out of the hotel last month. I've been sleeping in the car while I figured out where to go next. Same old story, right, Mom? Trusty Rusty finally died. Puttered out on the side of the road in some Podunk town called Wishing. So, I'm stuck here until I can get her fixed or find a new ride. I hope you're good. I miss you and love you. Talk soon."

TWO

THE HARSH MID-MORNING SUN BROKE THROUGH THE dingy gray curtains. It tickled my eyelids and slowly forced them open. I rubbed the sleep away from my eyes and blinked. For a moment, I forgot where I was. I glanced around the room, taking in the gaudy floral wallpaper and gold picture frames adorning outdated watercolor landscapes. Beams of light made the dust appear to be dancing across the room. The off-white comforter covering my body scratched what little skin I'd left exposed. I'd fallen asleep in my jeans and T-shirt. A habit formed from sleeping in one too many dirty motel rooms.

I tossed the blanket aside and stretched my arms over my head. For once, I didn't have any random kinks or tight spots. I'd slept comfortably, and it was a welcome change. Slithering out of my two-day-old clothes, I grabbed the hotel soaps and shampoo and headed for the poorly lit bathroom. The mirror, rusted and stained, accurately reflected everything I felt. Tired. Exposed. My skin pulled tight across ribs as my stomach growled. When had I eaten last? The banana at noon yesterday? Maybe a bag of Doritos at ten? I couldn't remember. I wondered if Eddie had bagels or saltines somewhere in the office. I could grab a quick bite to fill me up before finding a ride to the bus station.

As rested as I felt, I wanted out of this town. The wanderer life wasn't conducive to tiny towns like this. Too many nosey people exposed secrets. They asked questions. They studied faces and demanded answers, like Officer Trigg had last night. Answers I didn't have and didn't want to give. Besides the curiosity of strangers, small towns had little to offer in the way of jobs. I needed decent cash, and I needed it fast. The tiny wad of cash in my backpack wouldn't get me far.

I lingered in the shower, allowing the water to cleanse and refresh me. The hot water ran out before I was fully ready, but even the cold felt good. My skin soaked in the water, sucking the ice into my veins and burning the sting of memories I wished would fade. Motel showers were my favorite, and also the worst. My favorite because they washed off the stink and filth of the road, but they also hold years of dirt and grime. Thousands of naked bodies once stood in them, cleaning away the sin and regret. Inside, they were dark and covered in filth, but once I stepped back out, I was a new woman. When I was little, I longed to take bubble baths and play in the tub like the characters in the books my mother read to me, but she never allowed it. Her nose, usually held humbly in place, would turn up at the mere notion of her offspring soaking in a tub covered in other people's lost skin cells.

Lint flicked off the coarse white towel when I rubbed it over my skin. The tiny bottle of potent floral lotion did little to soothe my dry skin, but I slathered it over every inch of my body. Lotion was a luxury I rarely took for granted. Some months, when I had a few extra dollars, I'd wander into a department store and spend an obscene amount of money on a jar of rich, thick body butter. I knew how to milk every last drop from those jars, making them last months longer than my peers. That is, if I had any peers to speak of.

The road was a lonely, unforgiving place to grow up and live. Since my mother and I hadn't spoken in years, I relied on coworkers, bartenders, and random strangers for small talk. When I needed something more in-depth, I turned to the local library. The library was the one place I always felt at home. Every town had one, and each one I'd been to welcomed me with open arms. When I was too little to stay in the motel alone, my mother would find a kind librarian who would let me sit quietly in the corner and read. My mother assured them that I was more than self-sufficient and wouldn't be a burden. And I wasn't. I kept to myself. I knew how to navigate the shelves to find my favorites. Once engrossed in a book, I'd get lost inside the pages for hours. I taught myself how to read sitting in libraries.

Deep within my suitcase, underneath the tattered books, was a shoebox filled with library cards. One for every city and town I'd called home for the last twenty-five years. There were well over a hundred. As welcome as Eddie and Officer Trigg made me feel, I didn't anticipate adding a Wishing, Missouri, library card to the collection.

Last night, in my final glance back at Trusty Rusty, I'd bid her goodbye. Her final resting place would be here in this town, but it would not be mine.

Throwing my dirty clothes into my backpack, I slipped the soap, lotion, and shampoo into the bag along with a towel. Those always came in handy. It wasn't quite ten, but it was time for me to leave. I gave the quiet room one final glance and silently thanked it for the restful night of sleep before heading out the door.

"Mornin'," a young woman greeted me the instant I stepped outside the room. "Checking out?"

"Yeah," I answered. I lifted my hand to shield my eyes from the sun to get a look at this chipper human. "Excuse me."

She stood directly in my path and gave little indication she was planning to move. "Eddie's got cinnamon rolls this morning. He sent me to come getcha. Said you'd be hungry."

I nodded, acknowledging her, but didn't respond. As tempting as a cinnamon roll sounded, a ride to the bus stop in Springfield was more up my alley. I took a step past her.

"There's coffee, too," she added.

I turned back. She smiled, shrugging. "Thank you," I said.

"I'm Mary. You're Shay, right?"

I stared at her, confused. Had we met?

"I'm Eddie's niece. I clean the rooms here. We don't get many out-of-town guests, so he was excited when you checked in." Her ponytail bobbed back and forth as she bounced. Every word punctuated by a tiny hop. Her cheerfulness was off-putting.

"Officer Trigg set me up here," I said.

"Trigger's a good guy."

"Seems to be, yeah," I said, desperate for the awkward conversation to end. "Well, thanks for the breakfast info."

"Sure! See you later!" she said, flipping a strand of her strawberry-blonde hair over her shoulder.

You won't, I wanted to say, but kept my mouth shut. The broken wheels of the suitcase struggled over the gravel in the parking lot. I yanked it behind me as I walked into the office. The smell of cinnamon tickled my nose. My stomach lurched, reaching for the source.

"Good morning, Miss Lane," Eddie greeted. He'd changed out of the flannel pajamas he wore last night and into a baby-blue polo emblazoned with the Wishing Well Motel logo. A fresh pot of coffee sat on the counter next to him. I grabbed a cup and helped myself. "Sugar? Creamer?"

"Both, please," I said, yawning. "This smells amazing. Do you always have coffee and cinnamon rolls in the morning?" Not sure why I bothered asking, as I had no intention of staying.

"No, but special guests deserve special treatment."

"Special guests?" I asked and looked around the quiet lobby.

Outside, the parking lot was empty. No cars. No people, other than Mary.

"You, Miss Lane."

"Oh, I'm not special. Just a stranded stranger."

"Well, here in Wishing, you'll find that no one is truly a stranger."

This was my exact fear. "Are there any taxis here? I need to get to Springfield."

He shook his head and asked, "Springfield?"

"Officer Trigg mentioned the bus station was there."

"Sure is," he said. "Trigger mention that it's an hour or so away?"

"He did."

"I know Mary and some friends are heading up there Friday if you wanna wait."

It was Saturday. I didn't want to wait a week. "So, no taxis? Anyone else head that way? Deliveries? Trucks?"

"Oh, I'm sure someone does. Just don't know off the top of my head. It'll cost ya a pretty penny, though. Gas ain't cheap, and folks here are nice, but they'll expect payment."

I felt the thin wad of cash in my pocket. "How much?"

"Fifty, maybe? I don't really know though." That wouldn't leave me with enough money for a bus ticket.

"Know anywhere a girl could make some quick cash? Honest cash," I clarified. I wasn't my mother.

He thought for a moment, rubbing his chin. I poured a teaspoon of sugar into the coffee and added cream. Normally, I preferred black coffee. It was easier and faster, but the promise of a cinnamon roll made me want to make my coffee indulgent too. Stirring it, I watched his face, waiting for a hint at his thoughts. His gaze filtered out the window, past my shoulder, avoiding my face entirely. Sweet, hot liquid burned my tongue when I took a sip. Eddie slid a paper plate across the counter. A cinnamon roll the size of my face sat dead center. Icing oozed over the sides. It took all I had to not shove the entire thing in my mouth in one bite.

"Well, let me think," he said as I took a small, respectable bite. "If I didn't have my niece here helping, you could clean a few rooms for me. Ever tend bar or wait tables?"

"Done both," I said, my mouth full. I closed my eyes and let the cinnamon and sugar roll over my tongue. Soft, gooey warmth melted in my mouth. *Oh. My. God.* This was the best cinnamon roll I'd ever had. I chewed slowly to savor the taste. "You make these?"

He laughed a deep belly laugh that roared through the tiny office. "No, my sister Rayna did. She runs Lace & Grit, the bar just up the road. You know, she did just lose her waitress last week. Might be hiring, if you're interested."

If she kept cinnamon rolls like these on the menu, I was definitely interested. "It wouldn't be permanent, just long enough to get on my feet so I can get back on the road."

"Well, it's just a few minutes down the way. I can get Mary to drive you, but it's a quick walk."

"I can walk. Thank you for the coffee and breakfast," I said over my shoulder.

"Be sure to tell Rayna I sent you," he called after me. "Take a right out of the parking lot and you'll be there before you can say *hogwash* ten times."

I waved, thanking him, before heading back to my room to unload my suitcase. No point lugging it around if I was going to be staying for a few more days. Back in my room, I found the bed made and the carpet vacuumed. She'd even replaced the stolen toiletries. Mary worked fast.

Dropping my backpack on the bed, I dug through it, feeling for my wallet. Once I found it, I shoved it in my pocket along with the hotel key. Wishing I had more than my ripped jeans and old tank top, I gave myself a quick once over in the mirror. My hair, cut short so I didn't require product, had air-dried. It fluffed from the summer humidity, but it looked decent enough. I never bothered with makeup. Seeing how I couldn't afford lotion, makeup was a luxury I didn't waste time or money on. My skin glowed as a result. Blemish- and wrinkle-free, I looked just a bit younger than my twenty-five years. Most would assume the years on the road and stress would have aged me, but I was blessed with good genes. Or so my mother always told me.

I gave myself one final nod of approval and ventured back outside. My body tensed, waiting for Mary or Eddie to pop out and ambush me with more cheerful conversation. But neither appeared. If my ratty tennis shoes provided little protection from the jagged rocks in the parking lot, they were even more useless on the sunburned pavement of the road. The heat pushed my feet forward. I didn't bother thinking or saying *hogwash* as Eddie had instructed, but by the time I was certain my feet would burn up, a small brick building with a flat roof appeared on my right. The wooden sign out front confirmed this plain structure was Lace & Grit.

Here goes nothing.

THREE

I expected Lace & Grit to be like every other dive bar I'd ever worked in. Dark. Depressing. Bathed in the stench of urine, beer, and desperation. Old, half-rotted floors with mismatched tables and barstools. Cracked mirrors. Faded photographs of local celebrities and national has-beens. But Lace & Grit had none of that.

Beyond the institutional brick exterior, the inside was well-lit and airy. Windows lined the walls—clean windows without a fingerprint or watermark in sight. The floor was freshly polished. My reflection danced in the rich mahogany. Crisp white linens draped over the two- and four-top tables. Clean, wooden chairs sat neatly at each table. The walls, painted a faint shade of blue, were adorned with minimal decor. A few mirrors, all spotless, and a handful of paintings.

At the back of the room, there was a stage with a karaoke machine and a keyboard. A few small spotlights hung above it. The bar sat catty-corner to the stage and was likely the source of the grit in *Lace & Grit*. It was old. Older than the building itself. Made of sturdy wood, it appeared to be handcrafted, the edges rough and unpolished. Ten mismatched bar stools in red, black, and white were checkerboarded in front of it. Behind it, a petite, slender woman with long silver hair flowing freely behind her stood with her back to me.

"We're closed," she snapped, not bothering to look up when the sound of my footsteps echoed through the empty room. Her tone stopped me. I froze. "We open at two."

"Are you Rayna? Eddie sent me," I said, clearing my throat. "He said you needed a waitress?"

"Yes, I'm Rayna. Who are you?" she asked, turning around. Her head remained down, her hands busy cleaning a beer glass.

"Shay Lane," I said. She slowly looked up. Her face, leathered and tan, scrunched as if she were searching for something familiar.

"Shay? You the girl Trigger rescued last night?"

I laughed. Word got around fast in Wishing. "*Rescued* might be a stretch. I was just fine."

"*Humph*," she mumbled. "You sticking around?"

"Just need to get back on my feet, then I'll be moving on."

"That's what they all say."

"Excuse me?" I asked.

"The girls. They start saying it in middle school. Then in high school, they scream and shout it. Some do move on, but most stay put or move back."

This wasn't an earth-shattering revelation. I'd read enough books to know small-town girls have big city dreams. I didn't fit into that archetype as I'd never had a home to flee.

"So, are you hiring?" I asked, taking a step towards the bar, now that I knew she wouldn't be kicking me out.

"You ever waited tables?"

"Many times."

"Tended bar?"

"Yep."

"Can you make fancy drinks?"

"Name a drink, and I can make it." I'd worked in bars all over the Midwest and was confident there wasn't a drink out there I couldn't make with my eyes closed.

"Free-pour a perfect shot?"

"In my sleep."

"How old are you?"

"Twenty-five, but I've been working in restaurants since I was sixteen." A few times, I lied about my age so I could make more money behind the bar. She started rattling off a list of drinks, quizzing me on the ingredients. With each correct answer I gave, she offered a nod of approval.

"Start tonight?"

"Tonight?" I repeated. "Two o'clock?"

"How about one? Give me an hour to show you how to take orders and teach you the menu. You've got two weeks to prove yourself."

"Two weeks is all I need," I said, certain I could make what I needed and be on my way before the two weeks were up. "Is there a dress code?"

She did a quick scan of my outfit and said, "Jeans and a black T-shirt. You'll need sleeves. There's a general store a mile or so up the road. They'll have what you need. Maybe a pair of black shoes, if you can." Her voice grew softer as she spoke. She walked around the bar and held out her hand. "Welcome to Lace & Grit."

"Thanks," I said and shook her hand. "So, it'll just be us tonight? Is there another waitress?" I didn't know this town or this bar, but Saturday night was never slow at any restaurant or bar I'd worked in. For all I knew, this was the only place in town to grab a beer and burger. I already knew their food couldn't suck. That cinnamon roll was still on my mind. The hundred or so liquor bottles that lined the wall told me that had a decent bar business. Sixteen taps of local, domestic, and international beers stood proudly at the center.

"You, me, and Toby, my line cook. Menu is limited, but we'll go over that later."

"Cinnamon rolls?" I asked with a smile.

She grinned. "Legendary, but we only serve them on Sundays."

"Eddie had some at the motel this morning. Best thing I've ever tasted."

"Easy now, girl, you got the job. Brown-nosing may get you places in big city establishments, but here in this town, it'll get you a black eye." The welcoming tone faded from her voice. My mouth fell open. "Alright, then, we'll see you at one."

"Thank you, Rayna." I didn't dare risk saying anything else. I gathered what was left of my pride and turned towards the exit. Rayna wasn't much different from other bar owners I'd met, but there was something safe and familiar about her. She had a mothering vibe. Not that I was an expert on what being mothered should feel like, but she seemed like the type to look out for her people. She had a hard exterior, but no woman who baked cinnamon rolls like hers could be as harsh as she appeared.

Back outside in the unforgiving sun, I once again cursed my current lack of a car. If Trusty Rusty were as trusty as she once was, I wouldn't be here. I'd be in Arkansas or Oklahoma. Maybe Tennessee. Anywhere or nowhere. But I couldn't dwell on that. Truth was, I didn't know where I wanted to be. I'd rarely been in one place for more than a few months. Long enough to line my pockets with enough money to drive for a few weeks. Then, when the well ran dry, I'd work until the process was ready to repeat. I had nothing tying me to one particular map dot. I didn't know where my mother was, but I imagined her on a beach somewhere, sipping the fancy umbrella drinks she used to dream about. Wherever she was, she didn't want anything to do with me. Her radio silence made that perfectly clear.

She'd instilled a sense of adventure in me. Adventure or restlessness, I wasn't sure which it really was. Tammy Lane wasn't the type of woman who liked to settle down or dwell on the past. When she told me stories about her childhood or how I came to be, she kept her imagination wild and the details brief. I knew my father was older than her. She'd been seventeen, and, depending on the day she told the story, he was either a few months older or a decade older. He wasn't important, she'd insisted. He'd given her me, and that was all she wanted from him. Never mind what her daughter might have wanted or needed from him. I learned early on to never ask questions or challenge her memory. It was exactly as she told it, and there was simply nothing else to tell. Besides, if he was anything like the men she dated, I'd rather know as little about him as possible. She wasn't exactly known for her sound judgment around the opposite sex.

I swatted at a swarm of gnats. The bugs hovered at eye level, taunting me. "Shoo," I said and waved my hands in front of me to clear a path. There were few things I hated more than summer bugs. As if the air weren't heavy enough without the weight of thousands of tiny bugs that stuck to your skin. My mother hated them too.

Sometimes, late at night, Mom would whisper a confession into the darkness of the car, her voice bumping along with the road, barely audible. Those nights she assumed I was fast asleep in the backseat. It was during those confessionals that I learned the most. Those were the secrets she didn't even like to tell herself. The truths she would never admit to again. His name, I knew, was Ken. He had a wife. At the time, he'd been the love of my mother's life. That is until I came along. I ruined everything. Her dreams and plans all died when she missed that first period. Nothing was the same after, and everything that happened before was ancient history. She was ashamed of having me when she was so young. It wasn't until I was much older that I realized she regretted me. Perhaps not the actual, real-life me who was a child eavesdropping on her mother's deepest, darkest secrets, but she regretted the idea of me.

I suppose that's what made it so easy for her to walk away and leave me to fend for myself. At seventeen, with a baby in tow, she'd walked away from everything she'd ever known. Surely, she thought I could do it at nineteen without a needy baby attached to my hip. In her eyes, I didn't need her anymore, and she didn't need or want me. She assumed the years spent on the road trained me for a life of solitude and running. Her lessons on self-sufficiency, deceit, and seduction should have set me up to follow in her footsteps. Tammy raised a strong and independent daughter, that much was true. But, unlike my mother, the road wasn't enough for me. I used to dream about a house with a yard and a dog and a bed that was mine and mine alone. All the things I never had—stability, security, and safety.

Instead, I spent my days and nights fighting to stay a step ahead. I never knew what the sunrise would bring, but as long as I had a car and a few bucks for gas and food, I could make it to the next stop.

It was with this thought that I headed for the general store, prepared to spend a few precious dollars on a black T-shirt so I could wait tables and earn a few more dollars. With those dollars, I could get a bus ticket. To where I wasn't sure. It would be as far away as my yet-to-earn dollars would take me. From there, who knew? That was the answer I craved. Where was the end of the line? Where would I settle down? Was there a home out there for me? A home without wheels? Surely the road ended somewhere.

I dreamed the dreams my mother never would allow. Now, without her there to kill them, I could daydream and wish. Even if I knew it was fruitless, I could pretend. And, when reality stepped in to squelch those dreams, I had my suitcase of books and library cards to turn to. The very books she'd given to me as babysitters were the things that planted those silly notions within me. Those pages gave me hope. There were homes with dogs in the backyard. There were families with mothers and fathers. Kids who went to school and got to be little. All the things she'd denied me.

I kicked a loose rock in front of me, unleashing the silent rage

I never let out into the world. It sailed ahead, landing in the middle of the road. A car passed, knocking it back to the shoulder. At least the rock came back for me. As much as I missed and loved my mother, I hated her. I hated the life she'd chosen for me. I hated the pessimism by which she lived. I hated her for abandoning me. I hated her for listening to all my voicemails and never coming to find me when I cried and begged her to.

I hated myself for needing her.

Tires crunched on the gravel behind me. The unmistakable squealing of brakes broke me out of my internal monologue. I turned around and found myself a few inches from the bumper of a police car.

"Officer Trigg," I said, greeting him when he stepped out of the car.

"Please, call me Trigger," he said.

"Trigger," I replied, liking the sound of the nickname. "Looks like I'm sticking around for a bit."

"That's good to hear. Your car, it seems, is beyond repair. Even Old Mack can't fix it, and he's resurrected all kinds of ancient automobiles."

"Well, she had over 300,000 miles on her," I said with a laugh. "I've replaced nearly every part and component over the years. But they can only last so long."

"I suppose that's right," he said. "Where're you headed?"

"To the general store. I got a job waitressing at Lace & Grit."

"That's a good place to work. My wife worked there when she was younger. Although once Rayna took it over, she completely changed up the place. Improved it, if you ask me. Some other old-timers might not agree."

"It's definitely not what I was expecting," I said. "Well, I gotta get moving if I'm going to be back there by one."

"I'm headed into town; I'll give you a ride."

I glanced behind me and tried to gauge how much further it was.

Trigger laughed. "It's about two miles."

"Sure, I'd love a ride," I answered. My feet were aching. If I intended to be on them all night at the bar, I knew I'd never survive if I didn't give them a rest now. He smiled and walked around the car to open the door for me. Our eyes met for a moment. He flinched and pulled back. A tear formed at the corner of his eye, but he blinked it away before it fell.

"Allergies are rough around here," he said when he caught me studying him. I shrugged in response, still unsure of how to read him.

FOUR

Trigger offered to wait while I shopped, but I insisted I'd find my own way back to the bar. As I sat in his car, the radio popped in and out with various calls and demands for his attention. He had better things to do than chauffeur me around town, even though he acted as if the opposite were true.

Once inside the store, I tried to quickly calculate what I could afford. I had no way of predicting how much I might make in tips tonight, so I wasn't going to bank on that. At sixty bucks a night, the motel would wipe out my funds by tomorrow. That is, assuming Trigger hadn't already paid. I made a mental note to check with Eddie and make sure he hadn't. I might be broke, but I wasn't about begging for help. Especially not from strangers who happened to work in law enforcement. He'd probably know how to track me down should I skip town.

If I paid for the motel tonight and tomorrow, I'd have fifty dollars left to buy a black shirt and a pair of comfortable shoes. I had black shoes back in my room, but they were flats with little support. Those shoes wouldn't do here. My last job hadn't required as much foot time, so I'd opted for cute over comfort—something I rarely did, but I'd allowed myself to get too comfortable. I truly thought Kansas City might finally be home. It wasn't. Nowhere ever was.

The general store had exactly one style of black T-shirt, and it was twenty dollars. The black tennis shoes I found were just under thirty. I grabbed them and checked the time. It was noon. I had an hour to hurry back to the bar. As soon as I stepped outside, I regretted telling Trigger to go on without me.

Heat radiated from the blacktop. My face beaded with sweat, and I could feel my hair lifting with the humidity. Being raised as I was, I was more than used to the elements. Rain. Snow. Freezing temperatures. But the heat was one thing I could not stand. Heat made life unbearable. Humidity added an unhealthy dash of misery. With the cold, there were always more layers to add. When the sun beat down on me, I couldn't remove any more layers. Laws and human decency required that I remain mostly covered. As a child, I used to get so mad when I saw boys without their shirts. *How come their nipples are fine to show off, but mine aren't?* I used to whine to my mother. She'd just sigh and remind me that sometimes being a girl meant things would never be fair. Back then, I'd missed the gravity of her words. Now, years later, I understood them.

The walk back was hot and slow, but it gave me time to watch the town moving around me. Wishing was as quaint as its name implied. There wasn't a Walmart or McDonald's as far as I could tell. Everything appeared to be local and homegrown. Every storefront was unique to its owners. Nothing lined up neatly. The roads curved and met haphazardly as if they'd never actually intended to be a town. From my vantage point, there were few stop signs and even fewer traffic signals. It was the kind of town you drove through without a second thought. You might blink and think *how cute* and then keep on driving.

It was exactly the kind of place I hated. Aside from the nosy neighbors, towns like Wishing held little opportunity for a girl raised on the road. Lace & Grit appeared to be the only bar. The main drag, which the motel, bar, and general store were all on, held a few small offices and led directly to the town square. There was a doctor and a dentist. A hair salon shared a building with an insurance salesman. There was, of course, an antique shop, and a diner that served breakfast all day. They had world-famous pancakes, according to the sign in the window. Granted, I'd never left the United States, but I'd been to nearly all forty-eight contiguous states, and I'd never heard of them. I imagined not many people here left Wishing in search of better pancakes. There was no one to verify or dispute this claim. I wasn't about to be the first.

Every car that passed me slowed with curiosity. The drivers popped their hands out the window and waved. I offered a polite smile in return, gritting my teeth behind curved lips, and waved back. A few shouted their *hellos* and *have a good days* as they drove by. Everyone seemed to already know me. A few even called my name, which seemed weird. I'd just arrived last night. Was it Rayna, Eddie, or Trigger who had the big mouth? My money was on Eddie. He seemed just the type to be an overeager town gossip.

After twenty minutes and a hundred or so smiles and waves, I pulled my phone out of my pocket. I don't know why I kept calling her. She never answered. I didn't even know if she listened to the messages I left. I'd left more than one desperate message begging her to just call me. In a few of them, I asked for money. Some were tearful and pleading and others contained a few moments of laughter. But she never called back. She never answered. When she drove away that night, I knew she was angry with me, but at the time, I'd misjudged her anger. I was her daughter, after all, surely she'd loved me enough to forgive my one mistake and answer the phone.

Each time I dialed her number, I held my breath, hoping this would be the call she picked up. It never was. At the familiar sound of the generic voicemail, I released the breath.

"Hey, Mom," I said, sighing when I heard the beep. "I know I called last night, but for some reason, this town reminds me of you. I'm still in Wishing, where apparently everyone really does know your name. The police chief is decent, unlike a few we ran into back in the day. I got a job at a bar called Lace & Grit. Rayna, the owner, is a no-bullshit woman who seems nice enough. She kinda reminds me of you. I start work tonight. I'm out of cash, so I'm hoping it's busy or I'll never be able to get a bus ticket out of this state. I think I might head to the beach next. I know, I know, fall is the worst time to go to the beach. No tourists. No money. But I could use a frivolous sunrise and my toes in the sand."

HONK! HONK! A car sped past me, honking, and then slammed on its brakes. It skidded to a stop a few hundred feet ahead of me. I quickly hung up the phone and stepped into the ditch. The tall grass grazed my knees, and I swatted at a bee. The car started to slowly back up, inching closer to me. I stood my ground. It wouldn't be the first time I fought off some asshole who thought I owed him something. Balling my hands into fists, I held them rigid at my side. The bag containing my new shoes and shirt dropped to the ground beside me. The car, a black 2000-something Camaro, stopped beside me. I didn't take my eyes off the tinted windows.

The door flew open. I held steady. I wouldn't show fear or weakness, despite my racing heart. Sweat poured over every inch of my body, though I wasn't entirely sure if that was due to the heat or anxiety. I watched, my eyes wide and unblinking, as a tall, lanky man with hair as black as his car stood and exited the vehicle. His face, tan and dotted with facial hair, turned towards me. Over the roof of his car, his gaze met mine. I kept my mouth firm, refusing to smile. The stranger grinned.

"You must be the new girl." His voice boomed. My shoulders relaxed slightly at his smile and jovial tone. I didn't respond. He closed his door and walked around the vehicle. I watched, mesmerized by his cocky, intentional strut. "Shay, is it?"

"And you are?" I asked. I released my fists and stretched my fingers. This man wasn't a threat. At least not to my physical safety.

"Toby Reynolds," he replied. "Want a lift?"

"No, thank you. I'm not in the habit of riding in death machines with grown men who still drive like teenagers. Especially not a stranger."

His laughter ricocheted off the thick, humid air. It was a deep laugh with a hint of Southern charm; the kind of laugh that sings. "Oh, doll, we ain't strangers."

"Have we met?" I asked, knowing full well that we hadn't.

"I'm Toby," he repeated. "Rayna's line cook. We'll be working together tonight. She called me in early to teach you the menu."

When he said his name a second time, recognition rang in my ears. When Rayna mentioned him, she'd failed to mention his ego, which was apparent in the confident way he kept walking towards me. I didn't offer a smile or encouragement, but he carried himself closer and closer. My body itched to walk towards him, but I refused to move. I wouldn't let him see any sign of weakness. I knew his type—arrogant, demanding, and entitled. There wasn't anything special about him.

Except, perhaps, his eyes. The closer he got, the more I noticed their unique color. They weren't quite blue, but rather a silver-gray. They danced when he laughed. *Get it together, Shay.*

"It's another mile to the bar, you know."

"I know."

"It's hotter than Satan's asshole out here."

"I know."

"I'm going there anyway."

"I know."

He was standing directly in front of me now. Holding out his hand, he waited. With much reluctance, I reached over and shook his hand. His fingers gripped tightly, squeezing mine.

"I promise I have no ulterior motives," he said, releasing my hand. "It's hot and miserable out here, and by the time you get to the bar, you'll be exhausted and useless. I'll have to pick up the slack and wait tables, which I hate. So, really, I'm being selfish. Put aside your feminist ideals for a minute and come enjoy the air conditioning. I've got it cranked low. It's a nipple raiser in there."

"Charming," I replied, rolling my eyes. For a moment, I tried to remember what cold air felt like, but couldn't. I'd give anything for a bucket of ice.

"I've been accused of a lot of things, but charming ain't one of 'em," he said, laughing.

A cloud shifted, exposing the sun in all its glory. The heat seared my skin. I glanced towards his car and gave in. "Fine."

He smiled wide; the ends of his lips met his eyes. "It was the nipple-raiser line, right?" he asked as he held the door open for me.

"Shut up and drive," I said. I kept my eyes on him as he walked around the front of the car and slid into the driver's seat. His six-foot-tall frame folded through the door with unexpected ease. As promised, the interior of the car was ice cold and inviting, despite its dark interior. Even the black leather seats were cool to the touch.

"How do you like Wishing so far?" he asked.

I shrugged. "It's like every other small town in the Midwest. Boring and predictable."

"Hey now, that's my hometown you're dissing. Sure, this place is small, but unlike me, it has its charms. You'll see."

"Doubtful. I'm just here long enough to get enough cash for a car or a bus ticket. I don't stay in one place too long."

"Running from the cops? You some big-time mobster?"

"Maybe," I said, turning to wink at him. When I didn't expand on my answer, he turned his attention forward and put the car in drive. An awkward silence fell over the car, and if it weren't for the cold air blasting on my skin, I might have preferred to walk.

But when he pulled into the parking lot of Lace & Grit a moment later, I thanked him for the ride.

"I couldn't just drive by and let a beautiful girl sweat her nonexistent ass off in this heat, now could I?" He somehow managed to compliment and insult me in the same breath.

There was no doubt, Toby Reynolds was the exact kind of trouble I didn't need.

FIVE

If I'd had any idea just how busy Lace & Grit would be on a Saturday night, I'd have had no qualms about my finances. From the moment the doors opened at two until they closed at one in the morning, a steady stream of customers flowed through the doors. Every table filled and turned quickly. The barstools were never empty, and the patrons tipped well. They were also surprisingly friendly. They all smiled and said *please* and *thank you*. No one complained about cold food. Everything was perfect. Almost too perfect.

I hadn't been wrong when I'd assumed everyone in town knew my name and that I was new. Part of me wondered if I'd been the reason we were so busy. With each new patron came a fresh set of eyes staring me down. Most seemed curious. A few lingered on me too long, wondering what lay beneath the tattered jeans and tight black T-shirt. Some glazed over with jealousy as their partner's gaze wandered a bit longer than they approved of.

When I mentioned this to Rayna, she released a big, hearty laugh into the air.

"Oh, Wishing loves a shiny new toy," she said as she sat at the bar. Her fingers worked quickly through the stacks of receipts and cash. "Don't flatter yourself, honey, we're always busy, shiny new toy or not."

I bristled at being referred to as a toy, but I bit my tongue. Instead, I focused on the heaviness of my apron. All night, I kept sticking my hand deep into the wad of bills. My feet were on fire. My back ached. My head was trying to murder me, but that stack of cash reinvigorated me. I was desperate to count it but was under strict instructions to wait until Rayna finished cashing out the bar.

Toby proved to be as annoying at work as he had been on the side of the road. Every order I called to him was answered by shouted questions or innuendos. I dreaded calling back *fried pickles*. The offer to see his pickle wasn't funny the first time or the hundredth. Still, I managed to ignore him and get every order correct. I could only imagine what he'd do if he had to remake a burger. Thankfully, after ten o'clock, few guests ordered food, and I spent much of the evening pouring beers and grabbing tequila shots from Rayna.

"This is the only bar within thirty miles that serves decent food and ice-cold beer," Rayna announced proudly as she slammed the register till shut.

"That explains the crowd," I said, slinking my way up on the barstool. I sighed loudly the instant my feet left the ground. I hadn't sat down in over twelve hours. I was ready for bed.

"Silverware," Toby said, grunting as he plopped the rack full of forks and knives in front of me. "I'll help you roll it."

"If I what?" I asked. His gaze drifted over my face and down my chest. I crossed my arms, covering my body.

"Nothing, I usually help the waitress with it. Otherwise, we'll all be here until four." He winked. "Unless you wanna do something later?"

"Nope, let's just roll this so I can cash out and go home." The word stuck in my throat. Motel. Go to the motel. It wasn't home. I didn't have a home.

He rambled on and on about nothing in particular as he rolled the silverware alongside me. Despite the years of experience he bragged on and on about, I rolled three to his one. We knocked out the entire rack in under five minutes.

"You've done this before," he joked.

"Once or twice," I said with a yawn. It was nearly 2:30 a.m. My body ached to crawl into bed and snuggle into the flat pillows. Even the scratchy comforter sounded like heaven now.

Rayna came out of the kitchen, snapping a dish towel at Toby. He yelped and jumped to his feet.

"Boy, if you don't get back there and mop those damn floors, I'm going to call your mama."

"Yes, ma'am."

"And stop trying to scare off Shay. She's the most competent waitress we've had in years."

I smiled. "Thank you, I think."

"It's a compliment, trust me. Rayna's never called anyone competent before." Toby took off running for the kitchen before Rayna could swat him again.

"How long has he worked here?" I asked.

"Five years or so? He went off to college but came back when his mom got sick a few years ago. She got better, but he never went back. Wishing has that effect on some of us. It'll make you want to run and then pull you right back in."

I nodded. Removing the cash from my pocket, I guessed it was at least five hundred dollars. Rayna didn't accept credit cards, so everyone paid in cash. Fancier bars I'd worked in held credit card tips until payday. I was thankful Lace & Grit wasn't that kind of fancy. There were a few who had tabs I wasn't sure she ever collected but she rang up anyway. I handed the stack to Rayna so we could go through my receipts. She fanned through the bills before passing them back to me. Her fingers worked quickly over the ancient calculator. The paper ticked off the totals as she typed them in. When she was finished, she ripped the paper off and ran through the receipts one final time, checking her math. She leaned back in her chair, tilting it up on two legs, and stretched her back.

"Looks like folks were generous tonight."

"Shiny new toy," I replied, laughing.

"Three-fifty," she said. "The rest is yours."

Sorting them into stacks by denomination, I counted out the bills and handed her half the stack. The rest fell in my hand like a pile of freedom. A few more nights like this and I'd be on my way to the bus station.

"Well, you passed," she said. "Sundays are brunch. You're welcome to come in, but usually my niece Mary and I run the shift with Eddie in the kitchen."

"He works here, too?"

"Just on Sunday, and sometimes on Friday if the motel is slow. We're only open for the after-church folks. No booze, just coffee and brunch."

"That must be the lace," I said with a smirk. "The grit is the rest of the week."

"Something like that, I suppose. My mama's name was Lacey. Dad named it after her. He added the grit after replacing the windows a few too many times after bar fights."

"How long have you been running the place?" I don't know why I asked. It's not like I was going to be here long enough to care.

"A few years now. Eddie took over the motel when our Uncle Mark died. Daddy retired from the bar not long after. Then when he and Mama died, it was passed down to me. Maybe eight years or so."

"So, it's always been in the family?"

"Twenty years now."

"Since you got laid?" Toby shouted as he walked out of the kitchen. He laughed at his own joke, unaffected by our loud groans of disapproval.

"Get on out of here!" She rolled her eyes. "Pay him no mind, Shay."

"What are you two talking about?" he asked, ignoring Rayna. He pulled out a chair, flipped it around and sat down with his arms draped over the back.

"I was telling Shay how the Lace & Grit got its name."

"Eh, that's a boring story. Why don't you tell us about you?" he asked, looking at me. "You're the mystery woman who showed up in the middle of the night and has the whole town buzzing."

Rayna shot him a look of warning. Shifting in my seat, I studied the silent argument racing between the two of them. She narrowed her eyes. He shrugged. Her left eyebrow arched slightly. His steel-gray eyes rolled deep in his head. Silence fell over the bar for the first time all night. It was heavy with secrets—mine and theirs.

"Where are you from?" he asked once Rayna's face relaxed.

"Everywhere," I said, giving my standard answer. It was a line I'd said more times than I cared to count. "I've lived all over the place, but never for very long."

"You had to be born somewhere."

"I was."

"Where?"

"Missouri, I think."

"You think? Don't you have a birth certificate?"

"I do."

"Where are your parents?" he asked, moving on to the second most common question I was asked.

"I don't know my dad, and my mom is off doing what she does best."

"Which is?"

I sighed heavily, tired of the questioning. This wasn't unusual. Most men I met wanted to know more. They all wanted to be the one to crack me and break down my walls. Little did they know, it wasn't a wall they had to break through. I'd let them in, I'd just never let them all the way in. I'd give them enough answers to get what I needed, but never enough to satisfy their hunger. *Always keep them thirsting for something,* my mother had once said. *That's how you keep them generous.*

"Living on the road."

"So you grew up on the road?"

Rayna sat back in her chair watching our tennis match. He'd yet to score a point, but he was keeping me on my toes.

"Yup."

"School?"

"Homeschooled and self-taught."

"College?" he asked. I didn't answer. Chewing the inside of my mouth to stop the flood of bitter memories. "No?"

I shook my head. "Got my GED a few years ago, though. I don't really need a piece of paper to wait tables or clean motel rooms."

"Don't you want more out of life?"

"Don't you?" I countered, tired of the game. He didn't answer. I counted the rest of the bills. Two hundred and three dollars. Plus whatever the base hourly rate was. I'd filled out my paperwork this morning but couldn't remember what she'd said. It didn't matter anyway. I wouldn't be around long enough to find out. I shoved the money in my pocket and stood. It was a ten-minute walk back to the motel, and I was ready to get out of here.

"I'll give you a ride," Rayna offered before Toby could. "You take tomorrow off. We are closed on Monday, but if you want to come and help me stock and prep for Tuesday, you can come in at ten. Otherwise, it'll be Tuesday at one."

"I'm happy to come in on Monday," I said. "How often do you issue checks?"

"We get paid every Friday. You'll get your first check the week after next."

If the rest of the week was anything like tonight, I wouldn't need it. I'd leave it sitting in the safe like I'd done a dozen times before. Checks were hard. Cash was easy.

"Great. I'll definitely take you up on that ride."

"I can take her, Rayna. It's on my way."

"That's okay," I said, trying to be polite, even though I was too tired to care, and he hadn't earned my respect.

"Alright, then. Well, I'll see you Tuesday." He slipped his sunglasses on, despite there not being a trace of sun left in the sky and let the door slam behind him.

"He means well," Rayna said. "But I get the sense you don't like talking about yourself all that much."

"I don't," I said. I stood and gathered my bags. "Could I grab a water?"

"Of course, take a couple from the fridge in the back. Eddie keeps some in the motel office, too."

"Thanks," I said and sprinted towards the kitchen. The walls were lined with old photos of the bar and its former employees. Old photographs with tattered edges and yellowed images. I ran my finger over a few, not lingering long enough to get a good look at any of the faces. Not that I'd recognize any, but the bar felt so much like home that I felt as though I already knew these people. Their stories all sounded alike, mirroring the tragedy of small-town life.

"Shay?" Rayna hollered into the kitchen.

"Coming," I shouted back. *What I wouldn't give for my own car right about now.* This place felt too comfortable, too safe. It felt like I belonged, which couldn't be true. I belonged nowhere and everywhere. Anywhere but here.

SIX

SSLEEP DID NOT COME PEACEFULLY THAT NIGHT. Memories dredged up by Toby's questions tugged at my consciousness. Flashes of faces. Snippets of final words and conversations. Every city and town along the way. The friends I'd made and left behind. When I was younger, I tried to make friends. Motel rooms and libraries could be lonely places. Sometimes, I put my trust where it didn't belong, but I came out of it alive. A few bruises and broken hearts were all I had to show from those few times I'd truly let my guard down. Now those lingered, turning into nightmares and wasted daydreams.

While I had every intention of sleeping until noon, neither my brain nor my body was up to the challenge. At seven, I groaned loudly and flung myself from the bed with an odd sense of displacement. Days off were rare. If I wasn't working to make a buck, I was on the road. My body always in motion. I didn't know how to go slow. So I didn't.

I defied my better judgment, ignored my mother's voice nagging in my head, and drew a hot bath. I was used to working long hours on my feet, but something about Lace & Grit tested me in a way I'd never been tested. Sure, it didn't help that I'd spent the last month sleeping in my car and avoiding reality. I hadn't worked since Greg fired me and kicked me out of the hotel I'd been staying in. I missed those five-star sheets and pillows. I missed his five o'clock shadow teasing my skin as his kisses trailed every inch of me. I didn't miss his wife or her rage when she found us in that exact position. I did, however, miss the stability I thought I'd found.

We met nearly six months ago. He walked into the restaurant where I'd been working. Impressed with my rack and customer service skills, he offered me a job managing the front desk at the boutique hotel he owned. His left hand was free of both a ring and the telltale tan line. He never mentioned a wife or family. Instead, he assured me I was the only one in his bed. He lied. He lied about owning the hotel as well. That belonged to his father-in-law. But I didn't know any of that then. I was too blinded by his attention and pearly white smile that I didn't even think to question him or his motives. The first and last time I will ever make that mistake.

When I met him, I was tired of the road. I wanted nothing more than to settle down and sleep in the same bed for months. I found comfort in his arms and promises. So I believed every word he said, even though his eyes betrayed them. His eyes were clouded in deceit. I saw it when he refused to make eye contact, or when they darted towards the door anytime he snuck a mid-day kiss in his office. I ignored every single sign. Desperation never did me any favors.

He kissed me for the first time at midnight on a random Tuesday. My second shift at the hotel. When his lips touched mine, I knew it wasn't my customer service he was after, but I didn't care. I wanted him as badly as he wanted me. Unfortunately, my need for him was greater than his for me. He had a home. He had a safety net. I had nothing. Then for a brief moment, I had him.

I've never been the type of girl who allowed a man to define her. My mother raised me to never be that girl. She taught me there was power to be had in relationships and sex, and she demanded I understood the difference between being powerless and being in power. It should always be the latter that drove my decisions, she'd said. Giving a man power would only lead to devastation. Looking back, I wished I'd asked for details. She wouldn't have given them, but I could have learned a silent lesson.

I never fully learned that lesson until Greg. He held all the power over my job, my financial security, my sleeping arrangements, and my body. It was all given at his convenience. Never when I needed it, but only when he deemed me worthy or useful. I knew this, and I didn't care. I craved what he had to offer. The familiarity of his touch became a drug. The nights I spent with him were never long enough. He was gone before the sun rose. At work, he rarely acknowledged me. Unless, of course, he was horny and in need of a lunch-hour quickie. His pleasure came first. Mine was a bonus.

If I were being honest, I'd admit that part of me didn't care. I just wanted to be his. I wanted to belong to someone, and anyone who would have me would fit the bill. By the time I met Greg, I'd been on my own for almost five years. Five years was a long time to live without physical touch. Sure, I could have done as my mother had and found a random stranger, but random strangers didn't warm me. I needed more.

Greg gave me just enough to provide me with the more.

The night it ended, I'd decided what little he gave wasn't enough. I begged him to stay longer. I pleaded with him to give me more than just his body. For the first time, he gave in. He invited me into his bed. I should have known the home I walked into didn't belong to a bachelor, but I was too busy being in awe of him. He became a different man inside that house. At the hotel, his touch was rushed and urgent, but in the California king bed with luxurious Egyptian cotton sheets, he was slow and attentive. It was as if he suddenly had all the time in the world. In my naive mind, I thought I'd finally cracked him. My tearful pleas caused a shift inside him. He was mine.

Then, the door opened. A woman, older and taller than me, walked in. Her belly round and filled with a life he'd given her. I'd been too shocked to feel shame. I didn't cover myself. As her screams blended with his insistence that I was no one and meant nothing, I shut down and the walls closed back up.

In the aftermath, she came into the hotel, fired me, and refused my last paycheck. I didn't even get to pack my own bags. She'd done that for me. In black magic marker, she'd written exactly what she thought of me on every piece of clothing I owned. Then, to add insult to injury, I had to listen to him yet again tell her and everyone in the hotel that I'd been the shameless slut that seduced him. He conveniently left out the part where he stalked me and insisted I come work for him. Or the many seductions he'd initiated while I was on the clock. All of that remained unmentioned.

I didn't fight. I'd seen my mother go through similar situations with various lovers and wives. I knew the drill. I didn't belong. I never did and never would. In their world, I didn't exist. I was disposable. And soon, they'd forget all about me. At least until a marriage counselor asked why she no longer trusted her husband.

With my tail safely tucked between my legs, I walked out of the hotel with my suitcase of books and the few articles of clothing that survived her rage. I climbed into Trusty Rusty and drove to the first rest stop I could find. There, I slept in my car and studied my Rand McNally. Prepaid cell phones didn't usually come equipped with navigation apps. Plus, there was something primal about reading a map and using your fingers to trace your route. My tears blurred and stained the pages.

How could I have been so stupid? So vulnerable? I didn't bother leaving my mother any messages then. She'd have shaken her head and said she told me so, assuming she listened to them. I'd been disposable to her, just like I'd been disposable to Greg.

My pity party lasted far longer than it should have. I blew through my meager savings with cheap cocktails. My meals consisted of Snickers bars and peanut-butter crackers. Then, three days ago, I picked myself up, got in my car, and headed south. I put Greg behind me. I buried the memory of that weak, pathetic girl, and I drove.

Lifting myself from the tub, I stood and let the water drip off of me. Looking in the dingy mirror, I promised myself I'd never allow myself to fall victim to anyone again. Not my mother. Not Greg. No one. I alone was responsible for my happiness. I didn't need anyone's pity or love. Not when I'd only lose myself in the process.

I pulled on a pair of shorts and a T-shirt, skipping undergarments. I desperately needed to wash my clothes. Last night, I'd noticed a tiny laundry room next door to the office. I didn't have laundry soap, but hot water should do the trick. It wouldn't wash the stink of beer and smoke from my T-shirt, but I could cover that with perfume until I found a way to get back into town for supplies. Rayna offered to drive me any time and gave me her cell phone, but she'd be busy prepping for brunch.

Stepping outside, the air felt significantly lighter than it had yesterday. A walk into town wouldn't be so bad. I pulled the door shut and slipped the key in to lock it behind me. Aside from a red Nissan, the parking lot was empty. I gave the door one final shove to ensure it was locked. It was then that I first noticed the white envelope with my name on it. It was taped to the door. I glanced behind me. Not sure what I expected to find, I confirmed I was alone. Turning back to the door, I balanced my bag of clothes on my hip and reached for the envelope.

It wasn't heavy, but it felt like more than paper. I slid my finger beneath the seal and opened it. Inside, a shiny metal key caught my eye. The familiar logo caused me to pause for a moment. I rotated my head to face the parking lot again. Then, looked back at the key. *Nissan.* I slipped the paper from the envelope and opened it. It was a title for a 1994 Nissan Sentra. Red. In my name.

I shook my head and blinked. Surely there had to be a mistake. I studied the title a second time. Then a third. The facts in front of me didn't compute. Was the car mine? How did it get here? Who sent it?

Rather than dwell on the envelope or its contents, I taped it back to the door and continued my walk to the laundry room. I could deal with it later.

But I couldn't stop thinking about it. After I loaded the wash, I flipped open my phone. I stared at the call log. Sucking in a deep breath, I dialed her number again. Like always, it rang once before flipping to voicemail. The computer voice read my mother's number back to me and I waited for the beep.

"Mom?" I said, pausing to steady my voice. "Are you out there? Are you here? Did you leave me the car? It's a 1994 Nissan Sentra. Just like the one you had in Oklahoma, but red. Remember the banana yellow? God, I hated that car. It was so embarrassing. But we had fun with it, didn't we? We drove all over Oklahoma. You taught me to drive in that car."

I hesitated, thinking through my next words. "Mom, if you are listening to these messages, I'm sorry. I didn't hate our life. I don't wish I'd had any other mother. I just want to hear your voice. So, if you're listening, please let me tell you I'm sorry. Please pick up when I call. Or call me. Please, Mom?"

SEVEN

THE JAGGED EDGES OF THE SHINY KEY DUG INTO MY palm. My fingers knotted around it, terrified to let go. Slowly, I released my hold and stared down at the key. The metal, no longer cold, held an ominous promise. I desperately needed the freedom it held, but what stipulations did it come with? Who had given it? What did they want?

I lost half the day Sunday gazing at the damn thing. When my eyes grew tired of the lifeless key, I walked to the window, peeled back the curtains and stared outside. There she sat. Clean. Red. A few years newer than the car I'd left on the side of the road just outside of town. I wanted nothing more than to run outside and climb in. To feel her steering wheel in my hands. My foot on the gas. She solved so many problems, but I feared she'd create even more.

Trigger had given me his phone number when he dropped me off at the general store. I knew I should call him. If he didn't know who my benefactor was, I was certain he could trace the car's origins. Look up the title history, or whatever it is cops do when they need to investigate.

By three, my laundry was done, and I had the key's teeth pattern memorized. My stomach ached, begging for food. The money I'd earned last night was safely tucked into my pocket. One bottle of water remained in the fridge. I needed to go into town. Standing, I made my way back to the window. The car was still there. I sighed. It was mine, according to the title and the key in my hand.

Fuck it. I grabbed the key and my wallet. Holding my breath, I yanked open the hotel door. Humidity and heat gripped my lungs, holding them hostage for a moment. I exhaled sharply and fixed my gaze on the car. Every step I took toward it was slow and measured. I wanted to run to it, but I didn't know who might be watching. The motel seemed empty. The red Nissan, the only visible car. Still, I glanced around me to see if I could catch anyone in the act. But nothing moved. It was still and quiet outside, as if the world had pressed the pause button. The wind didn't blow. It was just me and the car. My car.

I turned the key and the locks clicked free. The door glided open without a creak of protest. Inside, the car was clean. It even smelled new, despite being a quarter-century old. Gray cloth seats welcomed me, inviting me in. Obliging their request, I slid in. My legs, bare aside from a pair of cut-off jean shorts, brushed against the soft, worn cloth. Like polar ends of a magnet, my hands found the steering wheel. Despite the heat, I didn't pull back. I wrapped my fingers around the soft, black helm.

It felt like home. A long-lost friend. It had only been two days since I'd driven, but it was the longest I'd gone. Even in Kansas City, when I thought I was settled, I still drove every day. The road was the only place I felt truly safe. Being back in the driver's seat soothed the anxiety. Turning the ignition, I didn't care where she came from or what stipulations she came with. Everything about her felt like mine. It felt right.

"Cherry?" I whispered into the lonely air. "No, too cliché. You need a name. A proper name."

I thought for a moment and ran through every name I could think of. I said each one out loud and waited for her to respond. My fingers worked their way over the dash and radio, memorizing her every curve. "Wanda," I said at last. "Wanda is your name."

The engine roared to life beneath the hood as I shifted her into drive. Despite being nearly as old as me, Wanda purred. The engine didn't shake as Trusty Rusty's had. A quick check of all the essentials told me her lights, brakes, and blinkers were all in working order. Gingerly, I pressed the gas, waiting to see how she'd respond to my touch. I smiled when she inched forward, slowly at first, then with more enthusiasm as I found my way. Much like riding a bike, a driver never forgets the feel of the road but knows to take it slow with a new friend.

The drive from the motel to the bar was much shorter than the walk; my feet silently thanked my anonymous benefactor. I quickly hushed them. No need to give thanks for something I couldn't possibly keep. I was already indebted to Trigger for whatever he was covering at the motel. I didn't want to think about what debt I might owe, and to whom I might owe it, to for a car. Even one as old as this one.

From the driver's seat, Wishing seemed much smaller than it had on foot. I arrived at the general store in significantly less time, with less sweat pouring out of me. *God, I missed driving.* I parked Wanda and headed inside, careful to lock her behind me. Once in the store, I did a quick loop to gather some essentials— shampoo, face wash, body wash, and lotion. I calculated my total carefully and made sure to grab the generics or sale items. I just needed enough to make it through the week. The general store had little to offer in the way of food, so I asked the cashier to direct me to a grocery store.

"There's the Wishing Market right off the square," she said, pointing out the store's large windows. "Take a left at First, and it's about a mile down the road. Can't miss it. The building is banana yellow."

"Interesting," I said and thanked her. I handed her two twenties and shoved the change in my pocket.

"You must be Shay," she said. Her left eyebrow cocked slightly. "Everyone's talking about you, but I can't honestly see what the fuss is all about."

"Me neither," I said, forcing a smile. "And you are?"

"Lorelei," she replied. She flicked a strand of her long, blonde hair over her shoulder. "Toby's girlfriend."

Of course he had a girlfriend. He seemed like just the type to flirt with a new girl without ever mentioning he was already spoken for. She gave me a look that told me all I needed to know. I could only assume Toby mentioned his new coworker. "Nice to meet you." I wasn't sure what else to say. It would have been tacky to mention I'd turned down her boyfriend's flirtations.

"Mhm," she hummed. "Have a good day. Be sure to mind what's yours."

I smiled again and nodded, saving my eye roll for after I'd turned away. This was exactly why I hated small towns.

I followed her directions, taking a few detours along the way. Few things taught me more about a town than getting lost within its streets. Wishing was no different. Half a dozen neighborhoods sprung off of the town square, each filled with cookie-cutter houses. I passed an elementary school, a middle school, and a high school. All three shared a name and took up just two buildings. *Home of The Wishing Bobcats,* the sign out front read in purple letters. Beneath it, they proudly proclaimed their football state championships. Five in total. Wishing was just like every other town I'd ever been forced to stop in. Like me, there wasn't anything special about her. At least not as far as I could see.

For as much as I hated small towns, my mother loved them. The cities terrified her. Small towns felt like home, she always said. Yet she never made one a permanent home. When I was younger, I falsely assumed she'd grown up in a city. When I asked her as much, she laughed and said she was a small-town girl. Though she refused to give me the name, I knew it was somewhere in Missouri. It was why we rarely spent more than a month or two here. Something about it always set her off into one of her spells. Much like questions about my father, I learned to never ask about where she grew up. That was one secret she never revealed.

Driving through Wishing, I tried to imagine her here. She'd have loved it. The perfectly manicured lawns. The neighbors that wave hello to every person who passes. The way no one was a stranger. I bet she'd have adored Rayna and Trigger. She'd have called them *good people* and told me she could see the pureness of their souls in their eyes.

I missed my mother often but touring this new town brought on an onslaught of memories I hadn't been prepared for. Blinking back tears, I shoved all thoughts of her aside. I didn't have time for feelings or emotions. She'd taught me that. Always push forward. Don't get attached. Guard your heart and pocket.

The Wishing Market was indeed banana yellow. The bricks were painted that unnatural color at least a half-century ago. The paint was chipped and peeling. As I walked closer, the imperfections caught in the sunlight. If I hadn't had a bad taste from my tour of the town, I might have laughed. I couldn't. This town wouldn't get my tears or my joy. Both would link me to it in a way I wasn't prepared for. I would feel nothing here. I wouldn't get stuck. Not here.

"Miss Lane," a familiar, warm voice called behind me. I pushed my buggy ahead, away from the voice. As I turned the corner of the breakfast food aisle, I bumped right into him.

"Trigger," I said, greeting him with fake surprise. "I wasn't sure if that was you I heard."

"The one and only. How was your first night working with Rayna?"

"Good, busy."

We stared at each other for a few awkward seconds. Wanda's key burned a hole in my pocket. I didn't want to engage in small talk, but I needed to ask.

"So," I said, breaking the silence, "do you know anything about a red Nissan Sentra?"

"Huh?" he asked. His eyebrows furrowed.

"This morning I woke up to find an envelope taped to my door. Inside were the keys and title to a 1994 Nissan."

"That is strange," he replied.

"Very. Any idea where it might have come from? I have the title. Maybe you could run it in a database or something?"

"Whose name is on the title?"

"Mine," I answered. "Just mine."

"I don't know how much help I can be, then."

"It's a small town," I said with more than a hint of accusation. "I just figured with as much as everyone pays attention to the new girl, someone might have noticed. Or, maybe, that you recognized the car."

"The car doesn't sound familiar, but I am happy to ask around and do some digging."

"I would appreciate that, Trigger."

"You're keeping the car?" he asked.

I hedged. "It just seems odd."

"How so?"

"How would it not? I just showed up Friday night. It's Sunday, and someone's left me a car. My mother and seemingly everyone in this town are the only ones who know I'm in need of one."

"It does appear to be a gift, though. I can see if the title is legitimate, but it sounds like the car is yours. You need a car. Now you have one."

He said it so matter-of-factly, I almost didn't question it. I did need a car. Badly. This afternoon's errands proved as much. Plus,

I wasn't planning on sticking around this place much longer. Having a vehicle would expedite my exit. But I couldn't silence the nagging question about where it had come from. And what did they want in return?

EIGHT

IF I'D HAD THE TIME TO OBSESS OVER THE CAR AND ITS origin story, I would have. After groceries and exploring on Sunday, I came home and read my favorite book, *Flowers for Algernon*. The pages were tattered and worn from a decade of reading and rereading. Turning those delicate pages always brought me a familiar comfort. Monday was a blur of searching the map for my next stop and budgeting how much I'd need to get back to my nomadic life. I'd popped into the bar for a few hours to help Rayna, which only managed to distract me further. Tuesday and Wednesday weren't much better. The town was officially obsessed with their newest resident, and Rayna was reaping the benefits. From the moment the doors opened at two until Rayna yelled last call at one, every table was full. Beer flowed, but so did the iced tea and hamburgers. If Rayna was enjoying the rewards, Toby was not. He cursed every single order I called back to him. His curse was usually followed by an innuendo and an invite to grab drinks after we closed. I told him no every time, but it didn't deter him.

I was in a rhythm, though. I thrived in the chaos and loved every miserable second. Aching feet were nothing compared to the questions my brain would have had if I'd had time to think about them. Instead, I was meeting every single resident of Wishing, and a few from neighboring towns. If I thought they were curious on Saturday, Tuesday and Wednesday were an entirely different game. Any shyness they'd had was gone. Their questions were flung at me faster than Rayna could sling drinks. I'd been asked out to dinner no less than ten times. One elderly woman was convinced I was destined to marry her grandson.

Every one of them asked where I was from and if I was staying. Vague answers simply would not do. They asked and asked until I finally gave in, needing to turn my attention to another table. So I'd tell them I grew up all over and wasn't sure if I was staying. I learned quickly this was the wrong answer. For the next three minutes, they'd launch into a speech about how great their little town was.

Great schools! Affordable houses! Eligible bachelors and grandsons! And on and on.

This was why I never stopped in small towns. In a big city, no one cared. Every face that passed was both new and invisible. It was easy to fade into the scenery. Too many people provided camouflage. Unless you had something to offer them, they turned a blind eye. I could blend in. Not here. The Wishing townsfolk wouldn't have it. Not for a second.

If it hadn't been mildly endearing, it would have been suffocating. But they weren't asking out of morbid curiosity. They had a genuine desire to get to know me. No detail was too small. In their eyes, there was nothing insignificant about me. I was like a brand-new book, and they couldn't wait to crack open the spine and see where the story began and ended. Even the middle engaged them.

One thing I knew for certain was the instant I had enough cash in my pocket, I was out of here and on to the first big city I could get to. Maybe I'd finally make it to Nashville. Ever since watching *The Thing Called Love* over and over in some random motel in Indiana, I'd been in love with the city. I always begged my mother to take me, but she never would. In the six years since she'd left, I intended to go but never made it. I'd yet to even make it to Tennessee. Instead, I stuck to the states I knew, where she and I had visited before. As much as I hated familiarity, part of me longed for it. I made a point to not visit the cities or towns we'd been to before, but I passed through them along the way. Sometimes I stopped long enough to ask if anyone had seen her, but they never had. By the time I settled in Kansas City, I'd given up on finding her. She clearly didn't want to be found.

I patted the phone in my pocket, vowing to call her once I made it back to the motel. It would be nearly three in the morning, but it wasn't like she'd answer anyway.

"You look oddly familiar," the dark-haired woman said. She propped her elbow on the table and rested her chin in her hand. She gazed up at me with a strange curiosity. "Doesn't she look familiar, Hannah?"

Hannah barely glanced up from her phone. "Mom, you think everyone looks familiar. Leave the poor girl alone."

"I do not. Put that blasted phone away. I swear, you kids are always on those damned things. Posting your dinner plates and duck lips."

"At least I'm not posting chain letters and memes on my friends' walls all day."

I'd never been on social media, but I'd overheard enough to know what they were talking about. I refilled the mother's iced tea and offered the daughter another glass of wine. She declined.

"Where did you say you were from, dear?" she asked, ignoring her daughter.

"Just came from Kansas City," I answered for the fifteenth time tonight. Surely this town gossiped enough to know these answers by now.

"Yes, I know that. But where were you born?"

I paused, debating my answer. "Somewhere in Kelb County."

"That's not far from here, you know."

I did know. Well, after studying the map on Monday, I realized the proximity. I obsessed over that county for much of my teen years. I knew the roads in and out of it better than I knew my own name. This particular part of Missouri was one area my mother refused to come near anytime we ended up in the state, which wasn't often. But there was something about it that pulled me in. More than once, I'd pointed my car south and intended on driving to Kelb County, but every time something stopped me. I'd run out of gas money or get sidetracked. It's quite possible I'd been heading there when I left Kansas City, but whether that was my intended destination or not was a question even I couldn't answer.

"What did you say your last name was? I've got some kin out in Kelb. Maybe they know your family?"

"I didn't," I said and excused myself. As curious as I was, I didn't know if I was ready to find out. I didn't need anything else to keep me here. I made a point to avoid their table as much as possible. There was plenty to do to keep busy. Food to run. Drinks to fill. Stares to avoid.

"I just don't get it," I mumbled to Rayna. We stood shoulder to shoulder in front of the row of beer taps. "Why is everyone in this place so damn curious?"

"Bitsy over there is the town gossip, and she's decided it's her business to be in everyone else's private lives," she replied. "Wishing is a small town. Small towns love to gossip."

"I'm aware."

"Everyone knows everyone, and if they don't, they feel a need to."

"But I'm not even sticking around."

"Well, perhaps that is why they care."

"Because I'm leaving soon?"

"That, and maybe they don't want you to leave." Her sentence hung in the air as if it were missing a word or two.

"They don't get much say in that, now do they?" I snapped. "I'm not made for small towns. Too many noses in my business."

Rayna shrugged and patted my arm. "They are just loving people. Something tells me you could use some of that."

Before I could argue, another table called my name. I plastered a smile on my face and forced aside my annoyance.

"There you are, Shay," the middle-aged man sighed in relief.

"What can I get for you?" I asked. His drink was more than half full, and his meal seemed to meet his expectations, as he'd eaten more than a third of it.

"The name is Edwin."

"Edwin," I repeated. "Can I get you another beer?"

"No, ma'am."

"How is your food?"

"Well," he said, pausing to scratch his nose. "The burger is a bit overdone."

"Oh dear. I requested it to be medium." He lifted his plate to show me the burger. It was still a bit pink, not quite mooing, but pink nonetheless. "Would you like me to have it remade?"

"Could you?"

"Of course, let me get you a slice of Rayna's chocolate cake for the trouble."

"That would be wonderful." I offered a slight smile and took his plate.

"Toby," I called into the kitchen. "Table fifteen needs a remake. More moo, less grill."

"What?" he asked.

"The bacon cheeseburger for table fifteen is overdone. He wants more pink."

"Edwin?" he asked, looking over my shoulder. I nodded. "That cranky old man is never fucking happy."

"Whoa there, tiger, it's just a burger."

"Just a burger?" he hissed at me. "I've got five other burgers on the grill and seven orders of chicken tenders to make."

"And?" I asked.

"And remaking your burger is going to throw everything off."

"Would you like me to come make it?" I threw my hands up and gestured behind me. "You can take all these tables and answer their nosy questions."

"Oh, sweetie, they don't give two shits about me. You're the reason we're so damn busy. They'll all leave if I go out there. Then how will you make your great escape without all those tips?"

I huffed in response and rolled my eyes. After Saturday night, he hadn't bothered asking me any more questions, but he was sure to throw all of his assumptions at me.

"The way I see it, you should be grateful for their curiosity. You're the one gettin' rich off 'em."

"Rich?" I snorted. "It's going to take me a month to scrape together enough money." Six weeks to be exact. Five weeks longer than I'd hoped. Especially now that I was paying Eddie sixty bucks a night for my room. His and Trigger's generosity ran out on Monday. Just as I'd folded my last eighty bucks into my pocket. That meant I only cleared about fifty or sixty dollars each night I worked. I'd definitely be sticking around long enough to collect my paper checks. I'd need them.

"Poor you," he said, pouting. "I'll have Edwin's burger in five. Here's table six's fried pickles." He shoved the red basket through the window. I glared at him for a moment before grabbing them.

"Thanks," I said with little sincerity. Between my sour mood and his, a cloud fell over the bar. It shifted everything, including Rayna's normally calm demeanor. By the end of the night, we were snapping at each other with little regard for the other person's feelings. The customers picked up on it as well. Their tips got smaller, and their questions ceased. As much as I missed the big piles of cash left on the tables, I enjoyed the silence more.

At one-thirty, Rayna locked the door behind the last guest and sighed. "What a shitstorm that was."

"You can say that again," I replied, sinking into the first chair I saw. My feet throbbed, and my head pounded. Toby shut off the music and joined us in the dining room.

"I can't wait for your newness to wear off," he said. I raised an eyebrow. "What?"

"You'd rather be slow?" I asked. I enjoyed the rush of busy-work, but I too wanted their fascination with me to die down.

"No, I'd rather have a nice waitress that doesn't snap at me."

"I'd love a cook that didn't look at my ass every time I walked away."

"Good luck with that one. I'd rather look at your ass than listen to you whine about customers all night."

I rolled my eyes. "Don't be a dick. I wasn't whining about customers, just their interrogation techniques."

"Get used to it."

"Alright, you two. No more bickering."

"Yes, Rayna," we replied in unison.

"Let's get cleaned up and get out of here. Tomorrow's only going to be busier."

Toby headed back to the kitchen, and I bused the last few tables. We cleaned in silence. His apology came in the form of a shoulder bump at the dishwasher, followed by a sly smile.

"You could just say the words," I said.

"What words?"

"An apology," I replied.

"You first."

I winked and turned back to the dining room where Rayna was standing with her hands on her hips.

"Shay," she called over her shoulder. "You've got a visitor."

NINE

"Trigger, what brings you out this late?" I asked. He stepped forward and offered an awkward handshake that shifted into an even weirder hug. I stepped back and brushed my hands over my shirt.

"Trigger never stops working," Toby said as he passed us. "I'm heading home. Need anything before I go, Rayna?"

She waved him off before excusing herself and leaving me alone with Trigger.

"Can I get you an iced tea or water?" I offered him out of habit. He shook his head. "Did you get a chance to look into the car?"

"I did. It was sold in a private sale a week ago. The title is clear and in your name."

"Who bought the car?"

He shrugged. "They paid cash and put it all in your name. There is no record other than that."

"Isn't that odd?"

He lifted his shoulders again, releasing them with a sigh. "I've seen weirder."

That didn't exactly answer my question. "So, what do I do?"

"Take the car down to the county clerk's office and get your tags transferred. I had the guys down at the junkyard pull the tags off your old car. Left 'em with Eddie at the motel. They're still good, so you'll just have to get them transferred."

"You don't find it at all strange that someone left me a car?" I asked again, pressing for an answer. Surely, I wasn't the only one that found all of this to be too convenient.

He shook his head. "It's yours. Keep it or sell it."

I opened my mouth to object once more, but he held his hand up as a call came over his radio. I listened with him as the dispatcher shared the coded message. He closed his eyes as he listened, the lines in his forehead creasing. When the message was delivered, he opened his eyes again. I tried to look away before he noticed but failed.

"Listen, kid, it sounds like someone is looking out for you. Perhaps you have a fairy godmother."

He was gone before I could offer my rebuttal. *Fairy godmother?* No way. If I had a fairy godmother, where had she been when I need her all these years when I was alone and broke? When my own mother walked out on me? Where was she when my mother and I went days without eating and slept in our car? Why now? Why here?

I didn't have time to wallow in the questions. Rayna called me over to cash out. Despite the atmosphere, I still managed to clear over $100 in tips. So far, that seemed to be the trend. It still wasn't enough. Paying nightly for the motel would drain my funds, and Eddie wouldn't offer a weekly rate no matter how much I begged. He was firm in his rule that the motel was no place to live. I left the bar wondering how I'd ever get out of this town and back on the road.

If I were still with my mother, she'd have found a way to make the extra cash. She always did. Just when things seemed to be the worst they could be, she'd show up with a purse full of cash, throw our things in the car, and we'd be gone. When I was younger, I never asked questions. I just ate my Happy Meal or whatever treat she bought me and kept my mouth shut. It wasn't until my thirteenth birthday that I learned the truth.

My mother cleaned a lot of toilets and motel rooms in her day. It was how we almost always managed to have a roof over our heads. If she wasn't housekeeping, she waited tables and tended bar. Much like I did now. But when times were especially rough and the money ran out, she turned to other means to keep us fed and clothed. She never talked about these things, but she was never ashamed of them either. Even when I confronted her.

That night was the first time I got a glimpse of the woman who would later abandon me. Her eyes held regret and rage, and for the first time, those emotions were directed at me.

It was early May 2007, and we were in Lincoln, Nebraska. It was also my thirteenth birthday. I'd known we were out of money. We hadn't had breakfast, and lunch was crackers she'd found in the bottom of her purse. She left the motel room at noon, kissed the top of my head, and promised to be back by dinner so we could celebrate. I think I whined about making sure we had cake or something equally selfish. I sat alone in that room and waited. I waited until midnight before I fell asleep. She stumbled in a few hours later. Her sobs woke me from whatever dream I was lost in.

Mascara ran down her cheeks, leaving inky black trails. Her eyes refused to budge from their hold on the floor. Her body shook. Rain dripped from her hair all the way down to her knees. Her dress, the blue one she loved, was ripped. Practically torn to shreds.

"You promised," I'd whined, begging her to look at me. "You said today would be special." At the time, I hadn't noticed how disheveled she was. All I knew was that she'd missed my birthday and she'd come home without cake. Nothing else mattered to me.

"Where were you?" I shouted. "You promised!"

My mother never kept promises. Not once. I knew better than

to believe them, but I always did. She rarely made them, so when she did, I let myself believe her. She only used them when things were desperate, and she needed to placate my protests. At first, the promises were small—a new book or toy. They got bigger as I got older. A real school. Answers. None of it ever came.

But birthdays were different. She always made a show out of celebrating my birthday. It was the one day of the year I felt her full affection. Birthdays were special. This wasn't just any old birthday; it was my thirteenth. I was exiting childhood and entering my teen years. To me, it was a big deal. Nothing else mattered.

"You ungrateful, selfish brat," she spat at me. She finally lifted her head, and when her eyes met mine, I regretted it instantly. There was a coldness there I'd never seen before. "Do you have any idea what I do to keep you safe?"

I shook my head, unable to speak.

It was then she told me about the men. There in the early morning hours of my first day as a teenager, she told me all about the birds and the bees and how a woman could profit from them. In great, painful detail, she explained to me exactly how she planned to pay for my birthday cake and surprise. Then she shared how it went wrong, horribly wrong, so she hadn't been able to. She screamed that while I was asleep in a comfortable bed, she was being deprived of both comfort and sleep. I couldn't hear her over my tears. I didn't want to stare, but I couldn't take my eyes off of her. She looked different. Older. Sadder.

"Oh, stop your crying, girl," she said. Her words slapped my face. I gasped for tiny breaths as I tried to calm myself. "Save your tears. No one gives a shit about them or you."

"I'm sorry, Mommy," I whispered.

"Enough with the *Mommy*. You're a woman. My name is Tammy."

"I'm sorry, Tammy," I said. Her name felt like poison dripping from my lips. Bitter and sour.

"You've got a lot to learn, Shay," she said with exasperation that spread through her entire body. "I don't need your sympathy or apology."

She tossed the cash at me. I didn't reach for it. As it fluttered to the floor, something on her face shifted. "Don't ever be like me, Shay. Promise me you'll never do the things I've done."

I nodded my head and promised. She sighed and pulled me into her arms. She held me and rocked me as we stood together. Her hand brushing through my hair. Then she kissed my cheek and sent me to bed.

The next morning, we loaded into the car and left Lincoln. We drove for three days until she found a motel we could barely afford. The clerk, a chubby man who always smelled of body odor and cigars, told her there wasn't a housekeeping position available, but a silent look passed between them. She sent me to the room by myself that night. When she joined me a few hours later, she informed me there was a housekeeping job. We'd be staying in nowhere Nebraska for a few weeks until we had enough cash to get to Kansas or Oklahoma.

When she crawled into the bed next to me, I recoiled from her touch. I couldn't look at her the same way. If she noticed, she didn't say anything. But after that night, she never again mentioned her work. The hug she gave me the day after my thirteenth birthday was the last one she ever gave me. I should have known then that things wouldn't ever be the same again. We became strangers in that motel. The woman I'd known as my mother my entire life as my was foreign to me. She'd been the only constant in my life, and I didn't recognize her anymore. We still spoke as mother and daughter, but it was all pretend. An act she put on until she could get rid of me.

I pulled the scratchy covers over my body and buried my face in the pillow. This bed, though hundreds of miles from that motel in Nebraska, felt just the same. Empty. Lonely.

In my hand, the key burned with a million questions. I held it tightly as if keeping it close would bring me those answers. I wasn't even sure I really wanted them, but they nagged at me. Now that the bustle of the bar was gone and I was alone with my thoughts, it was all I could think about. The only people who knew where I was were my mother and everyone in this damn town. No one here knew me well enough to care, though. I'd been here less than a week, and I hadn't exactly opened up to anyone.

Toby was the only resident I could think of who had anything to gain from giving me something as grand as a car. He hadn't bothered to hide his desire to worm his way into my motel room, so if he'd been behind the car, he would have said something.

I rolled onto my back and stared at the ceiling. No. It wasn't Toby. He wanted to sleep with me. He didn't really care whether or not I had a car. I couldn't imagine Rayna, Eddie, Trigger, or anyone else I'd met this week buying me a car, even a cheap one.

That left my mother.

The thought should have been comforting, but it wasn't. I'd been more desperate than I was now. I'd been devastated and broken so many times before. She hadn't shown up then. She'd not been there any other time. Flipping to my side, I reached for the phone on the nightstand. I held my finger over the call button, hesitating. The familiar rush of heat spread through my face as my heart raced. This used to happen every single time I called her. The what-ifs and ludicrous hope that maybe she'd pick up this one time. Calling her became a habit—a drug, almost. It wasn't even her voice on the recording. I wasn't sure I remembered what her voice sounded like anymore.

"Mom. Are you there? Where are you?" I had more to say but couldn't force the words from my throat. My eyes burned. My body ached. My heart broke. I had so much I needed to tell her, so many questions to ask, but in that dark motel room, I clung to the phone, unable to speak.

When the message timed out, I hung up and rested back on

the pillow. My eyes tried to close, but I forced them open. I didn't want to dream tonight. All I wanted was my mother. More specifically, the mother I'd had before I turned thirteen. I'd give anything to have that innocence back. Anything to have her back. Not Tammy, but Mommy. I wanted to undo whatever I'd done that night. I wanted to take back what had happened to her.

TEN

As Rayna promised, Friday night was busy. Not just busy, but pure insanity. Mary came in to help with expediting and delivering food. Eddie popped in during the dinner rush to help Toby in the kitchen. It still wasn't enough to keep things under control. The mood was lighter than it had been on Thursday. Toby was back to his usual flirty self, and Rayna barked orders in her semi-happy clip. I tried to ignore everything that nagged at me. I was mostly successful.

At ten, Eddie and Mary left, leaving me alone with my familiar crew. After almost a week together, the three of us fell into a rhythm. We each knew how the others moved and had our own dance we performed each night. It felt almost comfortable, a feeling I wasn't sure I'd ever get used to. For me, comfort meant fear. At any moment, the peace it brought could erupt into chaos and I'd be left broken again.

"Order up!" Toby shouted from the kitchen. I dropped the towel I was holding onto the table and rushed back to grab the plate. "Please, for the love of God, tell me that is the last table."

"Last one. They already asked for to-go boxes, so I don't think they plan to linger."

"Just don't tell them you're new in town."

I stuck my tongue out at him.

"Promises, promises."

I took the plate out to the table and returned to my closing tasks. All the tables were cleaned, and the silverware was mostly rolled. When it slowed down around midnight, I was able to catch up and get things settled. I also didn't want Toby to sit down with me to help. As comfortable as we'd gotten over the past few days, I wasn't up to another night of relentless flirting.

Despite my best efforts, he plopped down at the table after the last customers left. Rather than help me gather the plates and glasses, he leaned back in the chair and propped his feet up on the table. His arms flanked his head like wings, and I could tell by the look in his eyes that he was up to something.

"Whatever it is, my answer is no," I said, swatting his feet with a towel.

"You don't even want to hear the question?"

"Nope."

"It's a good one."

"I doubt that."

"Come on, Shay."

"No."

"I'm going to ask anyway," he said with a smirk. "Let me show you around town. I've got a six-pack of beer and can make us some burgers."

"I don't drink," I replied.

"Ever?"

"Never."

"Why?"

"Because I don't," I snapped, exasperated. Tonight's customers were less inquisitive, and I naively thought I'd get a break from twenty questions and curious eyes. Leave it to Toby to prove me wrong.

"Okay, I'll grab some iced tea."

"No, thank you."

"Oh, we're narrowing down our choices and getting some-where. No beer. No tea. Water?"

"No, Toby. No matter the question, my answer is no."

"You don't think I'm sexy?" he asked, lifting his hips suggestively.

"Gross, put your pelvis down."

"I see you looking at me."

"You don't. If I'm looking at you, it's because I need an order or you're being so ridiculous I'm checking to see if you're still human."

"So you were checking me out."

"Don't you have dishes to do or a grill to clean?"

"Already done, just waiting on you, darling."

"You shouldn't bother," I said. I gave the table one final wipe down before turning to Rayna. "Ready for me to cash out?"

"Yeah, Rayna, cash her out so I can show her around town."

"Give it a rest, Toby," Rayna replied. "Got your receipts?" I nodded and left Toby sitting at the table. He promptly followed me to the bar.

I handed Rayna the receipts and tried to ignore Toby. He didn't say anything while Rayna added or while I counted, but I could feel his eyes on me.

"Go home, Toby," Rayna said. "Have a good night?"

"Yes, very good. Better than Saturday."

"Glad to hear it. You're doing a great job, Shay. I know you ain't sticking around, but you should know I'm happy to have you as long as you need."

"Thanks. The motel is killing my budget," I admitted before I realized what I was saying. "I just mean, it's taking most of my tips. Makes it hard to save up."

"Why don't you find a month-to-month lease?" Toby asked.

"I don't know how long I'm going to be here."

"That's kind of the point of month-to-month."

"What if I'm not here for a month?"

"All the more reason to let me take you out tonight." I should have known he'd twist my answer.

"Listen, Toby, I don't mind working with you, but I'm not going out with you."

"Why not?"

"For one? I don't make it a habit to date boys with girl-friends." *Or wives. At least not anymore.* "Second, I don't date coworkers."

"Whoa, whoa, whoa," he said, throwing his hands up. "Who said anything about a girlfriend?"

Rayna chuckled. Something told me she was all too familiar with Toby's escapades.

"Lorelei."

"Oh, good God." He laughed and rolled his eyes. He ran his hand through his jet-black hair. "She's not my girlfriend."

"She seems to disagree."

"We broke up months ago. I've made my position clear to her. I can't help it if the ladies love me." He wagged an eyebrow and winked.

"Get over yourself." I groaned. I knew his type. I despised every Toby I'd ever met. They all assumed a girl on the road was a loose girl. The truth was, until Greg, I'd mostly kept my hands to myself. I wasn't my mother. I was never going to be her. Men had their usefulness, and I knew how to flirt to get what I needed, but I rarely ever took it beyond that. Greg had been the one excep-tion, and that didn't exactly end well for me. I didn't need a man, and I sure as hell wasn't going to make the same mistake my mother had. To be clear, that mistake was me. I wanted none of it. I didn't need it. I could take care of myself in more ways than one.

"I will get you to say yes," he said. The cockiness in his voice was nauseating.

"You won't. This whole keep-asking-until-a-girl-wears-down

is a tired game. No means no. We can be friends. That's it. I'm not looking to make a mess of things over some stupid boy."

He hopped off the barstool and put his hands on his hips. Rayna glanced at him and then at me with an amused smile.

"I'm guessing you're a hot commodity in this town, but I'm not like the girls here. I don't want to settle down. I don't want to hook up. I just want gas money and a few bucks to live on. Then, I'm gone. I'm not leaving any baggage behind, and I'm not taking any with me. So if you want to keep up this game, by all means, keep wasting your breath. Just know my answer is no. It will always be no." With that, I handed Rayna her cash and turned to go.

"Wait," he called after me. "I'm sorry."

"What?" I stopped and asked. There wasn't even a hint of sarcasm in his apology.

"I'm sorry, Shay. You're right."

"Well, that's something I've never heard before," Rayna said with a chuckle.

He ignored her. "Friends? Can we be friends?"

"Sure, but I'm still not letting you show me around town."

"I know."

"No more flirting?"

"None." He sounded sincere, so I nodded.

"Friends, then."

"See you tomorrow," he said.

"Alright, have a good night, guys." I waved and headed for the door.

If I were being completely honest with myself, I'd admit to feeling something towards Toby. He was attractive, but he also made me laugh. His jokes and flirting distracted me from every-thing else. I didn't want him to. I didn't need a distraction, but I welcomed it. If I allowed myself to think too much, I'd drive myself insane. Kansas City. Greg. My mother. The car. This town. None of it made sense. Everything used to be simple.

Maybe simple wasn't the right word. Predictable. I knew what to expect before Kansas City. The road used to be all I needed. I'd given up on my silly childhood fantasies of having a home. But Greg gave me hope again. Stability wasn't something I understood; I wanted it, but I didn't know how to achieve it. For me, instability was stable. It was all I knew. Until Kansas City, I'd never stayed in one place for more than a few months. I'd never had confidence that I'd have a bed to sleep in or food to eat. I'd never had comfort.

Now, I was feeling it again. In only a week, Wishing gave me that unfamiliar comfort. It held me in its arms and begged me to stay. Everything about this place screamed stability. Even working in the bar provided some level of security. It was almost like a home. Rayna wasn't exactly the mothering type, but she made me feel like I belonged with her. Maybe I did.

No. I shook my head. Turning the key and walking into the motel, I refused to allow myself even a second to think that I belonged here or anywhere. My life was on the road, chasing an imaginary finish line.

My phone tugged at me like a brick in my pocket. I'd called her every single day since I'd been here. Out of habit, I dialed her number from memory, not bothering to use the saved entry. I'd made myself memorize it in case I ever ran out of money to buy minutes for the phone. Or if it was ever stolen.

"Hey, Mom," I said with a deep sigh. "I'm going to tell you something that I'm scared to admit. You were right. You were right about small towns. I think I'll always prefer the anonymity of a big city, but there is something warm about small towns. Or maybe it's just this particular small town. I know we've never been here, it's too close to Kelb County. Sorry, I know I'm not supposed to mention that place to you, but it is. Maybe that's why I feel drawn to Wishing. Do you believe in fate, Mom? I don't. Never have. You taught me that we are responsible for ourselves and shouldn't depend on luck or anyone to look out for us. But this place feels different. It feels like I belong here. Not this motel room, I definitely don't belong here. I know it sounds insane, but I want to stay here. Maybe find a little apartment to rent? I've never had an apartment, Mom. I can't remember if we ever slept anywhere other than motels or rundown trailers. I'd ask you, but you won't answer. You never do. I know I'm on my own."

The voicemail clicked off. I'd run over my allowed time. I considered calling her back but couldn't find the energy. I replayed my message over and over in my mind, wishing I could delete it. Did I really want to stay here? Was I really considering making Wishing my temporary residence? I thought about Rayna, Toby, and Trigger. I'd already shared more with them than I ever had with Greg. Greg and I never talked. So, it wasn't like it took much to share more with them. Unlike Greg, they seemed genuinely interested in me.

I yawned. Sleep took over my thoughts. Tomorrow, I decided; tomorrow I'll flip a coin. Heads, I stay. Tails, I go. I'd let fate decide.

ELEVEN

MY MOUTH WATERED AT THE SIGHT OF THE STACK OF pancakes in front of me. An hour ago, Rayna had banged on my motel door, jarring me from a restless sleep. She'd rushed me to get dressed, brush my teeth, and meet her outside. For someone who worked until two in the morning, she had far too much energy. I'd have loved nothing more than to sleep the day away, but she had other plans for me.

The sun, still far too bright for my preferences, blared through the wide windows of the Diner on the Square. This restaurant and Lace & Grit were the only two dining choices for the residents of Wishing. As a result, the diner was just as busy as the bar. There were several familiar faces sitting at neighboring tables. This morning, their cups were filled with coffee rather than beer, but their faces bore the same expressions. I knew a few of their names, but mostly I just knew their occupations. Librarian. Teacher. Plumber. Truck driver. Farmer. And so on.

In the early morning hours, without the added confidence of alcohol, they appeared to be far less interested in me. Only one or two acknowledged me with a nod, which was a welcome change. I sat back in the chair, allowing myself to relax a bit.

"Eat up, girl," Rayna said and pointed at my plate. "They won't stay hot long. Syrup?"

I shook my head. "I'm a plain pancake girl."

"Butter?"

I said no again.

"Interesting."

"We didn't get pancakes often when I was little. The rare times my mother made them, there wasn't money for syrup or extra butter."

"Well, that's the saddest thing I've ever heard," she said as she poured an unhealthy amount of syrup over her pancake stack. "I get the feeling you're like an onion. Full of stories and flavor when the walls and layers are peeled back."

I dropped my head forward and focused on my plate. Eggs. Bacon. Pancakes. Coffee to the right. Plenty to look at other than the questions in Rayna's eyes. I should have known there was more to this breakfast than a free meal. I know better than anyone that nothing comes free.

"You know Mary, Eddie's niece, right?"

"Yes," I mumbled, not looking up. "She worked with us last night."

"She's my daughter," Rayna said. This got my attention. Mary called her Aunt Rayna and gave no indication that she was anything more. In their interactions last night, they'd kept their distance and didn't talk much. "I was twenty-one when I had her. Married my high school sweetheart, but we both loved the bottle more. Drank ourselves silly nearly every night. Having Mary didn't change that. He got bored a year or so in and left us, which meant double the liquor for me. My big sister, Helen, stepped in and took Mary. Raised her as her own. Took me ten years to put down the booze. By then, Mary called Helen 'Mama,' and I was running the bar. Ironic that I quit drinking when I started slinging drinks, but I couldn't see I had a problem until I saw the same problem in everyone else. My life was in a better place, but Mary didn't know me as anyone other than Aunt Rayna. We didn't tell her the truth until her senior year. She'd figured it out, of course. Kids are so much smarter than we give them credit for."

"Why are you telling me this?" I asked, knowing full well that her intent was to get me to open up and share.

"I know all about complicated relationships with mothers and daughters. My own mother was tough as nails. She'd beat the curse words and back talk right out of you. She wasn't afraid of the switch or a harsh word. But she was my only mother, and I loved her. And she loved me, flaws and all."

"Did Mary forgive you?"

"For what, Shay?"

"Abandoning her."

Rayna's eye twitched, and her lips turned down. "I didn't abandon her. I realized I was no good for her and put her in the care of someone who was. Someone capable of love and self-lessness."

"I wish my mother had done that," I admitted. "Instead, she regretted me."

"I doubt that," Rayna said, lifting her coffee to her mouth. She took a sip and closed her eyes as she swallowed. "Being a mom is hard work and not all of us are cut out for it. I'm sure your mother loves you."

"In her way, maybe," I conceded, not wanting to dive into the complicated ways my mother showed her love.

"She took care of you and raised you. Made pancakes when she couldn't afford syrup."

I knew she meant it to reassure me, but the guilt ached inside of me. My mother had gone to great lengths to take care of me, and I'd been nothing but ungrateful.

"What's on your mind, Shay?"

I let my gaze slowly drift across the table until I met Rayna's eyes. "The last thing I said to my mother was that I was ashamed of her and who she was," I said, biting my cheek to stop the tears

I knew were coming. "I told her I hated our life and how she raised me."

"You were angry?"

"Very. My mother did so many things that embarrassed me. She did anything and everything she could for a buck. She left me alone in hotel rooms while she was out with her flavor of the week. We slept on strange men's couches. We moved from motel to motel when their wives found out. There was always some new guy and a new town. She followed them around, using them while they used her." I didn't want to tell Rayna any of this. I didn't want to tell anyone. Saying the words out loud made them true. It made every awful thing she'd done real. But I couldn't stop myself. Rayna made me feel safe. Her brown eyes were soft and inviting, a stark contrast to the harshness the rest of her held. "I'm pretty sure my dad was married, too,"

"It sounds like your mama was hurting," she said. She reached across the table and squeezed my hand. "When women have babies, they're still women with needs."

"Yeah, but most of them don't fuck an entire town for a free motel room." I covered my mouth, not believing I'd said the words out loud. "I'm sorry."

"No four-letter word bothers me, child. I work in a bar. I've heard it all before."

"She wasn't always like that, I don't think," I said, continuing the confession I hadn't meant to make. "It got worse after my thirteenth birthday. That's when she told me the truth. I stopped calling her mom. I couldn't look at her. When I did, all I felt was shame. Shame in myself for being the reason she did what she did. Shame in her for doing it. She saw it, I know she did. She flinched when she looked at me. At the time I thought it was because I disappointed her, but now I know she was disappointed in herself."

"When was the last time you saw her?" she asked gently.

"Six years ago. The day before my nineteenth birthday."

"Birthdays haven't been good to you, have they?"

I laughed and shook my head. "Not at all."

"What happened?"

"What didn't happen?" I asked with a subtle smile. "Everything blew up."

Then, I told her the story I vowed to never tell anyone. The one I never wanted to remember. "We were in Iowa," I started. "We'd been there for almost five months. I'd just taken my GED and was starting to think about college. It was a long shot, I knew, but I wanted so desperately to be done with this life."

I'd never known a life that didn't involve living out of suitcases. It was no secret to my mother that I wanted and needed more. I was tired of the road and smelly motels. I was sick of the rotating door of men who smelled worse than the motel rooms. Now that I was eighteen, they'd started looking at me more and more. Their eyes would drift between my mother and me. Sometimes their thoughts were left unspoken, but most of the time, they weren't. My mother always brushed them off, insisting her daughter wasn't up for grabs.

At the time, my mother was working at a little farmhouse restaurant that was owned by a man named Will. His wife, Susan, ran the restaurant while Will managed their family farm. They had four kids, all within a few years of each other. Their eldest, Adam, was my age. The three daughters were younger than me, and they all hated me. Somehow, my mother had wormed her way into their lives. We lived in an old trailer parked on their land. It was the first time she'd found honest work. Susan and Will took her in and were mentoring both of us.

Susan, despite her daughters' dislike for me, took a special interest in me. She helped me study for my GED and drove me to take the test. All the while keeping the secret from my mother. What Susan saw in me, I'll never know, but she encouraged and supported me in a way my mother never could have. My mother was selfish and only saw how I could benefit her. Susan had the foresight to see a promising future for me. I'd given up on myself, but Susan pushed me to see there was more.

"I like Susan," Rayna interjected with a smile. "You are definitely worth the effort, Shay."

"I wish I could tell you that is where this story goes," I said. My cheeks flushed as I let the memories in. "I'm more like my mother than you know."

The night it fell apart, Will, Susan, and my mother were busy at the restaurant. Their daughters were visiting their grandparents. I was sitting alone in the trailer, reading. I don't remember what book, but I do know it is no longer in my suitcase. Around seven, a light knock on the door disturbed my reading trance. I ignored it at first, but the person on the other side was persistent. Dropping the book onto the floor beside me, I got up to answer the door. Adam was on the other side.

I'd noticed Adam more than once. We'd flirted and teased each other. Part of me assumed that's why his sisters didn't like me. They were protective of their brother. His hair was a shade of dark blond that complimented his farmer's tan. His blue eyes danced when he laughed. And I did everything I could to make him laugh.

"I've always been a sucker for blue eyes," Rayna said when I paused to take a long sip of water before getting to the *good* part. She was listening attentively, captivated by every detail. Not in the way that said she'd be hungry for gossip, but she was genuinely interested to know me. Her eyes studied my face, reading ahead and trying to put the pieces together. It wasn't hard to predict where this story was going.

"He had a six-pack of beer and a few wine coolers. We'd both snuck a few sips of a stolen beer after dinner a few nights before. After everyone left the table, he'd whispered in my ear that he liked me. I'd been too shy to say anything back." I can still remember the way his breath felt against my skin, followed by a gentle brush of his hand. He didn't say another word but lingered beside me for a moment. That was the first time I remember feeling wanted. It was addicting. I needed more.

When he walked through the door of the trailer, he lifted the bottles. I remember smiling as the heat rushed through me. I'd never so much as kissed a boy, but something about him warmed the chill inside me. Looking at him standing in the doorway, I suddenly understood my mother's need for attention and touch. I wanted him more than I'd ever wanted anything or anyone before.

"I drank every last wine cooler," I said. My eyes drifted to the floor; I didn't dare look at Rayna. Shame washed over me. "After all the things I'd ever judged my mother for, all it took was a few drinks and one boy's attention to become just like her."

Adam drank the beer and offered me one when the wine coolers were gone. I didn't, and still don't, like beer, but I took it. I drank it as if I'd never had a sip of water before. I was parched. Starving. I didn't even bat an eye when he reached for my shirt. His hand burned against my skin. Everything about his touch was wrong, but it felt right. I let him in further and further until there wasn't an inch between us. After, he held me, brushing his fingers through my hair and thanking me for allowing him to be my first. He acted as though it was a great honor. He made me feel important—special, even. I knew he wasn't a virgin, but he acted as though I were the only one he'd ever touched. He marveled at the sight of me. I glowed under his eyes. Most girls will tell you their first time was horrible or painful. Not mine. Adam, though I knew he couldn't have loved or cared about me, was slow and patient. He made sure to take care of me. Maybe he was just as nervous, but he seemed to know what he was doing.

"I knew deep down that I should have been ashamed," I admitted, "but I wasn't. I was well aware of what I'd done and the consequences. I didn't care. For once, I gave in to what I wanted without a care for anyone else. I may have been young, but I was neither dumb nor naive. I was as much to blame as he was. I have no doubt he would have left if I'd told him to."

The consequences came quickly. Adam and I lost track of time. Neither of us noticed the sun going down or the voices growing louder. When the door opened and my mother and Susan walked in, I didn't hide. Adam tried to. He'd been caught in bed with the trash.

"Adam insisted I'd seduced him. He told his mom everything was my fault, and in the same breath, he accused me of stealing the drinks. When Will showed up after hearing the commotion, he called me and my mom trash. I'll never forget the way Susan looked at me. In her eyes, I'd ruined her son. It wasn't until I saw how upset Susan was that I felt embarrassed or ashamed. She'd trusted my mother and me. She'd gone out of her way to be kind and welcoming to me, and I betrayed her," I said, wiping away the tears I couldn't stop. "She told me I wasn't worth the time of day or effort she'd put into me. Then, she kicked us out. My mother couldn't even look at me."

I felt nothing towards my mother that night. Not pity or shame. I wasn't angry with her. I finally understood her. Or, at least, I thought I did. She didn't see it that way. I'd never seen her so angry with me.

The fight we had in the car was the worst we'd ever had. Everything came out. Her true feelings toward me. The truth that I'd ruined her life. My hatred of her and the way she raised me. I blamed her for everything, and she blamed me. She'd insisted we had a good thing with Will and Susan and my actions took it all away. She conveniently forgot everything I'd seen her do. When we reached the Missouri state line, she stopped the car.

"It was midnight. Everything was dark. I saw the words in her eyes before she said them." I fought the urge to keep staring at the floor and lifted my head. Rayna was watching my face intently. There wasn't an ounce of judgment in her eyes. "She gave me a few dollars and told me to get out of the car. I didn't believe her at first, but she reached across me and opened the door. I cried and begged her to at least take me into town, but she was done with me. I could see it. I took the money, my suitcase of books, and my backpack. Then I screamed those hateful words at her and slammed the door."

"She just left you on the side of the road?"

"Yes," I said, sobbing. I felt the restaurant grow quiet. Rayna's hand rested on top of mine. She patted it softly. "I haven't seen or heard from her since. I still have her number and leave her messages every once in a while. But she never answers or calls back. I doubt she even listens to them."

"I bet she does," Rayna said. Her voice was calm and soft. "Have you tried to find her?"

"At first I did. As soon as I had enough money for a bus ticket, I took one to Kansas. When we first got to Iowa, she mentioned she wanted to go to a small town outside Topeka. I went and asked around, but no one had seen her. After that, I kept visiting towns she'd once talked about. I apologized over and over. Every message I left, I begged for forgiveness. But she never answered."

"You didn't give up, though."

"No, I still call. More so now that I'm here. This place makes me miss her more. But I do it more for me than her. Just knowing she might be listening gives me hope."

"Keep calling. Don't give up on her. I'm sure she hasn't given up on you. A mother never forgets her children. Our pride can get in the way sometimes, but we always love our babies. We never stop fighting for them."

I smiled, grateful for her words, but I didn't believe them. My mother had stopped fighting for me long before Iowa.

TWELVE

Rayna leaned across the car and wrapped her arms around me. Normally, I wasn't a hugger. My mother and I rarely hugged or cuddled. We barely ever touched each other. My brief history with intimacy taught me it wasn't worth the headaches that came after. But there was something in Rayna's hug that soothed me. She smelled like coffee and maple syrup with a hint of lavender. I rested my head against her shoulder, not wanting to let go.

"Thank you for listening," I said when she released me. "See you at one."

"Shay, I'm here anytime you want to talk."

"I appreciate that." I meant it. I'd never opened up to anyone like I had during breakfast. In those few hours, Rayna was more of a mother to me than my own mother had ever been. She gave me one final smile before driving off.

At the door, I found a white envelope with my name written in familiar handwriting. It was the same handwriting as the envelope with the key. I pulled it off, peeling the tape carefully so as not to rip the paint off the door. This envelope was lighter than the one before. I tucked it against my chest and unlocked the door.

Once inside the room, I fell onto the bed. I closed my eyes and tried to ignore the voice nagging me to call my mother. I'd heard Rayna's words. I knew she was right. My mother did love me. She sacrificed her body to care for me. The way she left me didn't change that. Well, not entirely. My last memories of her clouded everything. Every sweet moment we shared over our nineteen years together now ended with the look of rage on her face.

Sighing, I sat up and opened my eyes. I slipped a finger under the flap of the envelope and ripped it open. Folded inside was a black and white newspaper page. Carefully, I tugged at the corner and shook the paper open. It was a page from the classifieds. An ad in the top right was circled in red ink.

1br studio garage apartment. Kitchenette. Unfurnished 1ba with shower. $200 per month. Available now with first month's rent.

I ran my finger over the words again and again. The address, listed below, was just off the town square. I was fairly certain it was one of the streets I'd driven on the day I got the car. The same person that left me the car wanted me to see this particular ad. They wanted me to stay. But they'd given me the car I needed to leave town. It seemed they were as conflicted as I was.

Reading the ad a third time, then a fourth, I found myself drawn to it. I pulled out my phone and put it back in my pocket. Did I want to call? Would seeing the apartment help me make up my mind? I decided it would. Taking my phone back out, I flipped it open and dialed the number in the ad.

"Hello?" a timid voice answered.

"Hi," I replied. I wasn't sure what to say next. My mother hadn't taught me how to do this. "I'm calling about the apartment in the ad. Is it still available?"

"Oh, of course. Yes, yes it is. Would you like to come see it?" she asked, her voice more confident.

"Please. Could I come today?" I asked.

"Sure. How about in an hour?"

"That works."

"Great," she replied. "Oh, wait, I need your name. Mama wants to know who all is interested."

"Shay Lane."

"Shay!" she said excitedly. "Oh, Mama will be so thrilled. You may not remember me, I'm Hannah. I was in with her at Lace & Grit a few nights ago."

While the name seemed vaguely familiar, it didn't elicit a strong memory or image of a face.

"My mama was the one asking you where you were born. Kelb County. We've got family there."

"Oh, right, I remember," I replied and instantly regretted making the call.

She picked up on my hesitation. "Don't worry. The house is mine, well I mean, my grandparents own it, but it's mine for all intents and purposes. Mama is just helping me get the garage apartment ready to rent. She won't be around much."

"Oh, alright then. I'll see you in an hour," I said and hung up before I could change my mind.

With an hour to kill and a nap out of the question, I took a quick shower and towel-dried my hair. It was in desperate need of a trim, but I didn't want to waste a single dollar on it. I liked to keep it no longer than chin length, but it was almost to my shoulders. The sand-colored strands fell in loose waves, framing my face. It was hard not to see my mother when I looked in the mirror, so I rarely lingered. My cheekbones sat high like hers. I had her hazel eyes and slightly upturned nose. My thick eyebrows, she claimed, came from my father. The one thing she gave him credit for without a hint of disgust.

I ran my fingers through my hair one final time, shaking the curls so they didn't get stringy or tangled. With one final look in the mirror, I considered Rayna's words again. How could I find my mother? She could be anywhere. By the time I did find her, she might have moved on to the next town. For every reason I had to find her, I had an excuse to not bother.

I had just as many excuses for not going to see the apartment. But I shoved them aside. It wouldn't hurt to look, I reasoned. Looking didn't mean I was taking the leap and staying. The ad didn't mention month-to-month, but I was sure I could negotiate the option. I had the money for the first month's rent, and it would save me money in the long run. The motel was quickly draining my funds, and I was tired of itchy towels and sheets. With the money I saved on lodging, I might be able to buy my own blankets. I relished the possibility.

Hannah was waiting for me when I parked outside her house. When I saw her sitting on the porch, I realized I did recognize her from the bar. The unassuming two-story brick house had a bright pink door and a flowerbed covered in weeds. To the left of the house was a long gravel driveway that led to a detached garage. When I got out of the car, she met me on the sidewalk and shook my hand.

"Thanks for making time," I said.

"Oh, yeah, no problem. The apartment is back here." She nodded over her shoulder. I followed her down the driveway. "It's $200 per month with the first month due up-front. After that, rent is due on the fifth of the month. There isn't a long-term lease. We can do month-to-month or whatever you want."

"Great," I replied. She unlocked a dark red door on the side of the garage. When she opened it, she guided me up a narrow, steep stairway. At the top, she opened a second door.

"Here we are." She moved to the side, letting me pass. The space was much larger than the outside let on. "It's a studio, so pretty much what you see is what you get. My dad just finished all the work up here. To be honest, I'd move in here myself if I didn't need the space in my house."

I took a timid step around her and stood in the middle of the room. The hardwood floors sparkled in the sunlight.

Looking up, I could see a large skylight. Two ceiling fans hung on either side before the ceiling sloped down. The kitchen was off in the far right. A black refrigerator stood in the corner. It had an ice maker and water dispenser on the front. I'd always wanted one of those. The stove and microwave matched. Granite countertops adorned the island and space around the appliances. Deep cherry cabinet doors with simple silver knobs lined the walls.

At the other end, a walk-in closet sat next to the bathroom. It was the nicest living space I'd ever been in.

"It's not huge, but the shower is pretty decent. There is, of course, central air and heat. The utilities are built into the rent. That may change, though. If the bill gets too high, I'll ask you to pitch in," she said, pausing to look at me. "I mean if you decide you want it."

"I want it," I blurted. It was exactly what I'd always wanted in my own space. Clean appliances. Free of stale cigarette smoke. Private. I reached into my pocket and pulled out the cash I'd counted out carefully. "First month's rent."

She laughed and reached for my hand. I took it. Gripping tightly, she jerked it up and down. "Fantastic! Mama gave me some paperwork for you to fill out. It's over in my house."

I followed her back down the stairs and across the yard to her house. The paperwork consisted of a handful of questions and two signatures. Hannah took a photo of my driver's license with her phone while I filled it out.

"I'm guessing you don't have any pets," she said. I shook my head. "I'm cool with small dogs or cats, just let me know beforehand. I've got a cat, Ollie; he's hiding somewhere. You may see him lurking in the yard. If he scratches at the door, just ignore him. He'll go away eventually."

Hannah's house was a mess. Books and papers scattered across the dining room. Bolts of fabric lined the walls and covered every exposed surface. When she caught me looking around the room, she smiled. "I'm in school for fashion design. I've gotta get out of this Podunk hellhole."

"That's cool," I said nonchalantly. I wanted to ask her more questions, but I wasn't sure where to start. The brightly colored fabrics intrigued me, as did the seemingly organized chaos that was her house.

"If you want any clothes, let me know. I'm always looking for models."

"Really?" I asked, surprised. "Aside from these jeans and a few T-shirts, I'm running low in the wardrobe department."

Her eyes lit up. "Follow me!" she exclaimed and jumped from her chair. I had to jog to keep up as she ran upstairs. She opened a door to reveal her sewing room. Even more fabric cluttered this room. Piles of pants, shirts, dresses and other articles of clothing were stacked on the floor. With the energy of a toddler who'd just eaten a pint of ice cream, she started digging. She'd hold up a piece, gauge my reaction and toss it into a fresh pile if she thought I'd like it. We played this game for an hour before I realized I was going to be late for work.

"I'll look through a few more pieces," she said when I stood to go. "I'll put them in your closet."

"This is more than I need," I tried to argue, but she stopped me.

"Please, my mom's been on my case to clean this place up, but I couldn't bear the thought of throwing these clothes out. Anything that doesn't fit, just bring back. Oh, before I forget, here's your key. I have one, too, but won't use it unless it's absolutely necessary. It's your space now."

"Thank you, Hannah," I said and took the key. I pulled the Nissan's key from my pocket and added the new key to the ring. I'd never had my own house key before. Motel or hotel keys, sure, but never anything that was mine. The weight of it tugged at my heart, pulling me towards a future I wasn't sure I wanted but knew I needed.

I had no idea who'd left me the car or led me to this apartment, but I was confident whoever it was knew my innermost secrets. The voicemails I left my mother contained hints of those desires, but never the full depth of them. If she was behind the gifts, I knew I needed to find her. It meant she was nearby. Maybe Rayna was right. My mother was still looking out for me. She was still fighting for me.

I had to find her.

THIRTEEN

Eddie was understandably disappointed when I checked out of the motel, which I did as soon as I got back. I threw my things into the car, deciding to sleep on the hard floor of my new apartment rather than spend another night in the motel. *My apartment.* My brain repeated that sentence over and over. During my shift Saturday night, the newness never wore off, nor did my smile. I didn't tell Rayna or Toby about the development; I didn't want them to get their hopes up that I was staying.

But I was. Somewhere between signing the lease with Hannah and getting back to the motel, the decision was made. I couldn't fight it anymore. Wishing would be my home for now. Or, at the very least, where I parked my car and rested my head. *Home* wasn't a word I liked to use. Home meant permanence—a guarantee of sorts. It was also the promise I couldn't keep, not even to myself.

I finished my side work and cashed out in record time, practically throwing my money at Rayna. She raised an eyebrow but didn't ask any questions. I kept expecting her to bring up our conversation from the morning, but she didn't. Grateful to not have my mood soured, I didn't mention it either. Instead, we focused on drink orders and customers. Even Toby left me alone, which was a small miracle in and of itself.

After Rayna locked the door behind me, I hopped in my car and sped into town. The apartment—*my apartment*—was five minutes from the bar, doubling my commute time. I parked to the side of the garage, where Hannah had directed me. Turning off the car, the song the jangle of my keys sang made me giddy. *You're home*, they chimed over and over again. I allowed myself a small celebration before remembering that everything good usually ended badly. *Don't get too excited.*

The key turned smoothly in the lock. I climbed the stairs, carefully lifting my suitcase behind me. The books were heavy, and I hoped I wouldn't be making this trip up the stairs with them again any time soon. I unlocked the second door and held my breath. This was mine. I had my own place. The thought was intoxicating. I wanted to savor it and never forget this moment. This was a feeling I wished would never wear off.

Dropping my backpack to the floor, I reached around the corner to feel for the light switch. When the lights came on, I gasped. I looked down at the key to make sure I was in the right place. Then back down the stairs. The kitchen looked the same. The counters were the same white granite. Cherry cabinets. Black appliances. The shiny hardwood floors and bright white walls were all the same as before.

Now, though, furniture sat in the room. A couch. A bed. A table. Curtains hung from the window. I pulled the paperwork from my pocket and skimmed it. *Unfurnished.* I read it again. There was no mention of furniture. In the kitchen, I opened the cabinets to find dishes and pots and pans. In the pantry, the shelves were stocked with basic food items. Same with the refrigerator. I couldn't believe it. I'd been here twelve hours ago, and it was completely empty, now it was full. Had Hannah rented the space out from under me and taken my deposit?

I crossed the room and opened the closet. The clothes she'd

offered me were inside. Every piece we'd looked at together and a few others. I sat down on the bed; my mouth hung open in disbelief. My back stiffened as anxiety crept in. Glancing around the room one last time, my mind wandered over the possibilities. Either my anonymous benefactor was at it again or Hannah rented the space to someone else. The sense of peace I'd had moments ago was gone. This wasn't right. This couldn't be mine.

Knock! Knock! The sound jarred me back to present. "Shay?" Hannah called through the closed door, her voice muffled by the stairwell. I stood and rushed to the door.

"Coming!" I ran down the stairs and pulled open the door. It was three in the morning, and Hannah was still fully dressed and looked as though she'd been out. She hadn't been at Lace & Grit during the rush, so I assumed she had another bar she visited when she wasn't with her mother.

"I promise I won't make a habit of popping in, but I just got home and saw your car out here," she said, smiling. Her eyes darted around the space. "Wow! The movers sure got this set up quick."

"Movers?"

"Yeah, they came around two. I let them in, I hope that's okay."

"This isn't my stuff," I replied. My voice shook.

"What do you mean?" she asked. Her head moved from left to right as she scanned the room and avoided meeting my eyes.

"That suitcase and my backpack are the only things I own. I don't know who this stuff belongs to."

"They had your name and everything, I'm so sorry. I thought you sent them."

"Did you get their names?" I asked.

"No, Shay, I'm so sorry."

"First the car. Then the ad. Now this?" I mumbled to myself. I studied Hannah's face to gauge reaction. It didn't make any sense for her to be behind any of this, but at this point she was the only person who might have a clue.

"What?" She furrowed her brow.

"Someone is leaving me random gifts."

"Oh," she said, exhaling. "Does your family in Kelb County know you're here?"

"I don't know my family there or if that's where they are," I said.

"Oh! Look!" Hannah said, her voice loud with excitement, and pointed at the empty bookshelf by the window. "There's a note."

My eyes landed on the familiar white envelope. The same blue ink scrawled my name. I couldn't find words to speak. The furniture and appearance of yet another envelope rendered me speechless.

"Well, I'll leave you to it," Hannah said when the silence became too awkward.

"Thank you," I managed to whisper. My gaze fixed on the envelope. I listened to her footsteps, waiting to hear the door shut at the bottom of the stairs. The lock clicked into place. Paralyzed by a combination of fear and excitement, my feet remained rooted in place.

I don't know how much time passed. Tears blurred my eyes, and I lost focus on the envelope. Sighing, I took a tentative step forward. Then another, until I reached the envelope. My fingers tingled as I reached for it. In a motion that was now muscle memory, I carefully opened the envelope. This time, a tiny card was inside.

Welcome home, Shay.

I read it over and over, my mind lingering on one word. That one word, the one I refused to allow myself to reach for, was right there next to my name. *Home.*

Stillness surrounded me. The only sound was the empty echo of my feet padding over the hardwood floors while I paced through the room. I touched every piece of furniture and ran my fingers over the countertops. In the kitchen, I pulled a can of Diet Coke from the fridge. Whoever was behind this knew me well. Diet Coke was another luxury of mine. I couldn't always afford it, but when I could, I'd drink it slowly to savor the nectar. The pop of the can opening bounced off the walls. My eyes closed at the delicious sound. The sweetness poured over my tongue.

With the can in my hand, I walked back to the bookshelf and set it down. I stepped back and smiled. The one thing I'd always dreamed of, more than having a home or friends, was a bookshelf for my books. They too deserved a home. Their spines needed sunshine so they could be admired and loved, not shoved in a suitcase. Rather than push the heavy suitcase across the floor as I would have done in a motel, I lifted it and carried it to the bookshelf. These floors were mine. They were clean, untainted. I wouldn't ruin them with my old suitcase's broken wheels.

Carefully, I placed the books on the shelves. Each one filled with memories of the time I'd spent lost inside them. *To Kill a Mockingbird*. A librarian in Texas gave her to me. *The Babysitter's Club*. I had four of those tattered paperbacks that my mother gave me for my tenth birthday. *Shiloh*. I ran my hand over the spine, searching for the memory held inside its yellowed pages. The library sticker was still affixed to the side. I opened the book and slipped out the card. My name and the date jumped off the page, slapping me in the face. May 12, 2007. The day before my thirteenth birthday.

I opened to the first page; tears formed in my eyes as I read the words, just as they had the first time I read the book. The week before, a brown and white puppy with floppy ears and muddy paws showed up at our motel door. My mother was off at work at the time. Being just twelve, I didn't know any better, and I let him in. He was alone. His eyes drooped, heavy with sadness and hunger. He reminded me of myself. I recognized the brokenness in him. I shared my breakfast of dry generic cereal and water with him. After we ate, he curled up at my feet and cuddled into me. I can still remember the comfort his warmth brought. I named him Freddie. I don't know why or where the name came from, but I can still feel the way it rolled off my tongue.

When my mother came home, she was furious. She kicked Freddie out of the room, ignoring my cries. I'd never had a friend. Never had anyone or anything to call mine. Freddie held the promise of all of that. I tried to reason that he could stand guard and keep me safe while she was gone. He could keep me warm, and I'd always have him to play with when I started to annoy her. She heard none of it. My tears meant nothing. She wasn't having it. Tiny, desperate puppy whines filled our room that night. His paws scratched at the door, begging to be let in. At some point, my mother huffed out of bed and ran outside. I don't know what she did, I never asked, but Freddie was gone. I waited for him every morning. I set out food, but he didn't show up.

The day before my birthday, my mother grew tired of my moping and dropped me off at the library instead of leaving me in the motel room. She knew I'd find solace in a book, and she left me with two dollars for a vending machine lunch and the promise of a special birthday dinner the next night. I asked the librarian for a good book about a loyal dog, and she led me to *Shiloh*. Sitting in a quiet corner, I read the entire book. It wasn't until the librarian came by later that evening that I realized I'd been there all day. I'd skipped lunch, oblivious to the time. When she locked the door behind me and my mother was nowhere in sight, I walked back to the motel and waited. And waited. I read *Shiloh* again, thinking to myself that Freddie wouldn't have dumped me at the library. He wouldn't forget my birthday.

I never got to return the book. It's the one and only library book that I'd ever stolen.

Swiping the tears from my cheeks, I tried to wipe away the memories. As much as I loved *Shiloh,* and no matter how many times I'd read it and tried to cover the bad with a new, good memory, I couldn't. The underlying story lived in those pages.

"Hey, Mom," I said when the message picked up. "Do you remember Freddie? He was a great dog. Why were you so mean?"

Sobbing, the words stuck in my throat, choking me. "All I wanted was someone to love me and protect me. I wanted to feel safe. I wanted a warm body to cuddle with me. Mom, I was just a kid. Freddie was better to me in the five hours I had him than you ever were."

As soon as I said the words, I was desperate to take them back. "I'm sorry. That's not fair. I know you tried. Mom, all I ever wanted was for you to see me and love me. Was that too much to ask? I know the answer. It was. You didn't have any love to give, did you? Not even to yourself. I won't make that mistake. I won't. I'm capable of love, Mom. Giving it. Receiving it. Someone here cares about me, Mom. The car. The apartment. The furniture. Someone sees me."

I hung up the phone and stared at the screen realizing I wasn't done. I dialed the number again. "Maybe I'll get a dog now," I said. "A puppy. I won't name him Freddie. God, you never let me live that down. 'Who names a dog Freddie?' You mocked me. Actually, maybe I will name him Freddie, just to spite you. I'm sorry, Mom. I miss you and I love you, but I'm so angry with you. Where are you? Why won't you answer?"

I ended the call before I could say anything else. My words stung, devastating the sense of calm I'd felt moments ago. I returned my attention to the books, focusing on the ones that brought more positive memories. The Dr. Seuss books my mother read to me when I was little. The *Sweet Valley High* books a kind girl in Kentucky gave me.

When the suitcase was unpacked, I stepped back and admired the books. *Home.* We had a home, my books and me. Despite my protests, Wishing was home. At least for now.

FOURTEEN

"I MEAN, IT'S WEIRD, BUT NICE," I SAID. LEANING OVER the table, I ran the towel across the top. Crumbs scattered onto the floor as I flicked it back and forth. "But it's creepy. The car. The ad for the apartment. Now, the furniture. And it was everything I needed. Well, and more. A bookshelf? Diet Coke? How did they know?"

Rayna shrugged. "I think Trigger was right, you got yourself a fairy godmother."

"Either that or it's the Wishing Well," Toby said, coming up behind me. He reached around me and grabbed the stack of dirty plates I'd piled neatly on top of each other. His hand brushed my arm but pulled away quickly as if he'd been burned. I moved aside and removed myself from his path. He mumbled a soft apology.

"The Wishing Well? What is that?" I asked.

Toby looked at me with wide eyes. "No one has told you about the well?"

"No?" I replied, questioning his incredulity. I'd been here a week, and I hadn't exactly been eager to learn about this place I was supposed to just pass through. "Is someone going to tell me? Or are you going to keep looking at me like I have five heads?"

Rayna laughed. "Toby, she's been here a week. Give the girl a break. She can't possibly know everything about this town."

"But it's literally the only interesting thing about this hellhole."

Rayna gently swatted his arm. "There's plenty of fun here."

"Maybe in 1960, but in 2019? It's a bore."

"Sorry, Rayna, I'm gonna have to agree with Toby on that one," I interjected, smiling to show her I was teasing.

"You tell her," Toby said, pointing at Rayna. "You tell it so much better."

Rayna smiled. "Toby, go fry up that last order of pickles. Get yourself a beer. No alcohol for you?" she asked me. I shook my head. "Tea? Water?"

"Water," I answered. My fingers twitched. They'd piqued my interest with this wishing well, and I wanted to know more. I wasn't one to buy into legends or superstitions; the road removed my belief in anything more than a map or a book. Nothing good came from wishes or dreams. Every bump and crack on the road reminded me nothing was permanent.

She slid a glass across the bar and leaned forward. Her eyes met mine and held them captive. When she opened her mouth to speak, I held my breath.

"Back in 1840, the first settlers moved into this part of Paris County. They picked this patch because there was a natural spring that ran through it and formed a nice lake. Wilfred and Anna Benedict built their house west of the lake. The town started growing from there. The general store and library are still in their original buildings."

"With modifications of course," Toby added. He placed the fried pickles in front of me, and I grabbed a handful, dipping them in ranch before popping them in my mouth.

"The exact history on the well is up for debate. Some say Anna had it built after they lost two babies. She wished for more children once it was built and had two sets of twins after."

"That's the boring story." Toby yawned.

"Hush and let her tell it," I said.

"Thank you, Shay. Where was I? Oh, yes, the second and slightly more salacious version," she paused and took a sip of water, "involves murder and bank robberies."

"Oh, I take it back, Toby, she should have started with this version."

She launched into the new story with renewed vigor. The Tulleys, she said, were local criminals who usually kept their shenanigans limited to bar fights and cow-tippin'. Until one night when they grew bored and rode up to Springfield and robbed a bank on a whim. There was a shootout and a brief chase, but the boys made it back to Wishing and began drinking away their stolen bills.

Rayna knew how to tell a story. I'm sure Toby had heard this story hundreds of times growing up here, but he sat on the edge of his barstool and gasped at all the right places. Perhaps he was putting on a show for me, too.

"So, when Mr. and Mrs. Benedict learned of the Tulley's crimes, they built a jail just for them. Rumor has it, Mr. Benedict knew his daughters had their eyes on the Tulley boys. Before the boys could be tried or prosecuted, they escaped and fled for Springfield. They romanced the Benedict's eldest twin daughters, who fled with them. Around the same time, the town was growing and needed a better way to get water to the houses at the middle of town. This story claims it was Wilfred who built the well. He was desperate to have his daughters back and believed in the powers of the well. A local woman promised him the well was magical because of the natural springs that flowed beneath the town. His wife didn't believe in the nonsense of wishing wells and was ashamed her husband bought into the superstitions. She hated him tossing his pennies into the blackness. The Tulleys eventually came back after making brides of the Benedict girls. Marie Tulley, the librarian, is the last descendant to live here."

"So, when was the well built?" I asked, hoping to clarify which version was true.

"That's where it gets fuzzy. It was either in 1841 or 1861. The Benedicts weren't the greatest record keepers."

"Which story do they teach in school?"

"The one where the wishing well isn't an actual wishing well and the town just got it's random name because Anna Benedict liked the way it sounded."

"Which do you believe?" I asked Rayna.

"I believe the version that granted Anna her greatest wish."

"Babies?"

"To have a family and a home to raise them in."

"I never took you for a softie, Rayna," Toby said. "I prefer the bank-robbery-and-stolen-virgins story."

"Why am I not surprised?" I asked with a laugh. "Surely the well has granted more wishes since, or it wouldn't be town legend. Right?"

"There have been stories," Rayna said, looking at Toby. She raised her eyebrows, and he shrugged.

"I wished for my mom's cancer to go into remission."

"Was that the well or chemotherapy?" I asked.

"Both," he said. "I did a lot of praying, too. I didn't just toss pennies into the well."

"Rayna?" I asked.

"Oh, I don't talk about my wishes," she said, her voice dropping to a whisper. "I'm still waiting for it to come true."

Reading her face, I assumed she was talking about Mary. She wanted her daughter back. I wondered how much Toby knew about Rayna and her family. They seemed close, but Rayna kept him at arm's length. She'd only told me her story to get me to open up.

"Do you think the well is granting my wishes?" I asked, drawing the attention back to myself. I wasn't a fan of being at the center of the conversation, but Rayna's discomfort was worth the distraction. She smiled gratefully. "I haven't been down to the well, but I have spoken the wishes out loud to my mother."

"I don't think it works like that," Toby answered.

"Have you thought any more about finding your mother?" Rayna asked. I shook my head. "She knows where you are, right?"

"I've told her in the messages, so I guess she does."

"Where is she?" Toby asked. I shrugged. "Have you Googled her?"

I hedged. At twenty-five, I should know how to use the internet, but I didn't, at least not like everyone expected me to. When you live in a car and run-down motels, there isn't exactly money or space for a computer. I had no problem admitting that to Rayna, but I didn't want to see the look of shock on Toby's face. It would confirm to him that I was weird or strange or whatever. I'd never fit in. Between homeschool and living in motels, my life and upbringing were easy to mock.

"No, I haven't."

"What?" he asked, reading my face. "You do know what Google is, right?"

Of course, I knew what Google was. I'd just never used it. I hadn't ever needed to. "I mean, yeah."

"Shay… have you been on a computer?"

Shrugging, I sighed. "No. I mean, yes, if you count looking for books at the library."

"Facebook?"

I shook my head.

"Instagram? Twitter? Snapchat?"

"None of it," I said. He could keep naming stuff, but I had no idea what he was talking about after Facebook.

"She has a flip phone, Toby."

"What? I need to see this."

"Thanks, Rayna." Toby held his hand out. Reluctant to hand over my one lifeline to my mother, I clutched it in my hand. "I don't exactly need the internet or a fancy phone on the road. I've got my map."

"Like an actual map? A Randy Mac?"

It was my turn to laugh. "A Rand McNally? Yes, reading maps may be a dying art, but it's a valuable skill. What happens if you don't have cell service or data?"

For once, he didn't have an answer. His face twitched as he fought the urge to roll his eyes. "See," I said, "I'll be able to find my way, and you'll be lost."

"Point made."

"Do you want to find her?" Rayna asked.

"I don't know. Even if I did, how would I?"

"We can start with Google. I can show you how it works."

"I know how to use Google, I just never had a need for it," I said in an attempt to deflect his offer. I felt his eyes on my face, but I didn't look up from the fried pickle I was dissecting.

"Just to help. I promise, I don't have any nefarious motives."

Rayna laughed. "Nefarious? You get one of those word-of-the-day calendars?"

"Shut up," he said, his cheeks flushed. "I just meant that I'm not trying anything funny. I just want to help."

"I appreciate that," I said, meaning it. "But where would I even start? Tammy Lane isn't exactly the type of woman to leave breadcrumbs. If she doesn't want to be found, she won't be."

"Tammy Lane," Toby repeated my mother's name with a sense of awe and a hint of curiosity. I glanced at him, finally lifting my head. I dropped the pickle on the plate. My gaze shifted between

Rayna and Toby, and I tried to read the unspoken words that passed between them.

"Yes, her name is Tammy."

"Tammy Lane can't be a unique name," he finally said. "We can try, though. That won't hurt, will it? If we find her, great. If not, you're no worse off than you are now."

He had a point. "Okay. Tomorrow?"

"Library is closed on Sunday," Rayna interjected.

"I have a computer," Toby offered.

"No," I said. There was no way I was going to Toby's house. He'd backed off on the flirting, but I still didn't trust him. "Monday? I need a day to think about where she might have gone. Won't that help us narrow down how we look?"

"It's the internet. We can find her anywhere."

"If she wants to be found," I added. "Monday?"

"Sure," he said. "They open at nine. Meet there?"

I nodded in agreement. We finished eating the pickles. The conversation shifted to less heavy topics as Toby and Rayna talked about the upcoming school year and high school football season. I half listened, paying attention only when they said my name or offered up some new detail about this person or that person.

I envied the easy banter between the two of them and wondered what it would have been like to grow up somewhere like this. Or in Wishing specifically. My mother would have liked Rayna. Even Trigger would have connected with her. His kindness was the stuff of small-town folklore. Tammy would have loved Wishing. She'd have fit right in with the hustle and bustle of the local gossip. For a minute I tried to picture who she'd have seduced to find a job. I couldn't see her flirting with Trigger, but Eddie might have been her type. Or maybe there was someone more her speed that I hadn't met yet.

The story about the Wishing Well would've pulled her in. I could see her dragging me out to the town square to find it in the middle of the night. Her pockets full of pennies to toss in. She'd egg me on, begging me to make a wish. *Make it a good one, Shay, don't waste your wishes,* I could hear her say. Maybe Wishing would've been the place she finally opened up and let me in. If we'd come after my thirteenth birthday, I know what I would've wished for. The one thing I'd probably never have again.

One hug. One sign that she was proud I was her daughter. But I doubted even the legendary well could grant that wish.

FIFTEEN

I sat on the steps outside the library. The Wishing Well was a few hundred feet ahead of me. It was unassuming and looked like any other well. Well, any other well that was almost 200 years old. I glanced at my phone. It was five until nine, so I wouldn't have time to walk over and say what I needed before Toby showed up. There would be time after. For as much as I didn't believe in the legends of the Wishing Well, I couldn't help but feel the pull of its optimism.

Focusing on the well distracted me from the million questions racing through my mind. My mother. The gifts. Toby. This town. Everything punctuated by a question mark without any hope of finding an answer. I wasn't even sure I wanted to find answers. There was a certain comfort in the unknown. The unknown I could ignore. Once I knew the truth, there was no going back. It wouldn't matter if I liked the answer or not. I'd know without a doubt that my mother just chose to ignore my cries for help.

I chewed my thumbnail and watched for Toby, wishing I'd never agreed to this. I rarely let curiosity get the best of me. When you're constantly running, it's easy to forget what you miss. Hunger and exhaustion speak louder, demanding attention.

Survival trumps all else. That was the world I was used to. Having an entire day to stay inside and read wasn't normal. Waking up in a comfortable bed in my *home* wasn't something I ever thought I'd get to do, and I still wasn't convinced it was permanent. Nothing ever was.

Whether it was my mother's actions or decisions that blew everything up or mine, it didn't matter. The Lane women had a knack for ruining everything good. I never knew my grandmother, but the way Tammy spoke of her, I assumed she was just as disastrous. My mother rarely spoke of her family but when she did, it was filled with contempt. Whatever she'd run from, she'd made sure to leave the memories far behind. Or maybe she held on to them and kept them close, too afraid to let go of them. If she spoke them out loud or shared the stories, they'd be real. Much like the truth I was hiding from.

"Ready?" Toby asked, out of breath, as he approached me. He offered his hand to help me up, but I stood on my own.

"I suppose so."

Once inside the tiny library, he led me over to the information desk. He introduced me to Marie, the librarian, and explained that I was new in town.

"So we need to get her a library card," he finally said after a few minutes of flirting and bantering with Marie, who was at least ten years older than him. For her part, she giggled and played with a loose strand of hair. It took all I had to not roll my eyes and groan.

"Ever had a library card?" he asked me.

Smirking, I said, "This will be my one-hundred-twelfth library card."

"Wait, how many?" His eyes were wide in disbelief. I repeated my answer. Both he and Marie gawked at me.

"I told you we moved around a lot. I spent more time in libraries than anywhere else."

"And you never used the internet before?"

"I never needed it." I had no practical use for the internet. I had maps. And aside from recent events, I wasn't a curious person by nature. Curiosity led to trouble.

"Well, consider me your tutor today. I'll be sure to save the lessons on finding porn for next time."

"Or never," Marie suggested.

"You're no fun. Ready?" I nodded and followed him to one of the computer terminals. He walked me through the process of logging in. Once online, he directed me to Google and showed me how to set up and check email. Then, he moved on to the search function. I watched as his hands moved over the keys and mouse at a speed I envied. I memorized the movements and clicks he made, making sure to note how to navigate between the various tabs and pages.

Toby sat in the chair beside me. His breath blew a loose strand of my hair with every inhale and exhale. It tickled my skin. The slow, steady rhythm of it was a stark contrast to the vibrating nerves inside me. I wanted to send him away, but I wasn't sure I could handle the search on my own. I stared at the open browser. My fingers hovered over the keys. Each letter a piece of the puzzle I wasn't sure I wanted to complete. Was I really ready for answers? If my mother was behind everything but couldn't bring herself to answer the phone or come see me, I wasn't sure I wanted to know that.

"You just type her name in that search bar there," he said, pointing at the screen. Though he sounded calm, I sensed a hint of irritation. "Do you know how to type?"

I groaned. "Yes. Can you go somewhere else while I do this?" As much as I needed his help to figure out how to work the search and what to do when something came up, he was making me more nervous. "If I have questions, I'll find you."

He hesitated for a moment. "Okay, I'll be over there." He nodded towards the information desk where Marie sat. Before he walked away, he turned and smiled. I got the feeling he didn't want to leave, but he also didn't want to wear out his welcome. I waited until I couldn't hear his footsteps or feel his eyes on me before I put my fingers on the keyboard. They fell onto the home keys and rested. In a library not too different from Wishing's, I'd learned to type thanks to an elderly woman who, as they all did, took pity on me. Muscle memory kicked in, and I typed out my mother's name.

Tammy Marie Lane. Fourteen letters. The cursor blinked after the final one, daring me to hit Enter as Toby had instructed. My pinkie rested over the return key. I tapped it lightly. Adrenaline coursed through my veins. *Tap. Tap. Tap.* Each tap daring me to press harder. I closed my eyes and drew in a deep, slow breath. Lingering for another second until the muscle twitched and pressed the key. I counted to ten before opening my eyes again.

A million results. More. Pages after pages of Tammy Marie Lane. *Specific.* Toby had suggested I be as specific as possible in order to get the best results. I moved the mouse arrow back to the top of the page and clicked. After her name, I typed her birthday. *Tammy Marie Lane 12/25/1976.* This time, I hit enter before my fear could stop me. I scanned the results. Two news articles from Dickson, Tennessee led.

Jane Doe identified. My pulse raced as the blood drained from my face. It flowed down my fingers and out into the world. I couldn't breathe. The air entered my nose and stopped. My lungs constricted, reaching for life. I blinked to clear my eyes and read it again. Shaking my head, I refused to process the words. I clicked into the article. My vision blurred and the words mangled together. I swiped the tears away before they could escape and forced myself to read.

January 31, 2017

Victim of Hit and Run Identified

TBI confirms the identity of the body found on I-40.

DICKSON, Tenn. On Tuesday, authorities identified a Missouri woman found dead in a ditch at mile marker 170 in late December. The woman, estimated to be in her early forties, was discovered on Christmas Day by local teens. An autopsy revealed the cause of death was blunt force trauma from being hit by a car. At this time, authorities believe the cause of death was an accident but are still investigating and asking any potential witnesses to come forward.

While there is no available next of kin, DNA from the scene allowed investigators to positively identify the woman as Tammy Marie Lane of Gaines, Missouri. It was not immediately known where she resided before her death.

I READ THE SHORT ARTICLE AGAIN. AND THEN AGAIN. The sentences flowed, but their meaning drowned between the screen and my brain. Sitting back in the chair, I pulled my hands to my mouth. I didn't bother stopping the tears as they flowed down my cheeks. Each tear a memory. The voicemails, every single one I'd left, played back in my mind. What had I told her on Christmas in 2016? Did I tell her I loved her or to have a happy birthday? Did she hear the message? Who had her phone now? Where was she buried? Questions and regrets filled me with emptiness.

"Shay?" Toby whispered behind me. I jumped at the sound. I couldn't respond to him; it took every bit of energy I had to lift my hand and point at the screen. His chest brushed my shoulder as he leaned forward. I felt him tense beside me as he read. He reached around me and grabbed the mouse. My eyes followed as he clicked back to the search results. I read the words he typed. Obituary. Funeral. Realizing he was looking for the answers to questions I hadn't asked. I slid away from him.

"Stop!" I shouted. "What are you doing? Bring it back. Bring her back!"

He didn't stop. He kept clicking and typing. Article after article opened in new tabs. Body found. Body identified. No next of kin. No funeral. Cremated. Everything flashed quickly. He wouldn't stop. My tears and sobs echoed through the library. Marie pushed past me and pulled Toby away from the computer. He held out an arm, offering me balance or support, but I turned away and ran for the door.

Shoving it open, I ran into the sunlight, gasping. Steel cages gripped my chest, refusing to release me. The humid air burned my throat. I needed to get out of this town and away from Missouri. I needed to put distance between me and the truth I'd just learned. The car door bounced when I yanked it open, ripping itself from my grasp. I could hear Toby behind me, calling my name. I didn't dare turn around and look at him. I couldn't go back in there.

The key twisted in my hand, starting the car. I was on autopilot. No destination. No chains or ties. That was my comfort zone. I pulled my phone from my pocket and dialed. I couldn't stop the shaking. My hands weren't listening to my brain. I tried to tell myself to calm down, to breathe, but the instructions never reached their destination.

"Mom!" I cried as soon as the message beeped. Searching for what to say, I couldn't speak. For the first time in six years, I had confirmation that she wasn't listening to my words. She couldn't. She was gone. Dead. Blunt force trauma. Body in the ditch. Gone. Dead.

With the open road ahead of me, pavement flying beneath my tires, I searched for the words I'd wished I'd said to her. The years of anger built with every passing mile. I should have been with her. I never should have let her leave me. I should have sent Adam away that night. Everything I did or didn't say or do piled on, dragging me down. Every truth confirmation that I'd let her down. I was to blame. She was gone, and it was my fault.

My hand slammed into my face, scratching at the tear-stained rivers trying to wash away the guilt. She couldn't be gone. I'd been so convinced she was the one behind the car and the apartment. If she were gone, wouldn't I feel it? I searched my memory for any sign I missed. A feeling of emptiness or loneliness. Anything that would have clued me in that my mother was gone. Nothing. She'd been gone for nearly three years, and I hadn't known.

I tried to ignore the questions and focus on what was ahead of me. *Focus on the road,* my mother's voice whispered. *Just drive, Shay.* She'd tell me to press the gas as if my life depended on it. Run away. Flee. Escape. Go.

A faded orange sign stood on the right side of the road. *Now Leaving Wishing. We wish you well. See you soon!*

SIXTEEN

Heat filled the car as the midday sun soaked through the windows. The trees beside my car offered little shade or relief. I'd pulled over when the tears became too blinding to drive any further. I couldn't blink or wipe them away fast enough.

I didn't recognize my surroundings or the road but knew I hadn't made it far from Wishing. Seeing the sign did little to slow my car until I realized all I wanted was the comfort of my bed and Rayna. She'd know what to say.

My head pounded. Between the harsh sunlight and my inability to stop the flow of tears, everything inside me itched to break free. I reached for the handle and pushed the door open. The ancient steel creaked, whining. It didn't want to open any more than I wanted to get out of the car. The comfort of the car tempted me, begging me to stay put.

Swinging my legs through the frame, I stretched my body back, extending the full length of the car. The open road was calling me, but I couldn't hear her. The words I'd read jumbled and clanked inside my head. I stepped out of the car and glanced around me. I knew Wishing wasn't far behind me; I could still feel her pull. The look on Toby's face as I ran past him. The way I instinctively slowed as I drove past Lace & Grit. Trigger's patrol car sitting just beyond the city limits. I could feel his eyes on me, but I refused to look his way.

"Mom," I whispered into the humid air. A light breeze teased and tugged my hair. It was a near-perfect summer day. A great day to enjoy a book under a tree or to put the car in drive and head nowhere. *Mom.* The familiar, yet distant, name hung in the heaviness. It floated around me, tugging and whispering in the breeze. Leaves rustled with the dancing trees and grass. Yet, it remained still and silent.

I leaned against the car, the hot metal piercing through my thin shirt, and rested my head on the roof. The sky was a brilliant shade of baby blue. No clouds. Just bright sunshine and a clear sky. This was my mother's favorite kind of day. She loved to roll the windows down and let her hand ride the air. When I was old enough to drive, she'd give me the wheel while she hung her feet out the window. Unlike me, she kept her hair long. She'd let the wind tie it in knots without a care in the world. The road was her home, and she loved everything about it.

I think I always knew it would be the road that took her from me. In a way, it took her long before she died alone. I'd held on to the small hope that she'd find her place in some small town along the way. Maybe she did. Maybe Tennessee was where she finally found the happiness she was looking for. Or she was headed to Nashville to wait for me.

Despite the daylight surrounding me, darkness filled my being. It consumed my thoughts, bringing me to my knees. As the tears I'd been afraid to release for six long years broke free, memories of my mother flooded my mind. Happier days. Back to when she wasn't consumed with bitterness and anger. When our days were spent playing I Spy in the car or reading her favorite books before bed.

There were happy times. Days, weeks, and months where we

bonded. She smiled and laughed, amused at something silly my younger self had done. My mother used to love to watch me play in the park. I'd sit on the top of the slide, pretending to pout until she came to rescue me. She'd stand at the bottom with her arms wide, ready to catch me. Her words would fill my ears and explode inside my heart: *I'll always catch you.* An empty promise, as it turned out. What I wouldn't give to have that moment back.

I tried to think of our days together in Kansas, Illinois, and Ohio. Those were the places we were the happiest. I still called her Mommy, and she called me her baby ladybug. We were a team. I'd have done anything to make her happy back then. My love of books came from my desire to understand and share with her. Some of my strongest memories were the ones of her sitting beside me in a random motel bed. I'd curl into her body and rest my head against her chest. She'd lazily drape an arm over me, pull me in, and read the pages as if she were on a stage.

"Do you remember reading *Green Eggs and Ham?*" I asked the wind, hoping the echoes would catch a ride and be carried to her wherever she was. "Your Sam-I-Am used to make me giggle."

When I learned to read, I'd picked up that book first. I held the tattered pages in my hands and stumbled over the words. It took me nearly an hour to read it, but she sat patiently in front of me smiling as I mimicked her voice. She made the words come alive.

"Or *Anne of Green Gables?* We would make up our own dream house with green gables. You never called it a house, though. Mom, why was that? It was always *home.* One day we'd have a home and a yard. You wanted horses; I just wanted a swing set and a dog."

We each had a long list of things we wanted in our future home. Sometimes she wanted a husband. I never asked for a dad. My mother was enough for me. This was long before she insisted I call her Tammy. Before she ever considered abandoning me on the side of the highway. Back then she was my entire world. She taught me everything she could and would teach herself what she didn't know. I felt love from her then. Now, standing on the side of an empty highway, I reached for that feeling. I wanted to wrap myself in it and never let it go. The good memories were the ones I'd keep. I'd use them in moments like this where nothing made sense and all I wanted to do was run away and hide.

For the first time, it wasn't the open road calling me, it was Wishing. I wanted to find Rayna or Trigger. Hell, even Toby. Someone to sit with and talk about all the good times I used to have with my mother. But I couldn't. I'd spent the last week or so telling them all the horrible things. They'd likely celebrate her death and reassure me that I'd finally be free of the chains of her memory. I wasn't free, though. Regrets tightened their grip. Their boney fingers stretched around my throat, pulling until I couldn't breathe. The thick air caught between my lips and tongue. Sticking to me like a plague.

I could have tried harder to find her. Looking her up online hadn't been hard. I'd had the opportunity before. Maybe if I'd been more genuine and apologetic in my messages, she'd have called back. There were a million different what-ifs I could focus on, but only one kept replaying. If only I'd been with her that Christmas. Would we have been on the side of the road together? Could I have warned her? Or saved her? Did her car break down? Was it the radiator? The one engine part that terrified her but I was confident enough to tinker with and fix?

The questions rolled around, knocking into each other like pinballs. Every time they clanged together, my head throbbed. Guilt, fear, and regret seeped into every memory, threatening to taint them. I slipped the phone from my pocket and called her number.

"Mom," I said, fighting the tremble in my voice. I held my breath and waited for the shaking to subside. Silence permeated my mind. Calling her now that I knew she was gone was almost calming. I savored the emptiness on the other end of the line knowing there would be no consequences for my words. "I'm sorry I wasn't there. I'm sorry I didn't try harder to find you. I hope you weren't alone, Mom. I hope you saw my face before you closed your eyes. Me at five or ten, when everything still made sense and my innocence still amused you. I miss you, Mom, more than you'll ever know. I love you. You knew that, right? I loved you. Even when I watched you drive away, I loved you. I never wanted anything more than to be your baby ladybug."

The message clicked off. I'd run out of time, but I wasn't done. I dialed the number again.

"Mom, do you remember when we talked about having a home? Where people were kind and they cared? I think I've found it. I wish you could see this place. It is everything you would have loved. They even have an old wishing well. My apartment is perfect, too. I don't know who helped me find it or how they knew exactly what I'd want. I thought it was you, but it couldn't have been. Who has your phone, Mom? Who is listening to these messages?"

I gasped for air and wiped away the last few tears. "Anyway. I love you. I miss you. I don't know if I'll stop calling. I feel like you're still somehow getting these messages. I would give anything to hear your voice one more time." My words trailed off. I didn't know what else to say, so I hung up and shoved the phone back in my pocket.

Wrapping my fingers around the door handle, I pulled it free. Wanda welcomed me with open arms, warming the chill of my final goodbye. The engine roared to life, and I swung her back towards Wishing. It was Monday. The bar was closed, and Rayna was likely home with her soaps or doing chores. I'd left Toby dumbfounded at the library, though he'd probably reread the article and every other one he'd found. He knew, which meant Rayna surely did. They'd be worried about me. They cared. People cared about me. The feeling, though strange and new, filled me with relief.

Driving past the motel and the bar, I felt an unfamiliar surge of happiness. This was where I belonged. Every fiber of my soul called to this place. A slow smile crept over my face. My mother was gone. She'd been gone for years. But I couldn't help but think she'd directed me to Wishing. Perhaps that was her final gift to me. A sense of belonging. A home.

I looped around the square and parked in front of the well. I didn't have much change but found a penny in the console of the car. I had no memory of putting it there, but as with everything lately, it was there when I needed it. The well looked as old as Rayna said it was. A tiny plaque dedicating it to the town stood to the side. Stopping to read it, I held the penny in my hand, rubbing my thumb over its surface. There was no mention of either rumor, nor was there a date of dedication.

I stepped up to the edge and leaned over. The penny burned in my hand. Closing my eyes, I whispered my wish into the air and released the penny down into the blackness.

SEVENTEEN

A sense of relief washed over me as I pulled into the driveway. *Home.* My entire body was exhausted. It was as though the news had drained my own life out of me. A crucial piece of myself was lying in the ditch where she'd been found. All I wanted now was to escape in a book and forget for a moment that I know the truth.

Once inside, I grabbed *Anne of Green Gables* off the bookshelf and opened it. My fingers ran over the yellowed pages, trying to pull the feeling of my mother's hugs from within them. If I could only find her voice or touch, I'd be okay. I settled under the covers, the book resting on the pillow beside me, and started reading. I made it two pages before there was a sound at the door. At first, I ignored it, but it was followed by a light scratching. I assumed it was Ollie. It wouldn't be the first time Hannah's cat tried to beg his way into my apartment.

Groaning, I rose from the bed and padded across the hardwood floors. The scratching was accompanied by a persistent whine.

"Hold on, Ollie!" I shouted as I bounded down the stairs. My eyes and cheeks were still puffy from the morning. I hoped

Hannah wasn't home to see how much of a wreck I was. I pulled open the door and looked down. It wasn't Ollie. A chocolate-brown puppy stared up at me with big brown eyes. A bright pink collar was on her neck. Attached to it I found a note. My hand shook as I reached for it. There wasn't an envelope this time, just a small square card with a black ribbon tying it to the collar.

Aside from my car, the driveway was empty. No cars were parked on the street either. Hannah's lights were out, and she didn't appear to be home. The puppy and I were the only living things in sight. My heart thudded in my chest as I reached for the card. It took extreme effort to stop the trembling in my fingers so I could untie the ribbon. The puppy sat patiently, staring at me. Beside her were a bag of unopened food, a water bowl, a dog bed, and a crate. Whoever left her thought of everything.

"Where did you come from?" I asked, my voice soft. At the sound, she leaped to her feet and licked my face. I knelt beside her and read the card out loud. "In case you need a reading buddy."

I read the words again before slipping the card back into my pocket. It was too hot to stand outside, so I picked up what I could and carried it upstairs. The puppy followed me back down to gather the rest, not leaving my side for a second. Her tiny paws click-clacked across the floor. I couldn't help but smile at how comforting the sound was. Reassuring, almost.

Once I had everything upstairs, I filled her water bowl and poured the food into the dish my anonymous benefactor left behind. She looked up at me and then back down at the bowls. Her head bobbed between us for a moment until I sat down beside her. I crossed my legs and leaned back. She gave me one last look before diving into her food. The crunching filled the silence. I reached over and scratched the sweet spot behind her ear. She paused for a moment and looked at me before turning her attention back to the food.

I watched her for a moment to make sure she was content,

but with food in front of her, she was no longer interested in following my every move. Too distracted to read, I sat on the couch and watched her eat. If I'd had questions before this morning about where and who the gifts were coming from, the puppy's arrival combined with what I'd learned this morning multiplied them exponentially. Someone had my mother's phone. The need for a car, home, and home furnishings were obvious; my car died as I arrived in town, and I was living in a motel with two bags to my name. The only place I'd even uttered a word about the dog was on the voicemail tied to my mother's phone number. I knew now without a shadow of a doubt that she was gone. She wasn't my fairy godmother.

The harder I tried to make sense of everything, the less I understood. My mother lived her life in private. When we left a city, she left everything about it behind. I don't ever recall her keeping in contact with the people who'd been a part of our lives while we lived in a particular city. Nor did I remember her mentioning anyone from the past. *Don't live for yesterday, Shay, live for today and hope for tomorrow*. Those were the words she said to me often, especially when we were leaving somewhere I wanted to stay or if I were missing one of the rare friends I'd made. Nothing from yesterday mattered to her. It was always about what was next and which direction to point the car.

Then again, we usually left when things blew up. Someone caught her with their husband or with money she hadn't earned. We were always running. Until Iowa, we'd always run because of her. Iowa had been entirely my fault. My mistake was so severe, she'd never forgiven me for it. So unforgivable that she left her daughter on the side of the road. Tammy held Susan and Will in high regard. She'd been so proud of the honest work she had there. More than once she promised me that she'd turned a new leaf. From then on, she swore she'd live her life honestly. No more affairs. No more stealing. No more manipulation.

It was entirely possible she'd gone back to Susan and begged for her job back. Perhaps she'd stayed in contact with the family. When I was younger, she kept a piece of paper with a name and phone number on it. She always told me to give that to the police if anything ever happened to her. I never asked her whose name was on the paper, and she never told me. I'd been too young to think anything of it. When I turned eighteen, she stopped carrying it, reasoning that I was old enough to take care of myself. Maybe she replaced it with Will and Susan's information before she drove to Tennessee. If she had, Susan might have my mother's phone. It had been six years since the night I ruined everything. Maybe time and the loss of my mother softened Susan's feelings towards me. Perhaps she'd been listening to my desperate calls and decided to do what my mother would have done. Susan had a giving heart; she'd always been kind to me. Well, until I slept with her son.

If I'd managed to find my mother with the help of the internet, I was certain I could find Will or Susan. Maybe even Adam. I shuddered at the thought, wondering if he'd even remember me.

The puppy started to whine. She nudged my leg with her nose.

"Do you need to go outside?" I asked. She whined louder. "Alright, let's go. Maybe we can come up with a name for you."

She yelped in response and ran towards the door. I grabbed the leash off the counter and clicked it onto her collar. We walked down the stairs, and she pulled me behind her as she rushed for freedom. The instant we made it outside, she led me to my car where she promptly marked her territory.

"Don't pee on Wanda!" I called after her.

"Wanda?" a familiar voice called from the street.

"Rayna!" I replied. "What are you doing out here?"

She stepped onto the driveway and walked towards me. "Oh, I live just 'round the corner over on Maple."

"Why didn't you mention we were neighbors?"

"You didn't tell me where you'd found an apartment," she

said and shrugged. "Who is this?" She leaned down, and the puppy promptly pawed at her legs.

"She doesn't have a name yet. She just showed up today. There was a card and everything she needed."

"You alright?" she asked, studying my face. Rayna leaned in closer. I flinched when I realized I hadn't bothered to clean my face.

"I got some news about my mother today," I said. "Toby helped me get on Google, and I found a news article."

Before I could finish, my throat tightened, choking me and stopping the words from coming out. I shook my head and wiped my eyes. The puppy—my puppy—rushed to my side. She jumped up and down until I picked her up. Her wet nose nuzzled my cheek, and she licked the tears. I giggled as she kept licking.

"What is it, Shay?" Rayna stepped closer and placed her hand on my shoulder.

"My mother died, Rayna. Two years ago." I opened my eyes wide to avoid picturing the words again. Every time I closed my eyes or blinked, I saw the headline. "She died alone on the side of the road, somewhere in Tennessee."

"Oh, Shay," she said, "I'm so sorry." Before I could look at her, she wrapped her arms around me and pulled me into a tight hug. Her hand rubbed my back. I leaned into her, letting her attempt to comfort me and soothe the internal screaming I was desperate to silence. The puppy laid at my feet, curled against my legs. Both she and Rayna held me until my breathing slowed and I was able to stand on my own.

"Do you want to come up?" I asked Rayna once I was able to speak again. "I have Diet Coke and cookies."

"I'd love to. By the way, what are you going to name this sweet girl?"

"I was thinking Brownie or Four," I said, verbalizing the names I'd been mulling over.

"Brownie I get," she said as she patted my overeager pup. "Why Four?"

"Lucky like a four-leaf clover. She's also the fourth gift," I said. "I think I like Four."

"It's perfect."

"I can't stop thinking about the gifts," I said. I opened the door at the top of the steps and led Rayna into my home. "This is it. See all the furniture? Another gift, and from someone who knew exactly what I needed and would love."

"Do you have any idea who it might be from?"

I hesitated for a moment. "Now that I know it isn't my mom, I don't. The only other people I can think of are Will and Susan."

"Really?"

"I mean they knew my mother and me better than anyone. Maybe she went back?"

"What about your father?" she asked in a whisper, almost as if she didn't want to say the words. "Didn't you say your mom grew up in Missouri? Maybe he's nearby."

"I don't know. From what little I know, I don't think he'd care too much. How would he know?" *Was his phone number the one my mother kept in her pocket?* "I need to figure out who has my mother's phone. That's got to be the key."

"Can you track it?" she asked.

"I wouldn't know how. We've always had prepaid phones. So, whoever has it keeps the minutes loaded."

"I say start with the people you know. Will and Susan. If that comes up empty, are you ready to find your father?"

"I wouldn't even know how to begin. I only know his first name. I don't know where in Missouri he is."

"Have you considered one of those DNA tests?"

"What?"

"A DNA test, like through one of those family tree websites. They're not too expensive. You just spit in a tube and mail it off."

"And it matches you to your family?" I asked, not believing what I was hearing. It sounded so simple.

"If someone in your family has done one, yeah. My cousin did one a few months ago and found out she has a sister she never knew about. Blew up the entire family."

If she was trying to sell me on the idea, it wasn't working. She must have picked up on my hesitation because she smiled and said, "Look at it this way, what do you have to lose?"

Nothing. I have nothing to lose.

EIGHTEEN

"FOUR!" I SHOUTED, RUNNING DOWN THE ROAD. THE leash dragged behind her, bouncing off the pavement. Her head turned and she stopped. Her eyes darted between me and the squirrel that had stolen her attention. "Sit! Four, good girl."

She plopped onto the ground, dropping her chin. Her big eyes looked up at me, mourning the loss of her promised playmate. Four kept me up most of the night. Her eagerness to please was exactly what I needed. Rayna stayed until she felt I recovered from my afternoon breakdown but excused herself just before dinner. Four and I ate cheese crackers on the floor in the kitchen. When I went to bed, she curled up against my stomach. I naively believed she'd stay there, comfortable, for the night. But around midnight she started whining and playing, demanding my undivided attention. She finally fell back asleep just before three. I was beginning to wonder if someone hadn't trained her with my bar shifts in mind.

After an emotional two days off, I was ready to get back to the bar. I was not ready, however, to see Toby and confront what he'd witnessed the library. I cringed thinking about what I might have looked like fleeing from a newspaper article.

I let Four run and play a little longer before making our way back home. My shift didn't start for another six hours, and I wanted to get to the library to do a little more research before I had to go in. Much of my night, aside from playing with Four, was consumed with dreams about Iowa and the Rhodes family. I couldn't get them off my mind. I'd convinced myself they were behind everything. Maybe they were working with someone in town to coordinate. If it wasn't them, I was out of ideas.

When Four and I got back to the apartment, we found Hannah sitting on her porch drinking a cup of coffee. She waved me over, her arm flailing about as if she were stranded on an island and flagging down a ship. "Shay!" she called out to me.

"Hey, Hannah!" I said. I forced as much cheerfulness into my voice as I could muster at this early hour. "I was going to call you today." I pointed down at Four.

"You got a dog!" she squealed. "Oh-em-gee, he is adorable!"

"She," I corrected. "Her name is Four."

"Come here, Four." Her voice flipped into soft, practically unintelligible baby talk. "Oh yes, you're a sweet girl, aren't you? Such a good baby."

Four lapped it up, jumping up and putting her paws on Hannah's thighs. She licked my landlord's hand and panted happily. "We just went for a walk, and she found a squirrel, so she's a bit hyped."

"She's perfectly adorable, Shay. How rude of me! Do you want a cup of coffee?"

I shook my head. "No, thank you, I'm planning on heading to the library shortly."

"One cup?" She folded her hands in prayer, begging me to stay. "I can't promise I won't talk your ear off, but I make a mean cup of coffee."

"Sure, why not." I wanted nothing more than to go back upstairs and get ready to go to the library. Her eagerness was contagious, though. "Just one cup. I do need to get some stuff done before work."

"One cup coming right up. By the way, that top looks great on you!" She smiled as she gave me the once over. I'd thrown on one of the shirts she'd given me, pairing it with the one pair of leggings I owned.

"Thank you," I said. My cheeks flushed when her eyes didn't move away from me.

"You really are pretty, Shay. No makeup and all, you've got great skin." I squirmed under the compliment. It wasn't that I didn't appreciate her words; it was that those kinds of words rarely came without a *but* or some other expectations. I smiled, hoping she was finished with her observations. She gave me one last look before bouncing into the house. A moment later, she returned with a silver tray loaded with coffee, creamer, sugar, cups, and milk. "I didn't know how you liked it."

"Black is perfect," I replied.

"How are you liking the apartment?" she asked.

"It's fantastic. Close to work. Quiet and comfortable."

"Did you ever find out who sent the furniture?"

"No," I replied, not wanting to expand on my answer.

She took a sip of her coffee, her eyes peered over the top of the mug, watching me. For a moment, neither of us spoke. Sensing she wanted to ask more questions, I raised my shoulders and dropped them. I didn't have any answers, and I didn't want to share my suspicions. There wasn't anything to share, anyway.

"So, tell me about yourself," she asked when she realized I wasn't planning on offering more of an explanation. "Friends? Boyfriend? Hobby?"

I laughed. For years, I made up answers to these standard questions. But now, I didn't have any desire to pretend. So far, Wishing had accepted me for who I was. I hoped Hannah was willing to as well. "I've lived my entire life on the road, which isn't really conducive to friendships or relationships. So no friends, unless you count Rayna or Trigger. Maybe Toby. Definitely no boyfriends." Images of Adam and Greg flashed through my mind. Their kisses and brief embraces didn't count as relationships. "Reading and driving are really my only hobbies. Never had time or money for anything else."

"What about Toby? I've heard he's been flirting and making eyes at you."

"Oh, please," I said, laughing. "He's not my type."

"What is your type?" she asked the question I knew she would, but I'd hoped she wouldn't.

"I honestly don't know. Not Toby, though. I don't know if I even want all of that right now. Boys just cause headaches. Not sure I have any use for one."

"Mama said you were strange," she replied. Unlike her compliments, those words didn't faze me. I'd heard them before. "Oh, sorry! That was so rude!"

"It's okay, you're definitely not the first person to tell me that."

"I didn't mean it like a bad thing. It's just that you're so different from my friends and the folks here. Trust me, that's good."

"Then, thank you." I smiled, hoping it appeared genuine. Small talk wasn't my specialty. I didn't know how to do it casually. More often than not, small talk for me was a means to an end. When I needed work or money or food or a place to sleep, small talk was required to negotiate. "What about you? Boyfriend?"

"I'm between boys currently. Sam lives up in Springfield and can't be bothered with this small town or the drive to get here. Eric is my boyfriend from high school, but he's more of a hookup at this point."

"Friends?" I asked, eager for her to do more talking. The more she talked, the less I had to.

"A few here in town and some at school. My best friend

should be here shortly. We ride up to Springfield together on Tuesdays to shop for fabric. She's not in school with me, but she likes to help me with the designs and assignments."

"That sounds fun."

"Usually. Lorelei can be a bit much sometimes. She takes this small-town stuff a tad too seriously."

I tried to hide the look my face pulled. I remembered that name and how nasty she'd been to me. "I met her at the general store."

"She mentioned that."

"I should probably head home before she gets here."

"Don't be silly. You're my friend, too."

Friend. I mulled the word, letting it toss and turn inside my head, wondering where it might land. She'd said it so sincerely, it felt warm inside my ears. The single syllable danced and tugged, attempting to thaw the frozen core of my heart. I'd never had anyone call me a friend before, at least not like that. There was usually an awkward pause before the word, as if it fought to break free, urging its speaker to release it into the wild without meaning or intention. Hannah barely knew me, yet she was willing to put herself out with another friend to preserve whatever we had. That wasn't a feeling I was used to or comfortable with.

"If you're sure."

"I am. Besides, it's too late. She's already here." She stood, clutching her coffee mug close to her chest. Leaning forward on her tiptoes, she held her free hand in the air and waved. The wave she offered Lorelei was far more subdued than the one she used to get my attention.

Lorelei climbed the steps leading up to the porch. She glanced at Hannah and back at me. Eyes narrowed and lips pursed, she turned to Hannah and groaned loudly. She didn't seem to care that I was sitting right there, watching her display her obvious disgust towards me. "What is she doing here?"

"Her name is Shay," Hannah said and crossed her arms over her chest. "And she's here because she is my friend and she's renting the garage apartment."

"So she's your tenant."

"And my friend."

The two stood across from each other, arms folded, legs wide. Neither flinched nor backed down. Hannah was full of surprises. She seemed light and fun, not one to like confrontation. Her eyes held a softness I'd rarely found on the road. She listened intently and cared about what people said, but she also kept her nose buried in her phone. Though she never did that when she talked to me, only at the bar when she was with her mom.

"I'm sorry," I mumbled, trying to extract myself from the tension. "I should be going. I want to get to the library before work."

Lorelei snapped around to face me. Her blue eyes steeled. "I heard you were all over Toby yesterday."

My nose scrunched in annoyance. "You heard wrong."

"Mhm," she hummed. Hannah stepped forward and placed her hand on her friend's shoulder, but Lorelei shrugged it off. "Stay away from him."

"She's not interested in Toby," Hannah said. "And Toby isn't interested in you. You broke up. You really need to move on."

I braced myself, waiting for Lorelei to react. As little experience as I'd had with girls and girlfriends, I knew this interaction wasn't going to end well. Girls like Lorelei got what they wanted; they weren't used to hearing the word *no*. And they especially weren't used to their friends confronting them.

"Whatever, Hannah. I'm bored. Are we going into Springfield or not?"

"Well, you all have fun," I said. "Thank you for the coffee, Hannah."

"Where did that puppy come from?" Lorelei asked, her attention pulled away from me as Four jumped to her feet when I took a step forward. "That looks like one of …"

"Oh, that dog?" Hannah interrupted her and grabbed her arm. "That's Four, she's Shay's puppy."

"But where did she get her?"

"Who knows. Let's go before traffic gets too bad." Hannah grabbed Lorelei's arm and pulled her towards the house. "I want to show you some ideas I had so we know what to look for. Bye, Shay. Maybe we can grab drinks one night this week? I'll be by the bar with Mama for dinner. See you later!" Her ramble exploded through her lips. The words ticked louder and faster until she tripped over them. Lorelei's face twisted in confusion, but she didn't dwell. She gave me one last squinty-eyed look before following Hannah inside.

The door snapped shut behind them, and Four tugged on her leash, pulling me towards our home. I stopped to let her squat next to my car. Back inside, I filled her food and water bowls and laid out a pee pad—another gift—hoping they worked. That last thing I wanted was my new home smelling like dog pee.

"Be a good girl, Four," I whispered, leaning down to let her kiss my cheek. "I'll be home before work, and we can go on another walk."

At the last word, she leaped to her feet and cocked her head towards the door. "Later," I said, laughing, "I'll be home later. Then we go."

She lay her head back on the dog bed and lifted her eyes to me as if she'd understood. Sadness filled them at the realization that she'd be left alone.

"Don't worry, girl. I'll be back. I'm not going anywhere anytime soon."

NINETEEN

Trigger's patrol car was parked outside the library when I arrived. I found him leaning against it with a coffee in his hand.

"Good morning," I said.

He looked up and smiled. "You're out and about early."

"I have some research I want to do," I said, hesitating. I wasn't sure I could handle talking about my mother again.

"Rayna mentioned you learned some bad news yesterday." Rather than trust the words I wasn't sure I could speak, I simply nodded to acknowledge him. "I'm very sorry to hear that your mother is gone. She was—"

He stopped himself. "She was what?" I asked.

"Sorry," he replied, hesitation. "I lost my mom a few months ago, so it's hard not to think about her."

"Oh," I whispered, not sure what else to say. "Well, I'm in a time crunch. I'll see you around?" A small part of me wanted to ask him to help me get to the bottom of the gifts, but he seemed uneasy talking to me. He shifted his weight from his right foot to his left and back again. Normally, Trigger made eye contact and held it, but not today. He kept his eyes on the ground to hide the tears brimming in them.

"Of course. Shay?"

"Yeah?"

"I'm sure your mother loved you, and if she were still here, she'd definitely be doing everything she could to help you."

"I appreciate that, Trigger." His words did little to soothe the burning emptiness in the pit of my stomach. "Well, then, have a good day."

"You too," he said with a gentle smile. The edges of his lips twitched, threatening to turn down at any second.

I waved goodbye and hurried up the steps. I was running out of time. I had less than two hours before I needed to return home to walk Four and get ready for work. If the library was as empty as it had been yesterday, I should be able to sneak in and out without much fanfare. Waving at Marie as I entered, I rushed past a few people I recognized from the bar. They were too lost in conversation to notice me.

In front of the computer, I tried to remember the steps Toby showed me. I managed to log in and get the internet open from memory. The cursor hovered over the search bar, and I typed in what I was looking for. *Will and Susan Rhodes Nevada Iowa*. Images of the farmhouse and restaurant popped up in seconds. Seeing them again sent a tingle over my skin. So many good memories tainted by one night. A photo of Adam and his sisters sat in between the farm pictures. I let the mouse drift over it but couldn't click on it. His blue eyes, though aged a few years, still called to me.

In the days and weeks after our one night together, I would lie awake at night and wonder what might have been. If we'd taken the right steps and I'd let him court me. The Rhodes family was as traditional as they come. Will and Susan were high school sweethearts, and Susan and I had many conversations about saving yourself for marriage. She'd never even looked at another man, she once told me. Will was the love of her life, and she couldn't imagine another man or home. I envied her for that. I'd never known the feeling of being connected to a place or person. Not even my mother. Susan gave me a glimpse into what could be possible. She did the same for my mother. Tammy and Susan would spend hours on the tiny couch in our trailer talking about life and possibilities. I think Tammy saw the life she always wanted on that farm. She'd earned her job and place by hard work, and she'd gained their respect.

Seeing her daughter become just like her and fall victim to the judgment of people who were supposed to care for and love her broke something in my mother. She thought the Rhodes family was different. She believed she was different with them. I reminded her she wasn't. She saw all of her shames and failures in me that night, and she didn't like it. She hated it. She hated me. No matter what Trigger said, my mother wouldn't have done anything to help me. If she would have, I wouldn't be sitting in a library in Wishing, Missouri, staring at a photo of the boy I gave my innocence to.

I clicked through a few articles before venturing onto the restaurant's website. Stalling, I browsed through the menu and read the family history, though I already knew it. Some new information jumped out. Will retired a year ago, and Adam was running the restaurant with his mother. He'd graduated valedictorian and studied agricultural science at Iowa State, where he also graduated with honors. *See*, I whispered to the picture of Susan, Will, and Adam at his graduation, *I didn't ruin him.*

The restaurant would be open by now. I could picture Susan standing at the host stand, welcoming her neighbors and friends, greeting them with a hot cup of coffee. I imagined Adam in the kitchen calling orders to the staff. Maybe Will was in the corner booth with a hot cup of coffee and the local paper.

I dialed the restaurant's number but couldn't press the button to make the call. I needed to be away from the library and my new neighbors before I did, just in case. I quickly logged out of the computer and grabbed my backpack. I'd wanted to check out a few books but wouldn't have time. I had to make this call. I needed answers. I thought about the car, the apartment and furniture, and Four. Everything was becoming too much. I needed to know.

Inside my car, I turned the key and put Wanda into reverse. Once I was back on the road, I hit the green call button, pressed the phone to my ear, and held my breath. My heart pounded in my chest. Nausea gripped me in waves.

"Rhodes Diner, this Adam, what can I serve you?" His voice sounded just as I remembered it. Gruff but soft, with a slight twang. He probably had the phone cradled between his ear and shoulder. "Hello?"

"Sorry," I mumbled. Words stuck in my throat, itching to escape, but my fear choked them back. "Adam?"

"This is Adam."

I took a deep breath to steady myself and said, "Adam, it's Shay Lane. I don't know if you remember me. My mom and I stayed with your family a few years ago."

Silence filled the line. I couldn't even hear the usual bustle of the restaurant in the background. After a moment, the sound of his breathing returned.

"Shay," he whispered. My name sounded just as sweet on his lips as it had six years ago. I pulled the car into the driveway and leaned my head back into the seat. My eyes fluttered shut as I held on to the sound. He'd hurt me, but he still held a vulnerable piece of me.

"Are you busy? I can call back," I said to fill the silence.

"No, no. I'm just surprised to hear from you."

"How are you?" I asked, forgetting everything I wanted to say.

"Good. You?"

I sighed, unsure how to answer. "I'm in Missouri now. Working in a restaurant here." *Bar,* I mentally corrected myself.

"That's great. You sound just like I remember."

"So do you."

"How's your mom?" he asked after a beat.

"That's actually why I'm calling. She died a few years ago."

"I'm very sorry to hear that. How are you holding up?"

"Okay, I guess. I just found out yesterday."

"Wait? What?"

I took a deep breath and prepared myself for what I had to say next. "After that night, when we, well, you know. Mom left me. She drove me to the Missouri state line and left me on the side of the road. I haven't seen her since. I've been on my own."

"Oh, Shay." Pity filled the space between us. His voice dripped with regret. "I was a stupid kid who was terrified of his parents. What happened between us was just as much my doing as yours."

"I know. It doesn't really matter now."

"I liked you, Shay. A lot. You were all I thought about back then. I still think about you."

"You do?"

"I do."

"I think about you too, sometimes," I admitted, leaving out the part where the memory of him was tainted by my mother's abandonment. "Anyway, I was wondering if my mother had any contact with Susan after that night?"

"Not that I know of."

"So she never came back?"

"No."

"Did anything from her arrive in the last few years?"

"No, why are you asking?"

"I've been leaving my mom voicemails for the past six years. She never answered or called back, but I was always updating her on where I was. When I got to Missouri last week, weird things started happening."

"Weird how?"

"Random gifts started showing up. A car. A lead on an apartment. Furniture. A dog. All things I told my mom I needed. I left her personal messages. But she's dead, and I think someone has her phone."

"And you think it's my mom?"

"I don't know. It was the next logical choice."

"It's not my mom," he said bluntly. "She's been in the hospital for the last month. Cancer."

"Oh, Adam, I'm so sorry."

"Thank you. She's been fighting for a couple of years, but it's gotten worse over the last few months."

A million questions raced through my mind, each chasing the other. Susan wasn't the answer I was looking for, but hearing Adam's voice brought something I wasn't expecting—peace and closure. For years I lived with the notion that what we'd done had been so horrible that a mother was willing to abandon her daughter. That somehow I'd done something wrong. Hearing him speak to me as if we'd never left the bed that night made me realize I'd been holding on to the wrong guilt. We'd done nothing wrong. It was our mothers' irrational reactions to something natural that caused the problem. I may have been young, but I had feelings for Adam. I wasn't using him nor was he using me. I wasn't my mother.

I ran my fingers through my hair, pulling out a few tangles. It was getting far too long, and I was desperate to cut it. When we stayed with Susan and Will, I grew it out. Back then, I had more time to care. As we were lying in bed together, Adam had twisted the long strands between his fingers. Over and over, he'd gently pull a small chunk into his hand and work up and down. At the time, the sensation and movement mesmerized me.

"She probably doesn't want to hear this, but can you let her know how much she meant to me? She believed in my mother and me when no one else did. She really made a difference."

"Until she banished you for sleeping with her son," Adam said with a slight laugh. His ability to make light of the situation confirmed my conclusions. What we'd done wasn't a mistake.

"Well, that's the past."

"I guess so. Listen, Shay, I'm really sorry about what happened here and after. I wish I had more to say or offer, but I can't help you."

"I know. I appreciate you talking to me and not hanging up."

He exhaled slowly. "It's really good to hear your voice, Shay. If you ever find yourself up in Iowa, please stop by. I'd love to see you, and I know Mom and Dad would too."

"Thank you, that means a lot."

"Is this your phone number?" he asked. "Could I maybe call or text you sometime?"

"Yeah, it's just a basic cell, no texting or anything. But, if you do call, I'll answer."

"Great. Well, I hope you find what you're looking for, Shay."

TWENTY

I couldn't stand the way Rayna kept looking at me. Pity was one emotion that made my skin want to crawl. I could handle rage or disappointment, but not pity. Especially not from someone as strong-willed as Rayna.

"Please stop looking at me like that," I said under my breath. Rayna flinched slightly. Her eyes darted between my face and the bottle of vodka in her hand. The entire night had been nothing but awkward conversations with her and Toby. Business was slow, which only made it more uncomfortable. Toby tried to mention the library incident but stuttered until he gave up. Normally it was me who didn't know what to say. Rarely was I on the other end of a loss for words.

"I'm sorry, Shay," she said. *I'm sorry* was a phrase I was over hearing.

"Rayna, I'm fine."

"Are you sure you don't want to take the rest of the night off?"

"I'm fine," I snapped.

"Okay, we're just worried about you."

Sighing, I closed my eyes. They meant well, but every sideways glance and frown reminded me that my mother was dead. It pushed the truth back to the surface, forcing me to pay attention. I couldn't. The truth was I lost my mother a long time ago. Long before Iowa. Before my thirteenth birthday. She'd never been mine, just as I was never hers. We'd been brought together by the fate of birth. Knowing she was dead didn't change any of that. I couldn't allow myself to idealize her life or our relationship; all that would bring was more sadness and tears. I was done crying. I wanted to move on. For now, moving on meant getting settled in Wishing and finding out what was next. And solving the mystery of my mother's phone.

There wasn't anything I could do other than survive this shift and start my research again tomorrow. Although I wasn't sure where to go next. Mom was dead. Susan was dying. The two women who could have possibly cared enough about me to send the gifts weren't the ones sending them.

The more I thought about the gifts, the more I wished my mother were here so I could discuss it with her. She'd be able to think outside the norm and come up with leads. She was always good at that—finding solutions to problems. Granted, the problems were often of her own volition. If there was ever anything unorthodox that needed fixing, my mother would shine. She found food when there was none and ways to make money when everyone else was broke.

An hour before closing, after Rayna and Toby had their last smoke breaks, I requested my own fresh-air break. The dining room had thinned out, and I only had one table left.

"Sure, take all the time you need," Rayna said. I suppressed an eye roll and rushed through the kitchen to the back door, avoiding Toby altogether.

Once outside, I sucked in a healthy dose of air that was free of stale beer and body odor. The night, just like the morning, was hot and humid. My clothes clung to me, making my phone stick inside my pocket.

"Hey, Mom," I said when the familiar beep sounded. "Well, I

guess I shouldn't call you *Mom*, whoever you are. But I can't stop. I still can't believe she's gone."

I stopped myself. I wasn't calling to rehash my feelings. This message, unlike all the others before, had a purpose. "Look, I don't know who you are or how you knew my mother, if you knew her. All I know is you have her phone and have been listening to these messages for more than two years now. So, why now? Why are you acting on them now? Who are you? What do you want?" Anger bubbled just below the surface, waiting for an opening. It flowed through my words. My hand trembled as they gripped the phone.

"I will find you," I said, clenching my fist. "I will get my answers."

I hung up quickly, unsure of what else to say. Though I knew they wouldn't call back or answer, I held on to hope that whoever was listening would hear the desperation and need in my voice.

"Shay!" Toby called out the back door. "Edwin is ready to cash out. You got his check?"

"Yes," I replied and wiped my eyes. "Give me a minute."

Reality called me back. I could stand out here and stare at my phone all night, or I could go in and finish the shift. Maybe Rayna could offer some advice. She was no Tammy Lane, but I had a feeling she'd solved a problem or two before. I knew she'd be eager to help, or at the very least, listen.

After close, Toby brought out an order of nachos for us to share. We'd started our own tradition of chugging water and eating whatever appetizers Toby could pull together at the end of the shift. Mostly, we talked about me and my gifts, but tonight, Toby dominated the conversation.

"I just don't get it," he whined into the beer he'd begged Rayna for. *Just one*, she'd said when she gave in. "Lorelei dumped me. It's been months. Now she wants me back?"

"That's the understatement of the year," I said, laughing.

"What do you mean?"

"Your ex has threatened me twice now, instructing me to keep my distance from you. I'll never understand the territorial need to stake a claim on someone you aren't even dating."

"There's your answer, Toby. She's jealous." Rayna smiled. She leaned back in her chair and folded her arms over her chest, resting them atop her stomach. "Nothing makes a girl realize what she's lost like another woman entering the scene."

"But Shay and I are just friends."

"She doesn't see it that way. Shay is a beautiful, interesting girl. She's competition."

"Thank you," I said, beaming at the unexpected compliment. "A little damaged, though."

"Your stories and life are what make you so appealing, Shay. Don't cut yourself down because of them," Toby said.

This compliment sent a flush to my cheeks. "Spin it however you want, but my life is a disaster."

Rayna reached across the table and squeezed my hand. I waited for her to offer her own version of Toby's statement, but she didn't. Instead, she locked her eyes on mine as if she were attempting to send a silent signal.

"Speaking of disaster," I whispered to her when Toby excused himself for the bathroom. "I talked to Adam today."

"Adam, Adam? From Iowa?" she asked. With one eyebrow raised, she cocked her head to the side.

"The one and only. I thought maybe my mother had gone back to Iowa after she left me. To make amends, you know. She was so happy on the farm and with Susan and Will, I figured there was a chance."

"Did she?"

"No. I was kinda hoping that Susan or Will were behind the gifts. Like maybe she left instructions for her phone and personal things be sent to them. When I was little, she kept a phone number and name in her pocket, so they'd have someone to call if anything ever happened to her. My mom wasn't much of a planner, but she always made sure I knew there was a plan, just in case."

"That's very sweet."

"It was practical. Anyway, when I got older, she stopped carrying it. I assumed maybe she'd replaced the old number with Susan's. She didn't. So, I'm back at square one."

"Did you get to talk to Adam much?"

"A little. He was at the restaurant. Talking with him did make me realize a few things," I said, not expanding. "Let's just say I feel better about Iowa and what happened between us."

"That is good. Where are you with everything else?" she asked. Toby flopped into the chair beside me and reached for his beer. "Before you ask, no, you can't have another."

"Yeah, yeah, I know. I'm meeting friends in a few anyway."

"It's nearly two-thirty," I said with a yawn. "Where are you going?"

"Night fishing."

"Sounds lame." I yawned, fighting to keep my eyes open.

"It's not."

"Shay," Rayna interrupted. "Let's finish up our nachos and conversation before you fall asleep at the table."

I grabbed a chip and shoved it in my mouth. She waited patiently as I chewed. Toby watched with a mixture of awe and horror as I plowed through another handful of chips. "I'm good," I finally said. "I don't have any answers, and I don't know where to look next."

"What about your dad?" Toby asked. Rayna took a big, long drink of her ice water.

"I don't know him."

"That article said your mom was from Gaines. That's in Oak County. That's not far from here. Do you know anything about him?"

"His name was Ken." I ignored the mention of the article. I'd assumed he read it and memorized the details to his memory just as I had done, but hearing him confirm it made me uneasy. It's not as if it were personal. The story had been on the internet for two years. I'm sure it was on the news in Tennessee, too. Maybe even in Missouri. A million or more random people had known about my mother's death before I had.

"So, Ken from Oak County. Not a lot of people live there; I'm sure you could find him."

"So, I just call every Ken who lives there and ask if they slept with my mother? That assumes she didn't lie about his name. Or that he lived where she did and still lives there now."

"Did you give any more thought to the DNA test I mentioned?" Rayna asked. I looked over at her and shrugged. "Seriously. We can order one. I don't think the general store carries them. Pull it up on your phone, Toby; mine's in the office."

Toby flipped his phone over and started tapping the screen. "What's it called?"

"Lineage Kit," Rayna answered. Her leg shook, causing the table to vibrate, but her face remained calm.

"How do they work?" I asked. She'd mentioned it earlier, but I'd forgotten the details.

"You know, you just spit in the tube and then send it off. They match you with relatives and tell you if you have any genetic markers for diseases and shit," Toby answered.

"How much are they?" Any excuse to shoot down this idea was fair game. I wanted answers, but I wasn't sure I wanted that specific answer. My mother had mixed feelings towards the man who had given me to her. I didn't know the full story, but I knew it didn't have a happy ending.

"Look, they're on sale! Sixty bucks. Normally, these things are a hundred or so."

After the apartment and groceries, I had a few hundred dollars set aside. Enough to keep me safe for a few more weeks. My tips were consistent, so I had some idea of what to expect. While sixty dollars wasn't a fortune, it wasn't insignificant either. "I don't know."

"I'll cover it." Rayna got up and pointed at me. "Don't you dare argue. Let me go get my credit card."

"Rayna, I can get it, it's not that much." She turned her back to me before I could argue further. I pulled my tips from my apron and counted out the cash.

"I wouldn't do that if I were you," Toby warned. "Rayna wasn't kidding. She won't touch your money."

"I don't need her charity."

"It's not charity. She wants to help you find answers. This is something small she can do."

"Not another word, Shay. Here," she said and handed the card to Toby. "What's your address?"

I hesitated, still not convinced this was a good idea. The look Rayna shot me changed my mind. I could decide whether or not to take it and send it in later, but it was clear I didn't have a choice now. I gave Toby my address and watched him type it on his phone. Chewing my thumb to keep myself from arguing, I glanced between Toby and Rayna. They huddled over his phone, completing the purchase.

"Done," Toby announced.

"Thank you, I think."

"Hush up, child," Rayna scolded. "You want answers. This will get your answers."

Answers were something I could use more of, but I wasn't sold on the idea of my dad being behind any of this. What little I knew of him wasn't good. He'd hurt my mother in a way that she carried to her death. It could have been his number she kept. When I was a kid, I used to imagine it was. I would fantasize about ways to steal it from her so I could call him. If I was mad at her, I'd picture her injured or sick—never deathly so, but enough to justify needed to call her emergency number. As I grew, I believed this fantasy less and less. If she'd had his number and kept it all this time, she'd have called him. No matter how much he'd hurt her in the end, she'd loved him. When she talked in her sleep, she sometimes called out to him. Mostly wishing for him to come. Occasionally, his name was laced in hatred and anger, but it was usually doused in love. She'd never wanted me, that I knew for certain, but she'd always wanted him.

TWENTY-ONE

It took exactly four weeks to get the results back. Granted it had taken me nearly a week to work up the courage to send it off. The email with the results had sat in my inbox for three days now. First the one with my heritage, and then one confirming a relative match. I'd opened the first email as soon as I saw it, though its contents weren't all that surprising or interesting. The other, I waited on. It arrived on Friday morning. I'd been sitting in the library reading a book while checking my email. When it popped up, I dropped the book. I read the subject over and over again. Excitement and fear flowed through my veins and wrapped itself around my ribcage, preventing me from opening it. I didn't open the email on Friday or Saturday, and the library was closed on Sunday. Instead, Four and I curled up on the couch with the last *Lord of the Rings* book.

After weeks of early mornings in the library, Marie was used to me. She knew I didn't like small talk, so she avoided it. She learned my tastes in books and usually greeted me with a coffee from the diner—despite Wishing Library's strict rule banning beverages at the computer workstations—and a book recommendation. When I told her I'd missed the whole *Lord of the Rings* hype because my mother refused to allow me to read fantasy novels or any book that encouraged a wild imagination, she promptly pulled out every book in the series and sent me home with them. I allowed her fifteen minutes each morning for us to discuss the books. Then she left me alone.

On Monday morning, fall was starting to settle into Wishing. A soft chill hung in the air. I welcomed it after weeks of unrelenting heat and humidity. My hair, now past my shoulders, was appreciative. I had two goals for my computer time this morning: to find somewhere to get my hair cut and finally open the email. I started with the haircut. Marie offered up her stylist and gave me a few other leads. I meandered through the search results, ignoring the tab I kept open with my email. I looked up pictures and debated letting my hair grow out even longer. I'd settled in Wishing and had a routine, I reasoned. My old excuses didn't apply. Real shampoo and conditioner sat in my shower, and I'd tossed out all the old hotel and travel bottles I had. Tips and wages from Lace & Grit more than allowed me the funds to buy a blow dryer and other accessories. Closing the final tab of hairstyle photos, I decided to just play it by ear. The time I'd spent served as little more than a distraction from what was waiting in my inbox.

The only tab that remained open was my email. I stared at the email from Lineage Kit. *Relative Match Found.* I knew from my research of the kit's literature that I had to accept the connection in order for them to see my name and for me to see theirs. For the last three days, I let the weight of the news sit on my shoulders. I didn't tell Rayna or Toby. Hannah, though we talked nearly every day, had no idea I'd even done the test. But we usually limited our conversations to fashion, her dates, and whatever gossip she had to share. Hannah was the one person who didn't constantly remind me that my mother was dead and some random stranger with an unhealthy obsession was trying to fill in for her.

I hadn't left my mother a message since the day we'd ordered the kit. There wasn't anything left to say. Whoever had her phone knew I'd learned the truth about Tammy. They likely knew I was looking for them and for answers, but they never called back. It had been nearly five weeks since Four arrived. They hadn't left any more surprises or gifts. I was starting to wonder if they'd given up. Or if my need to find them scared them off. I should have been grateful that they weren't leaving more things to remind me I needed them, but I wasn't. I missed the surprises. Mostly, I missed knowing someone was out there looking out for me. Someone cared.

I leaned forward, squinting as I read the subject again. This time, I didn't hesitate. I took a deep breath and clicked the email. It opened, and the contents flashed in my face. The words didn't register at first, despite having a hint about what they'd be communicating. I read them again. *A DNA match has been found. Paternal link confirmed.* Again, I pushed aside the fear and clicked the link to confirm my desire to know more. Logging in to the Lineage site, I gave myself a second to reconsider. I shook my head. *No.* I'd waited long enough. Anticipation tingled in my fingers as I typed my password. When the page loaded, a giant blue button sat at the center, asking me if I wanted to connect with my half-brother. I did. At least I thought I did. I was ninety-five percent sure I did.

Within seconds his profile appeared. He'd already clicked his blue button and was waiting on me to do the same. *Chris Alan.* A small photo sat to the right of his name. I clicked on it. Looking at him, there was no denying we were related. We had the same thick eyebrows. Sandy blonde hair. Blue eyes. His smile only curved up on the right, like mine often did when I smiled on command. He was twenty-four—a year younger than me.

The tab with my email open blinked. I had a new message. I studied his photo for a little longer, searching for any indication that I'd been wrong. But I couldn't deny it. Chris Alan of Gaines,

Missouri was my brother. *Brother.* I rolled the word over and over in my mind trying to make sense of it. I had a brother. It didn't seem real.

In my inbox was a message request from Chris. He must have been anxiously waiting for me to confirm. I opened the message.

Hey sister! It started. Immediately my stomach turned. That was quick. *Sister.* I was someone's sister. I had a family. The news should have comforted or excited me, but it didn't. I'd just learned his name, and he was already claiming me. The email continued.

I guess this answers the questions about Dad, huh. The rumors were true.

That was it. No curiosities about me. Just a confirmation of a rumor about our shared parental linkage. Did that mean the people of Gaines knew me? Or knew of me?

Rather than respond to his email, I opened a new tab and typed in his name and city. A few clicks in, and I confirmed my dad's name. Ken Alan. Born October 10, 1972, in Joplin, Missouri. Pastor. Gaines Baptist Church. He'd joined the congregation in 1992 as a youth minister and stayed with the church while he attended seminary school in Springfield. He graduated from college in 1996 and was promoted to associate pastor. In 2009, he took over as head pastor. Ken and his wife, Bethany, married on Christmas Eve in 1993. The day before my mother's seventeenth birthday. She was probably four or five months along at that point. Chris, their first and only son, was born May 11, 1995, and was exactly one year and one day younger than me. His sister, Ava, was born two years later. I found all of this on the church's website.

A large photo of Ken and his family stood prominently on the church's website. Smiling faces. Thick eyebrows. Blue eyes. Sandy hair. Ken and his two children looked alike—they all looked like me. My heart pounded inside my chest. I touched the screen and ran my fingers over their faces. Bethany had brown hair and hazel eyes and looked eerily similar to my mother. Not close enough to be sisters, but definitely related. The internet didn't have much to offer on Bethany or Ava, other than Facebook pages. Toby wasn't here to help me figure out social media, but he'd offered more than once. I wasn't ready to take him up on that offer just yet, so I focused on Ken.

Article after article about Ken and his community work in Gaines and Oak County filled me in on who my father was. *My father*. I let the word roll over and over in my mind, marinating. The longer it sat, the more the truth sank in. I had a father. He appeared to be a good man, despite whatever rumors Chris had referred to. No one was perfect, I reasoned.

I plugged in the headphones the library kept beside the computers and opened one of the videos from the church's website. My mother and I didn't attend church often, but we'd been to a few, usually because her boyfriend of the month invited us. In Iowa, we went to church with the Rhodes family every week. Wednesdays, my mother helped Susan host a Bible study group. I hadn't set foot in a church since then.

The video I clicked on was entitled "Redemption." I listened, entranced by his words and voice. The deep tones soothed the worries that filled me. I forgot all about Chris and his stupid rumors. I ignored the warnings in what little my mother told me about him and focused on the evidence in front of me. His long, lanky body—not too dissimilar from mine—paced the stage with confidence and familiarity. He carried himself with a level of comfort and knowledge that neither my mother nor I had. Through his words, I felt his passion for his beliefs and his church family. He spoke with conviction and kindness.

He was nothing like I'd imagined. I'd always pictured a monster who'd taken advantage of my innocent mother. This man couldn't be the same one she whispered about in her sleep. The one whose mere mention would cause her to flinch and retreat into herself. The Ken Alan that stood at the pulpit of his small-town church seemed like the good guy. My mother, on the other hand, was the wayward teen who'd seduced him. The new pastor in town, handsome and wide-eyed, could have easily been drawn astray by my mother.

All the stories left untold gave me room to fill in the gaps with my new knowledge. Perhaps Bethany was my mother's cousin or relative and the reason Ken and my mother met. Or maybe Ken moved to Gaines for Bethany, and my mother swooped in and tried to steal him away for herself. Knowing my mother as I once did, it seemed entirely possible.

"Oh, I adore Pastor Ken," Marie said, leaning over my shoulder.

I slipped the headphones off my head and turned to look up at her. "Do you go to his church?"

"Sometimes when they have revivals. Gaines is only an hour or so away from here."

"Do you know his family?" I asked. I wondered how ingrained in Wishing he was.

"Not really. He's kind of a local celebrity there in Oak County. Our Baptist church and theirs are sister churches. So sometimes we host their revivals here. Other times, we take the bus up to Gaines."

"He seems well respected."

"He is." She smiled, but her eyes told a different story. *The rumors were true.*

"I was thinking about going up next Sunday," I said.

"You should. I think you'd like the church and town. Just don't go movin' on us."

Laughing, I said, "Let's not get ahead of ourselves."

I put the headphones back on, hoping she'd get the hint and let me get back to my research. She lingered for a moment but turned and walked away. In the hour I had left, I listened to a few more short sermons and read every news article I could find. Church events. Fundraisers. Every single word a glowing endorsement of Ken Alan. I scoured the Gaines Register's website for engagement or birth announcements that might mention my mother, but the paper's archives didn't appear to go earlier than 2001. I did find a note on his fifteenth wedding anniversary and the charity dance they hosted at the church to raise funds for a teen pregnancy clinic. The irony was not lost on me.

Back on the church's website, I found the address for the church and wrote it in my notebook. Toby's voice filled my head for a moment as I clicked on the *Get Directions* link. I'd never understood the purpose of online maps when printed ones worked so well, but the step-by-step list of driving directions was extremely helpful. I jotted them down below the address. Sunday was five days away. Five days to talk myself out of the drive. Five days to figure out what to say to my father.

Five days.

TWENTY-TWO

GAINES BAPTIST CHURCH LOOKED JUST AS IDYLLIC IN person as it did online. The pristine white building stood bright against the clear blue sky. A thick forest filled with tall oak and pine trees lined the back of the property. The gravel drive was surrounded by a white picket fence. Wanda, as much as I love her, stood out like a sore thumb against the shiny pickups and minivans. I parked her at the very back of the parking lot, avoiding the visitor parking spots. Easy exit and she'd stand out a bit less being hidden under the cover of trees.

Like my car, I relegated myself to a back pew, close to the aisle. My legs trembled as I sat down. I tucked the gray dress, another of Hannah's designs, under my legs and smoothed the skirt over my knees. My tattered black flats felt out of place too, but I ignored the embarrassment stinging in my cheeks. I was used to wishing for clothes that made me fit in. Something without holes that exposed every flaw of my life. Frayed hems to match the lack of a stable career. Ripped knees for all the times the road bottomed out beneath me. Loose strings. Pilling sweaters. Aside from the gifted clothes from Hannah, I'd never owned anything that fit well or was free of blemishes.

A frazzled mother with two teenagers who clearly did not want to be there climbed past me. The eldest, a girl no older than fifteen, glared down at me. I'd encroached on their territory. When they sat down, all three turned towards me and scowled. I pulled the old Bible, a long-forgotten gift from Susan, from my backpack and opened it to the verse mentioned in the program. The topic of the day appeared to be forgiveness. Reading through the verses mentioned, I wondered if Chris had told our father about the match. I wasn't sure I wanted Chris to be the one to tell him about me; that was my truth to speak. Did Ken know he had a daughter out there? Had Mom told him about me?

"Good morning, neighbors," a friendly voice said over the speakers, interrupting my thoughts. "Let's all stand and turn to page 55 and join the choir in singing praise to our God."

I set the Bible on the pew beside me and reached for the old, worn hymnal. I tried to ignore the curious eyes glancing towards me, but I felt them following my every move. Oak County was small, and Gaines was even smaller. The packed church likely represented more than two-thirds of the town's entire population. Keeping my eyes to myself, I stood and focused on the organ playing. The notes filtered through the sanctuary. Rather than call more attention to myself, I mouthed along with the words. No one needed to hear my pathetic and terrifying attempts at singing.

Two songs later, a tall, lanky man with sandy blonde hair walked to the pulpit. I recognized instantly that he was my father. Aside from seeing his photo earlier, I knew exactly who he was. I saw those tiny pieces of myself in him. The eyebrows. The hair. The slight slouch in his shoulders. There was no denying I was his. My cheeks flushed as I wondered if anyone else noticed the similarities between the stranger sitting in the back of the church and the man at the front.

I leaned forward in my seat, hiding my shoes under the pew. The instant he opened his mouth to speak, I was transfixed.

Every word spoke to me. His smooth cadence practically sang the verses as he read them. The message in his sermon seemed directed right at me. Forgiveness and love. Caring for your community and neighbors. But instead of seeing my father in those words, I imagined Wishing. Trigger, Rayna, Toby, and Hannah. Everyone who'd been my rock for the past few weeks, guiding me through the loss of my mother and helping me feel welcome in a strange place.

Wishing, and maybe even Gaines, was the small town where I would have loved to have grown up. It was the exact place my mother spent her life searching for. As I sat in the pew, I began to wonder if my mother had sat in this very pew. Had I been in her womb when she did? Did she sit here and listen to Ken speak just as I was, hanging on every single word he spoke, watching with awe and admiration along with the rest of the congregation?

I didn't know their story, but I could imagine a young Ken and Tammy sitting there, secretly holding hands or sneaking into the woods after the service to make out. Ken was exactly the type of man my mother fell for. Confident, but approachable. Strong. Well-spoken and passionate. Taken.

Though her back was to me, I knew Bethany was sitting in the front pew, flanked by her children. I recognized her vibrant, perfectly coiffed hair. Chris sat on the aisle. Ava was to her left. They sat close enough to tell me they liked each other, but far enough apart to seem casual. While I couldn't see their eyes, I had a feeling they conveyed the same messages. The Alan family cared deeply for each other. Their love filled this church and attracted the entire town to them. This was their home.

As hard as I tried to picture myself sitting with them, I couldn't. My hair, which I'd combed and curled for today, was still a mess. My dress, though new, was drab compared to their brightly colored outfits. Even Chris wore a bright purple shirt. Happiness surrounded them like a bright cloud against an even brighter blue sky. I was the rain cloud threatening to ruin their perfect day. I was the secret confirmation of a rumor that could destroy them.

It was hard not to daydream about what life might have been like had my mother stayed. Would the Alan family have accepted me, or would I have been shunned? As kind as they seemed, I didn't get the sense that they'd welcome me with open arms. But I was desperate to pretend they would. With my mother gone, I felt aimless. If it weren't for Wishing, I'd be completely lost. It had been weeks since I'd last heard the road calling me. I didn't itch to drive towards the end of town any longer. I wasn't chasing something. Maybe knowing she was gone took that determination from me or maybe I was finally settling. I'd been in Kansas City for more than a few months, in what I thought was a normal relationship, and it never felt like home. Even with Greg, I always felt the urge to keep running.

As the service came to a close, my heart raced. I'd come here with the intention of talking to him. I didn't know what I'd say or if I'd tell him, but listening to him speak changed my mind. I couldn't ruin his life. His son already knew about me, but I didn't know if Bethany did. I wasn't even sure if she knew about my mother and Ken. If she did, she might not take too kindly to my presence. If she didn't, my being here and showing up out of the blue could destroy her.

When the final song was sung, everyone stood. Ken and his family walked hand-in-hand to the back of the church. I held my breath as they passed. Bethany kept her eyes trained forward and a massive smile on her lips. Watching her, I realized her joy was real. She wasn't faking a smile or putting on a show. Her hand rested comfortably in Ken's. Warmth radiated from her. Just looking at her, I could tell she was everything my mother wasn't. She held her kids when they cried and soothed their nightmares. She shielded them from life's harsh truths. She was the mother I used to dream of.

The congregation filtered out behind them. Chatter filled the room. Laughter echoed as ladies gossiped and shared their news. I let the scowling family pass me. I wasn't ready to leave the comfort of the sanctuary. My mind replayed Ken's sermon over and over. Forgiveness. Love. Had he meant it for me? Did he want me to hear him today?

Sweat dripped from my hairline into my eyes. My stomach tightened. Anxiety surged through my nerves, pushing me forward and pulling me back all at once. I didn't know what I wanted. The words I could say to him tumbled into my throat and caught. I needed to get out of here. The plan I thought I'd made crumbled to pieces with every breath I couldn't catch. I shouldn't be here. Seeing him with his family—his real family— confirmed that I didn't have a home here. I'd let my optimism get the best of me. I stood to join the rush towards the door when a familiar face walked past me. Lorelei narrowed her eyes and paused. I tensed, waiting for her to approach me. But she just shook her head and kept walking.

I moved to fall into line, but my foot caught on the edge of the pew. I pitched forward and lost my grip on my bag. It clattered to the floor, and its contents onto the ground. My heart raced as I watched my entire life spill onto the floor. The sound of my keys, phone, and everything else rolling across the hardwood echoed through the church and out the door. Chris was the first to look over. His eyes squinted as he studied me. There were no photos of me online, but I sensed that he felt the connection between us. Recognition flashed in his eyes. I quickly looked away.

"Excuse me," I mumbled as I chased my belongings across the church. I needed to get out of this church and out of this town before Chris or anyone spoke to me. I thought I was ready for this. I thought I wanted to know more, but today didn't feel right.

I pushed past Lorelei, hoping she didn't call even more attention to me and moved towards the exit. Chris's attention was pulled elsewhere. I hoped it stayed there.

"Such a great sermon today, Pastor Ken," a petite elderly

woman said as I passed. "I felt like the Spirit himself was speaking through you."

"Thank you, Agnes," Ken replied, his voice followed me as I passed. I didn't dare look up. I felt his eyes on me. "Forgiveness and love are messages we all need to hear from time to time."

TWENTY-THREE

"Mom," I whispered out the window as the car raced toward Wishing. "I found him."

I'd given up on her voicemail. I refused to share any more secrets with whoever had her phone. Instead, I'd taken to talking to her when I was in my car. The road was where I felt her the most. She was gone and wouldn't hear what I had to say, but the words needed to get out. There was so much more I had to say to her. Stories about Wishing and the people I'd met. My newfound love of the internet and researching the people we'd once met.

"He's right where you left him. But I think you knew that. I don't know why you took me away from him, but I understand why you avoided Missouri all those years. Your secrets are buried here. Do you want me to find them? Mom, I don't know what to do. I want answers. I need to know where I came from and why you ran."

The whispered confessions and questions to my mother were a way to free myself of the chains the truth held on me. But I didn't have anything else to say to her. Shame filled me. My mother kept me from knowing a man who could have been a good father. She'd stolen my chance at a normal, happy childhood. If I let myself venture down that confessional, the resentment I already felt could fester into an infection. It could seep into every good memory of her I had left. Those daydreams would destroy me. I couldn't shake them, though. Even when I wasn't thinking about them, they hovered at the edge of my consciousness and teased me. Taunting me with everything that never was but could have been. They strangled me. Holding the air hostage. Keeping me from moving forward.

My breathing didn't return to normal until I saw the sign welcoming me back to Wishing. The hour-long drive felt like an eternity. Normally, the road soothed me. Not that drive. All I wanted was to get home and back to my dog. Wishing called to me, and it was the only sound I could hear. I pulled into the parking lot, grateful to see two familiar cars. It was almost two, which meant the bar was closed.

I threw my car into park and jumped out. Running towards the door, I ignored the gravel digging through my thin shoes.

"Rayna!" I shouted. Pounding on the locked door, my entire body trembled. Tears burned in my eyes. I'd kept them at bay the entire drive, but the instant her name escaped my lips, the tears broke free.

My friend greeted me with concern. Her brows furrowed, and a frown spread from the corners of her lips all the way to her eyes.

"Shay, what is it?" She ushered me inside. I blinked and rubbed my eyes, desperate for clarity.

"My dad," I whispered. "My dad."

"Oh, no." She shook her head and took me in her arms. Trigger joined her and stood beside me. He rested his hand on my shoulder but didn't speak. "Come sit down. I have cinnamon rolls and coffee."

The scent that had convinced me to stay in Wishing wafted through the air. That first morning felt like a lifetime ago. Since that fateful day, I'd lost my mother and found my father. I'd discovered a sense of belonging and stability that I never knew was possible. My life filled with people who saw the real me and didn't run or judge.

Trigger guided me to a chair and pulled it out. I sat down, forcing a smile. "Thank you."

"Here, eat up. We can talk once the cinnamon works its magic."

I steadied the fork in my hand and dipped it onto the soft roll while Rayna poured a cup of coffee.

"So," she said, sitting down next to me. Trigger sat across from her. "You went to his church?"

I flinched. Had I mentioned the church to her? I couldn't remember. "I did."

"What did he do?" Trigger asked. His body straightened, tensing as if ready for a fight.

"He was amazing. Everything about him seemed perfect. His wife. His kids. The church. Even his sermon, it was like he was speaking directly to me."

"Then what's the matter?" Rayna asked. A silent look passed between her and Trigger. He shook his head and turned away when he caught me watching them.

"I can't help but wonder 'what if?' What if she'd never run?"

"Asking 'what if' won't get you anywhere good, child."

"I know. I keep seeing her face. The sadness in her eyes when she talked about him. What if she really did love him?"

"I'm sure she did. Nothing as good as you could come from any place other than love." Rayna smiled, but I didn't believe her words. I wasn't good. I was a burden.

"Then why the years of running? Why not come home?" I asked.

"Sometimes there's more to a story than what you see," Trigger added.

"No," I said, shaking my head. *Rumors*. Chris's email rang in my head. What rumors? Did it matter? "I'm sure a lot can change in twenty-six years, but not a person's soul. I could see his goodness in his eyes."

"Did you talk to him?" Rayna asked.

"I planned to but didn't." Rayna's mouth curled into an amused smile when I rolled my eyes. "What?"

"Nothing."

"What if I didn't belong here or there? I'd never have fit in in a place like that. There's too much, I don't know, perfection."

"Shay, you belong here just as much as anyone born here. You're exactly what this town needed." I tried to ignore the comment, but it wormed its way into my heart and nestled deep inside. It felt warm and unfamiliar. No one had ever said anything so kind about me. The cynic in me had a million reasons why it wasn't true. But the part of me that had always longed to belong was desperate to believe every word.

"What if my mother isn't who I've always thought she was? What if she was the bad guy here and she kept me from him?"

"Trust me, Shay, there is nothing perfect about Pastor Ken or Gaines," Trigger said.

"You know him?" I asked Trigger. Questions filled my mind.

"Not personally."

"Then how can you say that?" Had he heard the rumors too? Did he know more than he was letting on?

"I'm a cop. I have gut instincts about people, and no one who seems as perfect as you claim he is, is actually perfect. We all have flaws."

"I know that."

"What Trigger is trying to say," Rayna interjected, "is don't get your hopes up. He could be a great man, or he could bring more hurt."

"Are you planning to go back?" Trigger asked.

"Yes." The answer came before I could stop it. No matter how out of place or guilty I'd felt, I still had questions. I deserved answers. For the first time in my life, I wasn't going to take what someone else spoon-fed me without asking for more.

"I don't know if that's a good idea," he said.

"Why?"

"Look how upset you were today."

"I'm not upset. Besides, I can't stay away. I've lived my entire life making up stories about him. Imagining him to be this monster, but he's not. He's nothing like that at all."

Trigger dropped his head into his hands. His fingers rubbed his beard. It looked as though he was about to cry. "Just be careful."

What wasn't he telling me? The threat behind his words lingered in the air, but I couldn't catch it. What he was saying didn't match what I'd witnessed with my own eyes.

"Trigger is right. You don't really know him, Shay. You've seen one version of him. Arguably, the version of him that is for show. I'm not a church-going lady, but I know from years of tending bar that men of God can be men of the bottle. It's easy to throw them on a pedestal and idolize their words, but the gospel they speak might not be their truth."

"I appreciate your concern and advice, but I have to know. I need answers."

"I know, and I won't try to stop you." She looked at Trigger with an intense gaze. "We won't try to stop you."

I watched the two of them have yet another conversation without words. I trusted Rayna more than anyone else. More than my mother. Trigger too. They both had shown me nothing but respect and honesty. But sitting between them, I felt trapped between what they wanted to say and what they couldn't.

"What?" I asked. I couldn't ignore the tension.

"It's just," Rayna said with hesitation. "We're worried about you."

"I can take care of myself."

"We know that."

"Then what?"

"Do you think he's the one behind the gifts?" Trigger asked. His voice had grown tired.

"I do," I said. "It makes sense. My mom always kept an emergency contact on her in case anything happened. I think now it was his number."

"And you think he has her phone?"

"Yes, it's the only thing that makes sense. Who else would do something like that?"

"Someone who loved and cared for you," Rayna said.

"Exactly. A father." Another look passed between them. "Look, I get it. I know you're worried about me, but you have to let me do this my way."

"Just promise me you won't get your hopes up."

I nodded. "I won't. A lifetime of disappointment has taught me to never do that. I hate to run, but I've got to go let Four out before she pees everywhere."

"Alright," Rayna said, standing. She pulled me into a hug, holding me close. "You do belong here, Shay. Please don't forget that. Don't let anyone tell you otherwise."

"Thank you," I whispered. "For everything."

I leaned over the table and took one last bite of the cinnamon roll. They walked me to my car, both offering more hugs. I told Rayna I'd see her Tuesday and drove away. Gravel kicked up from my tires. On the drive home, I rehearsed everything I wanted to say to him. More than just questions, I wanted to tell him how I used to dream of having a father. I'd reassure him I wasn't here to ruin his life. As much as I wanted him to be the man I'd dreamt of, I also didn't want to scare him off. Trigger was right, I didn't know the whole story. My mother, even in her late-night confessions, never shared everything.

Secrets weren't always meant to be exposed; I knew that better than anyone. And I was learning there were a lot of secrets to uncover. My mother's life after she left Gaines. Where had she gone? Why did she run? I looped through town rather than driving straight home. I didn't believe in the Wishing Well or the legends around it, but seeing it sitting unassuming in the middle of town square gave me hope. I parked my car in front of it and fished a penny from the ashtray.

I stood at the edge, looking down. How many wishes had been made by people standing exactly where I stood? How many had come true? The penny weighed a ton, holding more than the copper it was made of. My fingers rubbed the surface. I didn't come here to make a wish. There wasn't anything I wanted or needed. I was safe. I had a job and food to eat. My car got me where I needed to go. Four kept me from getting too lonely at night. Rayna, Hannah, Toby, and Trigger were like family. For the first time in my life, I wasn't chasing a feeling. I was home.

I leaned over the old brick wall and closed my eyes. "Please don't let me screw this up. Don't ruin this, Shay."

It wasn't exactly a wish, more of a commandment. But I opened my eyes and dropped the penny into the well. It fell quietly, taking my plea along with it. My stomach tightened as I watched it fall into darkness. I tried to picture Ken's face, but all I saw was Wishing. The town that had welcomed me and pulled me to safety. I wasn't sure what else I'd find in talking to him, but knowing I had this place to come home to calmed my fears.

TWENTY-FOUR

"WEAR THE FLORAL DRESS," HANNAH SAID. SHE SAT ON the edge of my bed, her legs swinging like an impatient child. "The pink sandals you got yesterday will look great with it."

Hannah was the only person in Wishing who supported my decision to talk to my father. I was hesitant to tell her about him and what I'd learned, but Thursday night she'd shown up after work and we'd started talking. Once the words trickled out, I couldn't stop the flood. Lorelei told her she'd seen me at church, and Hannah wanted to know why I'd been there.

Rayna and Trigger hadn't brought up my father or my planned visit at all during the week. Trigger stopped at the bar for a post-shift appetizer every day. He sat at a table, drank coffee, and picked at his food, but he didn't say a word about Ken. He barely even spoke to me. Rayna brought it up a few times, mostly to caution me not to get my hopes up. It was too late for that. I was more than ready to solve the mystery of my mother's phone and the gifts, which had stopped at the same time I stopped calling her phone.

The soft cotton dress slipped smoothly over my head. It fell delicately around my frame. The cap sleeves, complete with tiny ruffles, did little to warm the chill on my skin. "Are you sure it's not too short?" I asked, tugging it down. It hit just at my knees. All the dresses I'd seen last Sunday fell well beyond the knees of their wearers.

"It's perfect, Shay. You look innocent and sweet."

"In a good way or like a slut?"

"Don't say that," she said, shuddering. "Slut is worse than bitch. Women shouldn't be ashamed of their desires."

"Okay," I said, sighing. "Does it make me look like a decent person deserving of his time?"

"Shay, it's not the dress that does that. It's you. I really wish you could see yourself the way the rest of us see you. Your father is lucky to have the chance to know you. If he doesn't see that today, the problem is his, not yours."

"You sound like an old lady," I replied, deflecting the compliment. Her words filtered through my mind. Instead of calming me, they made me uneasy. She saw someone who didn't exist. She didn't see the girl who'd lost her mother and the best chance at a future because of a boy. She didn't see the woman who spent half of last year being someone's mistress. I wasn't a woman worthy of anything. I was the other woman.

"Shay," she said, standing and walking towards me, "you are a good person. You are worthy of love and a home. I don't care what you did before you walked into our lives. You've become a friend to me, and you care about this town and the people. Focus on the good."

"I don't know how," I admitted.

"Tell the negative voice in your head to shut up."

Easier said than done. I forced a smile and turned towards the mirror. I'd curled my hair and let Hannah do my makeup. I barely recognized the woman staring back at me. She looked confident. I'd need to channel her later today. Four came up and sat beside me. She rested her head against my calf. Her warm fur tickled my leg, and I bent down to scratch her head.

"You better get on the road. Shay, you look amazing. Remember, you are worthy."

"Thank you, Hannah." She followed me down the stairs and hugged me. "Can you check on Four if I'm not back after lunch?"

She nodded and sent me on my way. I could have stayed in the driveway staring at the rearview mirror for hours. I knew what was behind me—home, my friends, my dog. Ahead of me was the road to my father and, hopefully, the answers I needed to find.

I'd planned to arrive at the church towards the end of the sermon. I wasn't going in today. If I heard him speak and watched his family again, I'd find a way to talk myself out of what I needed to do. The plan was to wait outside and join the line of people waiting to greet him. I would wait at the end until everyone else was gone and ask for a private meeting. It was crucial to get him alone. The last thing I wanted to do was ambush my father and his family.

By the time I pulled into the church parking lot, it was full. So I parked along the road behind a row of pickup trucks that dwarfed my Sentra. I'd timed it perfectly. Just as I put my car into park, the double doors opened, and people flowed out. Ken and Bethany were first. I watched from my car a safe distance from the church. Today, her eyes seemed darker, less happy than last week. She still held his hand but fell a step behind him. Ava and Chris weren't here. Or, if they were, they weren't with their parents.

The line formed quickly. Once it stopped growing, I turned off my car and took a deep breath before crossing the parking lot. The wind rustled the trees and tugged my dress, pulling it behind me. I held my arms at my side and used my hands to keep the skirt in place. The last thing I needed was a gust of wind to show my father and the congregation what was under my dress. I took my place in line behind an elderly man in overalls. His wife turned and offered a sweet smile. She opened her mouth to speak, but I turned away before she could. I'd rehearsed the words I planned to say to him and couldn't risk speaking out of turn. Anything that didn't go according to plan would ruin my momentum. Small talk with old ladies wasn't on my agenda this morning.

The line moved slowly. After the first dozen or so people, Bethany kissed Ken's cheek and walked away. My eyes followed her as she made her way across the parking lot. She climbed into a shiny, silver Lexus SUV and quickly drove away.

"How are you today, Mrs. Grant? Lovely to see you." He greeted everyone the same way, listening patiently as they shared what was on their mind. "I'll keep you in my prayers," he said as each person turned to leave. He seemed to genuinely engage with them. His words, though repeated over and over, never lost their sincerity.

"A new face," he said to me when I stepped up. I glanced behind me to ensure I was still the last person in line. "Welcome."

When my eyes met his, I flinched slightly. The smile stayed on his face, the edges twitching into a mischievous grin. My mouth turned to cotton, and the words I'd rehearsed faded to dust. There wasn't even a hint of recognition in his eyes. There was something else entirely. Something I didn't want to see.

"What brings you out?" he asked, placing a hand on my arm. His skin burned hot against mine. I fought the urge to pull away from him. I'd seen him do this with every other person in line. I wasn't any different.

"I was wondering if I could, um…" I stuttered. Drawing in a deep breath and releasing it quickly, I said, "Could I have a word in private?"

His eyes scanned my face and worked their way down. Every inch of my body they passed felt exposed. The smile on his face widened. "Anything for a beautiful girl."

My stomach knotted as I followed him back into the church. He led me past the pews and pulpit to a private office at the rear of the church. I followed him in, and he brushed my arm gently. His fingers grazed the skin, sending a chill over me. The door clicked shut behind me.

"Have a seat, sweetheart." He gestured towards a brown leather couch at the center of the room. I sat down and crossed my ankles as Hannah had taught me. The dress flowed over my legs, covering my knees. I was grateful for the coverage. Rather than sitting at the desk across from the couch, he sat next to me. "You were here last week."

"You saw me?" I asked, shifting away from him. The kindness was still in his voice, but something in his eyes changed as he watched me. He inched closer, ignoring my obvious aversion to closeness.

"I always notice new faces."

"Oh," I said, unsure of what to say.

"What's your name?" he asked, placing a hand on my knee. The cotton brushed away, leaving no barrier between our skin.

"Shay." My name fell from my lips, catching at the tip of my tongue. I wished I'd brought my water in. I watched his face, hoping for a hint that he recognized my name. If he did, he didn't let on.

"Are you new in town?"

I shook my head. "I live in Wishing."

"What brings you all the way down here?"

"I saw your sermons online, and I wanted to meet you," I said. His eyes lit up, catching mine in their grasp for a moment before slipping down my body again. The meaning in them was clear. He'd misread my intention. Disgust ached inside me, breaking the resolve and killing any illusions I'd had about how this would go.

"Oh," he said, breathing heavily. His fingers moved up my leg, and I jerked away from him. I jumped to my feet. "What is it?"

I stood in front of him, his eyes lingered at my chest. I shook my head. *The rumors were true.* When his eyes met mine, every nasty word my mother said about him rushed back to me. He wasn't who I thought he was.

"I'm your daughter!" I said, forcing the sentence past the catch in my throat. I'd planned much more delicate words to make this announcement, but the way he was looking at me and touching me made my skin crawl. Even if he hadn't been my father, I would have been disgusted.

"My what?" His eyes grew wide as they studied me with a new intensity. Before I could answer, realization lit up his face. Flames of red flushed his cheeks. His chest puffed forward. The left side of his mouth curled into a snarl. The transformation was jarring. I stepped away from him.

"Your daughter. My mother was Tammy Lane." The words choked me as they came out. I gasped for air, feeling the room close in around me.

He stood. His height loomed over me. I felt his eyes bore down into me, but I didn't dare look up. The air in the room grew heavy. "What did you say?"

"I'm your daughter. Yours and Tammy's."

"Don't you say *that* name in my presence. That bitch," he spat at me. His curse echoed through the room. Shaking my resolve and fanning my anger. My shoulders slouched forward as I shrank away from him. At his full height, he was imposing. "What does she want now? Twenty-six years later and I still can't get rid of her."

"She's dead," I replied. I pulled out from under from his shadow, determined to take my power back.

"Good riddance. She send you to do her dirty work? Was her dying wish to ruin my life again?" I shook my head, keeping my jaw square. He wouldn't get a reaction out of me. "That's just like her. Even in death she is a vindictive bitch."

"Don't talk about my mother like you know her."

"Oh, girl, I know her plenty well. She tell you what she did?"

I shook my head. Everything shook. My knees threatened to

give way. Everything about him was wrong. The man standing in front of me wasn't the man I'd seen a week ago. He wasn't the same man who greeted and prayed for the people who turned to him for guidance. This was a man so broken by his past, he was dangerous.

"How dare you come into my church and threaten me."

Bile rose from deep within my stomach. "Threaten you? I came to get to know you. You're disgusting. No wonder she ran."

I glanced around the room, trying to get my bearings and find the door. I took a step towards it, but he grabbed my arm. His grip dug deep into my flesh. He yanked me towards him and put his nose to mine. His eyes burned red.

"You came to *my* town and walked into *my* church. You have no right to be here, girl. I don't give a shit what your mother told you. She's a liar."

"She didn't tell me anything," I hissed back at him. "I found you. I took a DNA test."

"You what?" His anger rose, and his hold on my arm tightened. A slight hint of fear glinted in his eyes. This time, he stepped away from me. He didn't loosen his grip. His fingers dug into my skin. I latched on to the slight advantage of his shock.

"A DNA test. Your son already knew all about your past and the rumors. I just confirmed them," I said with false confidence. Inside I was shaking, but I refused to let him see the fear. I was playing with fire. I tried to free myself from him, but he pulled me closer.

"You listen to me real good. You stay away from my family. Your mother did enough damage. Trying to ruin my life and Bethany's when all we did was take care of her. She used me. She used Bethany. She used you to try to manipulate me."

"You don't know what you're talking about," I said. I chewed the inside of my cheek to tamper back the tears. "She loved you!"

"Lies, you stupid girl. Everything Tammy did and said was a lie. As if ruining my life wasn't enough, she had to go and get knocked up just to prove her worth. Like I'd ever marry trash like her."

The harshness of his words sparred with the images, Bible verses, and crosses that decorated the dark room. I suddenly understood the contradiction in my mother's various stories. She'd loved him, I was certain of that, but she also knew it wasn't reciprocated. If he'd treated her the way he was treating me, it would have destroyed her.

"Listen to me," he said, snarling his lip. He grabbed my other arm and lifted me towards him. I strained to maintain balance on my tiptoes. "You leave this town and never come back. You forget all this nonsense about being my daughter. Sure, I slept with Tammy. Everyone did. But I never loved her, and I won't have that mistake coming back to take away everything I've worked for. You're nothing, little girl. Nothing. You don't belong to me, and I owe you nothing. Your mother ran. Follow her lead."

Tears flooded down my cheeks. My eyes blurred. I wanted to turn, but he held on to me, refusing to release his grip or gaze. I didn't want him to see my tears. He didn't deserve them. He wasn't worthy. Looking back into his eyes, I didn't see a trace of myself. There may have been physical similarities, but that was it. He was nothing to me.

"Let me go!" I screamed. I pulled my body back, away from him. Twisting my arms, I tried to break free. "I'll leave if you let me. I don't want anything from you. Coming here was a mistake."

"Get the hell out of here," he said, dropping me. He took a step towards me. "If I ever see your face in this town again, you won't walk out on your own. I made the mistake of letting your mother walk away free, I won't make the same mistake with you."

TWENTY-FIVE

RED AND BLUE LIGHTS FLASHED IN MY REARVIEW mirror. I glanced at the speedometer. Ninety-five. I let off the gas, slowly bringing the car to a stop on the shoulder. I swiped at my face to clear the tears. I didn't know where I was. The road was unfamiliar. I'd left the church so quickly, I hadn't bothered to look for highway signs. I just needed the road. The escape should have pulled me out of reality, but I couldn't stop hearing his words. The threat he'd made and what he'd implied about my mother.

The car stopped, and I rested my head back against the seat with my eyes closed. Ken Alan was my father. Before he'd learned he was my father, he planned to do God knows what with me in the basement of the church he led. Moments before that, he was offering prayers for little old ladies and preschoolers. The harshness of his words still stung. *Trash. Stupid. Lies.* He'd been even crueler than she ever let on. How could a man like that be my father? I'd spent my entire life imagining him to be my savior. The one to finally bring me home. But he wasn't, and he never would be.

Tap! Tap! Tap! The loud rapping on the window startled me. I should've expected it, but my mind wasn't here. I rolled down the window, not bothering to look at the officer I knew was there.

"Shay, what the hell?" Trigger shouted. "Do you have any idea how fast you were going? You didn't even slow down at the four-way stop."

I turned to face him. My face scrunched, twisting with the devastation of the morning. He took one look at me and pulled the door open. I stepped out and into his waiting arms. They wrapped around me, pulling me close. His touch felt comfortable. Not like the repulsive burn of my father's hands.

"What did he do to you? That son of a bitch."

I shook my head, leaning against his chest. My arms were sore from the bruises left by Ken's fingers, but all I wanted was for Trigger's embrace to pull tighter. I sank into him, breathing in the scent of gasoline and coffee. My tears soaked through Trigger's uniform.

"Shh, Shay, it's okay. You're safe now. He can't hurt you."

"He—" I whispered, unable to find an adequate way to describe the man who'd given me to my mother. "Monster."

Trigger stepped back, releasing me. Our eyes met, but shame pulled mine away. They'd warned me. He and Rayna both had tried to stop me. "How did you know?" I asked when I composed myself. I leaned back into my car and folded my arms over my waist, hugging myself.

"Gaines ain't far from here," he said, sighing. "Rumors spread."

"About my mother?"

He shook his head slowly as if lost in a memory. "About Ken."

"And what? What are the rumors?" I didn't have the patience for his slow-paced non-answers.

"That he isn't faithful to his marriage or in his beliefs."

"That he's a pervert?" I offered, shivering at the lingering feeling of him on my skin.

"Among other things." Trigger shifted on his feet. Discomfort turned his soft face hard.

"Abusive? A cheat? What, Trigger? He's my father. I have a right to know."

"You do, Shay. I wish I had more answers for you, but I don't."

"Who does?"

He shrugged and knelt in front of me as I sat back in the car. A passing truck slowed, and curious faces gazed out the window at me. I could only imagine what we looked like. Me in my pretty floral dress and tear-stained face, and Trigger in his too-small uniform, kneeling in the gravel beside my car. Hands folded in front of his face, he bowed his head.

"I don't know how to help you, kid, but I will help however I can. This is a journey you're going to have to take on your own. I can't give you all the answers."

"Some of them? My mother was a minor when she left Gaines. No older than sixteen when she was in a relationship with him. He says she ruined his life. What does that mean?"

"I don't know."

"How can you help?"

"I could look into his records, see if anything lines up. But are you sure you want to know?"

I thought about my mother and the way her eyes squeezed shut anytime I mentioned a curiosity about my father. The disappointment on her face when I would make up stories about who he was. All the times she'd sacrificed her own safety to ensure mine.

Closing my eyes, I pictured his face. The way his eyes had studied my body. His fingers on my skin. The memory coiled out from me, rounding itself into a snake ready to pounce. His final words to me played over and over as I contemplated Trigger's offer. I wanted answers, but at what cost?

"I don't know," I admitted. "I wish she were here."

I'd missed my mother countless times over the years but

never like this. Over the past week, I'd spent countless sleepless nights imagining what she'd say to me if she were here. I debated whether or not she'd have allowed me to find him. Something told me she wouldn't have stopped me, but she wouldn't have encouraged it either.

Trigger handed me his handkerchief. I held it in my hands and studied it before using it to wipe my eyes. Black streaks of mascara stained the pristine white cotton. The streaks tore through the innocent fabric, leaving their mark of forever damage. The black might wash out, but it would never be pure again. I held it towards him and offered him an apology and a thank you. A single *I'm sorry* to cover every dark spot I'd brought to him and to Wishing.

"No need to apologize or thank me, Shay. It's just a hand-kerchief."

But it wasn't just anything. It was more. His small gesture today compounded by every act of kindness he and his town had shown me since I arrived here.

"Not for that, Trigger, for everything."

"Everything?" His eyes shifted past me.

"For welcoming me here. For showing me there was more to life than the road."

"Oh, don't get all sentimental on me, kid."

"I mean it, Trigger. I'd have been okay on the road by myself, but you and everyone here gave me a second chance."

"We didn't give you anything, Shay. You've found that on your own."

I lowered my eyes. The contrast between this man who barely knew me and the one who was supposed to be my father was stark. Trigger had no obligation to help me, yet there he was.

"Thank you," I whispered. "I should get home. Four is waiting for me."

"You good to drive?"

"Yes. Promise I'll stop at stop signs and follow the posted speed."

"I should give you a ticket."

"I know. I appreciate that."

He braced his arm against the car door and stood. I gave him one last hug before getting in the car and heading home. Despite Trigger's kind words, I still felt lost. I wasn't sure what today had accomplished, but it wasn't what I'd hoped. I had more answers, but I was nowhere closer to solving anything. My father was even worse than my nightmares predicted. There was absolutely no way my mother had her phone sent to him. Nor was he behind the gifts. I was back to square one.

I wasn't sure I cared anymore. The gifts had stopped. It was clear that whoever left them didn't want anything from me. I still didn't believe things like that came without strings, but the evidence was clear. They wanted to stay anonymous and didn't expect anything in return. Even knowing this, I couldn't shake the questions. I did still care. I wanted to know. At the very least, I owed them a thank you.

Driving by the motel, my mind flashed back to the first night I spent in Wishing. I'd been more than lost. My will to keep going was gone. Trusty Rusty dying was just the cherry on top. But she'd died in the exact right spot—right outside of Wishing. Somehow, she'd known I needed to be here. When I left Kansas City, I had no destination in mind. Yet I found myself smack in the middle of the one place I'd be able to find answers I didn't even know I needed.

My mother remained on my mind that entire drive. I weaved down the back roads screaming at her, begging her to answer me. I must have dialed her number a hundred times. No matter how many times I called, she'd never have answered—she couldn't. I didn't know that then. I just needed to hear her voice. Any hope of finding her died that night. No mother could have ignored that desperation in her child's voice. I'd told her I was over it. That I didn't want this life anymore. There was nothing ahead of me, that's what I'd told her on the message I left before my car died.

I had no plans. Nowhere to go. No one to depend on. I'd spent much of my life alone, but I'd always had her to lean on. When she left me, I was aimless. I knew what to do to survive, and I did it. But a few months ago, I was done. The fight was gone. Whatever hope I'd found in Greg and Kansas City died. He'd been the final straw. The last proof that I wasn't worth someone else's love or time. My mother not answering the phone when I needed her most was the final nail. It all faded into nothing that night.

Then I found this place. Or it found me. I wasn't sure which. It didn't matter, though. I'd found something in Wishing that I thought I'd never find. Optimism. There were things to look forward to. I actually felt stable, and it scared me. There was too much to lose here. If something happened and I lost it all again, I wouldn't recover. I loved this place and its people. Perhaps those were the strings the gifts came with. I wasn't used to being tied to a place. Fear poured like lava through me, burning its truth and leaving behind delicate scar tissue. I couldn't stay. I couldn't risk the devastation of losing it.

Terrified, I pulled the car into Lace & Grit. Rayna's car was alone in the parking lot. The bar was closed, and she was probably about to head out. I wasn't ready to leave Wishing yet, but my time was coming soon. Stepping out of my car and walking towards the door of the bar that had given me my life back, I knew I'd do what I always did. Say goodbye in my own way and leave before they had a chance to realize what I was doing. A clean break.

It was time to get back to what I knew. Solitude and the road. I just needed a few weeks to figure out where I was going and make a plan. That plan included learning everything I could about my mother and her childhood in Gaines. I'd leave here with closure so there would never be a need to look back. No regrets.

TWENTY-SIX

"W HAT ARE YOU DOING HERE?" RAYNA ASKED WHEN she opened the door. She took one look at my face and shook her head. "I'll resist the urge to say I told you so."

"That'd be great." My stomach growled. The bar smelled of bacon and cinnamon. "Got any more cinnamon rolls?"

"I may have saved one." Of course she knew I'd be here today. There was a good chance she'd been waiting on me. Sadness gripped me, pulling and squeezing the air from my body. I'd miss Rayna the most when I left. My attachment to her was one more reason to leave. If I'd learned anything from my mother, it's that others cannot be counted on. Everyone leaves eventually.

"So," Rayna said as she set the place in front of me, "do you want to talk?"

I shook my head no, but the words spilled out of me. I hadn't intended on telling her everything, but the instant I saw her, the confession bubbled out from below the surface. How he'd touched and looked at me. What he said about my mother. Rayna listened intently as I spoke; she didn't interrupt or offer her opinion. I only paused long enough to take bites or drink the coffee she poured me. When I finished, she reached across the table and brushed my hand.

"All that to say, I still don't know who sent me the car or the furniture. I don't know who has my mother's phone. If anything, I left with more questions." I'd also left with a new resolve, one that I couldn't share with her or anyone. It was bad enough knowing I'd be breaking her heart; I didn't need to see it happen. I couldn't tell her I planned to leave.

"Do you want to know the answers?" she asked. Her hand rested on top of mine for a moment before her fingers curled around it. She squeezed gently.

"I don't know. Trigger offered to help, but I need to digest everything that's happened. I still don't know if I've fully processed what happened to my mom."

"What do you mean?"

"She died alone in a ditch while I was gallivanting across the Midwest."

"You were trying to survive, Shay."

"So was she. But she was alone."

"So were you."

"I had her voicemail. Then I had Greg."

"Greg?"

"My boyfriend in Kansas City."

"You've never mentioned him before."

Her eyes locked on mine. I shrunk back into my chair. "It ended badly."

"Is that why you're here?"

"I guess? I don't know. Do you think it's weird I ended up here?"

"What do you mean?"

"Here, somewhere my mother likely visited. A place where my father has ties. Less than a hundred miles from the place they lived. Near where I was born."

She thought for a moment. Her eyes closed and eyebrows furrowed. "Did your mother ever talk about her childhood?"

"Not really. Her parents rarely came up. I always assumed they'd disowned her because of me. But she never talked about the town she grew up in, just that it was in Missouri."

"Do you think she'd want you digging into her past?" she asked. Her tone was neutral, but I felt like she was projecting her own feelings onto me. If she were my mother, she wouldn't want me resurrecting ghosts.

"Honestly? Probably not, but it doesn't matter. She never told me the truth about where I came from, and I think I have a right to know."

There was no way she'd have ever given me the answers. Instead, she'd have let me find them on my own. That was always her way. Never give way to the easy route. My mother didn't take shortcuts, and she wouldn't allow me to either. I taught myself to read. I taught myself how to drive. Tammy Lane refused to have a lazy daughter. If I needed answers, I was on my own. Now as an adult and back when I was a child. At least she was consistent.

"What if the truth changes things?" Rayna asked and topped off my coffee.

"What do you mean?"

"Shay, your mother may have demons in her past that aren't your business. Dredging those up could alter your history or future. Is it worth it?"

I didn't even have to think about the answer. "Yes," I said with no hesitation. "The truth is worth everything."

"Even the hurt you experienced today?"

"Rayna, pain is like a second language to me. I'm fluent in it. Pain and disappointment are the only two constants in my life. And it only gets worse when I have time to build up hope or dream."

"That's a terribly sad outlook on life." She frowned.

"Well, it's all I know." I stood up and cleared the plates and mugs from the table. I'd already said more than I'd intended to. "I need to get home. Four is waiting for me."

"I'm glad you stopped in, Shay. I know you're not used to having people to lean on, but I've grown pretty fond of you these past few weeks. I care about you and what happens to you."

My heart sank. The tightness in my chest hugged closer. I couldn't speak. Swallowing back my tears, I simply nodded and turned my back to her. Tears stung in my eyes as I walked to the kitchen. Her footsteps trailed behind me. She walked around me and stopped in front of the dishwasher. My cheeks burned under her intense gaze.

"I've got these," she said and reached to take the dishes from me. She read my face and flinched. I didn't have to say anything. She already knew I was leaving. The brimming tears and tight smile told her everything she needed to know. "This is your home."

Her whisper floated through the air between us and landed on my gut, punching me. We stood in silence for another moment. Her face inches from mine. After a pause, she leaned forward and pulled me into her arms. She wrapped me tightly against her, forming a shield around me.

"I understand" was all she said. She released me and shifted her attention to the dishes.

"I'll see you Tuesday," I said quietly. My voice trembled. I made a beeline for the door. I needed to get outside before the tears exposed my decision. Rayna saw me in a way no one ever had. She could read into what I wasn't willing to say out loud. Like my mother, Rayna could see through my eyes into my soul. In a way that was nothing like my mother, she was able to take what she learned and use it to comfort me. Her words always came out right.

I slammed the car door shut and jerked the seatbelt across my shoulder. It clicked into place. I blinked. Once. Twice. Three times. Then the tears started. Tears for my mother and the loss of the father that never existed. Tears for Wishing and everything I planned to leave behind. The car shook with my sobs. Slamming my fists into the steering wheel, I unleashed every ounce of rage and sadness that swelled inside me. It came out in a burst, screaming from my lips. When I looked up, Rayna was standing in the doorway watching me. Tears streamed down her face. Not only could she read my pain, but she felt it too. Her pain was that of a mother who'd disappointed her daughter. Had she seen me as a second chance?

I dragged my hand across my eyes, clearing away the evidence, and started driving. I pointed the car towards home and Four. Hannah would have let her out by now. Thankfully, Hannah was also headed to Springfield with her mother and shouldn't be home when I got there. I couldn't face any more humans today. Just my dog and a book. I had a pile from the library waiting for me. Tonight and tomorrow, I'd allow myself to get lost in the pages. Tuesday I'd start planning.

At home, Four was waiting by the door. I could hear her paws clicking on the floor as I climbed the steps. I took my phone from my bag and dropped my keys and the bag onto the counter and took her outside. She wasn't interested in Hannah's yard or her usual spot. She dragged me out to the sidewalk and led me through the neighborhood. The hot air did little to cool the raging fire inside me. But the walk with her distracted me long enough to clear my head. Everything seemed to be happening so fast, yet I felt like I'd been here forever.

"Let's go home, girl," I said. We'd been walking for nearly an hour. The heat from the pavement seeped through the sole of my sandals. Four tilted her head toward me, and her eyes dropped. "Okay, one more block."

Four barked in response. A slow smile crept over my lips. She bounded forward, pulling me behind her. I glanced down at my phone in the other hand and sighed. "Should I call again?"

She didn't respond, but her pace slowed enough to allow me a second to flip open the phone. When I didn't dial the number, Four stopped and sat on the sidewalk. Her back to me and ears raised, she waited. I hesitated for another moment.

"What do I say?" This time, Four barked impatiently. "Okay, okay."

The sun was setting on the horizon ahead. As it dipped behind a cloud, the summer air cooled; orange and red splays of light glimmered in the sunset. The wind danced around me, pushing my dress against my skin. My mother and I had spent many summer nights walking and enjoying sunsets and breezes. At least we had before it all went to shit. Those nights she'd hold my hand as we walked, and she'd tell me about her dreams. She'd settle down on the coast one day, she said. That was her biggest dream—to find a small ocean town and finally park her car for good.

"Hey, Mom," I said after I finally got the courage to call. "I wish you could see this sunset. It's just like the ones we used to love. Remember your beach house daydreams? I hope you made it to the beach before you left. At least to dip your toes into the ocean."

My throat tightened. I clenched my teeth and bit back the tears. "I met him, Mom. He's awful. Worse than you ever said. He hurt you in a way I'll likely never know or understand. But Mom, I need answers. I want to know who you were before all of this. Before Ken. Before me. I know you can't hear this now, and I don't know who has your phone. Whoever you are, if you have answers, can you help me find them? Who was she?"

The message beeped indicating I'd run out of time. I wasn't sure who was on the other end, but I was certain they'd have answers. I closed the phone and pressed it into my chest. Four pushed herself off the sidewalk and guided me back home. On the walk back, she stayed beside me. Even as cars and squirrels raced by her, she didn't waver. Our steps were matched. She remained calm until we got back home. At the edge of the driveway, her nose dropped to the ground, and she jerked the leash from my hand. She ran full speed towards the house and clawed at the door. I chased after her, calling her name.

I pulled it open, realizing I'd forgotten to lock it. Four was at the top of the stairs before my foot hit the first step. I ran up behind her and pushed open the door. She barked frantically and leaped towards the kitchen counter.

Beside my bag was a box with my name on it. It hadn't been there when we left.

TWENTY-SEVEN

FOUR SAT NEXT TO ME, HER NOSE AGAINST THE BOX. IT took me five long minutes to calm her barking. She raced around the apartment and sniffed every surface. It wasn't until I grabbed the box that she came back to me. I sat cross-legged on the floor with it in front of me. I didn't have to open it to know what was inside. There were answers.

I opened the flaps and reached inside. The familiar white envelope with my name in perfect penmanship sat on top. I tore it open and slipped out the card.

I hope these help.

I studied the handwriting for a moment and tried to remember what Rayna's looked like. She scribbled out the nightly specials on the board. Her handwriting was chaotic where this was precise and intentional. I didn't recognize it at all. Aside from Rayna and Trigger, I couldn't think of anyone else that could be behind all of this.

Tossing the note aside, I pulled out the first stack of papers. A note instructing me to read them last was stuck under the rubber band that held them together. Placing them beside me, I reached back into the box and pulled out a book. Each time my hand went in, Four lifted her head to watch with a mixture of confusion and concern. I leaned over and gently brushed her head with mine.

"It's okay, girl." She panted in response but dropped her head back to the floor. "Nothing in here can hurt us. At least not physically."

Drawing in a deep breath, I clutched the book to my chest. The book with the white cover and gold lettering was just the book I used to dream of being a part of. There weren't yearbooks for kids raised in motels and libraries. *Gaines High School, 1991-1992.* Quick addition told me this was my mother's freshman year of high school. She wouldn't have met my father yet, but if I was going to start somewhere, I wanted it to be before. To see who she was before she met him. I reached into the box and pulled out the rest. There were two more. Her sophomore and junior years. This made sense. My mother never graduated high school, and as far as I knew, she didn't even attend her senior year. I was born the month she should have finished her junior year. It was tempting to open the one for that year, but I went back to the beginning.

I opened the book and scanned the pages. As my years of reading told me, the early pages were filled with notes and signatures. People who'd once been her friends left clichéd sentiments scribbled on the blank pages. I traced the writing with my fingers, skimming for names that might be familiar. I only knew two people from Gaines: Ken Alan and Tammy Lane. Neither of those names was scribbled inside.

A few pages in, I found the first photo of my mother. Her face in the middle of a group of girls who all appeared to be her age. Even in black and white, she looked as full of life as she always had. Her hair pulled into a high ponytail with a big scrunchie on top. An infectious smile I didn't recognize spread across her face. The caption listed her and her friends—Lizzie Gable and Miranda Price. According to the caption, Miranda was a senior and Lizzie was a freshman like my mother. I studied their faces and the way they seemed to be looking at my mother for guidance. Both girls' faces were turned towards her, a look of awe danced in their eyes. The caption didn't reveal much more, but I knew these two girls were her best friends, their closeness clear even in a faded black and white photo. I stood and retrieved a pen and paper from my bag to make a note of their names.

I flipped through more pages and found pictures of her sitting at lunch and at football games. Halfway through, I saw her face in a sea of cheerleaders. She sat in the front between Miranda and Lizzie. She'd been a cheerleader. I tried to picture my cynical mother doing cheers and shaking pom-poms. The woman who didn't even listen to the radio in the car. The one who refused to let her daughter join anything. I tried to imagine the Tammy Lane I knew joining the cheerleading squad. I couldn't. But there was the evidence, plain as day. A smile spread across my face.

"I knew you were hiding something big, Mom," I said giggling at the photos of her flying in the air and lifting her pom-poms over her head. I closed my eyes and stretched back into my memory. Laughter wasn't something we shared much of, but when she did laugh the sound would boom and echo through the car. It was better than any song on the radio. When I was little, I would do everything I could to make her laugh just to hear that sound.

Her class photo appeared next. Her hair was even longer back then. The chunky layers fell softly around her face, framing the high cheekbones I shared with her. Snapping the book shut, I reached for the second book and repeated the process. Tracing the signatures inside this book took less time. There were only a handful. Lizzie and Miranda signed the cover. It was inside that I found another. But why had he signed her yearbook? They'd never attended the same school. What he'd written made even less sense.

We'll always have Paris. Love, Ken.

Paris? I knew there was no way he meant the city in France.

The only logical answer was Paris County. The very place I was sitting now. I tried to picture her and Ken and their younger faces walking through town. They'd stop at the Wishing Well and toss their pennies in along with a wish for their future. There was a kindness in those words he'd written her. They hid the truth of what was to come, but they proved that at some point, the relationship was one with mutual happiness. I couldn't help but wonder if Wishing had been at the beginning of their relationship or the end. Did they start here?

When I turned the pages, I found fewer photos of my mother. She wasn't pictured with her friends. Nor was she listed among the cheerleaders. The one photo I did find, her class picture, was drastically different from the year before. Her face, clear of makeup, was lacking the smile I'd seen in her freshman book.

I held my breath as I picked up the next one. Her junior year. The year she had me.

"I'm not sure I'm ready for this," I whispered. At the sound of my voice, Four sat up and shifted so she was laying on my lap. She nuzzled into my leg, pushing me slightly.

This yearbook was lighter than the others. Inside, I didn't find any notes from friends or Ken. Not a single photo of my mother. Not one. I went back to the beginning and scoured the pages. She wasn't there. Her name was listed as *No Photo* under her class. Aside from that one mention, she didn't exist. A girl lost and forgotten. That was the Tammy Lane I knew.

I blinked away a fresh set of tears and turned my attention to the stack of papers. Taking extra care to not rip anything, I slipped the rubber band off and lifted the first piece. It was a copy of an arrest report. Skimming it, I found Ken's name. *Statutory rape* was listed beside his name. The accuser's name was blacked out, but I knew what name was under the ink. Tammy Lane. The report was dated January 3, 1994. There weren't a lot of details listed, most of the information was blacked out or blank. I set it to the side and moved on.

Wedding Announcements. The newspaper clipping was thin and yellowed, aged from time. I knew without reading further that the smiling couple in the photo were Ken Alan and Bethany Lane. Lane? So, she was related to my mother in some way.

Another photo framed the bottom of the page. In it, a smiling Bethany and Ken stood between a man I didn't recognize and my mother. Her eyes weren't looking at the camera like the rest of the wedding party. She was listed as the maid of honor. Her hands rested on her belly. It wasn't yet swelling, but I knew I was in there, waiting to ruin her life. The young girl smiling for photos and posing with friends was gone by the time the wedding photo was taken. The man in the tux had stolen her.

I resisted the urge to take the paper and rip it to shreds. Someone had taken care to save these for more than a quarter-century; I couldn't let my anger destroy them. They were all I had left of my mother. More newspaper clippings were below the announcement. These were filled with stories about Ken and his work at the church. They alluded to the police report, but nothing concrete was mentioned. Almost every word focused on what a saint he was. Small-town gossip didn't make its way into the pages.

The last article contained a photo of my mother wearing cut-off shorts and a T-shirt emblazoned with the Gaines High School mascot. In it, she was smiling and looking off to the side. It appeared someone was cropped from the photo. *Local Teen Missing.* I read the words, devouring each one as if I were starving. Tammy Lane had run away from her parents' house. Bob and Sally claimed to be frantically searching for their daughter. Their quotes read like distraught parents, but I knew better. They hadn't looked for her. If they had, they'd have found her easily. According to my mother, they'd kicked her out as soon as they learned she was pregnant. I didn't know where she went when they did, but based on my birth certificate, she didn't make it far. Kelb County was just a few miles from Gaines.

The last line in the article alluded to a scandal and the rumors that surrounded Tammy. They didn't mention Ken by name. Nor did it mention her pregnancy. The final line contained a quote from an unnamed *friend*.

Tammy was always a good girl. She followed the rules, but lately, she'd started rebelling. She made some mistakes and spread lies about a respected man in our community. I wouldn't be surprised if she'd run away in shame.

Those were the last words they'd included, and they essentially blamed my mother for the affair with Ken and accused her of lying. Gaines had no idea what kind of man he was. They'd buried the arrest report, likely the second my mother turned up missing. There wasn't a single news article or clipping about him. I'd found nothing bad about him online, and this box confirmed the evidence didn't exist.

What I didn't know was who'd gone to the police. Someone reported him for the relationship with my mother. I couldn't see her doing that. Even if he'd hurt her, she'd loved him at one time. If she was anything like the woman she became, she never would have blamed him for his mistakes. She'd have carried them herself.

The story of my mother's life before me was a bit clearer now, though still incomplete. Where had she gone? Why did she run?

I made the mistake of letting your mother walk away free, I won't make the same mistake with you. Ken's final words to me rang in my ears. He threatened her. Had he learned about me and realized I was proof she'd told the truth. Rage filled me, bubbling up into a scream I couldn't release.

Maybe Rayna was right. Some secrets were better left buried. My mother never shared her past with me. Whether it was because she was ashamed or because she was trying to protect me, I'll never know. But someone wanted me to know the truth. They'd taken the time and care to keep these mementos. Yearbooks and newspaper clippings that only painted half of the picture. They'd neatly stored them in a box and organized them for me. There was no way they could have known I'd end up in Wishing one day, but they held on to hope that I would. Someone wanted me to know her story. Someone here cared about her and me enough to preserve this history.

I pulled the box back to me and turned it sideways so I could slip the books and clippings back in. A color Polaroid photo slipped out. I picked it up. My mouth fell open, and I dropped it as if it burned me. It landed face up in front of me.

Ken and Tammy stared up at me. His arm snaked around her waist. She gazed into the camera, a look of puppy love danced in her eyes. The bright, infectious smile stretched across her youthful face. They stood so close that there wasn't even air between them. In the background, a building I knew all too well.

The neon sign behind them illuminated the words *The Wishing Well Motel*.

TWENTY-EIGHT

"Jesus, Shay, another one?" Toby groaned as I slid a half-eaten burger into the window.

"Sorry, I forgot Edwin doesn't like mustard."

"Just like you forgot the other five special orders?"

"Yes," I snapped. I was well aware of the million-and-one mistakes I'd made tonight. Wrong beer. Wrong wine. Wrong order. Wrong table. Everything was wrong. Every time I blinked, I saw the photo of my parents smiling in front of the motel.

"What's with you tonight?" he asked. He didn't bother masking his annoyance. His question wasn't one of concern. I got the impression that he didn't really care what was going on.

I didn't bother answering. I wasn't ready to share what I'd learned. Word travels fast in small towns, so I was certain Lorelei had already told him she'd seen me in Gaines. He probably knew from Rayna that Ken was my dad. I hadn't shared any of it with him, but he knew. I could tell in the way he looked at me with pity.

"Sorry, Edwin," I said when I returned to the table. "Toby is making you a fresh mustard-free burger right now."

He nodded but mumbled something under his breath. I chose

to ignore it and move on. Hannah and her mother were in as well. I grabbed their fresh glasses of wine from the bar and set them on their table. Hannah tried to catch my attention, but I ignored her. She'd shown up Sunday night and knocked on the door. I didn't answer, and she didn't come up. I assumed she knew it didn't go well with Ken. She hadn't bothered stopping by on Monday. She was probably waiting for me to come to her. I wasn't planning to, though.

I couldn't shake the feeling that everyone in this town knew me before I ended up here. Their looks of confusion when I showed up may have been recognition. My mother spent time here. My father came through town often as a pastor. He preached to them. Aside from that, twenty-six years ago, my parents carried out their inappropriate affair under their noses. How much did they know? Who knew?

As ready as I'd been to leave on Sunday, by Tuesday morning I'd decided to stay. I needed answers, and they were buried some-where in this town. It was clear someone wanted me to find the truth, but no one wanted credit. I had to know what they were hiding.

"Order up, Shay!" Toby shouted.

"Thank you," I said and took Edwin's burger out to the table.

Hannah and her mother stood to leave. I waved and smiled, acknowledging them, but busied myself cleaning tables. Rayna waved me over to the bar. I groaned but obliged her request.

"I didn't expect to see you tonight."

"Why not?"

"You seemed ready to run when you left on Sunday."

"I was," I admitted.

"Why didn't you?"

I sighed. "I'm not ready yet."

"Okay." She tried to smile, but it didn't quite reach her eyes. "You can talk to me, you know that right?"

"I did talk to you." I wasn't mad at Rayna, but the more I sat and thought about everything, the more I realized she had to be hiding something from me. Trigger too.

"Yes, you did."

I waited for her to speak up again because she looked like she had more to say, but she didn't. After a few awkward seconds of silence, I headed back to the floor to refill drinks and finish up the tables. We were approaching closing time, and I was more than ready to get back to the silence of my apartment. I had big plans to curl up with Four and read my mother's yearbooks again. I'd all but memorized her classmates' names and faces. Monday, I was tempted to go to the library and research them to see where they were now, but I didn't want to do it with Marie hanging over my shoulder. I needed privacy. I needed my own computer.

I'd intended to ask Toby to help me find a cheap one, but we hadn't been on the best of terms tonight. I knew buying one would set back my funds and force me to stay in Wishing a little longer, but it would also help me find answers faster. I could always pick up Sunday shifts at the bar to help make up the difference. Rayna had been asking me to help lately.

Five minutes before close, Trigger walked into the bar. His eyes darted around the room until he found me. A look of relief filled them when he did. I smiled back. Seeing his familiar, warm face reminded me of everything good about Wishing. No matter what I learned over the next few weeks, I would miss this place.

"The usual?" I asked him when he sat down.

"No, just coffee please."

"Long day?"

"You could say that."

"Listen, Trigger," I said before getting his coffee, "I wanted to talk to you about the other day."

"Coffee first?"

I nodded and walked back into the kitchen to get his coffee.

"Is he ordering food?" Toby asked. He stood in the middle of the kitchen, which he'd already cleaned.

"No, just coffee. Hey, I wanted to ask you something?" I asked, taking advantage of the good news I'd just shared. If Trigger wasn't ordering food, he'd get to leave sooner than expected.

"Sure."

"What are you doing tomorrow?"

"I'm going fishing with my old man, why?"

"I wanted to see if you could help me find a laptop."

"What for?"

"I want to research colleges," I lied.

He smiled and said, "I'd love to, but can't tomorrow. Thursday morning?"

"That would be great."

"We can head up to Springfield. There are a few stores that sell refurbished laptops that are pretty cheap. Do you have the internet at your apartment?" he asked. It was clear that my asking him for help was more fun for him than the burden I assumed it would be.

"I think Hannah mentioned there was Wi-Fi or something? I can ask her tomorrow."

"Great, we can head up early, and I can help you set it up."

"Eight?" I asked.

"It's a date," he said and frowned. "Sorry, I didn't mean it like that."

"I know. Thank you, Toby."

I pulled a coffee mug from the rack and returned to the dining room. Trigger was deep in conversation with Rayna when I walked up to the table. I heard her say my name, so I waited before approaching the table. Their voices were low, and I could barely decipher what they were saying. I set the mug down. As soon as they saw me, they stopped talking. Rayna patted my shoulder before walking away.

"What was that about?" I asked.

"Nothing, really. Rayna just asking about my wife."

"I didn't know you were married." Maybe he'd mentioned it? I couldn't remember. He wasn't wearing a ring, though.

"Going on twenty-seven years now."

"Why don't you ever talk about her or wear a ring?"

"The ring gets in the way at work, so I don't want to risk it snagging on anything. And you've never asked."

My stomach flipped. I'd never asked him about himself. Every interaction we'd had was all about me. In reality, I knew very little about Trigger. I didn't know if he had kids or pets. I made a note to at least make an effort to get to know him before I left town, even if I planned to dig deeper into my mother's past in the process.

"You're right, I didn't. Maybe we can talk more about you when I come into the station tomorrow."

"Tomorrow, huh?" He lifted the coffee mug to his lips and peered over the top.

"I wanted to see if you could help me track my grandparents down."

"Find out more about them?" he asked.

"Sort of. I know their names, which is something, I guess."

"I'll be happy to help. Why don't you come by before lunch tomorrow."

"Thank you, Trigger," I said, smiling. He handed me the cash for his coffee and my tip. Not bothering to finish his coffee, he stood to go and waved to Rayna. She came over to help me clear the last few tables.

"What were you and Trigger talking about when I walked up?" I asked her.

"Oh, just some county business," she said, contradicting what Trigger said earlier. She must not have heard him when he answered me. I ignored the lie because I didn't know which of them hadn't been honest, or if neither of them had. I could only assume they'd been talking about me. "What did you two talk about?"

"He's going to help me find out about my grandparents."

"You found them?"

"Just their names," I replied. I hadn't told anyone about Sunday's box, and I didn't intend to.

"I'm sure he'll find something," she said casually. "He's good at digging up people."

I wasn't sure what she meant by that, and I didn't care enough to ask. Finding my grandparents might not help me answer my questions, but if they were still alive, I might be able to meet them. I could easily research them online, but I needed an excuse to grill Trigger to see just how much he knew. It wouldn't be easy; he'd done a great job pretending to know nothing about my mother or father, despite having grown up here. And knowing what I knew now, I didn't believe he'd never crossed paths with her. They were close to the same age—he was probably a few years older. I didn't have anything concrete to prove it, but sometimes when he looked at me, it was as if he was looking deep into the past. Maybe he saw her in me.

Everything was too convenient here. The gifts. The people. Answers appeared just as it occurred to me to ask the questions. It was both comforting and unsettling. While I appreciated the seemingly free gifts and information, my past reinforced the notion that there was no such thing as a free meal. Someone was expecting something from me; I just didn't know what that was.

Since arriving in Wishing, I'd learned more about my mother than I had in the nineteen years I'd spent with her. This was also the place where I'd felt closest to her, despite learning she was gone. I could feel her in the air around me. This kept me steady. The urge to run was strong, but I felt her arms around me, begging me to stay.

Rayna had assumed the secrets I was learning were things my mother didn't want me to know, but I think she did. She'd guided me here that night; I believed that with every fiber of my soul. I didn't believe in ghosts or premonitions, but I'd felt her that night, just as I did now. She wanted me to come here and unravel her story. This town played a role in her life, though she never spoke of it to me. Not even in her whispers when she thought I wasn't listening. Yet now she wanted me here to learn the truth.

This realization did little to comfort the unease that consumed me. I'd noticed everyone's stares and unspoken sentences, but I ignored them. I wanted to belong here, to fit in and be a part of something. I let myself get caught up in the emotions of finding a home. Even Four distracted me. Nothing here was an accident. Toby and Rayna urging me to find my mother and then my father. Trigger's reluctance to my meeting my father. Even Hannah's friendship felt staged.

What didn't make sense were the contradictions. Rayna pushed me to find my father, but when I did, she'd hedged. She and Trigger discouraged me from meeting him. Before that, she suggested I find my mother, and then when I learned she was gone, she cautioned me about digging up the past. None of it made sense, and I needed to know why.

I needed to know whose truth they were hiding.

TWENTY-NINE

THE SUN PIERCED THROUGH THE BLUE SKY AND CAST A shadow in front of the unassuming police station. Both the Wishing Police Department and Paris County Sheriff's Office were housed in this small white building. I arrived thirty minutes early, which, in hindsight, wasn't smart. I'd given myself time to change my mind. In my car, I watched as officers trickled in and out of the building. Trigger wasn't among the crowd. His shift didn't start until noon, and from what I knew about him, I assumed he was already in the building, waiting on the clock. He didn't strike me as the type to show up late or right on time. For him, five minutes early was late.

At 11:50 a.m., I unbuckled my seatbelt and ignored the tightness in my chest. In the twenty minutes I'd sat in my car, I almost backed out ten times. Each time I thought about bailing, I'd look down at the picture of Ken and my mother. *I'm doing this for her,* I thought. I'd had time to go through every clipping and yearbook that had been left for me. The more I read, the less I wanted answers for myself and the more I wanted justice for her. I hated Ken. He'd gotten away with abandoning my mother and me. There were no consequences for his actions. My mother, the likely victim, bore every ounce of it. I would make it right, even if it meant staying in Wishing.

I just hoped I was making the right decision by asking Trigger to help. If I put my trust in him and it turned out he was on Ken's side, I wouldn't forgive myself.

"Good morning," a bright-eyed young woman greeted me. "You must be Shay. Trigger said you'd be stopping by. Can I get you a coffee or anything?"

"No, thank you."

"Alright, let me call back and see if he's at his desk. You can have a seat."

I didn't bother sitting. Instead, I paced the lobby and avoided eavesdropping while she called him. The walls were lined with photos of what I assumed were former officers or deputies. A large photo of Trigger hung to the left of the door. *Officer of the Year*. In it, he didn't smile, but the corners of his mouth appeared to be mid-twitch.

"Shay?" the receptionist called. I let my gaze linger on his photograph for a moment, still unsure of what I would say to him. "He's ready. Follow me."

I fell into step behind her, and we snaked through the hall-ways. It felt as though everyone was watching me. A feeling that hadn't stopped since I'd been in Wishing. When we reached Trigger's office, the door was open. She waved me in, and I thanked her.

Trigger had his back to me and was looking out the window. I knocked on his door. At the sound, he turned to face me and smiled. He stood behind his desk, which was clear of the clutter I expected to see. I assumed it would be littered with papers and empty coffee cups, or at the very least, a personal photo or two. But there was nothing.

"You're right on time," he said.

"I have to be at work at 1:30, so I wanted to make sure I had plenty of time."

"Great, let's get to it. What can I do for you?"

This was the big question. My backpack pulled at my shoulders, reminding me of what was inside. The actual weight of it was insignificant, but the heaviness dragged me to my decision. I slipped it off my shoulders and unzipped it. Trigger followed my every move. I kept waiting for him to sit down, but he didn't. He stood on the other side of his desk with his arms crossed over his chest. The smile shifted into a frown in the silence.

The paper shook in my hand as I passed it to him. "I want you to look into this."

"What is this?"

"An arrest report," I replied more sarcastically than intended. I assumed in his line of work things like police reports were pretty common.

He laughed and sat down. "I know what *it* is, but what is this relating to? Where did you get it?"

I sucked in a deep breath and held it for a beat. This was the moment of truth. "It appears to be an arrest report regarding my mother and father. His name is there, but the victim's name is blacked out. I believe it is my mother's name. Someone left it on my porch Sunday night."

He leaned back in the chair and rubbed his temples. "Shay, this document," he said and held it up, "should be sealed."

"How do you know?"

"Arrest reports that don't result in charges aren't public record."

"How can you tell charges weren't filed?"

"I've worked in this town for nearly three decades. If a pastor in a nearby country was charged with statutory rape, I'd know about it. Ken's never been charged, so this arrest report isn't publicly available."

"Then how would someone get this?"

"It looks like it's a copy of the original report."

"So only the person who filed would have it?"

"Or the arresting officer."

"So, whoever left this on my porch likely knew either my mother or the officer." I yanked the paper from his hand and scanned down the page. The officer's name was blacked out. I'd studied that paper for hours but didn't notice that important information. I lifted my head and met Trigger's eyes. He was watching me intently, but his face was expressionless. No hint as to what he was thinking.

"That is blacked out."

"That's unusual."

"Very. It's like the person who left me this doesn't want me to know the whole story."

"What would you like me to do?" he asked, avoiding my eyes.

"I want you to find out why charges were never filed and who the arresting officer was."

"Shay," he said, his tone filled with warning. "This is from Oak County. I don't have access to their files."

"Do you know people there?"

"I do, but again, these records aren't public."

"Trigger, it's my mother."

"I know, and I want to help, but I can't make any promises."

"Then don't make any. Just say you will try. That's all I'm asking."

He hesitated and then reached for the report. I held it in my hands, refusing to release it. He tugged gently, pulling it free. We sat in silence while he read it. Shaking his head, he glanced up at me and asked, "What are you hoping to find?"

"I want the truth. I want to know what happened to my mother. I want justice for her."

"Justice?"

I nodded. "I want him to pay for what he did to her."

"And what do you think he did?"

"At the very least, he committed statutory rape. She was just

16 when she became pregnant with me. He was 21. At worst, he forced himself on her and then threatened her life."

"Do you have evidence?"

I pointed at myself. "I'm proof of the statutory rape. DNA would prove he was my father, and my birth proves her age."

"And the rest?"

"I can't prove anything else. I only know what he said to me."

"Can you just tell me instead of dancing around the issue? If I am going to help you, I need to know everything you do. I get the feeling you're hiding something."

"That makes two of us," I snapped without thinking. I hadn't wanted him to know I was suspicious.

"What do you mean?"

I shook my head. I wasn't here to accuse Trigger of anything. I needed his help. "I'm sorry, I'm just frustrated. I didn't mean anything."

"Okay, then, tell me what he said to you." He leaned forward with his elbows on his desk.

"He told me he made the mistake of letting my mother walk away free and wouldn't make the same mistake with me." I studied his face as I spoke, looking for anything that might hint at his loyalties, but he didn't even flinch. No reaction. Either he was very good at acting, or he wasn't at all surprised by what I said.

"I can understand how that would feel like a threat, but it isn't exactly prosecutable."

"So, he'd need to actually come after me? Or have done it to her?"

"Yes, but there are limitations on cases like this. The rape has no time limit. But the threats of violence do. Aside from all of that, I can't exactly charge him without evidence."

"What can you do?" I asked, exasperated. I glanced at the clock. I had thirty minutes until I had to be at the bar.

"I will call a buddy of mine who works in Gaines and see what he can find."

"Thank you, that's all I'm asking for." I sighed. "Can I ask you a personal question?"

"Sure."

"How long have you been a cop?"

"Twenty-seven years."

"Always in Paris County and Wishing?"

"Yes, why?"

"Just curious."

"What are you getting at, Shay?" he asked, reading my face. "Do you think I'm hiding something?"

"Are you?"

"No. My name isn't on this report, and this is the first time I've seen it, if that's what you're implying."

My face flushed. Of course, he'd read into what I was asking. He was a cop. It was literally his job to read people. I wasn't fully prepared to play investigator and he'd seen right through me. "I trust you."

"Good," he replied. "Alright, I've got a meeting here in five minutes. Anything else you want to ask me? You mentioned your grandparents?"

"Oh, yeah. Bob and Sally Lane."

"What do you want to know?"

"Are they alive? Where do they live? Do I have any other relatives?" I knew I could Google the information, but I wasn't prepared to receive any more random devastating news in a public place.

He scribbled notes onto the notepad in front of him. "Anything else?"

"Nope."

"I'll see what I can find, but don't get your hopes up. Especially on the arrest report, it's a long shot."

"I understand."

"Can I walk you out to your car? I need to head that way anyway."

"No, thank you. I appreciate your time today. Next coffee at Lace & Grit is on me."

"Not necessary. I'm happy to help." He reached into his pocket and pulled out a card. He paused to write something on the back before handing it to me. "That's my personal cell and home address. I'm here any time, Shay."

"Thank you." I stood and met him at the side of his desk. Rather than accept the hug he offered, I shook his hand. I still wasn't entirely convinced I could trust him. He hadn't reacted at all to anything I said or revealed. Nor had he been too eager to help me investigate my father. I held the card in my hand. He trusted me with his home address and phone number. That said more than the stoic look on his face or neutral reactions. But it all still felt too convenient. Too easy. As much as I wanted to believe him, I couldn't shake the unease that slithered through my veins.

"Hey, Trigger?" I stopped at the door and turned around. He glanced up at me. "Why don't you have any pictures on your desk?"

"Of what?"

"Your wife or family?"

His eyes moved across his desk and for the first time, he shifted in his seat. I watched as his chest rose and fell with each breath, the rhythm increasing with every second of silence. My question about his wife and family triggered a reaction. I suppressed a victorious smile and leaned into the door frame.

"Um, I don't usually keep personal effects in the office."

"Why?"

"Not all the people who come in here have good intentions."

I waved and left him sweating at his desk. I flipped the card over and read his address until I had it memorized. I'd definitely be taking him up on his invitation to stop by anytime. It was time to meet Mrs. Trigg.

THIRTY

"WHAT'S YOUR BUDGET?" TOBY ASKED, SHOUTING OVER the music. I reached over and turned down the volume on the radio. He scowled and repeated the question.

"Under $600. Do you think that's doable?"

"Yeah, definitely won't be anything fancy. Maybe even more of a tablet than a laptop, but you don't need much, do you?"

"I don't know. You've been to college, what do you think?"

"You could get away with a tablet until you need more. There's always the library if you do. Will you want Excel and all that?"

I looked at him blankly, and he laughed. He was speaking a foreign language now.

"Okay, so we'll start with the basics, and you can add what you need later. Something like a Surface Go."

"How much is a Surface?" The word felt funny coming from my mouth. I knew what laptops and tablets were, I'd seen plenty, but I had absolutely no idea what brands were good or what the different options were. This was where I was leaning on Toby for advice.

"Maybe $400? Definitely under your budget and will get what you need."

"Okay, then. Let's do that."

He glanced over at me and smiled. "You can test out different ones in the store. Why don't you take a look before you make up your mind?"

"We don't have all day, Toby." Springfield was a roughly two-and-a-half-hour round trip. Rayna warned us not to be late when we closed up last night. We represented her entire Thursday staff; without us she wouldn't be able to open. We had less than two hours to shop. I wanted to be prepared.

"I'm just saying that it's a big investment, and you shouldn't rush it."

"I appreciate your concern, but I'm pretty decisive."

He glanced at me from the driver's seat, giving me the side eye. "Really?"

"What?"

"Decisive and female don't typically go in the same sentence."

"What?" I laughed, ignoring the sexism in his comment.

"Take Lorelei," he said. I groaned and shook my head. "You know how many times we've broken up?"

"Five?" I guessed, not really caring to play this game.

"Ten."

"Good lord, why do you put up with that?"

"She was my first everything, you know. Hard to let go of the past."

"Or she's possessive and only wants something she thinks she can't have."

"Why do you say that?"

"I've known many girls like Lorelei." Adam's sisters. My mother.

"She really doesn't like you, you know."

"She's made that very clear." I laughed. I was under no illusion about how she felt. Nor did I care.

"You know I'm not going to tell you what to do, but if I were you, I'd keep my distance. She can be pretty vindictive when things don't go her way."

A shiver ran up my spine. I'd gathered as much about her from our brief encounters. "Trust me, I don't plan on spending much time around her willingly."

He shifted in his seat and put both hands on the wheel. The blinker clicked and he pulled on to an exit ramp. "Can I ask you something?"

"Sure. I might not be able to answer, but you can ask."

"Why do you want to look at colleges now?"

I sighed and dropped my head back onto the seat. Toby didn't know about Iowa or Adam. Unless Rayna told him, he didn't know much about why my mom and I hadn't been speaking. Closing my eyes, I said, "It's a long story." Even if my needing a laptop was unrelated to college, the lie I'd told stirred things up that I didn't want to resurrect or discuss.

"We've got time."

"How about we get the laptop, and we can talk on the way back?" I suggested. Part of me hoped he'd forget and wouldn't bring it up, but I knew him better than that. Toby wasn't the type to let anything go. Especially after I'd already agreed to tell him.

"Sounds good. Ready to go spend all your money on a piece of technology that will be obsolete by the time you learn how to use it?"

"Yup," I said, grateful to shift the conversation back to the laptop. But my mind was elsewhere. His question stirred up more memories I tried to forget. Iowa wasn't somewhere I had fond memories of. At least not ones that hadn't been tainted by what happened when we left.

Susan was always surprised by how much I'd managed to teach myself. My mother told her she'd homeschooled me, but I'd confided in her that my mother's idea of school was dumping me at a library or leaving me alone in a motel room to read while she worked. At the time, I was eighteen. I'd never stepped foot in a school but seeing the Rhodes sisters lug home backpacks and homework made me long for something I never realized I wanted —normalcy and routine. Then, Adam announced he was heading off to college, and I snuck peeks at his course books. I wanted more.

Without telling my mother, Susan signed me up for a GED class and insisted they pay for it. I tried to resist, but she wouldn't hear it. She made sure it was during the time Tammy would be busy at the cafe. Will drove me to the school every day, and Adam would pick me up. For two months, we did this and hid it from my mother. I never uttered a word or hint to her. I knew she'd see it as a betrayal. When it was time to take the test, I was nervous. I'd never taken a test before. Adam spent hours showing me how to take the test and fill in the answers. I think those nights with him were what made me fall for him. He'd never once laughed at me or mocked me. He saw me for me, not as some helpless pet project.

Then something happened that I never expected. I passed. Not just passed, but I'd aced it. I outscored my peers in every single subject. I'd never felt prouder than I had sitting across from Susan and hearing her tell me the results. I was too nervous to open the envelope myself.

"You know what this means, right?" Adam asked. He leaned over my shoulder. I held the letter in my hand, my eyes scanning the words his mother had just read to me. I shook my head. I had no idea what it meant. "You can apply to college."

"College?" I asked in disbelief. The word tumbled out of my mouth and landed in front of me. The possibilities snaked through my daydreams. Four years in one place. A routine. Real classrooms. A chance at a future that didn't involve greasy spoons and motels.

"Why are you talking about colleges? What is that?" my mother asked, peering over my shoulder. I hadn't heard her come into the kitchen. Her voice sent my pulse running. She reached around me and snatched the paper from my hand. "Shay?"

Susan started to explain, but my mother held up her hand to stop her. Her breath was hot on my face when she leaned over me. "Let's go, Shay." My heart thudded loudly in my chest. I didn't want to go with her, but I did. I followed her out to the trailer. I could tell by her walk that she was more than angry. She was hurt.

She held open the door, and I followed her inside. The door slammed behind me, causing me to jump.

"I can explain, Mom."

"Tammy. None of that *mom* shit out here. We can put on a show for Susan and Will, but out here, nothing changes. My name is Tammy."

"Tammy," I said, "I can explain if you'd let me talk."

"No bullshit, Shay. I want to the goddamned truth. What the fuck is this?" She shoved the paper in my face. "GED? The education I gave you wasn't enough?"

"You didn't teach me anything!" I spat back.

"You're such an ungrateful brat. I always knew this day would come. Do you have any idea what I've sacrificed for you?"

"I do, M—Tammy." I remember thinking about every man and bruise she'd stopped hiding from me. The late nights. The stench of cologne and cigarettes on her skin. At eighteen I was under no illusions.

"Almost nineteen years, Shay. I've given you nineteen years of my life. And what do I get in return? A daughter who thinks she's better than me."

"I don't think I'm better than you," I whispered. "I didn't even think I'd passed." Self-deprecation was my go-to when she got like this. It was as if I wanted to prove to her that I thought as little of myself as the rest of the world did. I wasn't worthy of their time or hers. If it hadn't been for Susan, I might have believed it.

"So, what was your plan? You're all grown up now, so you're going to leave me?"

"No," I said. I can still remember the sinking feeling that settled in. My nineteenth birthday was days away. I think I knew how it would all end. That night, watching her look at me as if I'd betrayed her, I knew one of us would be leaving. I honestly believe Adam was an excuse for her. My sleeping with him gave her an out, but when she realized I was planning a life that didn't include her, she snapped. She'd have left me, one way or the other.

"Bullshit, Shay. I always knew this would happen one day. I tried to keep you safe and give you everything, but you never appreciated me. Your whore of a mother. I see the way you look at me."

Tears brimmed in my eyes, but I blinked them away. I couldn't look at her. I didn't want to see her disappointment, and I didn't want her to see that she was right. I'd hated her for the way she raised me. I hated that she'd stopped hiding the truth from me. She'd flaunted it in my face. Some nights, she'd give me lessons on how to seduce and use men to get what I needed. She expected me to follow in her footsteps and live my life on the road, hopping from bed to bed and job to job. Until Iowa, I thought that was my only way forward. But seeing her settle in and make an honest living there gave me hope that there was more. Susan encouraging me to see beyond what was in front of me proved it. She'd given me the confidence to strive for and to want more.

I hated that my final moments with my mother were filled with so much resentment and anger. I'd been devastated the night she left me, but standing in front of her trying to explain my dreams into nothing, I wanted nothing more than to be rid of her. I knew as long as I was with her, I'd never get anywhere or become anything more than she was. Years later, I wondered if it hadn't all been an act. Perhaps she wanted me to leave, and when I didn't leave on my own, she forced me.

"Shay?" Toby called my name, dragging me back to the present. "Ready to head back?"

I slipped the change into my pocket and tucked the receipt into the bag. He led the way outside and towards his car. "Yeah, let's go." The small laptop felt like a million pounds in the bag. It wasn't the key to unlocking the secrets of my mother, but it was the first piece of the puzzle.

"Want me to come by after work and help you get it set up?"

"That would be great," I said. "Thank you for your help today."

"Of course. You can thank me when you graduate and get a job that doesn't make you smell like fried onion rings at the end of every shift."

I laughed and pulled the seatbelt over my shoulder. "Can't wait."

THIRTY-ONE

My phone buzzed in my pocket. I glanced around
the dining room and waved to Rayna. She nodded. I slipped the
phone out and answered.

"Shay? It's Officer Trigg."

"Oh, hey, Trigger. What's up? Do you have news?"

"Sort of."

"I'm in the middle of my shift, but I have a minute," I said. I
heard him exhale.

"How about tomorrow? I'd rather deliver the news in person.
My shift starts at ten."

My heart raced at the possibilities of what he'd found. I
couldn't tell from his voice if it was good or bad. So I agreed and
said I'd see him tomorrow. Back inside, Toby and Rayna stood at
the bar enjoying a rare lull in business.

"Everything okay?" Rayna asked.

"Yeah, that was Trigger. He's helping me with a few things."

"Care to share?" Toby asked. He smiled slightly. Our two
hours of windshield time gave us an opportunity to get to know
each other a bit. In the end, I didn't tell him about the GED or

my mother's reaction to it. Instead, I made up a story about some ad I'd seen for online courses.

"Not yet. I don't really know what he has. I'm meeting him tomorrow." I spoke slowly and with intention to prevent my voice from betraying me. I'd tried not to obsess over the arrest report or Trigger's reaction to it. I couldn't get my hopes up or let my guard down. I wanted to trust him and this town, but the more I learned, the less I did.

I climbed onto the empty barstool next to Rayna. She'd been watching me with what I could only describe as eagle eyes ever since my visit to Gaines. It was as if she were waiting for me to disappear into the dead of night. Tonight, she was watching me even closer. Her eyes darted across my face. Every few seconds she glanced at the door. Any other night, she only ever bothered looking at the door if customers were coming or going. Tonight, there were so few customers that it was eerie. She was making me nervous.

Around midnight, she decided we'd close early. Our last customer left half an hour before, and the bar had been a ghost town since. I busied myself cleaning and rolling silverware. She trailed behind me, bussing and cleaning tables. Every once in a while, she attempted awkward small talk. She'd been off for a few days, but tonight it seemed even more unusual. My unspoken threat to leave had spooked her.

"Shay," Toby called as he came out of the kitchen.

"Yeah?"

"You still want to set the laptop up tonight?"

"Please. Especially with us closing early."

"Why don't you two go ahead and get out of here," Rayna suggested, though her suggestion sounded more like an order. "I can lock up."

"You don't have to tell me twice," Toby said. He threw his apron behind the bar. "Shay, meet you at your place? We can get everything set up."

"Sure. Twenty minutes?"

"Sounds good. Rayna need anything else from me?"

Headlights bounced off the mirrors behind the bar. "No, go on. See you both tomorrow."

I followed Toby out the back door and climbed into my car. He waved from his car and peeled out of the parking lot. His headlights illuminated my car for a moment before fading away. The lights behind the bar were dim, but the night sky danced with stars. I pulled the door shut and turned the ignition. My eyes drifted out my window towards the bar. Rayna had already turned out the lights. She kept her car out front, so there was no point in waiting on her. There was so much I wanted to ask her, especially after finding out that Ken and my mom had been to the motel her brother owned, but the timing wasn't right. I needed to see what Trigger had found.

Bang! The loud noise pulled me back. I jerked my head to the right to locate the source of the sound. A thin figure with long brown hair appeared outside my passenger window. *Bethany*. I'd recognize her anywhere. I'd obsessed over her photo. I'd seen her at the church. She had my mother's eyes and cheekbones. Tonight, her face filled with a rage I didn't recognize. She moved forward, reaching for the door. I felt the door for the locks, but she pulled the handle before I could click them. She yanked the door open and slid into the passenger seat. She studied me for a moment. I pulled away from her.

"Shay, I assume?" she asked calmly, the wild look in her eyes a stark contradiction to the steadiness in her voice.

"Bethany," I replied. My own voice gave away the fear that coursed through me.

"So, you know who I am?"

I nodded.

"Good, this will be so much easier." Bethany shifted in the seat and turned to face me.

"What do you want?" I asked. Her eyes trained on mine.

"Why do I keep hearing your name pop up?" she asked.

"Let me guess," I said, forcing a smile, "all those little rumors about your husband were confirmed."

She ignored me and kept talking. She gazed windshield and focused forward. "You should know that not only is my husband a well-respected man, but he's also very powerful. Some of our dearest friends work in the Oak County Sheriff's office. A few with the police department."

"And?" I asked, desperate to move this conversation forward.

"And we know you've sent that small-town pig Trigger to look into a so-called arrest report."

"It's not so-called. It happened."

"Because Tammy is a liar. My husband, despite his wandering eye, is a good man."

I laughed. "You're delusional."

She turned to face me, whipping her head sharply. A darkness fell over her eyes as her gaze intensified. "You need to disappear, just like your mother. You don't belong here any more than she did."

"I don't think you get to make that decision."

"Oh, I think I do, little girl. If you were smart, you'd leave before this town realizes just how toxic you and your mother are. Well, as she *was*. Surely, you don't want to end up like her. Alone and dead in a ditch."

Her words caught me off guard. The implication in them was as clear as the hatred on her face. "What did you say?"

"You heard me, Shay. Your little visit to Wishing and Gaines is done. It's time for you to leave. Go on your own, or we'll take care of you."

Her threat was real. The menace in her voice wasn't a joke. I'd misjudged her sweet nature. She was just like her husband. "We? You and Ken? Did he send you here to do his dirty work?"

"Trust me, Shay, you don't want him to be the one delivering this message. He won't be as nice."

"I'm not scared of you."

"No, of course not. You're too dumb to know what's good for you. Just like her. The smartest thing your mother ever did was run away. She just wasn't smart enough to stay away, now was she?"

I shook my head. I didn't know what she was talking about, and I didn't care. "Ken's a coward, and so are you."

"Tammy had no business keeping you," she said, ignoring me. Her dark brown eyes stayed trained on me. "Then again, my cousin never really had much understanding of what was hers, now did she? Ken didn't love her, you know that, right? She was easy. A game, almost. Ken's a bit insatiable, if you know what I mean."

My stomach knotted. I reached for the handle, but she grabbed my arm. "What do you want?" I snapped.

"You out of my life and this town for good."

"I'm not going anywhere."

Her grip on my arm tightened. She pulled me toward her. "You will. Either on your own or, well, let's just say it won't be pretty if you don't. This town doesn't like secrets, Shay. And trust me, they won't be too happy when they find out who you really are, or who your mother really was."

"Neither you nor Ken can run me out of Wishing," I said, laughing to prove a point. I wouldn't be intimidated. Not by her and not by my father. "Bottom line, Bethany, I'm here. This is my home, whether you like it or not. It's not my problem you couldn't satisfy Ken and he came looking for something from my mother." I cringed at my own words. I'd heard my mother shout them at other women whose husbands she had seduced. Hearing them come from my mouth shocked even me.

She grabbed a fistful of my shirt and yanked me closer. I could smell peppermint and vodka on her breath. "Your mother was a no-good whore who didn't belong. You're just like her. You don't belong here or anywhere. You never will. You'll pack your bags tonight, and you'll leave this town and everyone in it behind."

I fought back, pulling myself free. Despite my bravado, the look in her eyes terrified me. She might look sweet, but beneath the perfect skin and doll-like hair, she was just as evil as her husband.

Her laughter filled the air. She leaned back against the door and reached into her purse. The dim light from my dash caught the glistening metal. The instant I realized what is was, I shrunk away from her, flinching. My eyes stayed locked on hers. The tiny movement of her finger pulled my attention for a second. Her index finger twitched against the trigger. I gasped, sucking in all of the air from the car.

She released her trigger finger and laid the pistol in her lap. Her fingers caressed the cool metal. "Next time," she said, "I won't hesitate. Get out of Missouri. Stay away from my son and my husband. The next time we meet, you won't get as much as a single word in. I'll expose you and your mother for the liars, thieves, and whores you are. This town won't want you. You think they will appreciate knowing you manipulated and lied to them? I'll tell them all about how you came to my church to try and blackmail my husband. That you threatened me. No one will believe you, the bastard whose mother was a liar. It will be my word against yours, and I always win. Understood?"

My bravado wavered. I sank away from her, trembling in my seat. The casual way she'd held the gun against my skin told me she didn't have any regard for my life. She wouldn't think twice about pulling the trigger. If she came here to rattle me, she'd succeeded. Aside from the gun, I couldn't risk her hurting Trigger or Rayna. She'd say whatever she had to in order to get her way, even if she hurt good people in the process. I couldn't risk them. I knew what I had to do. "Yes."

"Yes, ma'am," she said, nodding at me.

I repeated her words, my voice barely above a whisper.

"Good girl."

I didn't trust my voice not to quaver, so I simply nodded. Her gaze lingered on my face for a moment. "You look so much like him."

I watched as she climbed out of the car and slammed the door. The chill from her remained. I shivered, trying to shake the image of the pistol from my mind. My entire body shook as my heart raced, urging me to go back into the bar. But I couldn't face Rayna, not like this. She'd see right through me and the tears forming in my eyes. I blinked in a feeble attempt to erase them.

I waited for my heart to slow and the breath to return to my lungs. Once I felt steady enough to drive, I put the car in gear and pointed it towards home. I drove through town, throwing passing glances at the place I'd begun to call home. Bethany's words echoed in my mind. I didn't belong here. No matter how at home I felt, this place wasn't mine. She was right, but even if she wasn't, I knew they'd believe whatever lies she told them. My word meant nothing against hers.

Pulling into the driveway, I saw Toby's car. I blinked away one final tear and wiped my hand across my face, knowing I couldn't erase the evidence. Toby would take one look at me and know something had happened. The laptop would be a distraction, which I needed. I had to clear my head and come up with a plan. No matter how much I didn't want to believe her or let her bully me into leaving, Bethany's words left their mark.

As much as I wanted to send Toby away, he was determined to follow through on his promise. I rushed him through the process, insisting I could figure everything out on my own. He could see the fear in my eyes every time he asked if I was okay, but I ignored him. I couldn't tell him what happened or that I was considering leaving. When he left, I fell onto the bed, and Four curled up next to me, her head in my lap. "We're fine, girl. Everything is fine."

THIRTY-TWO

Every headlight of every car that passed sent a shiver down my arms. None of them slowed, but each one danced across the walls, taunting me. Four sensed my unease. She paced the floor, pausing in front of me each time. Her wet tongue darted out to lick my face each time she passed.

I'd already tried to go to sleep three times. Their faces haunted me with every blink. Ken was with Bethany in her threats. There was no way he didn't send her. He was too much of a coward to come threaten me on his own; he had to send his wife. I couldn't force away the images of our last encounter or the feeling his touch left on my skin. The intention of it lingered. Bethany's words echoed in the darkness, chasing my every move. As much as I wanted to erase both of them, I couldn't. He was a part of me. His role in my life, though limited, was undeniable. I couldn't erase Ken any more than he could me. Though both of us were desperate to.

The laptop balanced on my knees. I stared blankly at the first page of the search results. I'd tried every version of Lizzie Gable and Madison Price that I could think of. Nothing for either of the girls who appeared to have once been friends with my mother. No wedding announcements. No births. No graduations. Nothing. They were as invisible online as I was.

I logged in to the Facebook account I'd created to look up Ken and his family and tried searching there. Another blank spot. How did two women manage to hide themselves so well? Toby told me everyone was online when he started helping me. *Get on Facebook*, he'd said, *you can find anyone*. Apparently not.

The number two sat in a red bubble on the top of the page. I clicked on it. When the page loaded, a tiny photo of Hannah and one of Toby greeted me. He must have told her I'd created an account. As much as I didn't want to be on social media or online, I smiled at the thought of them wanting to be my friends. But I still didn't click *accept*. For over an hour, I went through their photos and public profiles. Toby didn't post much. At least not recently. Nearly a hundred photos of him and Lorelei still littered his page. I resisted the urge to click into her profile. There wasn't anything there for me.

Hannah Bridges posted more frequently and much more publicly. Pictures with words on them—Toby'd called them *memes* —news articles, celebrity gossip, horoscopes, and something called *Farmville*. Her page was even less informative than Toby's. She posted a few selfies with her friends. She mentioned her classes and shared photos of the clothes; some I recognized from the pile she'd given me. But nothing on Wishing or the two girls who once knew my mother.

After wasting an hour learning nothing, I slammed the laptop shut. I was no better off now than I'd been when I started searching. No answers. No leads. No clues. My mother's old friends didn't want to be found. Whoever was out there with my mother's phone didn't want to be found. Yet, somehow, they'd found me. Not only that, but they seemed to be leaving breadcrumbs for me to follow. Little tastes of the truth. Just enough to stoke my hunger for more, leaving me starved.

My phone burned beside me. I picked it up and dialed the familiar number.

"What do you want?" I screamed into the phone when the message beeped. My throat was raw from the tears I kept choking back, and my head pounded with the memory of Bethany's threat. The pressure point where she'd pressed the gun tingled. Whimpering, I cried into the phone, "What do you want from me?"

A sob escaped my lips. I curled myself around Four. Her warm body pressed into me. Fur tickled my nose. I didn't hang up. Instead, I let them hear what they'd done to me. Words couldn't convey what I needed to. I shuddered with each burst of tears. I couldn't stop them. I didn't want to anymore.

Despite being surrounded by the people I'd met in Wishing, I felt more alone than ever. I was vulnerable. Everything they'd given me tightened in a noose around my throat. The threat was there. Each breath a reminder of all they held over me. Someone here had the truth, and they wanted to control how I found it.

They *were* controlling how I found it.

The message clicked off, and I dropped the phone onto the floor. It clattered, bouncing twice before sliding across the hardwood and landing in the corner beside my suitcase. The tattered canvas case sat untouched. It called to me. Bethany's words rang in my ears. One more reason to run. Four panted beside me. Her breath as heavy as mine. When I stood, she leapt to her feet and followed me across the room. Her paws clacked with each step.

I wrapped my fingers around the handle and pulled the suitcase forward. The broken wheel skipped across the hardwood, and I no longer cared if the floors that used to be mine were scarred by them. The zipper creaked open, fighting the pull of my hand. Four jumped when it flopped open on the floor. Aside from a few books from the Wishing Library, my book collection remained the same. The only things new to add were my mother's yearbooks and the articles. I placed them in the suitcase first.

I could leave behind a novel, but those were coming with me. Once I cleared the shelf, I closed the top. Again, the zipper strained. Before adding the yearbooks, I'd been able to fill it completely, but now it bulged at the seams. I propped it up and wheeled it towards the door. It struggled under the new weight. I yanked it forward; it pulled me back. I ignored the tugging and dragged it along.

Like me, it had been worn and tattered before we arrived in Wishing. Now, it labored under the heaviness of new knowledge. We'd always carry the burden of what we'd learned here. Each step threatened to break us. Our wheels struggling with the weight. Unable to face the proof that lived within it, I was pulled under.

In the closet, I pulled my clothes from the hangers and drawers, leaving behind the ones Hannah had given me. There wasn't room in my backpack for them. I didn't bother folding the garments, I just shoved them in. Balling my fists, I punched them deeper into the bag to make room. I reached up on my tiptoes and pulled a shoebox from the top shelf. I held my breath as I lifted the lid. From inside, my entire life savings stared back at me. The receipt from my laptop rested on the bills. I couldn't return it because we'd opened the box, but if push came to shove, I could sell it. I placed the box on the bed, then turned back to the closet. Scanning the shelves, I grabbed a few more items and packed them.

I carried the backpack to the door and dropped it beside the suitcase. Four's crate, bed and food tucked neatly in the corner. I wouldn't need to pack those. They'd fit in my trunk. I reached down and patted Four's head.

"I hope you love the road as much as I do." She licked my hand in response.

I sat on the bed and dangled my feet over the edge, pulling my shoebox of cash onto my lap. Four jumped up and settled at my feet, her eyes heavy with sleep. It was nearly four in the morning.

I should at least try to sleep. We'd have a long day ahead of us tomorrow. My plan, though hastily thrown together, was to leave just after sunrise. I could be on the road before they noticed I was gone. I'd leave Hannah a note, thanking her for the room. I'd call Rayna once I was far enough away that she couldn't change my mind. By the time Trigger realized I wasn't showing up for our meeting, I should be in Arkansas or close to Tennessee, depending on which route I picked. Neither of them would be able to convince me to turn back. I'd be too far.

Two-thousand dollars. I counted the bills three times. Each time, the number was the same. I had enough to get far away from Wishing. It wasn't enough to sustain me for months, but I could get far enough away and settle into a quick job. Make a few more bucks. Hit the road again. Before long, I'd forget all about Wishing and the people here.

The rearview mirror is only for checking for dangers. Never use it to look back. My mother's words filled my mind. I could still see her sitting behind the wheel, her hair blowing in the wind. She used to smile at me when she gave me those little nuggets of wisdom. Her teeth would click as if she were tattooing it on her own memory.

In the bottom of the cash box, the photo I'd tucked away peered up at me. I lifted it and held it in my fingers. I studied it, searching for another clue. I couldn't stop thinking about the way she looked at him. Her cheeks pink, and her lips curled into a knowing smile. She'd seen something in him. I shifted my focus to his face. His eyes were lighter here. They didn't carry the years or secrets they did when I knew her. An overall weightlessness surrounded him in the picture. Carefree and young. Both of them. Neither aware of the future ahead of them. No baby or arrest reports. No threats. Just two kids in love.

I don't know what happened between that photo and my life. Was it me that broke him? That broke her? Or was there more to the story?

"Stop, Shay, stop," I whispered to myself. I needed a clean break, which meant stopping with the incessant questions. I couldn't be curious, or I'd always be searching for answers. Wishing would always be with me because I knew it held the answers.

I could stay and risk becoming stuck. Then I'd have a chance at finding the answers. Or I could let it go. I could let her go. Forget about Ken and Bethany. Pretend I was as insignificant as I'd always been. My mother was gone. My father didn't matter. For all intents and purposes, I was alone. Finding answers wouldn't change that. Knowing what happened between Ken and Tammy wouldn't make them better people. It wouldn't change my memories. My mother would have still left me in Iowa, and Ken would still be an asshole. I didn't need to know anything else.

The early hints of sunshine peeked through the curtains. It was almost five. I set an alarm on my phone for six. An hour of sleep would give me enough energy to drive for a few hours. Falling back onto the pillow, I didn't bother with covers. This time when I closed my eyes, darkness was all I saw. Bethany's voice and Ken's face were long gone. *Let it go. Let it all go,* I mumbled to myself over and over until the sleep won.

THIRTY-THREE

Scratch! Scratch! Four's paws against the metal door combined with her loud whining forced my eyes open. I grabbed my phone from the nightstand. 7:30. I'd slept through my alarm.

"Shit!" I slapped my hands onto the bed beside me. Four barked, pulling my attention back to her. Still dressed from my shift yesterday, I hopped out of bed and slipped my flip flops on. I jogged to the door, pausing for a second to study my backpack and suitcase. They stood as monuments to the decisions I made last night. I hesitated. The pull of the road fighting with Wishing and the life I'd built here. I hated how the light of day could change my mind so easily. I should have left last night when the need was fresh. Dreamless sleep lulled me back to the contentment I'd always felt here. I shook my head, fighting it off. I had to leave. I couldn't let this place hold me hostage another day. As much as I hated giving in to my fear, I refused to give Bethany a chance to fulfill her promise. With me gone, everyone else would be safe, I reasoned. I was running to protect Trigger and everyone in this town.

I clipped Four's leash to her collar and let her lead me down the stairs. "I hope you like car rides," I said. Her ears perked up, but she kept her focus on the front door. Her nose nudged it impatiently. I leaned forward, turned the knob and pushed it open. It resisted at first, so I pushed harder. I didn't have to look down to know what I'd find.

Another box. Exactly what I didn't need this morning. My bags were packed, and I had a plan. I was leaving Wishing today no matter what was inside that box.

Four sniffed at it and then licked the corner. She pawed at the top, but I guided her to the yard. The last thing I wanted was for her to do her business on the box. A slow smile crept over my lips. If she peed on the box, I wouldn't have to open it. I could throw it away and pretend that whatever was inside was soiled. I could shove it into the corner of my mind where memories go to die. Leave Wishing and put all of this behind me.

As Four walked through the yard to find the perfect spot, I trailed behind her. My mind wasn't here. I focused on the box. No matter how intoxicating it was to pretend the box didn't exist, I couldn't. Whatever was in that box called to me. It begged to be opened.

When she finished, I opened the door and removed her leash. She waited for me at the bottom of the stairs. My entire body was stiff and sore. Slowly, I knelt in front of the box. Instead of an envelope, my name was scrawled across the top of the box. The handwriting was familiar, but not in the way the others had been. I knew this handwriting. I'd seen it a million times over the course of my life. In notes left on the fridge. Letters to librarians asking them to keep an eye on me.

It was my mother's. *Shay Elizabeth Lane.*

Shaking, I picked it up and cradled it close to my chest. Tears stung my eyes. I scrunched my nose and squeezed my eyes shut, building a dam to stop them. After last night, I was amazed I still had any tears left to shed.

Like the time before, I sat in the middle of the floor with the box in front of me and Four beside me. She'd grown accustomed to my tears. When one rolled down my cheek, she jumped up to kiss it away. Just as my mother had when I was little. That was back when she was still Mommy.

Four scratched the box, urging me to open it. She smelled something familiar on or in it. Or she was just excited to see what was inside. Her nose worked overtime trying to get to it. Gently, I pushed her away and pulled open the flaps. I closed my eyes and took several deep breaths. This box was different. It didn't feel like the other gifts. Whatever was inside it was something from my mother.

When I opened my eyes, I found an old pink blanket. I lifted it from the box, taking care not to snag the edges on the cardboard. It felt comforting in my hands. My heart sped up, and I clenched it against my chest. The soft, plush material warmed my skin. I rubbed it against my cheek. I caught a hint of a smell I knew. Cheap Walmart perfume. It smelled of lilacs, vanilla, and alcohol. The scent swirled with moth balls and dust. There was no mistaking it. My mother's perfume.

I watched as the blanket absorbed my falling tears and wondered how many of my baby tears had this blanket dried.

Beneath the blanket, I found an old photo album. The cover, though faded with time, appeared to have once been the same shade of pink as the blanket. Underneath a pink and yellow baby rattle, my mother had written my name. The letters were drawn with painstaking perfection. Tracing my finger over them, I couldn't help but imagine the life she'd dreamed of for us.

That life, as I pictured it now, would have been in Wishing. I'd have grown up here. I could see us sharing a little house just like the ones on this block. She'd have raised me to believe in the Wishing Well and its magical powers. We'd probably have walked to school, hand-in-hand, as mothers and daughters do. At least until middle school, when I'd have demanded my independence.

I draped the blanket over my lap and placed the album on top of my legs. I gently opened the cover. The first photo was of my mother with a large round belly. Her hands folded together, rested atop what I assumed to be me. Light danced from her eyes as her smile stretched wider than I'd ever seen. She'd been happy. Happier than the last photos of her in the yearbooks.

Our time together was short. Too short. My youthful innocence, like hers, was stolen too soon. We'd shared a few good years, but none elicited the look of pure joy that I found in the photographs in the book. The woman in these pictures laughed often. She snuggled her baby, holding me close. She pushed me in park swings and placed gentle kisses on the top of my head. She looked at me adoringly and with pride. There wasn't a hint of shame in her. Everything in these photos indicated that our early life together was filled with love and happiness. The one thing she spent her entire life chasing. The one thing I stopped bringing her as we both grew older and more jaded.

I couldn't blame the road for that weariness, though I'm sure it contributed. My mother's loneliness was something I couldn't fix. The loss of whatever she'd once had with my father was a void a daughter could never fill. She chased it from town to town, seeking it out in the arms of strangers.

Sitting alone in my apartment with only a dog by my side, I finally understood the need to be close to someone. To have a person to share your thoughts and secrets with. The more I discovered about her life before me, the more I wished I could go back and change our ending. If I could rewrite our story, I'd write myself back into her life. My character would show up in Tennessee the day before her birthday. I'd stop her from getting in the car and driving down Interstate 40. She never would have been on the side of the road. Her body wouldn't have been found alone in that ditch. Instead, we'd be together. Our car pointed south. We'd have finally found that small town on the coast and settled down. She'd meet someone worthy of her love and find the missing puzzle piece. I'd go to school nearby and find a career I loved. We'd sit on the beach and read together, laughing at the roads and the memories we made along the way. Maybe she'd get married. Maybe I'd find a partner and have my own daughter. One night fifty years from now, she'd peacefully close her eyes and go. No pain. No loneliness. The life she lived would flash before her like a sweet movie, not the tragedy it actually was.

Holding my baby book in my hands, I wanted desperately for that version of the story to be our ending. She deserved it. *I* deserved it.

My gaze drifted back to the suitcase and bag by the door. Run away. It's what we always did. The road called us back. Or the place decided we didn't belong. Every once in a while, we were the ones to make that decision.

Push and pull. That's what Wishing was like. A yo-yo. Back and forth. Stay. Go. There was no clear answer. This time, it wasn't the random gift or box that was pulling me back. It was the daydream I'd just allowed. The one where my mother and I grew up here. Our lives would have taken a completely different turn if she'd raised me in Wishing. Perhaps Toby and I would have dated. Hannah might have been my best friend. Her mother and mine would watch us play in the yard while they drank wine or coffee. Lorelei and I would still be rivals, but we'd have always been that way.

"I don't know what to do," I whispered to Four. "I've never felt so safe and so terrified at the same time."

She climbed into my lap, burrowing her nose into the blanket. I leaned forward, rounding my back. My one companion fit into the curve of my body. I breathed with her, allowing the predictable pattern of her inhales and exhales to soothe the fire that still raged. I couldn't change the past, nor could I predict the future. If I stayed, Bethany, or worse, Ken, might show up again. The next time, I could be alone. He'd have an opportunity to fulfill his promise. If I ran, I'd hurt the people I'd come to care about. Staying could hurt them too. Nothing was black and white.

Despite my lack of trust, Rayna and Trigger had become like family. Even now all I wanted was to run to the bar and find Rayna. To show her the pictures of my mother and me.

Four shifted off of my lap, and I picked up the book to put it back in the box. Peering down inside it, I saw an old camera tucked into the corner. It looked like the old VHS recorders that my mother once dreamed about owning. She thought it would be fun to record our travels. We never could afford one, but she'd always stop to look at them when we were at the store.

I picked it up and pressed the power button. It was heavy in my hands. I could see a tape inside it, so once it powered on, I pressed play. At first, the screen was black. Static played over the tiny speaker inside the camera. Then, a tiny gurgling sound. A baby cooing.

"Sweet baby girl," my mother's voice sang. It sounded light and airy, not at all the gritty, ragged voice I remembered. The blackness faded and revealed a brightly colored room. In the middle, next to a crib, there was a rocking chair. The image shifted, tilting for a moment before settling into place. I didn't blink as I watched.

My mother, dressed in a long floral dress, walked into the frame. In her arms was a tiny baby—me—wrapped in the pink blanket I now held in my hand. Mesmerized, I watched as she sat in the rocking chair. One leg tucked under her as it always did. She cradled me in her arms and began rocking. Her soft voice filled the room as she continued singing. The words and melody were familiar. It wasn't a song I'd heard on the radio or in an old nursery rhyme. It was one she sang to me any time I awoke from a nightmare, or when I was scared during a storm.

"Sweet baby girl. Sweet baby Shay. Close your eyes. Go to sleep. Dream your beautiful dreams. Close your eyes. Go to sleep. The world will wait while sleep keeps you safe."

When she stopped singing, the creaking of the rocking chair was the only sound. My mother continued rocking, lulling me to sleep. Then, she stood and carried me to the crib. Laying me down, the faintest whisper was captured on tape.

"I love you. We're home, Shay. This is home."

THIRTY-FOUR

I knocked on the door and stepped back. My pulse raced. Sweat drenched my palms, and I wiped them on the front of my pants. I wasn't supposed to be here. I knew I shouldn't be, but I couldn't wait. I needed to know what Trigger had found. He'd been the one to give me his home address; I rationalized that he wanted me to stop by at some point. Now seemed as good a time as any.

The sound of feet padding towards the door filled the silence. They thudded along with the pounding in my chest. The footsteps were light and not at all like Trigger's. He walked with a heavy foot, clomping in his boots. These feet were a bit more timid. They came closer and then stopped. The knob twisted, and the door swung open. A petite brunette with bright green eyes accented by delicate crow's feet stood on the other side. Her eyes grew wide with shock when she saw me.

"Oh," she exhaled. She scanned my face, studying me. Like so many others in Wishing, a tiny flicker of recognition passed over her face. I hated that look. "You must be Shay."

"Mrs. Trigg?" I assumed the woman answer Trigger's door would be his wife.

"Call me Renee."

"Nice to meet you, Renee. Is Trigger in? I was supposed to meet him at the station at ten, but he gave me your address and said to stop by any time."

"He's upstairs getting ready for work."

"Can I come in?" I asked. She continued to study me. It was as if she were searching for an answer to an unspoken question.

"Of course." She stepped aside and waved me in. "Can I get you anything? I just made a fresh pot of coffee."

"Coffee would be great. Just black, please."

She disappeared into the kitchen. As soon as she exited, I did my own studying. Family photos of Trigger and Renee sat on the mantle. It was just the two of them. They didn't appear to have any children or pets. The house was immaculate, and the decor was minimal, with just a few knick-knacks and paintings. Their couch had a subtle floral pattern.

"Here you go," she said and handed me a mug. I followed her to the couch and sat down beside her. I could still feel her gaze on me. The intensity of it made me uneasy.

"Your home is beautiful," I said.

"Thank you. I'm in the process of redecorating. I finally got rid of all of Trigger's old hunting trophies."

I laughed, smiling slightly. I could only imagine all the deer heads and stuffed turkeys he'd had hanging on the walls. The image didn't fit the woman standing in front of me. Renee didn't seem like the typical rural wife my mother and I met over the years. She was softer and more feminine.

"Good for you. Those always creep me out."

"Me too."

For a moment, neither of us spoke. *Tick-tock, tick-tock.* I listened to the seconds flick away, desperate for Trigger to come downstairs. The silence was killing my resolve. I held the warm coffee cup in my hand and searched for something to say.

"Do you have kids?" I asked, aware of how rude the question

was. It just seemed odd that their house was devoid of anything other than vague pictures of the two of them.

"No," she whispered. Her sadness at the question was palpable. "We had plans to adopt, but it never worked out."

"I'm sorry to hear that," I replied, unsure of what else to say. I didn't know Renee, but she seemed like the type of woman who loved babies and kids. I could see her and Trigger chasing a toddler or three around the yard.

"How are you liking Wishing? I keep meaning to come up to the bar to say hi."

"Why?" I asked. She flinched slightly. "Sorry, I just don't get why everyone is still so interested in me."

"This town loves new faces," she said. "Trigger mentioned you a few times, and how much you've helped Rayna out down at the bar."

For the first time, she turned to me and smiled. Something about her felt familiar. Not in the way you recognize an old friend or family member, but I felt as if I'd seen her face before. I couldn't place it.

"Working for Rayna has been great."

"Has been?" she asked. She tried to sound light, but I heard the hint of trepidation in her voice.

"I think my time here may be coming to an end," I said. I hadn't meant to tell her, or anyone, I was planning to leave. My plan was to sneak out under the cloak of darkness and not make a fuss. But I'd slept too long and missed my chance. I wasn't supposed to be here. I should be halfway to Tennessee by now. Last night I dreamed about finding the town where my mother took her final breaths. I wanted to see where she might have walked or driven and find out what her final days had been like. Something told me whoever was leaving me boxes didn't have those answers. I wouldn't find them in Wishing.

"That's a shame. You just got here." Her warm smile silently pleaded with me to stay.

"I fear I've worn out my welcome."

"Because of the Alans?"

"What?" I stood, backing away from her. Hearing their last name ripped open the wounds I'd tried to ignore. I hadn't even looked in the mirror this morning. I didn't want to see the evidence of their existence. Not in Bethany's words that wouldn't leave my mind and not in the hair color I shared with Ken.

"Trigger mentioned Ken's wife was in town last night."

"He did? How did Trigger know?"

"I think he saw her leaving the bar. Shay, are you okay? You're shaking."

"Sorry," I whispered. How could they have possibly known she was there to see me? Or that she'd threatened me?

"I've known men like Ken my whole life. Him sending his wife to do his dirty work is the lowest of lows. He's been getting away with this kind of shit for far too long," she said. She spoke slowly and with intention. "Men like that seem to get away with just about anything. They can buy their get-out-of-jail-free cards and bribe the people they can't fool."

"Do you know him?" I asked. The anger in her voice seemed far too personal to be a casual mention.

"I know of him," she said, giving the same answer I'd heard a million times before.

"Is that what he does? Pay off people?"

"Ken's a charmer. He's the type that's used to getting his way. He thinks he's above the law."

I wrapped my arms around my waist and turned away from her. He was above the law. He had God and his reputation on his side. No one would believe me over him or his wife. Before I could respond, Trigger's unmistakable stomp echoed down the stairs. Flames raced through my blood, painting my cheeks red. As much as I wanted to ignore it, Bethany had rattled me last night. Her appearance and threat shook me.

"Shay? What are you doing here? Is everything okay? She didn't come to your apartment, did she? Did he?"

I shook my head. My mouth went dry. I couldn't speak. I had to get out of here.

"Then what is it?"

"Can we step outside?" The air in the room grew thick. Renee stood and moved towards me, but I turned away from her and reached for the wall to steady myself. I hated that the mere mention of my father's name elicited such a visceral reaction.

Trigger gently grabbed my arm, careful not to squeeze or pull, and guided me outside. Renee followed and stood on the porch beside him.

"Do you want to tell me what happened last night? Why didn't you call me?" He definitely knew more than he let on. Something in his eyes told me he knew all about Bethany's visit.

I ignored him. I didn't come here to talk about Bethany or Ken. I drew in a deep breath to calm the burning in my throat. The fresh air worked its magic. I took several cleansing breaths before speaking. "I need to know what you found."

"Why don't you come down to the station and we can talk?" Trigger glanced at Renee. A silent conversation flowed between the two of them. A few seconds passed before she nodded and returned to the house.

"It was lovely meeting you, Shay. I'd love for you to come by for dinner before you head out of town."

"You're leaving?" Trigger asked when the door swung shut behind her.

"It's time."

"Because of Bethany?" I nodded, not wanting to tell him the real reason. I was scared of what else I might learn here. "She won't be back, I can assure you of that. They can't hurt you."

"You don't know that," I replied. Something told me nothing would stop Ken or his wife. Not even Trigger.

"Shay," he said and reached for my hand. I let him take it.

Squeezing gently, he leaned closer. "I promise you that as long as I am breathing, that man will not come anywhere near you."

I didn't know what to say. He held on to my hand for a moment longer. When he released it, I let it fall back to my side. "Thank you."

"I'm guessing that's not why you're here, though."

"What did you find?" I asked, bringing the conversation back to where I needed it to go.

He sighed. "Unfortunately, not much. Your grandparents passed away a few years ago, and as far as I can tell, your mother didn't have any other family."

This didn't surprise me. I hadn't expected there to be news on my family. My mother didn't speak fondly of her parents, so even if they were alive, I doubted they'd be much help.

"And the arrest records?"

"Nothing. The records are long gone. The copy you have is all that exists."

"What does that mean?"

"As far as the Gaines PD is concerned, Ken Alan is a saint."

I rolled my eyes. "There has to be something."

"Shay, I know you're upset, but I don't have anything."

"Then why do they care so much? Why are they threatening me? I'm nobody. No one would believe me over them."

"I don't know, Shay."

"What are you hiding from me?" I shouted. "What don't you want me to know?"

Trigger reached for my arm again, but I pulled away. "Shay, I'm telling you there is nothing there. Nothing. Unless you want to tell me what happened with Bethany last night."

Shaking my head, I closed my eyes and swallowed back tears. "There's nothing there or there's nothing there you can share with me? Because those aren't the same, Trigger."

"I don't know what you think, but there is nothing to find."

"Who are you protecting?" I asked, pointing my finger at him.

"I know you're protecting someone, but I don't know if it's my mother or Ken."

"Did it ever occur to you that we might be protecting you?"

"We? Who is *we?*"

He didn't answer. He just shook his head.

"If you don't have anything helpful, then why did you call? What is it with this town? Everyone keeps jerking me around, but no one will tell me anything. I know you know something. You have to. I can see it in the way you look at me. The way everyone looks at me. But you're all too chicken to say something. What does he have on you? Why are you keeping his secrets?"

"I'm not keeping anyone's secrets."

I threw my hands in the air. "That's bullshit. I have to go."

"Aren't you tired of running? Running from town to town? Running from the truth that's right in front of you?"

"What truth?"

"This is your home. You belong here."

"No. I belong on the road. I was safe there. I'm not safe here. Not from Ken and Bethany. Not from whoever is leaving these random gifts and pictures. Everyone always wants something. Nothing is free. There's always a string attached. I don't want any of it! I never asked for this. Someone is dangling all these carrots in front of me trying to hold me captive here. Guess what, Trigger? I don't care anymore. This damn town can keep its fucking secrets for all I care. I'm done."

He staggered away from me like I'd punched him.

"I wasn't going to say goodbye. I was ready to leave. The car was loaded. Then this stupid box showed up with pictures and videos. It's sick! Who kept all of this stuff? I don't even know why I keep bothering. I don't want any of it!"

"Shay," he said. My name dripped slowly from his lips. Before he could say anything else, I turned my back to him and ran to my car.

I flung the door open and slammed it behind me. I didn't want to look back, but I did. Trigger stood on the lawn with Renee beside him. His arm was around her waist. Both of them locked their eyes on me. Watching them watch me drive me away gave me a surreal sense of déjà vu. I backed the car onto the street and headed towards my apartment one last time. It wouldn't take me long to put my things in the car and pack up Four. We could be on the road and out of Wishing within the hour.

As soon as I hit the main street, my car shuddered. The wheel vibrated in my hand. *The transmission.* I recognized the signs instantly. My arms struggled to steer the car onto the shoulder. I threw it into park and turned on the hazards.

"Shit!" I screamed into the empty car.

THIRTY-FIVE

$1,500.

Wanda needed a new transmission. I could have left her on the side of the road and found a way to the bus station. I could have left it all behind. I was ready to. The road had almost won me back. Then I remembered Four sitting alone in my apartment waiting on me. I couldn't abandon her. I'd been abandoned before, and I refused to do it to another living creature. Especially not the dog who'd comforted me so many nights.

So, instead of heading for the state line, I spent my night snapping at Rayna and Toby while I mentally calculated how many more shifts I'd need to regain my savings. Wishing had found a way to keep me. The town won. I was stuck for now. Part of me wondered if the transmission blowing wasn't planned. Had they known I was ready to leave?

It wasn't likely. Wanda had shown signs of a problem for a few days, I'd just ignored them. I knew better, but it was just another sign that I was too comfortable in Wishing.

"Trigger called me this morning," Rayna said, handing me a Bud Light draft for Edwin. "Didn't think you'd be making it in tonight."

"Wasn't planning on it," I said. "But my car broke down, and I can't bring Four on a bus."

"For what it's worth, I'm glad you're here. Even if your attitude is shit."

"Thanks, Rayna." I rolled my eyes and grabbed the beer. Edwin tried to make small talk, but I ignored him. He'd leave me two dollars and not a penny more. Every night, no matter how much he drank or ate, his tip was always two dollars. I needed Hannah and her mom to come in; they always left ten or fifteen dollars, depending on how much wine her mother drank.

The night went by in a blur. Every table the same group of people that came in every night. Every conversation the same as the one before. No one asked nosy questions. They ignored my puffy, red eyes. Wishing was a small town; I was certain everyone knew about Bethany and Ken by now. They all knew I was his bastard daughter. At least they had the dignity to not mention it. Small towns were pretty damn good at turning a blind eye to anything that threatened to darken their image or blurred the lines between right and wrong. No one asked, and I didn't plan on giving an answer if they did.

Toby did his best to keep the mood light. He didn't get grumpy when I made a mistake or snapped at him. He also refused to look me in the eyes. I wasn't sure if it was because of last night or because he'd heard I was leaving. Either way, I didn't care. I couldn't let myself get any more attached to this town or these people.

I half expected Trigger to show up. There was no way Rayna didn't call him to tell him I was sticking around. The two seemed to love talking about me and sharing gossip with each other. The bitterness flowed through me like a festering snakebite. Poison seeped into every open crevice. It soured everything and everyone I came into contact with.

At the end of the night, Rayna stalled behind the bar. She claimed to be doing inventory, but she normally did that on

Monday when the bar was closed. Tonight, she wanted me to stick around. She wanted to talk. Or maybe she sensed I had something to say to her. Toby didn't fry up any pickles or chicken tenders for us to share. When he finished cleaning the kitchen, he moseyed into the dining room and started mopping the floor around me.

"Rayna, can I cash out?" I asked, tossing the last set of rolled silverware into the basket.

"Sure." She didn't bother coming out from behind the bar.

"Can I ask you a question?"

"Of course."

I handed her my cash out slip and the money I owed. By now, she trusted me to count my own tips and checks. I bit my lip and debated my question. I hadn't intended on digging anymore, but my curiosity was getting the best of me. And I was stuck in Wishing for a little while longer. I couldn't just sit around and ignore everything around me.

"Did you know a Lizzie Gable or Miranda Price?"

"Doesn't ring a bell," she answered quickly without looking up.

"Neither name?" she shook her head. "Did you know my dad?"

"I knew of him, but not personally. Alcoholics like me aren't exactly welcome at the revivals around here."

"Who do you think is sending me all this stuff?" I asked, deciding to go all in on my interrogation. I hadn't mentioned the box from this morning to anyone. This one felt more personal than the others, and I wasn't ready to talk about what I'd seen. It contained items my mother wanted me to have.

"I don't know, Shay. I thought you didn't care anymore?"

"It's hard not to when it feels so personal."

"You need to make up your mind. I love you like a daughter, but this back-and-forth bullshit is getting old. If you're going, then go. But, if you want to stay, you need to leave that chip on your shoulder at the city limits sign. Wishing ain't done nothing but welcome you with kindness."

"My bullshit?" I repeated, my eyes wide. "What are you talking about?"

"Going off on Trigger this morning? That man would cut off his right arm to help you, but you can barely be bothered to thank him."

"Did he say that?" I asked, my heart broke a little more. Had I been ungrateful? I know my words were harsh today, but they were justified. Knowing I'd hurt Trigger filled me with guilt.

"He didn't. I may just be a barkeep, but I'm not an idiot."

"I didn't say you were."

"Shay, I need you to listen to me. There is so much here in this town for you. It's a place to call home, but you have to want it. We can't make you stay, and we can't help you find whatever it is you're looking for. You have to find those answers on your own."

"What do you think I've been trying to do?"

"I think you're trying to find someone to blame so you can run without guilt."

I couldn't argue with her anymore. Rayna was right. Even I was getting sick of my *am I staying or going* routine. Last night, I'd resolved to run. This morning, I'd already changed my mind before the box showed up. But I wavered and decided to leave again. If Wanda hadn't crapped out, I might have stayed anyway. I'd left my baby book open inside the box. It was the first thing I saw when I came home. It only filled me with more questions. Questions, apparently only Wishing could answer.

The person who had my mother's phone was still a mystery. The car. The apartment and furniture. The boxes. All of it dragged me back to Wishing. I kept seeing it as strings or chains. In a way, they were. But I didn't know if they were pulling me in or pushing me away. It was the fear that drove me the furthest away. Rayna had warned me that the truth might hurt worse than not knowing, and I was beginning to believe her.

She reached across the bar and took my hand into hers. "You need to ask yourself what you want, and you need to really listen to what your heart says."

My eyes locked on the top of the bar, studying the wood grain and ignoring Rayna's prying gaze. She squeezed my hand and pulled it up. My eyes followed. When they met hers, I flinched. There wasn't an ounce of anger buried in them. I'd expected to see disappointment or judgment. All I saw was compassion. Her words to me were genuine. I hated myself for not trusting her or Trigger, but I couldn't shake the feeling they were hiding something.

"What do you want, Shay?" she asked again. This time, she spoke each word slowly. Her mouth softened into a slight smile, but the intensity remained. She didn't want an answer, nor was she waiting for me to speak. We sat there, staring at each other, neither of us willing to break the gaze first. Her fingers curled around my hand, keeping it tight within her grasp.

What did I want? I couldn't answer Rayna or myself. The question clanked around in my mind, aching to be answered.

"Shay?" Toby slid up behind me and leaned around me. His elbow rested on the empty barstool beside me. "Need a ride back home?"

"Please," I replied. "Thank you for picking me up today." When the tow truck delivered Wanda and me to the body shop, Toby had been next door getting his hair cut. He saw me sitting on the curb on the verge of tears.

"See you tomorrow?" Rayna asked.

I nodded.

"Leave the attitude at home."

"Yes, ma'am."

Toby smirked beside me, and I slapped his shoulder. I

followed him out to his car. When he opened the door for me, he asked, "Are you really leaving?"

"Please don't ask me that tonight." I didn't want to talk about it anymore. I didn't have an answer for myself, much less for him.

"Do you trust me?"

"Right now, I don't trust anyone."

"Understandable." He reversed out of the parking lot and pulled on to the main road. "Mind if we take a detour?"

"Whatever." I leaned my head against the window. The cold air blasted from the vent blowing my hair. The vibration of the car rolling over uneven pavement rocked me. The road serenading me and sending my thoughts elsewhere.

When I arrived in Wishing, I was lost. Greg and Kansas City had devastated me. I didn't care about anyone, and no one cared about me. Then Trigger found me. He pulled me to safety. The motel and the bar gave me back my solid ground. When I found the apartment, I let myself believe that I'd found my home. Everything fell into place then. My life started to make sense. The routines and comfort gave me a sense of safety I'd never found before.

My curiosity got the best of me, and I had to start digging for answers. My mom was dead. My father was, at best, an adulterer and, at worst, a child-rapist married to a woman with a predilection for violence. I'd really won the lottery in the fucked-up parent department. At least my mother tried to protect me for a while. Then she abandoned me. I used to think she left me in Iowa, but she left me long before that. Adam wasn't the reason she vanished from my life. Maybe she thought she was protecting me by setting me free, but I was aimless without her. My compass broke the day she pulled away from me. It was still spinning, searching for its true north. If that even existed anymore.

I didn't know how to find that again. I'd give anything to go back to that first night in my apartment, to remember the feeling of contentment. I knew what I wanted that night. It was simple. I wanted a home.

I still wanted a home. Not even Bethany's threats could take that away from me. A home was worth risking it all for, because without it, what did I have to live for now?

THIRTY-SIX

"Toby, where are we?" I asked, taking in the unfamiliar landscape around me. I'd closed my eyes in the car, but I didn't think I'd been asleep that long. Long enough for him to drive me to the one corner of Wishing I hadn't yet seen, apparently.

"This is the football field."

"Okay," I said, dragging it out. "Why are we here?"

"This is where I go when I'm feeling lost or confused."

"Let me guess, you relive your glory days?"

"A little," he said with a laugh. "I did play football in high school and had many epic nights on this field, but that's not why I come here."

Outside the car, he stood in front of me. His arms were wide and from where I stood, it appeared that they spanned the full length of the field. His dark hair glowed under the moonlight. Sadness teased at the corners of his mouth. The Toby standing in front of me wasn't the same Toby that barked orders in the kitchen at Lace & Grit. This version of him was almost likeable.

"Then why do you?" He turned around to face me.

"This is where I decided not to kill myself." He said it with such nonchalance that I laughed and didn't believe him at first. When he looked at me, I saw the pain buried deep inside his eyes. "It was after I left college and came home. Mom was sick, and I was doing everything for her. Feeding her. Cleaning her. Managing the house. My dad was useless. He spent hours at the lake, fishing away his concerns. When she took a turn for the worse and we thought she wouldn't make it, I couldn't imagine a world where I'd given up everything for her and she still died."

"Killing yourself seems like a dramatic leap."

"There was more to it than that," he said, his voice low, as though he were afraid to say the words out loud. "Lorelei and I had broken up again. When I left school, I was flunking. Everyone thinks I came home for Mom. The prodigal son returning to duty, but the truth was I couldn't make it outside this damn town. Rayna's right, it always calls us home."

He took my hand and guided me to the ground. His legs stretched out in front of him. I sat beside him. The stars were brighter here than anywhere I'd been. Without light pollution from the city, they illuminated the black sky. Lying back, I propped onto my side and rested my head in my hand. He fell back beside me but didn't turn to face me.

"I'd been drinking more and more. Even tried a few things I never thought I would." He shook his head. I wanted to ask what he meant, but he didn't invite the question. "I was tired of everyone's expectant and sympathetic eyes. It was like they were waiting for her to die so they could show up with casseroles and condolences."

I knew what he meant, in a way. Everyone in this town looked at me like they knew me. They never stated expectations, but I saw it in their eyes.

"She was up in Springfield at the hospital. It was a Friday night. I remember because I was out with my buddies, three sheets to the wind, when they called. She'd woken up from her coma and was asking for me. I was too drunk to drive, so I just hung up and walked out here. I left my friends at the bar and walked the five miles alone. The entire time, I thought about what a failure I was and how disappointed my mom would be if she knew I wasn't cutting it at college. On the way out here, I stopped by the house to tell Dad she was better. He wasn't home. His truck and fishing boat were gone. I knew where he was, and it wasn't with his wife. I hated him. I hated her. I hated this town and myself. I grabbed his shotgun."

I pushed myself closer to him and leaned up. His eyes glistened with tears. Reaching toward him, I brushed my fingers over his cheeks. He turned away from me.

"But when I came out here and saw the field, I remembered every good thing about my life and Wishing. When I broke my leg after a nasty tackle, this place rallied around my parents and helped raise the funds for my hospital bills. When Mom got sick, they did the same. When Dad couldn't handle his wife's illness, they showed up to support him."

"Toby." I started to say that I knew what he was trying to do but things were different for me.

"Let me finish, Shay," he interrupted. "It started to rain while I was out here. The shotgun trigger burned under my finger. I was ready. Even knowing all that I had here, I didn't want to see what my future in this town would be. Just another washed-up small-town kid who couldn't move past his days on the field. It was such a boring cliché. I had nothing to look forward to."

I took his hand into mine and squeezed it. Our fingers laced together, he sat up and looked down at me. "I closed my eyes and braced myself. Before I could do anything, every light in this damn place came on. Even with my eyes closed, it was blinding. When I opened my eyes, Trigger and Rayna were standing in front of me. When I left the bar, Rayna called Trigger and sent him to find me. She left Eddie in charge and joined Trigger. When they found me, neither of them spoke. Instead, they sat down beside me."

I kept my eyes locked on his. "Trigger and Rayna seem to have a sixth sense about people."

"It's their job," he whispered, "to keep people safe and notice when there is a problem."

"What did they do?"

"They just sat with me for hours until the sun came up. Then, Rayna drove me home and waited while I got dressed. She drove me up to see my mom. Neither of them has mentioned that night since. I tried to thank them more than once, but they always shush me before I can. A week or so later, Rayna hired me at the bar and then helped me find someone to talk to. I've been working with Trigger on taking online courses in law enforcement."

"You want to be a cop?"

"I do. I'm heading up to the police academy in Springfield in a few months."

"That's great, Toby. I can't imagine you in a uniform or being all cop-like, but I can see you breaking up high school drinking parties and driving like a maniac in some police chase."

He laughed. When he did, his eyes danced. My heart did a tiny flip. I swallowed, shoving whatever reaction I'd just had away.

"What was it like growing up here?" I asked.

"Suffocating and amazing. It was like having a million aunts and uncles and cousins. Not everyone is close and not everyone buys into the whole community thing, but this town rallies around its people."

"And strangers."

"You're not a stranger, Shay."

"Why do you say that?"

He shook his head, and said, "Because you fit right in. When you got to town it was like everyone could finally breathe again. It's like you were the missing puzzle piece."

His words sounded nice, but they couldn't possibly have been about me. I wasn't the missing piece to anyone or anything.

"Can I ask you something?"

"Sure. Can't promise I'll have an answer, though."

"I feel like everyone is lying to me, or at least hiding something."

"That's not a question."

I exhaled sharply. "What are they hiding?"

"I can't speak for anyone but me."

"Fine," I snapped. "What are you hiding?"

"I know your father."

Finally, someone was admitting to knowing something. "How?"

"He's Lorelei's uncle. When you showed up at the church, she told him where you worked and lived."

"And you knew this?" I rocked back and rolled to my knees. The pit of my stomach dropped. How much had she told him about me? How much had Toby and Hannah told her about me?

"I'm sorry, Shay. I should have told you when you first mentioned him, but I didn't think it would matter. I had no idea Bethany would come here."

"Did you know about the rumors?"

"What rumors?"

"About Ken and my mother, Tammy?"

He shook his head. "No."

"How did he keep all of this hidden for so long?" I asked. I wasn't really looking for an answer. I knew. Men like him carried power and influence. He'd probably had the arrest records destroyed. He lied to my grandparents and convinced them that it was my mother who'd lied.

"He's a powerful man. Comes from money and is well liked and loved in Gaines. Most people there believe he is infallible."

"Do you know what Lorelei told him?"

"No, she wouldn't tell me much."

"Did she ever talk about him before I showed up?"

"All the time. She adored her uncle."

"Adored?" I asked, noting the past tense.

"You showing up kinda rocked the family a bit. None of them knew about you or your mother. When she learned what he sent Bethany to do last night, she lost it. I think she does blame you, but at the same time, she's pissed at her dad and uncle for keeping this from her."

"Of course, she'd make this about her," I said, rolling my eyes. "Thank you for telling me. Though, if you'd told me sooner, I might have avoided all of this."

"To be fair, Shay, I had no idea he was such a dick."

"Neither did my mother," I said dryly. I smirked. Toby stood and helped me to my feet.

"Look, I can't know what you're going through, but I do know how difficult it is to live somewhere like Wishing. But I also know how hard it is to leave it. This place isn't for everyone. I do believe Rayna when she says you belong here. You're part of what makes this place good for me."

"I've only been here a few months. You barely know me."

"That's not true." He reached up and tucked a stray strand of hair behind my ear. I felt his body inch closer to mine. I knew what he was going to do, but I couldn't move. His silver-gray eyes were transfixed on mine. "I see you, Shay. Your kindness, your vulnerability. All of it."

His lips brushed mine, and he snaked his arm around my waist, pulling me closer. I didn't resist. I leaned into him, welcoming the firm warmth of his chest. When his hand roamed down my back, I didn't stop him.

"Shay." He whispered my name. His breath tickled my skin. Leaning in, his kiss became more intense and urgent. I waited for a spark or anything that said he was more than just a friend, but there was nothing. Just his cool lips against mine. No tingles or flutters.

"Toby," I replied and shifted back. My hands pushed against his chest. He released me and pulled away. "I'm sorry, but—"

"Don't finish that sentence," he said, laughing. "I didn't feel it either. Friends?"

I sighed in relief. "Friends."

We walked back to the car, both of us giggling with nerves. Despite the lack of mutual chemistry, the kiss left an awkward pause in the air.

"Lorelei is going to be so relieved," I said when he opened the door for me.

"Shut up," he said with a chuckle. "I'm telling her we made out and you let me touch your boobs."

"No," I whined. "At least lie about where we were. I can't have people thinking I'm so weak in the knees over lame high school football stories."

"Don't worry, I'll think of something much less cliché to lie to her about."

"Thank you," I said. "Thank you for telling me the truth and bringing me out here."

"You're still leaving, aren't you?"

"Honestly, I have no idea. I was ready to go, and I probably would have if my car hadn't shit out on me. But you're right about Wishing. For all that I've learned here, it's hard to deny that something is pulling me in."

"If you ever want to talk, Shay, I'm here. I know I seem like a meathead who just wants in your pants, but I'm a good listener."

"After that lame-ass kiss, I don't think my pants have anything to worry about," I joked.

He started the car and turned to face me. "I really don't want you to leave, but I understand. If you do leave, promise me you won't just ghost us."

"I won't," I said. It was a promise I wasn't sure I could keep, but after tonight, I knew I owed this town more than my taillights.

THIRTY-SEVEN

"Ouch!" I cringed. I pulled my foot into my hand and leaned forward. I shoved the suitcase out of my way, cursing the books inside for nearly breaking my toe. For a moment, I just stared at the suitcase. My entire life on wheels. I stood alone in the middle of the furnished, comfortable apartment, alone with my thoughts for the first time since this morning. The itch to run I'd felt earlier had cooled.

I used to think my mother was weak for running. She never faced her problems head on, though she tried to teach me to do just that. *Don't run from pain, Shay. Let it make you stronger.* I used to laugh at those words. What a hypocrite, I'd think. She didn't know anything about strength. But I was wrong.

I rolled the suitcase over to the bookshelf and opened it. Just like I had my first night in the apartment, I unpacked them all. I put them back where they belonged. My fingers traced the familiar titles and names on the spines. When I finished, I took my clothes from the backpack and put them back in the closet. Four followed me through the apartment, matching me step for step. Her ears perked, her attention on high alert. Maybe she sensed the shift in me.

Toby didn't think he'd convinced me to stay, but in a way, he had. He didn't try to guilt me for leaving. He'd been honest with me about Ken and Lorelei. But what hit me was his love for Wishing, even though he saw the town's flaws. It was home, and that was the best blemish healer.

My mother hadn't been running away all those years. She'd been running forward. Home was like a beacon on the horizon. She chased it from state to state, but the target kept moving away from her. She was trying to get back here but the memories and threats she'd left behind wouldn't let her. Her fear of my father and what she knew he'd eventually do to her or me kept her away. I'd been wrong all these years. I thought I was following in her footsteps and doing what she wanted me to do every time I packed up my life and left another city or town behind. But I wasn't. I was living the life she never wanted either of us to live. She wanted to settle down; she wanted to find a safe place.

Wishing was her safe place. Or at least it had been.

Done with unpacking, I turned off the kitchen light and closed the curtains. I grabbed the baby book and camcorder from the box. I carried them to the bed and climbed under the covers. Four didn't jump up or try to get on the bed. Instead, she sat in the middle of the floor. She kept her ears alert and kept looking between me and the door.

"Do you need to go out again?" I asked. She dropped her head and didn't respond with her usual enthusiasm. "What is it, then?"

I knew she wouldn't answer, so I just assumed she was still on edge from this morning. I pulled the baby book onto my lap and opened. With fresh eyes, I opened it and studied the pages. I had to have missed something before. There were answers in these boxes, of that I was certain. Whoever was leaving them wanted to lead me to a conclusion. I no longer cared if they wanted to trap me here. All I wanted was to know my mother. To remember who she'd been before everything turned bad. I was desperate to unwind the good memories. These photos tugged at the strings.

A picture I'd missed before leapt off the page. It was my mother with me on her hip. I was around six months old. She wore a black T-shirt and jeans. A tiny logo in the corner pulled my eyes in. I peeled the photo from the page and brought it closer. *Lace & Grit.*

My mother wore a shirt emblazoned with the name of the bar I now worked at. The bar that had been in Rayna's family for decades. She wouldn't have been running it twenty-five years ago, but I was sure she'd worked there, which meant she knew my mother. She knew me. The pit of my stomach dropped, clenching tightly. I held the photo in my hand. Biting my lip, I forced back the anger and tears that threatened to return. I flipped the photo over, but there wasn't anything written on it.

The smile on my mother's face was just as bright and wide as the others I found in photographs in this book. She'd been happy. Though I was just a baby, the smile on my face was just as infectious. Every feeling of familiarity I'd felt here was justified. The lies and deception of the people here was not. Why hadn't Rayna told me? What were they hiding from me?

Before I could dwell further, the sound of tires screeching to a stop outside startled me. Headlights flashed on the wall for a moment and then shut off. Four hopped to her feet and ran to the door. *Bethany*. It had to be her. Or worse, Ken. All the air left my body in a single heave, and I slipped off the bed onto the floor. I crawled to the window, not daring to cast any shadows. Maybe he'd leave if he didn't see any movement or indication I was home. Careful to not be visible, I peered out the window, pulling the curtain back slowly.

The car outside wasn't familiar. I knew Bethany drove a Lexus SUV. I wasn't sure what Ken drove, but I was certain it wasn't an old Chevy. A petite woman with hair pulled back into a ponytail climbed out of the car and glanced up at the window. The streetlights were out, so I couldn't see her face, just an outline under the shadow of the blackness. She had a box in her arms and was walking towards the garage. I jumped to my feet and ran to the door.

My heart thudded a thousand beats per second. Four barked and chased after me. I pulled the door open and leapt down the stairs, skipping every other step. When I reached the bottom, I fumbled on the lock. The door caught on the rug, stalling me further. Yanking it open, I nearly tripped over Four as she raced ahead of me. The sound of a car starting forced me to run faster.

The box she'd been carrying sat on the driveway just outside my door, I ignored it and ran towards the road.

"Stop!" I screamed. The woman paused briefly. Her head turned slightly, and I felt her staring at me, but still couldn't get a good look at her. I reached the road just as she pressed the gas and drove away. "Come back!"

The taillights sped down the road, away from me. I couldn't catch up even if I tried. "Damn it!" I kicked a loose rock in the road and called Four. She stopped and turned toward me. Her head flipped back to the car and then to me. "Come on, Four. Let's go back inside."

My bare feet pressed into the gravel on the driveway. I ignored the pain and walked towards the box. Something unfamiliar under my heel stopped me. It wasn't a rock. I knelt down to examine it. It was as small flip phone, not unlike mine. I picked it up and slipped it into my pocket. Back at my door, I retrieved the box and called Four again. She was reluctant, but eventually followed me back into the house.

I didn't bother with the box. It was too light to contain much. The phone was of more interest to me. I returned to the bed and lifted Four onto it. She panted loudly, protesting. I climbed up and laid on my stomach beside her.

"It's okay, girl. They weren't here to hurt us." She dropped her head onto my back. She was shaking almost as much as I was.

Whoever was here had meant to leave the box undetected. They didn't think I'd be awake. And they certainly hadn't meant to leave the phone behind.

I took a deep breath and flipped the phone open. Being that it was older, there wasn't much more on it than the phone. No photos or games. It served a singular purpose. I clicked on the phone icon. Only one number appeared. All incoming calls. All missed. All my number.

I bit the inside of my cheek and scrolled through the history. Every single call I'd made to my mother was recorded there. Six years of calls. Dozens upon dozens of them. I wondered if they saved the voicemails. Without looking, I knew they had. As tempting as it was to listen to them, I couldn't. I knew what they said. There was only one I wanted to hear. I scanned through this history and searched for that night.

Christmas 2016. Her birthday. I knew I'd left one. I always did. When I found it, I hedged for a moment. It was the last message I'd left for her before she died. The next one was on January 5. I didn't want to hear that one. It didn't matter what I said after. I had to know what my final words to her were. I pressed play.

There was a brief pause and then, "Happy birthday, Mom. I don't know where you are, but I hope your toes are in the sand and the ocean is in front of you. I'm in Omaha. Probably leaving soon. Thinking about maybe Kansas City or somewhere in Oklahoma. Anyway, I'm good. I love you and I miss you."

Relief flooded me. I didn't remember leaving that message. Or where I'd gone after. I think I drove aimlessly for months, picking up odd jobs and sleeping in my car.

I went to close the phone, but something stopped me. A number that wasn't like the others. An outbound call at two in the morning on December 25. The area code was one I knew. Or at least one I knew now. 417.

Wishing's area code was 417. I didn't recognize the number,

though, and I couldn't tell if the person on the other end ever answered. The phone trembled in my hand.

My mother had called someone the morning she died. She called someone that wasn't me. Her dying words were shared with someone else. Sadness mixed with disappointment. My face burrowed into the blanket, muffling the sob I couldn't run from.

I lifted my head and sat up. My phone was on the nightstand. I looked at the number on my mother's phone again and dialed it into mine.

THIRTY-EIGHT

Nervous energy vibrated through every inch of me. My leg shook impatiently as I watched the clock. I'd barely slept the night before. I tossed and turned. When my eyes did close, my mind raced and buzzed me back awake. My mother's phone didn't leave my sight. I kept it tucked into my hand all night, only setting it down to go to the bathroom. At seven, I finally gave up and got out of bed. I took a shower. I got dressed. I cooked breakfast. I waited. And waited.

I checked the clock again. The minutes ticked by slowly. Each one more painful than the last. It was nine now. One more hour. I gave up on pacing and sat on the couch. Four curled up at my feet. I stared at the bookshelf and considered picking one up to read but didn't want to get too distracted and miss the small window I had to make a surprise visit to the police station. I picked up my laptop and opened it. The search results—or rather, the lack of results—on Lizzie Gable greeted me. I slammed the laptop shut. I didn't care about finding Lizzie or Miranda anymore. The number my mother called before she died was the only thing I could think about. Last night, I tried to dial the number, but couldn't bring myself to do it. The one time I hit the call button, I hung up before it rang. Whoever was on the other end had to know I had the phone. By now they would have noticed it was missing.

I typed the ten digits into the search bar. Rather than hitting enter, I turned my attention to the last box. I still hadn't opened it. I wasn't sure I wanted to, but knew I needed to. I reached forward and pulled it towards me. Four jumped up on the couch and sat beside me. Her nose nudged the box. She wanted me to open it too.

Knock. Knock. The sound ricocheted up the stairs. "Shay?" a voice called, interrupting me before I could get the tape off. I dropped the box beside me.

I groaned and lifted myself off the couch. She made it to the top of the stairs before I unlocked the deadbolt.

"Hannah," I greeted her. "What's up?"

"You okay?" she asked. She squinted and leaned closer, likely studying the dark circles under my eyes.

"Long night."

"Want to come over for coffee?"

I glanced at the time on my phone. I wasn't in the mood for small talk or gossip but could use the distraction. "Coffee sounds amazing."

"Besides, we haven't really had a chance to talk lately," she said and turned to go. I grabbed my backpack and followed her down the stairs. "I've missed hanging out with you."

"It's been a hectic few weeks." It wasn't a lie, but I'd been hesitant to spend time with Hannah. I knew she'd heard about my disastrous visit to Gaines and with Ken. Lord only knows what Lorelei told her.

"I'm sorry your dad turned out to be such a jerk." Yup, she'd heard everything.

"Yeah, I feel like everyone was trying to warn me, but I ignored them."

"I didn't," she said, almost apologetically. "I feel bad for encouraging you to contact him and to go to his church. I should have listened to my mom."

"You told her about that?"

"She asked how you were doing, and it just came out." She opened the door to her house and let me in. It smelled almost like Rayna's cinnamon rolls. My stomach growled. The scent of the buttery cinnamon pastries was like Pavlov's bell.

"What did she say?"

Hannah stepped behind the counter and reached into the cabinet for a mug. She turned her back to me and ducked her head. "Cinnamon roll? Mom dropped some off this morning. Apparently, she stole Rayna's recipe last time they met for poker night."

"A cinnamon roll would be great. Hannah, what did your mom say?"

"I don't know if I should tell you."

"You have to now."

"I want to, I do, but I can't."

"What is it with this town and secrets?"

"Some things are better left unsaid."

"Hannah, the man sent his wife to threaten me. They want me to disappear. If you know something, I need you to tell me."

She hesitated again. I folded my arms over my chest and refused to take the coffee mug she held out to me. Her lip trembled slightly, and she dropped her gaze. "I promised her I wouldn't say anything."

"Then why mention it?" I snapped.

"Because I feel bad." She offered the coffee again and slid a cinnamon roll across the counter. She avoided making direct eye contact, but I saw the sadness and regret in them. I couldn't stay mad at Hannah even if I wanted too. I took both and sat on the stool. I also knew she was stubborn. If she promised her mom she wouldn't tell me, she wasn't going to. No matter how bad I wanted to know. "I should've stopped you. Maybe they wouldn't have hurt you."

"I wouldn't have listened. I'm sorry I snapped at you," I apologized. "I'm just on edge this morning."

"Another gift?" she asked.

"Yes, but this time I saw the person leaving it."

She perked up at that and leaned against the counter, her eyes focused on my face as they grew wide with curiosity. "And?"

"I didn't get close enough to see who it was. I know it was a woman and that she drives an older model Chevy."

I watched Hannah closely, hoping she'd react, but she didn't. The crease between her eyebrows remained furrowed.

"They dropped a phone."

"Where is it? I bet we can find out who it belongs to."

"I know who it belongs to."

"Well?"

"It was my mother's." This sparked a reaction. Her mouth fell open, and she drew her hands up to cover it.

"Oh my God. Do you think she's still alive?"

I shook my head. "The only call she made on it was to a number here in Wishing. She made it the morning she died."

"What's the number?"

I wasn't sure I wanted to tell her. She was eager to play detective, but I wanted to find out on my own. "I don't know who she called."

"But you have the number. Shay, I know everyone here. I can help you figure it out."

"I need time to process, Hannah," I lied. She wasn't the only one capable of keeping secrets.

She pouted and said, "I understand."

I took a bite of the cinnamon roll. "These are good. Not as good as Rayna's, but close."

"I know, that's what I told Mama. I don't think she's ever

going to speak to me again," she said with a giggle. "Back to this phone thing, did you find anything else on it?"

"Just the voicemails I left my mother and that one number."

"I know you don't want my help, but if you change your mind, I'm all in."

"Thanks."

"Mom said you were leaving soon."

"Good God, this town sure loves to gossip."

"She's just worried about you."

"Why?" I asked. I barely knew Bitsy, her mom. When we talked at the bar, her mom asked me questions, but we never really spoke much. I usually avoided answering her and just went about my business. "Your mom hardly knows me."

"You're my friend, and she always worries about my friends."

"Even Lorelei?"

"Especially Lorelei. That girl gives my mom, and hers, heartburn."

"Me too. She may kill me before Ken gets a chance to."

"Why?" Hannah asked with her mouth full.

I took a sip of my coffee and grinned. For a moment, I wanted to talk about anything other than the phone and the gifts. Even if it meant listening to her squeal and grill me. Besides, what good was an awkward kiss on a high school football field at 2:00 a.m. if I couldn't gab to my girlfriend about it? It felt like one of those painfully boring and normal moments I used to crave. "Toby kissed me last night."

Coffee flew out of her mouth and hit me in the face. I wiped it with a paper towel. My cheeks burned red, but it wasn't from the coffee she'd just spit on me. "What?"

"He tried to talk me into staying in Wishing, so we went out to the football field." I left out the part about his confession. That story wasn't mine to tell. "Then he kissed me."

"Girl, you are full of juicy news this morning. Between the

phone and the kiss, this is the most excitement I've had all week."

If Bethany hadn't threatened to kill me less than forty-eight hours before, I might have agreed. Finding the phone and kissing Toby were definitely more gossip-worthy.

"Spill, Shay. You can't leave me hanging like that. I knew he liked you. How was it? Fireworks? Weak knees?"

"Meh," I replied and finished off the coffee. "No sparks. We're friends."

"Bummer. I was hoping to 'ship you two."

"What?"

"Sorry, I keep forgetting you don't text or use social media. By the way, you still haven't accepted my friend request," she scolded me.

"I know, I know. I'm never on it. Sorry."

"Anyway, I was hoping to set you two up. You'd make an adorable couple."

"Gross." Until last night, I'd assumed Toby was one-dimensional. He'd been so hot and cold with me. Flirting one minute, chastising me the next. But he'd also helped me. Last night, he showed me a side of him I'd never seen before or even assumed existed. "I mean, he's a nice guy sometimes, but there wasn't anything there."

"He's going to marry Lorelei anyway," she said.

"Why do you say that?" I glanced at the time. I needed to get going.

"Those two are made for each other. Do you need to go? You keep checking the time."

"Yeah. Hey, could you give me a ride to the police station? My car is in the shop."

"Sure, let me run up and put some shoes on," she answered a bit too enthusiastically. She grabbed my plate and mug and set them in the sink beside hers. "Why don't you wait in the living room? It's more comfortable there."

I slipped off the bar stool and walked into the living room. I sank into the plush leather couch and looked around the room. I'd been in it a few times, but never had the chance to take it all in. Hannah's walls were bare, but a few framed photos sat on the coffee table. One caught my eye. In it, a baby with Hannah's blue eyes and timid smile cooed at the camera. She looked to be about three months old. Another baby sat next to her. This baby was older, maybe a year old or so, and had significantly more hair. It fell in sandy blonde curls around her chubby cheeks. She was dressed in pink footie pajamas and she was staring up at someone behind the camera. Her hazel eyes sparkled under thick eyebrows. I recognized those eyes immediately.

"Ready?" Hannah asked and walked into the living room.

I jumped and dropped the photo. It crashed onto the coffee table. I flinched and stepped back.

"Shay?"

I studied her for a moment. My gaze shifted down to the picture. It landed facing up. My eyes darted between the photo and Hannah. She didn't react. She didn't offer an explanation or move to pick it up.

"Yes," I said, my voice shaking. "Let's go."

We rode to the station in silence. I couldn't find the words to ask about the photo or how she'd gotten it. If she'd noticed me looking at it, she didn't let on. Maybe she didn't know who was in the photo with her, but that didn't make sense. People don't frame photos unless they have some emotional or sentimental significance.

I thought back to every conversation we'd had and what she'd said earlier about her mom worrying about me. About the way she stopped Lorelei from asking about Four and how she stood up for me before we became friends. Hannah never looked at me like the others, but she'd latched on to our friendship quickly.

Had the answer always been right in front of me, sitting in plain sight? What else had I missed?

THIRTY-NINE

Hannah dropped me off outside the station. If she noticed me watching her nervously, she didn't show it. I tried to ask about the picture at least a dozen times on the short drive, but I couldn't find the words. The only hint that she'd seen anything was the faint glisten in her eyes when she said goodbye. I lingered for a moment and then slammed the door.

Inside the station, the receptionist was gone. I waved at a few officers I recognized from the bar. If I wasn't supposed to be there, no one even batted an eye. I found Trigger's office from memory. This time, he wasn't expecting me. He sat at his desk with his head down. He was making notes on a yellow legal pad. Unlike last time, his desk was littered with papers and folders. I even noticed a few picture frames that weren't there before.

"Knock, knock," I said. I didn't wait for him to invite me. Pulling the door shut behind me, I gripped the phone in my hand.

"Shay!" he said, surprised. "What are you doing here?"

"I need to know whose phone this is," I said, diving right in. I handed the phone across the desk.

"Where did you get this?" he asked. I dropped the phone into his open hand and sat down in the chair across from his desk. I watched as he studied the phone. I was getting pretty proficient at reading faces, though very few here wanted to be read. Everyone hid their reactions so well. Too well. If he recognized it, he didn't let on. The black device looked tiny in his hands. He turned it over and looked at it from a variety of angles.

"Whoever is leaving me shit dropped it outside my house last night. I know she is a woman. She's short with long hair and drives a Chevy."

He leaned back and held the phone in his hand. He examined it again and then looked up at me. "How do you know they dropped it?"

"I saw her. She ran from me."

"You chased her?" he asked, concerned.

"Sort of. She was already to her car by the time I got close enough."

"That wasn't a good idea, considering what happened the other night."

"I know, but I'm fine. She didn't seem interested in hurting me. She dropped off another box, but I haven't opened it yet."

"Did you get a good look at her?" I shook my head. "What kind of car?"

"A maroon Chevy Malibu. Maybe a 2010."

The pen scratched on the paper as he made a note. "License plate?"

"Too dark."

The room fell silent for a moment. Trigger flipped open the phone and started clicking through the call log. "It's only one number."

"Yup." I waited for him to recognize what he was looking at.

"Is that your number?"

"It is. That's my mother's phone."

"You're sure?"

"Check the voicemails," I said, "just don't play the last one." I cringed at the memory of me crying into the phone, desperate for my mother and broken over my father.

My voice played over the phone as he lifted it to his ear. He only listened long enough to confirm it was me. When he closed the phone, he glanced up at me. For a moment, his mouth curled into a slight smile. It faded as quickly as it had appeared.

"Can you find out who's had it this whole time?"

"It's a burner."

"I know, so is mine. Surely there are prints or something that can be pulled from it."

"Yours and mine, likely. I can try."

"That's all I'm asking."

"Will you be here long enough for me to investigate?"

I nodded. "My car needs a new transmission. Guess whoever left it didn't know that. Or maybe they did, and they wanted to make sure I stayed."

"Do you really think that?"

"I don't know what to think, Trigger. This phone confirms that someone here has been listening to the messages I left my mother. Someone here knew her and kept these things for me. I need to know who that is."

"Are you sure?"

"Why does every keep asking me that? I already know the truth about my father. I can't imagine it can be worse than that, right? It's not like they left rat poison in my food."

"I sure hope not," he said and chuckled. His focused shifted for a moment. I followed his eyes to the photograph on his desk. I picked it up and turned it towards me. After seeing the photo in Hannah's house, curiosity got the best of me. It hadn't been there when he knew I was coming, but magically appeared when he wasn't expecting a visitor. That in and of itself was suspicious.

"Your wedding?" I asked, smiling. I held the picture closer to get a better look at young Trigger. Trigger's signature potbelly was nowhere to be found. Renee's face was slimmer and more youthful. Her smile leapt off the photo. As with the photo earlier, I saw something I'd seen before that I missed when I met Renee. "Your wife—"

"Miranda," he said smiling. "We were so young."

"I thought her name was Renee," I said. I set the photo on his desk and pushed my chair back.

"Renee is her middle name," he replied quickly as he realized his mistake. "Everyone calls her Renee now."

"Do they? Why did you call her Miranda?" My voice trembled with realization and fear.

"Shay," he said and stood. I jumped to my feet and knocked the chair onto the ground behind me. "Are you okay?"

I shook my head. *No. No. No.* He called her Miranda. With the mention of her name, the picture from my mother's yearbook flashed in my mind. It all clicked into place. The look on Trigger's face when he met me that night. The way Renee—Miranda—watched me with sadness. He'd sat in front of me and gone through the motions of pretending he'd never seen the phone before or heard the voicemails. He lied to me. Everyone here lied to me. I'd known they were lying, but I ignored the signs. They were there. In the glances and unfinished sentences.

A wave of nausea passed over me, my head grew light, and the room spun around me. I closed my eyes and took long and deep measured breaths. Each time I counted to ten before exhaling. My thoughts were a jumbled mess, and my eyes blurred with tears.

"Is her maiden name Price?"

He didn't answer because he didn't have to. I knew it was. He stepped around the desk and moved towards me, saying my name again. I backed away.

"Stop," I said. "Answer my question. Stop lying to me."

"Yes," a timid voice behind me said. I hadn't heard the door open. "My name is Miranda Price Trigg."

I whipped around to face her. She stood delicately in the doorway, blocking the exit I was desperate to run toward.

"You lied to me," I whispered, biting back the sobs. The dam threatened to break and unleash a flood of tears. "You all lied to me."

"Shay, we had our reasons," Trigger said. He came around the side of his desk and stood beside Miranda. His arm looped around her waist. She leaned into him for support.

"Your mother," Miranda said. I stopped her before she could continue.

"You knew she was dead!" I screamed at Trigger, pointing my finger at him. I turned my attention to Miranda and snarled. She flinched and pulled back. "You knew her!"

"I did," Miranda replied, tears formed in her eyes, but she blinked them away. "Your mother was one of my best friends."

"Then why lie? Why sneak around?" I tried to move past her, but she wouldn't budge.

"Can you let us explain?"

"No." I shook my head and bolted for the door. Brushing past Miranda, my shoulder bumped her aside. I heard them calling after me, but I couldn't stop. I had to get out of there. I needed air. My lungs tightened. As soon as I pushed the door open, I gasped. The thick, humid air burst into my lungs so quickly, they ached. I kept running. I couldn't stop. Couldn't look back. Looking back would slow me down. I couldn't risk them catching up to me.

My feet hit the pavement and propelled me forward. It was two miles to my apartment. I knew I couldn't run the entire way, but I kept going, pushing through the pain in my legs and the thick air. Cars passed in front of and beside me. I ignored them all. My body ran without any direction from me. I was on autopilot. Unable to focus on anything, my mind rolled over what I'd just uncovered. Puzzle pieces floated in circles chasing each other, seeking their match. Blank spaces remained between them even as they fit together.

Miranda knew my mother. Trigger knew my mother. They

knew me. I'd already confirmed that Rayna did too. I assumed Hannah did at one time, though we were babies in the photo. That had to mean her mother knew too. Every one of them pretended to know nothing as they got to know me. They all acted as if I were a stranger. They feigned surprised when I learned my mother died. They claimed to not know my father, though that was impossible given what I knew now. None of them stopped me from finding him. Rayna had even encouraged it. I felt my stomach twist into a knot as the coffee and cinnamon roll threatened to reappear.

Even with all I'd just learned, I only had half of the answers. The rest would have to come from them, but I wasn't ready. I needed time. I needed to think. As tired as I was from the lack of sleep the last few nights, and considering I'd never run more than a few feet in my life, I made good time. The first mile was the hardest. My throat throbbed from choking back tears and gasping for air, and my muscles screamed at me, begging me to stop. But I pressed on.

My lungs were on fire by the time I made it to my neighborhood. I slowed to a jog and rounded the corner where I'd bumped into Rayna the first night I walked Four. My legs ached. I didn't want to take another step, but adrenaline pushed me forward. I vowed to pick up running or some sort of exercise the next time I settled down. I depended on my car too much and was out of shape.

When I reached my driveway, I dropped to my knees in the road. The asphalt ripped open my skin. Heaving forward, I struggled to catch my breath. Now that I wasn't in motion, I couldn't stop the tears. There wasn't anything to distract me. I couldn't hold them back. Angry drops of rain thundered from my eyes and rolled down my cheeks onto the gravel. The pounding of my pulse clouded my ears, blocking out the world. I sensed I wasn't alone, but I didn't care.

I kneeled in the driveway sobbing and screaming into the air.

A firm hand rested on my back for a moment, before wrapping around my waist and pulling me to my feet.

"It's alright, love; let's get you inside," a voice whispered in my ear. "Come on, Shay, I can't carry you. You have to walk."

"Mama, let me help," Hannah said. She moved beside me and helped her mother steady me.

I didn't want to go with them, but I didn't fight their help. One foot moved in front of the other, pulling me forward. Hannah and her mom guided me to my door and helped me up the stairs.

"Thank you," I whispered as I pushed open the door. I tried to shut it behind me, but they followed me in. "I'm okay, I promise. I just need some time."

Hannah stared at me, her eyes narrow with disbelief.

"I'm not going anywhere," I replied. It should've been a lie. The Shay who arrived in Wishing three months ago would have run today. She might have left everything, including her dog, behind, but not now. There was too much to lose by running. I'd never know the truth if I ran, and I was so close to it.

"Promise?" she asked. When I nodded, she turned to her mother. "Can I tell her now?"

FORTY

"Shay," Hannah said as she handed me the photo frame. "My mother's name is Elizabeth Gable. Everyone just calls her Bitsy now."

"Lizzie?" I asked, looking up at Hannah's mother. She nodded.

Bitsy stepped forward and handed me the box that had been left that morning. "Open it."

I hesitated for a moment before I pulled back the tape. The box was empty except for a single photo at the bottom. I reached in and picked it up. The photo was old and yellowed with tattered edges. In it, my mother held me in her arms. Miranda and Lizzie were on either side of her. Lizzie was pregnant, her smile as wide as her belly. Trigger stood behind Miranda with his arms around her waist. Beside him was Rayna. All of them younger and happier than I'd ever seen them.

"Why didn't you tell me?" I asked.

"I couldn't, dear," she replied. "We were given strict instructions."

"From who?" I asked.

"Your mother, of course," she said with a smile.

"I don't understand."

"You will soon, I promise. Why don't we sit down? Hannah, be a sweetie and get us some Diet Cokes."

I started to protest, but Bitsy waved me off. She'd come here to talk, and I wasn't going to stop her.

"I assume you've met Miranda. Silly girl dropped the phone when you caught her last night. Though something tells me that wasn't an accident. We're all a bit tired of waiting on you to put the pieces together."

Hannah handed us both a Diet Coke and went over to sit on the edge of the bed. Four followed her over and jumped onto her lap. I tried to silently beg her to come sit with me, but my dog forgot all about her loyalties and closed her eyes while Hannah scratched her ears. I couldn't blame her, though; I'd much rather sit next to Hannah than her mother.

"Now, where was I?" she asked herself. "Ah, yes. Your mother and I were best friends. We grew up in Gaines together. Two peas in a pod. You almost never saw one of us without the other. I followed her wherever she went. Back then she had this spark about her. She was as bright as the sun, and everyone kept their eyes locked on her. Myself included. We had some fun, I tell you. People saw Tammy and Lizzie walk into a room, and they knew the party was about to start."

I rested back into the couch, listening to Bitsy talk. I was mesmerized. I'd never heard anyone talk about my mother like she did. Tammy Lane sounded like a woman I'd have been friends with. She wasn't anything like my mother.

"Then, towards the end of our sophomore year, Ken showed up. He was dating her cousin Bethany. They'd met at some church camp, and he moved to Gaines to be closer to her. Everyone knew Ken and Bethany would eventually get married. Everyone but Tammy. That girl fell head over heels for Ken. Anytime he was near, her eyes glazed over like a girl on a diet who'd just seen cake for the first time. Miranda and I tried to talk some sense into her, but Tammy wouldn't listen. Your mother was always a stubborn one."

"Like you?" Hannah said, laughing.

"You hush up, child, this ain't about you." Hannah's cheeks flushed, and she turned her attention back to Four. "As I was saying, when Ken showed up, it changed everything. He didn't even try to hide Tammy from Bethany. Flaunted her right in her face."

Bitsy continued the story, her eyes focused on my face. Every word she spoke was chosen with intention. She wasn't one to mince or waste words. My father stayed with Bethany and proposed to her while keeping Tammy at his side. Everyone knew, she claimed. Everyone except my grandparents and the church. From the way she told it, Bethany wasn't bothered by the relationship as long as he promised himself to her in marriage. Bethany didn't want much from Ken. All she was after was a ring and a home. In return, she'd have his babies and turn a blind eye to his escapades. None of that surprised me. He proposed just after Tammy's junior year. Two months later, Tammy was pregnant.

"At first, Bethany ignored the pregnancy. I think she was naive enough to believe it wasn't Ken's. We all knew it was. Tammy was a lot of things, but she wasn't a tramp. She didn't sleep around. Ken may have been taken, but he was her only love interest. She gave him her virginity and stayed true to him despite everything. I really believe she loved him."

Despite all of this, Bethany asked my mother to be in her wedding. She stood beside her cousin and watched her marry the only man my mother ever loved. That night was when she told her parents about the pregnancy. They didn't believe her at first. My grandparents, like everyone else in Gaines, thought the young pastor was a saint. He was destined to lead their congregation one day. While Bethany and Ken were in Hawaii on their honeymoon, my mother brought proof to her parents. Photos and love letters from Ken to her. Evidence of their time together. In one, Ken mentioned the baby in her womb and promised my mother she wouldn't raise me as a bastard; he'd find a way to make it work.

"I really do think he believed he loved her too. In his mind, God had given him two women to love. One in the bedroom and one at the altar. He had his cake and his ice cream. He didn't see anything wrong with what he was doing."

When the newlyweds returned from their honeymoon, Ken was arrested for statutory rape. That's when everything went south. Ken denied everything. He made up stories about my mother coming on to him and throwing herself at him. He told Tammy's mom that her daughter was sleeping with anyone and everyone. Claimed my mother made up the letters and wrote them herself. Denied being alone with her. He did anything and everything he could to discredit his mistress. Bethany took his side. She lied to her aunt and uncle and told them Tammy confessed everything to her. That she'd set up Ken because she was jealous he never returned her attention.

"That was the lie that broke Tammy. She loved Bethany, and the two had always been close. Even when they shared Ken, the two were closer than sisters. When Bethany denied the truth and painted that awful picture of her, it killed her," Bitsy said. She dabbed the corner of her eyes with a tissue, wiping away a stray tear. "I tried to defend her. I went to your grandparents and told them everything I knew, but it was too late."

I wondered what kind of parents believed strangers over their daughter. Had they not known her at all? The wounds of my own mother's abandonment were still fresh, even six years later. Not even her death soothed those. It was a pain I knew my mother carried to her grave. I didn't shed a tear for her, though. Hearing her life being reduced to a series of mistakes put everything in perspective. She never even had a chance.

"The night they kicked her out, Tammy went to Ken. He was

at the church preparing a sermon for Sunday. It was early February 1994. Her belly swelled with you. She found him alone in the basement." I shuddered remembering my time with him there. "He hadn't been expecting her. She'd kept her distance after the arrest and its aftermath. The instant he saw her, he flew into a rage. The evidence of his lies was flaunted in his face, and he couldn't stand it."

As she continued, the tears I thought had dried returned and flowed freely. My mother begged him to help her. She promised to never let anyone come after him. She swore she'd keep their secret. He wouldn't hear it.

"He beat her so badly; we were certain she lost you. I knew she'd gone to the church, so when she didn't turn back up, I drove up there and found her. I called our old friend Miranda, who was a nurse in Springfield by then. Miranda and her new husband, Trigger, rushed her to the hospital. Obviously, you survived, but your mother never fully recovered emotionally. She'd trusted him with everything, and he'd tried to hurt her and you. But she refused to press charges. She wouldn't even tell Trigger what happened. She insisted on protecting Ken, convinced he still loved her and hadn't meant to hurt her."

"She spent a week in the hospital," Bitsy continued. "When she was released, Trigger and Miranda took her in. Tammy with them through the birth and for a year or so after."

Hannah stood from the bed and walked towards me. She sat beside me on the couch and took the photo of us from my hands.

"I found myself in my own trouble a few months after Tammy left. Though Roger was and is a decent man. Married me and we had Hannah here a few months after you were born. His family farm was in Wishing. I moved here, and the three of us were reunited."

"Obviously, I was too young to remember you," Hannah said, "but Mama always kept this photo of us in our house. She said you were my best friend."

"Tammy and I had dreams of raising you girls together. We imagined mini versions of ourselves growing up playing dolls and becoming cheerleaders like us. You girls would be smarter than us with boys, though. Thankfully at least one of those wishes eventually came true."

"What happened?" I asked. "Why did she leave?"

"I think you know the answer to that question, Shay."

"I want to hear it from you." I assumed it was something to do with Ken, but I didn't know much more beyond that.

"Your mother loved you, Shay, you need to know that. She'd have walked through fire for you. But being a single mom at seventeen ain't easy, and sometimes, love isn't enough. Babies need clothes, diapers, and food. She tried so hard to be everything to you, but it wasn't enough. She thought you needed more than her."

"She was too hard on herself," I whispered.

"All mothers are, dear." She patted my knee and continued. "She worked day and night at the bar trying to make ends meet. Miranda and Trigger weren't charging her rent, but diapers and formula aren't cheap. She tried to get assistance, but when she couldn't give them financial information on the father, she panicked. She was worried they'd start asking questions. When you were born, she'd lied and said she didn't know the father. She was always scared someone would show up demanding answers."

"What happened next was my fault," she said. "I knew better, but I hated to see her struggle. I thought he'd want to help. I saw the way Roger looked at Hannah and how he'd have done anything to keep her safe. I assumed, wrongly, that Ken would want to do that for you. He and Bethany had just had Chris. As a new father, surely, he'd have wanted to see his other child. To take care of the life he'd help create."

"You went to him?" I asked.

She nodded. "I was eighteen and stupid. Looking back, it's one of my biggest regrets. When I showed up at the church,

Bethany ignored me. Didn't even say hi. She just walked by. Ken refused to speak to me at first, but eventually I was able to get him alone. I showed him a picture of you. He took one look at you and knew immediately that you were his."

She paused to dab her eyes with the tissue again. Hannah wrapped her arm around my shoulder and pulled me closer to her. I had a feeling she'd heard this story before. She knew what was coming next.

"He called you an abomination. Said he should have taken care of you and your mother that night. He hated unfinished business. I left before I could even ask him to help. I drove home in a panic. I told Roger what I'd done, and he called Trigger. He was up in Springfield for training, and Miranda was at work. Tammy was home alone with you."

"What happened?" I asked, trembling at the ending I knew was coming.

"Ken drove to Wishing and found the Triggs' home. Your mother walked into your nursery and found him holding a pillow over your face."

I gasped. I didn't think my opinion of him could get any worse. I was wrong. I hated him. Even though I had no memories of that night, my face twitched. The breath caught in my lungs and pulled tight as if I were being suffocated.

"Your mother fought him off as best as she could, but he was bigger and stronger. By the time Roger and I arrived, Tammy was unconscious on the floor, and you were bluer than a full tick. He pulled Ken off of you, and well, I don't know what he did. I just worked on getting your cheeks rosy again. You didn't cry for what felt like hours, but when you did, that beautiful wail woke your mama right up."

"Who could do that to a baby?" Hannah asked, her voice tiny and childlike. "I just don't get it."

"He's an evil man, Hannah."

"Why didn't anyone tell me?" I asked.

"It wasn't our story to tell, Shay."

"You let me go to him."

"I didn't know you were going to see him until Hannah came home that afternoon and told me."

"Trigger and Rayna knew I was. Why didn't they stop me?"

"Neither of them were there to see what he was capable of. I think they believed Ken had changed, and that the years matured him."

"They didn't."

"I know that. From what I understand, they did try to stop you. They warned you that digging up bones rarely reveals the secrets we want to know. Would you have heard them if they had told you the truth?"

"No, I wouldn't have listened," I admitted. "What happened next?"

"A few days later, your mother packed the two of you up and left Wishing."

"That's it?"

"She left in the middle of the night. No note and no goodbyes."

"How did her phone end up here?"

"That's a question only Miranda and Trigger can answer. Why don't we take a drive?"

FORTY-ONE

IT WAS ALMOST THREE WHEN BITSY PULLED INTO THE Lace & Grit parking lot. The bar should have been open, and I was supposed to be inside waiting tables, but the Open sign wasn't flashing, and the only other car in the parking lot was Rayna's. Before we were even parked, the door flew open, and Rayna rushed out. She yanked open the car door and pulled my arm. Wrapping me in a tight embrace, she put her mouth to my ear.

"Don't you dare run off on me," she whispered.

"I'm not," I replied. This time, I meant it. I wasn't going anywhere.

"I've got coffee and sandwiches inside, come on. The others will be here shortly."

"Others? Who else is coming?" I asked.

"The rest of the story." She didn't say anything else. Rayna guided us inside the bar. "Let's sit here."

She'd pulled together a few tables and laid out sandwiches, chips, cookies, coffee, and tea. If I didn't know any better, I'd say she was planning a party.

"What is all this?" I asked.

"Lunch," she answered, "I assumed you'd be hungry after this morning."

"Do you all just have each other on speed dial? How does word get around so fast?" I knew Wishing was a small town, but damn, it was overwhelming to know your business made it from one end of town to the other in less than a few hours.

"Ham or turkey?" Bitsy asked, ignoring my question. I pointed at the ham. "I've got this. You go sit and listen to Rayna now."

Rayna patted the empty chair beside her. I was too tired to fight. I hadn't slept a wink last night, and this morning had been a marathon. I wasn't sure I'd ever process everything I was learning, but it definitely wasn't happening today. My entire life, I'd wondered about my mother's life before me, and now that I was finally getting answers, I wasn't quite sure what to do with them.

Rayna handed me a photograph. I looked down at it and recognized it as the one I'd seen this morning. "That's my mother and me."

"Yes. In this bar."

"I know," I replied. "I won't bother asking why you lied to me. I get the feeling you won't tell me."

"I won't, but I will tell you about your mother and her time here."

"Eventually, I need to know why no one could just come out and tell me you all knew here."

"In time, Shay," Bitsy said. She put a plate in front of me and poured iced tea into a glass. "Eat up."

I wasn't hungry; my stomach was twisted into knots. The mere thought of food repulsed me, but I knew telling Bitsy no wasn't an option. I lifted the sandwich to my lips and took a small bite. Bitsy watched me expectantly and waited while I chewed, swallowed, and then took a second bite.

"That morning you walked into my bar, it was like seeing a ghost. Eddie couldn't be bothered to call and warn me. I was just minding my own business, and then you walked in. I see your mama in you, Shay, but I also see him. There's no denying Tammy and Ken are your parents."

I set the sandwich down onto the plate and glanced at her. Her eyes brimmed with tears, but the smile on her lips stretched wide.

"Why didn't you warn me about him?" I asked her. "You knew what he was, and you still encouraged me to do a DNA test and find him."

She closed her eyes and sighed. "I just wanted to push you along and help you find answers. I knew I couldn't come out and tell you about him, but I could nudge you. I am sorry about that, for what it's worth."

I still didn't get it. They'd all known how awful my father was, yet they let me walk right into his trap. There wasn't anything I could say now that would change it, so I let it go. I was certain they had their reasons. They'd meant well. I wasn't sure I'd ever understand, though.

"So you recognized me?" I asked, bringing her back to the story she was trying to tell.

"I'd been waiting for that day for twenty-four years. When she left, Tammy promised me she'd come back one day when it was safe. I always assumed she'd bring you with her, but I never imagined you'd wind up in our town without her. And completely unplanned. What are the odds that out of anywhere in the world, you'd end up here in Wishing right when you needed us?"

"Fate is a funny thing," Hannah said. She sat across from me, taking tiny bites of a cookie. "I never believed in it before."

I didn't know what to say. That night was a blur in my mind. "I don't even remember driving here," I admitted. "I left Kansas City and just drove into the darkness. I think she was with me."

"I have no doubt she was," Rayna said. Her hand wrapped around mine and squeezed. "Your mama is always looking out for you, even if she's gone."

"She—" I started to say *she abandoned me and left me blind*, but Rayna held up her hand to stop me.

"I know you think she abandoned you. It wasn't right, what she did. I told her as much, but you gotta understand something about Tammy. She was hard on herself. Never believed she was a good mother or good for you. When she found you and that boy together, she thought she failed in raising you. She didn't want her daughter to grow up like her and fall victim to a boy's fake promises. All she wanted was a different life for you. We tried to reassure her that young love is normal and that she'd been a fine mother to you."

"You talked to her?" I asked. My heart thudded. "When?"

"She called me after she left you," Rayna admitted. "We talked a little over the years. Though, she talked to Bitsy and Miranda a bit more. We stayed in touch when she needed a friend."

"Why didn't she ever tell me about you all and this town?"

"I can't speak for Tammy, but I imagine she didn't want you getting any wild ideas about coming down here. You gotta remember, her last memories of this place were of your daddy trying to kill you and her. That ain't exactly a fond memory. No matter what happened before or how many people here loved her, she don't remember that."

"But her life here was good, right?" I asked. I needed to know that my mother had been happy once. Not just before Ken, but after. I needed to hear that she'd been happy being my mother.

"It was for a little while. She and I worked together here at the bar. She waited tables like you, and I ran the bar. My daddy still managed the place, but he spent his time in the kitchen. Tammy and I had some great nights here. Back then, we used to have live music. Your mama would dance and sing through the dining room while she worked. That girl's smile was so contagious, you couldn't help but laugh."

This was the mother I was desperate to know. "What was she like with me?"

"Miranda or Trigger stayed with you while she worked, but some days, she'd have to bring you in at the beginning of her shift. The customers loved it! When you were little, she'd strap you in one of those baby carriers and carry on with her work. As you grew, you'd crawl or walk all over this place. My daddy hated it, but even he was enamored with you and your mama."

Bitsy came up behind me and put her hands on my shoulders. "Seeing you as an adult walking in the same place you took your first steps is a bit surreal."

"I learned to walk here?" I asked. No wonder my mother never told me those stories. She'd raised me in a bar. Hearing it now, it made sense, but if she'd told me I'd learned to walk in the same place where she served tequila shots to drunk customers, I might have called child protective services on her myself.

"Right here," Rayna said. Her eyes danced as she laughed. "I'll never forget it. Tammy was at the bar waiting on a drink when the customers started shouting. We thought a fight had broken out. Tammy dropped that drink and turned around to find you. She was terrified you'd been caught up in the middle of something. But nope. There you were, on two wobbly, chubby legs waddling after Edwin, trying to steal his French fries."

Bitsy and Rayna burst out laughing at the memory. "His face! Oh, my Lord! He ran around this place, letting you chase him in circles. You never did get his fries," Bitsy said, wiping tears from her eyes.

"Did everyone know me?"

"Not everyone," Rayna said. "Most of our regulars did. Toby didn't. He still doesn't know your full story, just that your mama was from around here. Boy's got a big mouth, and I couldn't risk him breaking our promise for us."

Bitsy laughed and said, "Might have been easier if you had, Rayna. Took her long enough to put it all together."

"Are you mad?" Hannah asked.

"More hurt," I admitted. "I spent so much time looking for answers, and they were all right here in front of me."

I looked around the bar and tried to picture my mother there. It was easy to do. She always felt most comfortable in waitressing or bartending jobs. People were her element. She could talk to anyone about anything. Granted, she made up a million different life stories for herself, but none of them included this place. She'd left every detail out. I didn't know about her friends or family here. Nor did I know anything about my life before. She'd never talked about when I was a baby. I didn't know my first words or favorite toys. If I had a blankie or stuffed animal I loved, she'd never told me.

"What was I like?" I asked. "She never talked about me when I was a baby. Until you all left me that baby book, I'd never even seen photos of myself."

"You were colicky," Bitsy said. "Hannah here was too. You mama and I would cry to each other on the phone about the lack of sleep. We'd each try different tips and tricks to see what would work."

"You laughed a lot too. Always giggling and pulling Tammy's hair. She used to threaten to cut it all off just so you wouldn't have anything to grab," Rayna added.

"She loved her long hair," I said. "Even when we lived in the car, she found a way to keep it neat and pretty. She hated it when I cut mine off."

"I know," Bitsy said with a laugh, "she called me to bitch about it."

I stared up at her and met her eyes with mine. How had I not known my mother had friends she kept in touch with? She hid it all from me. She'd been happy here, I believed that now. Despite everything that happened with Ken, she had good memories from Wishing. She threw it all away and lived the rest of her life alone and longing for this place. It was all for me. To keep me safe. A million sacrifices were made, but the biggest one was her happiness.

"Your first word was *Mama*. I'm pretty sure you followed it with *Order up!* It's what my daddy used to yell when food was ready. You'd toddle around this dining room shouting *Order up!* at everyone. Even grouchy old dad thought it was adorable."

"Your daddy adored Tammy," Bitsy said. "Sometimes I think he wished she were his daughter too."

"Oh, he did. Used to tell me it all the time." She laughed. "Broke his heart when she left."

"It broke hers too," I whispered. Leaving Wishing was probably the hardest thing she'd ever done, and she'd done it for me. "I wish she could see me here with you all now."

Rayna and Bitsy each put a hand on my shoulder. "Shay, she loved you so much. She was so proud of you," Bitsy said.

"I let her down," I said, biting my lip. "I never realized how much she gave up for me."

The door opened, flooding the room with bright sunlight. Trigger walked in holding Miranda's hand. Her face was streaked with tears, and her eyes were red and puffy. I stood and reached for Rayna's hand. She intertwined her fingers with mine and held on tight.

"I'm sorry," I whispered to Trigger when he and Miranda came to stand beside me. "I didn't know."

"You weren't supposed to," Miranda replied. "We promised her that much."

FORTY-TWO

"I wanted to tell you everything," Trigger said. "So many times, I wanted to, but I remembered the promise we made to Tammy. We had to keep it."

"We never wanted to lie to you or hurt you," Miranda added.

Rayna stood and busied herself making plates for Miranda and Trigger. They sat down on either side of me, both turning their chairs to face me.

"That night I found you on the side of the road, I nearly had a heart attack. Still can't believe it." Trigger wouldn't stop shaking his head. It was as if he'd been holding them in for months. "Miranda had to keep reminding me how important it was to your mother."

"What?" I asked.

"For you to learn the truth on your own," Miranda said.

"I don't understand." My mother had always insisted I take care of myself and find my own answers, but it didn't make sense that she'd want everyone here to go to such great lengths to not just tell me the truth. "Why?"

Miranda slid her chair closer to me and put her hand on my knee. I turned to face her, her eyes pulling me in. "She always wanted to be the one to bring you here and tell you about the life you once had. To warn you about your father, but to also tell you about the good times they once shared. He wasn't always this way."

"He was," Bitsy said. "He's always been an arrogant SOB who thinks he's above the law and God himself. Tammy was just blinded by his smile."

"I'm sure that's true to some extent, Bitsy, but we don't know what happened between them before everything."

"He used her to get side action because Bethany was saving herself for marriage. Something her future husband couldn't be bothered with," Bitsy said.

"Let's not argue about that now. It doesn't matter." Miranda wasn't defending my father as much as she was trying to stick up for my mother.

"Just don't fill Shay's head with fairytales and nonsense. That's not what Tammy wanted."

"What did she want?" I asked. I was on information overload and ready to get back to my apartment to process and digest everything. All I wanted was to look back through my mother's photos and see them from my new perspective. I'd learned so much, yet it was still too fresh. I needed time. Alone time.

"She wanted you to have the life she used to dream about for herself here in Wishing. At its core, that's it. Your mother never had an easy life. Her parents were strict and never understood her. Then Ken came along and complicated everything. I assume Bitsy filled you in on their relationship?" Miranda asked, and I nodded. "He used to fill her head with promises of a life together. She knew they were lies, but she wanted to believe him, so she latched on to every last one. In her dreams, they'd settle down in Gaines and raise a family. She'd be the pastor's wife and finally have the respect of her parents. When that didn't work out, she found a new dream in Wishing."

Trigger stood and interrupted his wife. "Tammy was a smart

girl. She really was. Miranda and I tried to encourage her to go to school, but she was so worried about you and leaving you alone. We worked out a plan to where you'd always have one of us home with you. She was supposed to start nursing school in the fall. Then he showed up, and well, you know the rest."

This was news to me. When I'd tried to go to college, she'd basically disowned me. "She wanted to go to school?"

"Tammy wanted a bigger life so she could give you more."

"None of this sounds like the Tammy I knew."

"The Tammy you knew was a different woman," Miranda said with a sad smile. "She'd lost everything and nearly lost you. Her life became dedicated to keeping you alive and shielded from the past. That didn't leave much room for herself."

"She resented me for it, too."

"I can't speak for Tammy, but I wish I could say you were wrong. Trigger and I offered to take you in so she could chase her dreams for a bit, but she refused. She didn't want you anywhere Ken might find you."

"She never wanted to come anywhere near Southwest Missouri," I said, understanding her more and more with every revelation. A small part of me wished she'd taken the Triggs up on their offer. A life in a small town would've been better than growing up in the backseat of an old beat-up car, believing your mother hated you.

"I know. We tried to convince her it was safe so many times, but she wouldn't believe us. Ken hurt her in a way none of us will ever understand." Bitsy sighed and straightened her back. "But once Tammy left with you, he moved on. I can't say he was ever faithful to Bethany—the rumors say otherwise—but he fell into line pretty quickly. When he became pastor, some in the congregation that knew your mother's story protested and tried to get him fired. He again denied everything, but somehow word got to your mother, and it scared her. She stopped calling us all for a little while, afraid one of us would tell him where you were, but we wouldn't."

As enlightening as all of this was, it still didn't answer the question of why they'd lied. "How did my mom know I'd ever end up here?"

"She didn't," Miranda said. "Sure, she tossed a few pennies into the Wishing Well and tried to will you here, but she just hoped you'd find your way home."

"I think she always assumed you'd find your way to Kelb County where you were born and start asking questions. A few people there knew her and of you. They'd have sent you on to Wishing," Rayna added. She refilled my iced tea and slid a plate of cookies onto the table.

"So why couldn't you just tell me?"

The four of them looked at each other and then back at me. Hannah stood and walked towards the back of the bar, leaving me alone with Rayna, Trigger, Miranda, and Bitsy. She'd been so quiet, I'd forgotten she'd been with us.

"A few months before she died, your mother came back to Wishing. She'd been worried about you and wasn't sure what to do. Part of me thinks she came here looking for closure. She stayed for a few weeks and spent some time going through the boxes she'd left in our attic," Miranda said. Her hand pressed into my flesh as she squeezed my hand. Sweaty, trembling fingers interlaced with mine.

"We told her not to, but she went to see Ken," Bitsy said, her voice filled with anger. "He didn't take it well. Threatened her. Spooked her real good."

"She came into the bar after and told me she was leaving. Drank a few shots of tequila and drove back to the Triggs. She didn't tell me what Ken said, but I knew it wasn't good. He came through a month later for a revival and refused to allow Miranda or Bitsy into the church." Rayna laughed and added, "You can just imagine how well Bitsy took that."

"Hmph," Bitsy grunted. "That son of a bitch thinks he is God, but where he's going is a lot hotter."

"Where did she go after?" I asked. As entertaining as this was, it wasn't what I wanted to hear.

"I assume she went to Tennessee. She said you were always talking about visiting Nashville, and your last voicemail to her mentioned it."

"She really was looking for me?" I whispered. I'd intended to go to Nashville. I had enough saved to make the drive and get set up, but I never made it. I started trying to find her. I clenched my jaw, tightening the muscles to stop the tears.

"She was always looking for you, Shay. Leaving you that night was her biggest regret," Bitsy said.

"I always told her where I was. Why didn't she come for me?"

"She was ashamed," Miranda added. "She didn't believe she deserved you after that."

Whatever tiny piece of my heart still remained intact shattered. Her leaving me was the first fracture. It kept splitting further and further apart each day and month that passed until there was no chance of it ever becoming whole again. Hearing this obliterated what was left.

I shook my head, ignoring their looks of pity. Words wouldn't do justice to what I felt. I'd give my own life to have her back. So she could see that she deserved me. She deserved more than me. She gave up everything for me, and I'd been too blind to see it. It was me who didn't deserve her. Even in her darkest days, when I felt like a burden to her, she deserved more. If I'd known then what I do now, I'd have understood her better. I could have seen the weight she was carrying. But I'd been unable to because the truth was kept from me. Even in death, she'd tried to protect me from what she assumed I couldn't handle. She'd been wrong. I could have dealt with the truth. It might have brought us closer together if she'd just trusted me.

"Why couldn't you tell me this?" I asked. "Or about her time here?"

"We promised her. It was her dying wish."

"She called you the night she died," I said. Miranda nodded. Another tear rolled down her nose. It fell into her empty coffee mug. "What did she say?"

Miranda drew in a ragged breath. "She called to say goodbye."

"What happened?"

"She had a flat," Trigger said. Miranda was crying too hard to speak. "She pulled over and when she got out to check it, a car swerved and hit her. Shattered her hip, so she couldn't walk for help. We missed the first few calls from her, but when Miranda answered, Tammy knew."

"Didn't anyone stop? What about the person who hit her?"

"They never found them," he answered solemnly.

"I stayed on the phone with her," Miranda said, her voice meek and trembling through her tears. "She kept talking about you and how proud she was. Shay, you were her entire life. She'd have given anything to see you again."

"Why didn't she? All she had to do was answer or call me back."

"I know, but you have to understand how damaged your mother was. She truly believed you were better off without her."

"I wasn't," I said. Rayna nodded and walked towards me. She kissed the top of my head and wrapped her arms around my shoulders. I leaned back into her.

"She left a voicemail for you," Rayna said.

"She did?" I asked. "Can I hear it?"

Miranda nodded and handed me a small digital recorder. "I've been saving this for six years. You have no idea how difficult it is to transfer a voicemail."

I pressed play and held my breath.

"Shay," my mother's voice filled the room. Hearing her say my name sent me spiraling through time. This was the voice I remembered; it was the one that spoke to me on every car ride. The one that was quick to put me in my place, or to tell me a story. "I don't know how to start this. I miss you so much, and I'm so sorry. Not just for Iowa, but for all the years before and after. I wasn't the best mom, but I loved you more than even I understood. You need to know that I've listened to every one of your voicemails. I can hear how strong you are—you're the strongest woman I know. Keep fighting and driving forward, Shay. You deserve all those things you dream of."

The message cut off and there was a brief pause before she started talking again. I rubbed my eyes, wiping away the tears. "If you're listening to this, that means you're in Wishing with Bitsy, Miranda, and everyone. Let them love you, girl, like they loved me. If they've suffocated you with attention, embrace them. Let their arms hold you and keep you safe, like mine should have. I hope you find your home, Shay, even if it isn't in Wishing. But I know it is. This town is yours, just as it was once mine. Go and be happy, Shay. I love you."

I let the message play on, but she didn't say anything else. I could hear cars passing in the background. My mother's short, desperate gasps for air pricked through the speakers. I couldn't stop the tears even if I'd wanted to. Once the recording clicked off, I played it again. This time, I watched the faces of my mother's friends. Like me, their eyes were wet with tears, but they all smiled. They'd loved my mother; I could see that.

"She told me where to find the boxes she'd left," Miranda continued, "and asked me to get them to you. She begged me to promise not to call you or tell you what happened. She wanted you to find your way home on your own. She was adamant, Shay. When they found her, she'd wrapped her phone in a note with my name and number on it. Her dying wish was for us to keep an eye on you, but to keep our distance."

Rayna sighed and pulled me closer. "We all felt like that was one thing we owed her. We let her down so many times before, and I couldn't bear to do it again, even if she was gone. We also never thought you'd end up here. But she knew. She always knew."

For the first time, I saw the toll that all of this had taken on them. They'd carried my mother's secrets for nearly three decades. Then I rolled into town, unexpectedly, and they saw an opportunity to make things right for my mother. I couldn't fault them for any of that. No matter how much I wished they'd told me, I knew they were doing what they thought was right. They'd done exactly as my mother had asked.

"We also knew you'd run if we came out and told you," Bitsy added. "You were far more freaked out by the gifts than we thought you'd be."

"All of you?" I asked through my sobs. "You all did this?"

"The car was Bitsy," Rayna said. "As was the apartment. We all pitched in on the furniture. When your mother was here, she talked about you nonstop. She told us enough to help us figure out what you'd like."

"The boxes? That was you?" I asked Miranda. She nodded. "Four?"

"Edwin." Rayna said with a laugh. "He was desperate to do something. His old barn dog had a litter of puppies a month or so before you arrived. He insisted it was a sign. Then you left that voicemail about Freddie the dog, and Miranda called him."

"I don't know what to say." I sniffed back more tears. They were flowing freely now, though somewhere in the middle of the confession they shifted from sadness to gratitude. "I can't believe you did all of that for me. A nobody and a stranger."

"You're neither of those," Rayna insisted, her own voice thick with tears. "You're our daughter. You're Wishing's daughter."

"SHAY, WE'RE GOING TO BE LATE!" HANNAH CALLED UP the stairs. She didn't bother knocking. She never did.

"Sorry, one more thing and I'll be down." I stared at the submit button and hovered my mouse over it before scrolling back up to scan the application one last time.

"My mother is going to kill us if we don't leave now," she shouted.

I closed my eyes and clicked. When I opened them, the confirmation screen greeted me. It was done. I couldn't take it back now.

"Coming," I called down to her. I stood and patted Four on the head. She licked my calf and whined. "I'll be home before bedtime, girl. Don't you worry."

She dropped her head to the floor and pouted for moment. I knelt beside her and gave her a kiss on the head. She stopped whining long enough for me to grab my bag and keys. I threw open the door and bounded down the stairs. Hannah stood at the bottom, her foot tapping impatiently.

"Why are you smiling like that?" she asked.

"I did it," I said. I puffed my chest out and propped my fists on my hips.

"Yeah?"

"Now we wait."

"For what?" Toby asked. He leaned his head out the window of Hannah's car. His legs were propped up on the dash.

"Back seat," I said. "I called shotgun last night."

"You can't call shotgun more than an hour before the road trip."

"Bullshit," Hannah and I said in unison. He groaned and started to protest but climbed into the back seat.

"What are we waiting on?" he asked again.

I grinned and passed a knowing look to Hannah. "My college application."

"You did it?" he asked.

"I did. Hopefully my GED scores from Iowa are enough to get me in."

"Your essay should seal the deal," Hannah replied. "I mean, how many people can tell a story like yours?"

I smiled and leaned back into the seat. Hannah backed down the driveway. I watched as our neighborhood passed by outside the window. Everything familiar. A year ago, that feeling would have terrified me. Home wasn't something I allowed myself to dream of, much less want. But I'd found it anyway.

Wishing was my home now. I didn't have any plans to leave. The road no longer called my name. I'd found my true north, and it would always lead me back here. I still enjoyed a good road trip, but now Four and Hannah kept me company. We explored the back roads of Missouri, and I shared stories of my life as a nomad. She encouraged me to apply for colleges and use my life story to my advantage. I wasn't sure what I wanted to study, but I knew I wanted to work with at-risk kids. I couldn't change the world for all of them, but if I could help one kid like me, that was all I wanted.

What I found in Wishing was so much more than a home. Here I found a family. My mother was gone, but now I had Rayna. Miranda and Bitsy reclaimed their roles as unofficial aunts and fussed over me every chance they got. Trigger acted like the protective father, teaching me how to shoot a gun and defend myself. Not that I had much to defend myself from now that Ken was facing a long list of criminal charges. In addition to the disturbing allegations from young girls at his church, he'd also been dipping into the church funds. He'd used money he embezzled from the church to buy a new Cadillac for himself and a beach house for Bethany. It was hard not to sit back and smile any time I saw his face on the news or read the comments online.

"Ready?" Hannah asked as she turned out onto the highway.

"As I'll ever be." I smoothed my hands down the front of my long black dress that Hannah had sewn specifically for today. "Are they meeting us there?"

"Yeah," Toby replied. "Are they bringing, um, her?"

I laughed at his discomfort. "Yes, they have the urn. Miranda and Trigger brought it down from Tennessee yesterday."

After twenty-four years on the run, today was the day my mother was finally coming home for good.

ACKNOWLEDGMENTS

Each time I sit down to write acknowledgments, I am struck by how many people have stood by me and helped me through the publishing and writing process.

This book, in particular, was touched by many hands other than my own.

My mother, who does not enjoy my books (I get it, Mom) but actually read and loved Shay's story. In a way, Shay was inspired by my mother and her sense of adventure and wandering soul. Thank you for imparting your love for words onto me.

Leah, I honestly don't know what I'd do without you. Your daily texts and encouragement helped me not only survive 2020, but have also helped to keep the stories and words alive inside me.

Maria, I'll never stop being amazed by you. Your talent and drive are inspiring. Thank you for being my IABC partner.

Gwynne, your love for Shay and this novel gave me the confidence to release Out of Anywhere out into the world. Thank you for taking the time to help shape this novel into the book that it became. Your passion for writers continues to encourage and inspire me.

My husband and kids ... I'm not sure I'll ever be able to adequately thank you for your love and support.

Bookstagram. I continue to be inspired by this community. Thank you for always being there. I could never name everyone who's been a crucial part of this process, but to Torrie, Jamie, Kerry, Jamie, Becky, Hunter, Marian, Quinn, Phoebe, Leslie, and so many more - THANK YOU.

As always, to my readers, you mean more to me than I'll ever be able to express. I still cannot believe there are so many of you that invest time and money into me and my work. I love you all.

As always, please consider leaving a review! Reviews are crucial for independent authors and books.

ABOUT THE AUTHOR

Andrea is the author of women's fiction novels, including *Happily Ever Never* and *After Everything*. *Out of Anywhere* is her fifth novel.

Andrea currently lives in Nashville with her husband, Jeff, and two children, Jackson and Annabeth. She has a BS in Mass Communication from MTSU and an MBA from the University of Memphis.

When she's not reading, writing, or Bookstagramming, she enjoys pretending to know how to bake, swooning over Chris Evans, and scrolling Netflix without ever finding something to watch.

Andrea is the co-founder & co-host of the Indie Author Book Club and Podcast.

Follow Andrea on social media or visit her website (andreanourse.com)!

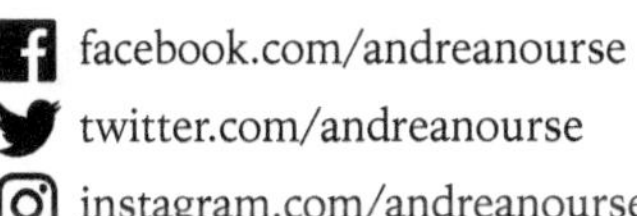

facebook.com/andreanourse
twitter.com/andreanourse
instagram.com/andreanourse

ALSO BY ANDREA NOURSE

Life is but a Dream

Happily Every Never

Lie Baby Lie

After Everything